The fiery brilliance of the Zebra Hologram Heart which you see on the cover is created by "laser holography." This is the revolutionary process in which a powerful laser beam records light waves in diamond-like facets so tiny that 9,000,000 fit in a square inch. No print or photograph can match the vibrant colors and radiant glow of a hologram.

So look for the Zebra Hologram Heart whenever you buy a historical romance. It is a shimmering reflection of our guarantee that you'll find consistent quality between the covers!

PASSIONATE SURRENDER

"I've always found the moon such a fascinating thing," she said, her attention focused on the night sky. "Lizzie used to tell me it was made of cheese, but I think not. What do you think?" It was then she lowered her gaze to Jason and realized what he was about to do. There was no denying the deep passion in his eyes. As he came closer, his lips parted, she was powerless to stop him, for she wanted his kiss. But it was more overwhelming than any kiss she had ever had, flooding her senses with its lingering heat, making her feel instantly lightheaded and weak-kneed.

Bravely she fought to still the emotions that had come to life within her. She brought her hands up against his chest in a futile effort to push him away, which only made him tighten his hold, pulling her closer. The more she struggled, the more demanding his kiss became, and the harder it was for Katherine to keep from being swept away. . . .

ZEBRA BOOKS
KENSINGTON PUBLISHING CORP.

ZEBRA BOOKS

are published by

Kensington Publishing Corp.
475 Park Avenue South
New York, NY 10016

First printing: December 1987

Printed in the United States of America

DEDICATION

This book is dedicated to the true heroes of this world—those who prove willing to risk their lives in order to protect the ones they hold dearest. To men like Kenneth Truitt and Red McDaniel, who gave up their lives in a valiant effort to save an entire Daingerfield congregation from the bullets of a crazed gunman that fateful Sunday. Tears can never fully wash away the sorrow. God be with them both.

Special Thanks

I'd like to express a special thank you to the Daingerfield Chamber of Commerce, and especially to Peggy Maxey, for helping me get over a few of the rougher spots. And to the Steel Country Bee for giving constant encouragement to an old hometown gal whose heart will never stray far. And as always, thanks must be expressed to my parents for the strong support they have given me from day one. And to my husband and my two sons for loving me, even though I burned the roast simply because my mind was no longer in this century.

Prologue

1902

Jeffrey Morris stepped quietly through the white picket fence that surrounded the family's small cemetery and carefully closed the narrow gate, taking time to latch it securely in place. When he turned back around, his green eyes swept the odd-shaped markers lined up in two perfectly neat rows and went immediately to the tall, blue-gray stone that he knew bore his father's name. He felt the familiar emptiness that ached deeply in the very core of his soul whenever he came to visit his father's grave.

A thin sheen of tears burned his eyes as he knelt beside the weather-worn fence and plucked a freshly budded yellow narcissus, the first bloom of the coming spring. Absently, he twirled the dark green stem with his fingertips while he fought to regain control of his deepest emotions. How he hated tears, such a sign of weakness, but he found it impossible to shrug off the sadness that engulfed him.

Slowly, Jeffrey stood and drew in a deep, steadying breath before he walked the short distance that still lay between him and his natural father's well-kept grave. A brisk March wind silently ruffled his dark brown hair. It blew the slightly curling locks into his face, then billowed it away. Unperturbed, his gaze lifted to take in the deep beauty of the nearby woodlands, always so serene, so special, so very close to God. The tall winter-faded grass and stately green pines that encircled the small cemetery had become wildly animated in the playful wind. He stared in momentary fascination at the lively performance nature had provided before letting his gaze fall back to the stark, blue-gray stone before him.

Although he usually tried to visit the grave every March, on the anniversary of his father's untimely death, it was several years since his last visit, and the impact of standing before the grave now seemed twice as great. Tears continued to well up in Jeffrey's green eyes while his mind sifted through memories of the man who had done so much for him in so little time. Though his own memories were few, they were nonetheless vivid, having faded very little in the years gone by. Franklin Edward Mason, known more commonly as Flint Mason, had to have been one of the most giving and caring men ever to grace this earth, yet one of the most misunderstood, right up until his death.

In a solemn but reflective mood, Jeffrey knelt before his father's grave and placed the small yellow wild-flower near the base of the stone. Lifting his hand to run a fingertip over the chiseled letters, he quietly considered the turbulent life of this man and how much that life, and especially his death, had affected them all.

Another gust of wind brought Jeffrey's attention back to the present for just a brief moment before his thoughts took another plunge back in time—to a day long ago—a day he had heard his mother talk of many times. The seeds of change had already been planted, and fate waited patiently to reap her harvest. . . .

Chapter One

March, 1878

The constant, hollow reverberations of wood banging against wood somewhere in the loft overhead sounded a harsh counterpoint to the high, perpetual whine of the cold wind, which forced its way relentlessly through the crevices of the old weatherworn structure. Surrounded by such eerie sounds, Katherine Mason became even more aware of how alone she really was—alone, and running from the only man she had ever dared love, but now feared.

A late winter storm hurried in from the northwest, boiling black, rumbling clouds in an angry gray sky. The abandoned barn seemed to be Katherine's only source of shelter from the onrushing wind and rain, and she felt lucky to have found it. It should at least help keep her dry, though it offered little in the way of comfort. Not much had been left inside the old barn, not even a small pile of hay in the loft for a makeshift bed. A few broken implements and rotting pieces of rope were all that remained. The building had not been used in years.

Forced to abandon her valise days ago, the burden not worth the clothes and articles she had packed inside, Katherine had nothing to lay across the earthen floor, nothing with which to make a bed; yet she was tired, so tired. Every muscle in her body ached. Her once lovely blue woolen dress was now torn and ragged. Her dark brown hair had fallen from its confines and now hung in a loose, tangled mass down her back. It felt as if she had run forever, yet it had been only a few days, barely more than a week. The bruises on her face and chest had not yet had time to heal. Even though she had only been running for such a short time, she sensed she was finally getting close to her destination, close to safety at last. She had to be.

Wearily, Katherine brushed away the sticky cobwebs before she settled into the southeast corner of the abandoned barn, where the sharp gusts of icy wind that whipped through the rotting, gray boards did not seem as strong. Huddled, with her arms wrapped around herself in an attempt to find warmth, she wondered how long the storm would last. Would she ever find her brother's ranch? How much further could it be?

Leaning back against one of the musty interior walls of what she assumed had once been either a part of the tack room or maybe even a small storage room for feed, she wondered what was to become of her. She dared not try to return to her father's house just yet. That would be the first place her husband would look for her. Closing her eyes to the misery of her situation, she realized that even if she had decided to go back home, it was unlikely her father would have let her stay.

In all probability, he would not even have let her into the house, and why should he?

A sob rose inside her and lodged deep in her throat as she thought back to the last time she had seen her father. His final words were still vivid in her memory, his expression still clear. How angry he had been when he learned that she intended to go against him and marry Flint Mason, a fancy drifter who had stopped in the small town of Gilmer, Texas, one hot summer day on his way west.

Her father had been furious with her, but she had refused to listen. She had not wanted to believe him when he'd warned that such a hasty decision to marry would eventually bring her misery. He had tried to tell her Flint was no good. If only she had listened, but instead, she had openly defied her father for the first time in her life. She had ignored him completely, though he'd warned her again and again that if she did such a foolish thing and married for anything but true, honest love, she would pay the consequences for the rest of her life. But she had believed her actions had stemmed from real love when she walked out of her father's house to join Flint, who had waited for her just outside. Her father had ordered her to stop right where she was or never again step foot inside his house, and he had meant it. She had never seen him so angry with her, and she had never been so angry with him. But her anger had quickly passed and had since been replaced by a deep, burning regret.

As she remembered that fateful night, a pathetic sigh slipped passed her sun-parched lips. Why hadn't she listened? Even as young as she had been then, how could she have been quite so blind? Now she wondered if she would ever find the courage to go to her father and try to patch things between them and to apologize—for he had certainly been right about Flint. But what if her father refused to even hear her out? What if he was still too angry with her? Too angry to listen to her apology. Too angry to forgive.

At least, she still had her brother, and although Flint knew that she had an older brother, Katherine could not remember ever having told him just where it was that Andrew now lived—after all, she, herself, was not completely sure. All she really knew was that Andrew had bought his own small ranch somewhere near Jefferson, Texas, just a little over two years ago. Her brother was her last, her only hope. If she could find Andrew, he would give her refuge, no questions asked. She was sure of it. She would be safe at last. Her husband would never find her there, or so she hoped.

Despite the growing discomfort of the cold, hard earth beneath her and the rough wood wall pressed against her back, sleep gradually overtook Katherine. With Flint foremost on her mind, her dream-muddled thoughts slowly drifted back to the day she had first met him. How wonderfully handsome she had thought him to be, and how easily he had won her young and inexperienced heart with his sophisticated charm and uncanny good looks. Never had she been shown such wonderful attention, never had she been treated with such tenderness, such complete kindness. He had fooled her totally with his flowery words of love and his overwhelmingly powerful kiss.

Slowly, Katherine's slender body sagged sideways across the coarse surface of the wall until she finally fell to the hard, dusty floor. Her dreams of Flint became more vivid as she slipped deeper into exhausted sleep. It was summer again, the air warm, the sun bright, and there he stood, just inside her father's smokehouse where he had stolen his first kiss from her. He waved at her to get her attention, and then, when he knew for certain she was looking at him, he smiled eagerly into her wide brown eyes, beckoning her to come to him. Although she knew it was wrong, she was unable to resist him. Timidly, she stepped inside the small building and watched with round-eyed fascination while he slowly closed the door and latched it.

Deep, curving indentations formed at the corners of his mouth when his smile deepened. His shining green eyes seemed to bear right into her very soul as, slowly, ever so slowly, he came toward her for that first kiss. Katherine's pulse quickened in her sleep. Flint's lips came closer, taunting her, teasing her, then suddenly, at the very moment she tilted her head back to surrender to the kiss, the image reshaped itself into the form of a dark, hooded man, tall and menacing. Terrified, she wrenched herself from the dark specter's grasp and ran into the surrounding shadows. The dark creature followed and stayed always right behind her, chasing her through a never-ending maze of smoky corridors. Then suddenly the last corridor she ran down came to an abrupt end. She was trapped. There was no place left to go.

Katherine came awake with a start. Her heart pounded against her chest, and her blood raced through her veins at a frenzied rate, causing her to gasp desperately for air. Drawn up like a frightened child in the furthermost corner of the barn, she was too terrified to move. Her eyes quickly searched the shadows for her dangerously violent husband; but slowly, she realized just where she was and why. She cried out with relief. It had all been a dream, just a bad dream, nothing more.

Drawing deep, quivering breaths, Katherine pushed herself back into an upright position. She wiped the dust from her hands onto her frayed skirts and forced herself to think of a happier time in an effort to drive the dark demon as far away as possible. She tried to envision her mother at the stove, cooking their Thanksgiving dinner. Thanksgiving was always one of her mother's favorite holidays and a day that Katherine could usually recall without trouble, but for some reason, the memory refused to come to her now.

Katherine continued to fight sleep as long as she could, for fear that the demon would return and haunt her dreams again, but her weariness eventually won out and gradually her lids drifted shut. At last, the happier images came. Katherine found herself a child again, back at her parents' small ranch, long before her mother had died and her father had grown so bitter. And there, while the little girl clambered onto a kitchen chair for a better vantage point, was her mother, bent over the cast-iron stove, carefully basting the plump tom turkey roasting in the oven. Such a wonderful aroma.

Eventually, the visions of untroubled childhood faded, then gave way to total darkness, and Katherine slept dreamlessly for hours. When next she woke, the harsh noises from outside had stopped. The storm was over. The only sound she heard now was the steady splash of water as it dripped through the roof in several places, forming large brown puddles on the dirt floor.

There were no other sounds. Slowly, she glanced around, trying to bring her surroundings and her thoughts together. Very little light came through the crevices in the thin, rotting walls, but before long she remembered where she was.

She realized that darkness had fallen, and rather than face the nocturnal dangers of the dense woodland that covered northern East Texas, Katherine decided to stay the rest of the night in the old barn. Though cold, hungry, and thirsty, she tried not to let her miseries get the best of her.

With the faint hope that she was no more than a few days away from her brother's ranch, Katherine lay down again on the dirt floor and willed herself to go back to sleep. She needed to get all the rest she could. Hugging herself against the cold night air, she somehow managed to drift off again, and slept this time until morning.

Bright shafts of light filtering through the tiny cracks high in the east wall eventually woke Katherine from her deep sleep. She blinked in confusion, and it was a moment before she could get her bearings. Slowly, she sat up and stretched her sore muscles, crying out at the pain the simple action had caused. The four-day trek through the wooded hills had taken its toll on her body. Even so, she forced herself to stand and walk around. It was a new day and she felt somewhat rested, though not much. Finally, she limped her way outside and into the fresh air.

The first thing she needed was water, but a quick look around revealed there was none to be had. Tears rose to her eyes for she had truly expected to find some accumulation of water from the rainstorm.

Her thirst was almost unbearable now, far outweighing her hunger, but there was no creek or pond in sight, only trees, bushes, and blackberry vines. When she gazed up at the sun-filled sky, she realized it had to be nearly noon. She had slept most of the morning. The warm sun had already dried whatever puddles the rain from the night before would have left, and, unable to find any receptacle that might have retained some of the water that had fallen, she knew she would have to forge on without any. There was no other choice.

It was now eight days since Katherine had run away, and four days since she'd had a decent meal. The last drinking water she had managed to find came from a small stream she had crossed early the previous afternoon. And because she could not travel by road, she had not passed a house in days. She needed both food and water, but she had no idea where she was, or where to go to find either. She knew only that she should continue heading southeast. She must find her brother's house, the sooner the better, for she was not at all sure how much longer she could last.

Moistening her chapped lips with her dry, sticky tongue, she started through the thick woods in the direction she felt Jefferson must lie and hoped she would come across a creek or a pond before long. When the dense woods finally thinned out and she could see farther ahead, she stopped and searched in the distance for some sign of water. She noticed a now-dry creek bed a few hundred yards away where the newly sprouted grass lay flat. When she got closer and discovered the grass was still moist, she realized that the previous night's downpour was what had flattened the grass. She decided to follow the narrow indentation until it led her to water, which she was almost certain it would. Chewing on a few blades of the damp grass, she hurried onward.

To her relief, Katherine discovered her guess to be right. The shallow ravine eventually led to a big, open field where a large herd of muscular black cattle grazed peacefully, scattered in liberal numbers across a wide green pasture; and there in the middle of the huge, rolling meadow, beside a small stand of budding elm trees, was a small pond that sparkled in the sunlight. There were several "no trespassing" signs posted along the waist-high wire fence that surrounded the huge pasture, but Katherine chose to ignore them. Quickly, she wriggled her way through the strands of wire, glad that only the top and bottom rungs were barbed, then ran toward the pond as fast as her tired legs would allow.

When she finally reached the edge of the pond, she found the water far too inviting. After a hurried search of the immediate area, she decided to take more than just a drink; she decided to take a much needed bath—albeit without soap. Her hands flew to the buttons along the back of her blouse and frantically began to work them loose, but she was too impatient for that. Also, it occurred to her that this was a good chance to get some of the dust and dried perspiration out of her clothing. Without another thought, she plunged fully dressed into the pond, gasping at the wonderful sensation of the cold water against her parched skin. When she had drunk her fill, she took off her clothing and carefully worked the clear water through each garment.

After she felt everything was as clean as she could get

it without soap, she looked for a place to hang the clothing so it could dry. A small clump of trees several feet from the water's edge seemed to be the only choice. But before she dared make a run for even the closest of those trees, she scanned the immediate vicinity again to be absolutely certain no one else was around. Except for the grazing cattle, she saw no movement. Bravely, she bit down on her lower lip and ran as fast as she could to the nearest tree. She took just enough time to arrange her clothes over one of the lower branches before rushing back into the water.

Although the water still felt briskly cold to her delicate skin, she soon became used to the temperature and found that the gentle pressure of the water soothed her sore, aching muscles. Slowly, she relaxed and allowed her thoughts to wander. As she floated just below the sun-warmed surface, her mind drifted into a pleasant daydream. She was a child again, floating in her father's pond out back of his house, in the pasture behind the barn, waiting for Andrew to finish his afternoon chores so they could play.

Katherine soon became lost in her fantasy, temporarily forgetting the fear that had driven her this far and the deep feeling of anger that had slowly been building inside her for months now. She was unaware of anything but the remembered images now in front of her. With her ears submerged just below the water's surface, she did not immediately hear the thudding sounds of something hard striking the earth, and when she did vaguely become aware of the noise in her dream-like state, she simply attributed it to the cattle—after all, they were huge, heavy animals. She was so preoccupied with her happy memories of a brother she was about to see again that she remained completely unaware of the lone rider headed straight for her.

When the thudding continued to penetrate her daydream, and it finally occurred to her that it was a sound far different from that generally made by cattle, it was too late. Her eyes flew open and she saw that the horse and its rider were already too close for her to run for her clothes. Wrapping her arms around her most private areas, she submerged until the water was level with the tiny cleft above her chin. She felt her heart quicken in alarm and hoped he had not yet noticed her and would quickly pass by, but judging by his direction and his speed, she realized that he had indeed already seen her and had no intention of passing her by. Her eyes went helplessly to her clothes, then back to the rider as she prepared herself for the worst.

Jason Morris had spotted something hanging in the trees the moment he first came over the rise on his daily check of the cattle. Then, almost immediately, he noticed someone splashing about in the nearby pond. Despite the fact that his land was clearly posted, it was clear that this was a trespasser.

Although he honestly expected the intruder to be little Tommy Monk from the ranch that bordered his to the east, he decided to check it out and be sure. He no longer took chances with strangers on his property. Not long ago, twenty head of his cattle had mysteriously disappeared in broad daylight. No, he definitely could not afford to take chances with strangers, and even if it did turn out to be Tommy, he wanted to ask him about his father's arm. If Craig's arm were really broken, Jason was going to offer him one of his hired hands to help with his spring branding. It was what any good neighbor would do.

But the closer Jason got to the pond, the more he came to realize that the trespasser was not little Tommy Monk after all. Tommy would have run out to greet him before now, buck naked if that be the case. Nine-year-old Tommy had no inhibitions whatsoever. Never had.

"This is private property," he began as he pulled his horse to a halt near the water's edge. The rest of his little speech was lost the moment he realized exactly what it was he had found. *A woman.* The head that protruded from the water's surface near the far side of the pond had to belong to a woman. Dark, silky hair floated out in every direction, and what features he was able to see were far too delicate to be anything but a woman's.

Stunned, he pulled off his hat and wiped his brow with his faded-blue shirt sleeve, unable to stop staring. A light breeze tugged at the ends of his thick brown hair as he continued to gawk. Finally, he realized he should say something more and began his speech again. "This happens to be private property, ma'am, and you are trespassing."

Angered and embarrassed by her predicament, Katherine glared at him a long moment before she responded. "Well, if you would be so kind as to toss me my clothes, I will gladly be on my way."

Glancing in the direction she had just indicated with a sharp nod of her head, he realized that what he had noticed dangling from the tree was actually this woman's clothes. His blue eyes grew wide. Even her undergarments were there, in clear view. The woman in his pond had to be completely naked. Intrigued, he put his hat back on, then leaned forward on his horse, peering into the water to see if it could really be true, but to his dismay, the reflection of the bright blue, sun-filled Texas sky above, prevented his seeing anything but bright blue, sun-filled Texas sky below. Glancing upward, he frowned when he saw there was not one hospitable cloud in sight. What he wouldn't give for a nice, big fluffy cloud about now—or even a tiny little cloud would do. He wasn't hard to please.

"But if I throw those clothes out to you, they'll get wet." He looked back at her as he pointed that fact out. He wanted to be as difficult as he could and keep her right where she was, in her present state of undress, for as long as he could.

"That won't really matter much because they are already wet," she informed him. All the anger that had been building inside her over the past few weeks was surfacing now. Her dark eyes flashed with anger as she waited for his response. Why was he so intent on making this situation worse than it already was?

"But they look about half dry to me," he said, tapping his dimpled chin thoughtfully. Slowly, he climbed down from his tall, chestnut horse and walked over to the tree to check. The torn and ragged appearance of her clothes did not escape his notice when he took them off the branch and carefully draped them over his arm. Nodding as he felt them with his hand, he spoke loudly enough for her to hear. "Yep, they're already nearly dry. You wouldn't want to get them wet all over again would you?"

"Believe me, I don't mind. Will you please just stop all this talking and toss them to me?"

"How about I promise to turn my back and not look while you slip out of the water and put them on? That way, you won't have to get them soakin' wet all over again."

"Toss me my clothes!" she screamed, slapping furiously at the water, which splashed up in her face, infuriating her further.

"Whoa, yes ma'am," he said quickly. His eyes sparkled with devilish delight as he fought to suppress the grin that twitched at the corners of his mouth. He sure liked her spirit. "Whatever you say, ma'am. Here, catch."

He wadded the clothes up into a ball and deliberately tossed them too high for her to catch, hoping she would make a leap for them, but to his disappointment she simply watched them sail over her head, then swam to where they landed.

"Need any help?" he asked and offered her a dazzling smile, watching as she struggled to put her clothes on underwater.

"No thank you," she muttered just before she ducked below the water in an attempt to pull up her bloomers and still stay below the water's surface. What she really needed was for him to take that arrogant smile of his, that probing gaze, and go away—the further the better.

Chuckling to himself, Jason climbed back on his horse and continued to watch the twirling water with interest, still glancing skyward every now and then in hopes of a decent-sized cloud. If only he could get rid of that blasted reflection, he could enjoy the view that much more. Even so, he had been able to make out the creamy whiteness of her skin whenever it came near enough to the surface, and he let his imagination try to figure out for itself what her body might look like. He sure hoped that when she finally emerged from the water she did not disappoint him with a shapeless form. A beautiful face like that deserved a full and womanly figure to go with it.

"You look like you're having problems. Sure you don't need any help?" he asked again and laughed when his taunt drew another glare from her. He knew he should be ashamed of himself for carrying on this way, but he could not seem to stop himself. An opportunity like this just did not present itself every day.

Finally, she started toward the opposite shore, and he rode around to that side to greet her as she emerged. To his extreme delight, her wet clothing clung provocatively to her shape like a second skin, and he was not at all disappointed with her figure. His imagination, as good as it was, had not done her justice. Her body was even more beautiful and appealing than her face.

"I'll be on my way now," she said through clenched teeth as she turned to head back the way she had come. The sooner she got away from this man's probing gaze, the better.

"No, don't," he called out before he even realized he intended to speak. Something stirred inside of him. He must not let her simply walk out of his life that way. He had to do something to keep her there. Something. Anything.

"Surely you don't intend to prosecute!" She turned back and glared at him once again. This was the final straw. She had already borne enough heartache. How much more was she expected to take? Well, she wouldn't take anymore. She refused to.

Never had he seen such fire in a woman's eyes. "No, I don't intend to prosecute. I just wanted to invite you to have lunch with me. You look as if you could use a good meal." He was almost as surprised by his invitation as she was.

"What's wrong with the way I look?" she asked and gazed down at herself as if she had no idea of her tattered appearance. When she did, she discovered just how revealing her wet clothing was, and she turned away again with her arms folded protectively over her breasts. She could feel the blood rush to her face.

"There's nothing wrong with the way you look, nothing at all," he told her quickly. "It's just that I may have acted a little . . . rude with you earlier . . ."

"A little?" she cried out, turning around to face him with an anger that demanded to be vented. "I've never been treated like that in my entire life, especially by a stranger, and I've never had a stranger dare look at me the way you are looking at me now. How dare you!"

"Sorry, ma'am," he replied guiltily. Then, raising his eyes to meet hers, he noticed the faint discoloration at the side of her face. He wondered how she had gotten such a tremendous bruise; it seemed to cover more than half her cheek. "It's just that your clothes are—well, they are—would you like some dry clothes to put on? It wouldn't be much, and I can't say any of it will fit, but I could find you something dry to wear while we eat. You could wash out your own clothes and hang them outside on the line. They would dry pretty quick in all this sunshine. What do you say? It would give me a chance to really apologize for the awful way I've behaved towards you."

"No, I think I'd better be on my way," she replied, though her hunger was quickly overriding her anger.

He sensed her reluctance. "I've got a housekeeper that makes a dandy beef stew. That's what we're having today—beef stew with lots of vegetables and piping hot sourdough biscuits," he said, hoping to tempt her. He could tell it was working by the way she ran her tongue over her upper lip. She was definitely hungry.

"You say you have a housekeeper? We won't be alone?"

"Is that what you're worried about? Sure, Minnie will be there to protect you the whole time. She won't let me do anything terrible to you, no matter how much I might want to." He laughed, then seeing her anger flare again, he quickly stopped grinning and said, as sincerely as he was able to at that moment, "I'm sorry. I guess I really do owe you an apology for the way I've behaved. It's just that I seem to have an evil streak in me today; but I promise to try to control it from now on. Please, come with me to the house and see for yourself what a great cook Minnie is. You won't be sorry you did. No one ever is."

"Beef stew?" she said more to herself than to him. Her hand went to her empty stomach. "All right, I'll stay for lunch. But I'm leaving right after I've eaten."

"Not if I have anything to say about it," Jason thought to himself. Offering her his hand, he helped her up into the saddle in front of him. With an inward smile, he slipped his arms around her and took hold of the reins, pressing his body closely to hers. Intrigued by the softness of her body and tempted by her wild beauty, he vowed to do whatever it might take to keep her at his ranch for as long as he could. This was one maverick he fully intended to tame.

Chapter Two

Trying to avoid any unnecessary contact with Jason's lean body, Katherine sat rigidly, keeping a tight grasp on the saddle horn with her left hand and gripping one of the leather tie straps with her right hand. She had tried shifting her position to a more comfortable angle, but when she did so, her outer thigh rubbed provocatively against his inner thigh, causing him to tense and lean a little closer when he was already close enough. She quickly decided not to try that again. Although the saddle was clearly not made for riding in this awkward position, she would try to bear the discomfort until they reached his house.

"You're trembling," Jason commented, sounding concerned. "Just as soon as we reach the house, I want you out of those clothes."

"I'll just bet you do," she thought, wondering if this Minnie person actually existed or was just someone he had invented to lure her into his house. She did not trust this man, but then why should she? Why should she trust any man? If she did not catch sight of a housekeeper the moment she arrived, she would run as fast as she could out of his house, and either find something to defend herself with or somewhere to hide, and she certainly did not intend to undress. She didn't care how much food he offered her.

"I'll be all right," she assured him, though she continued to tremble uncontrollably. He pressed his body more closely to hers, helping to shield her from the cool wind that whipped past them as they rode. Suddenly, her trembling grew worse. As she peered in the direction they were headed, eager to glimpse a house of some sort, she was not sure if it was the chill air brushing against her wet clothes or the sharply contrasting warmth of the man's body that was causing such a violent reaction. Despite all her efforts she was unable to stop shaking.

When he embraced her even more closely—though it offered her more of his warmth—the uncontrollable shivering pierced right through to her bones. To her dismay, she became aware of a slight smell of woodsmoke that clung to him, or was it tobacco of some sort? She was not sure, but knew it did not smell like the awful cheroots her husband and his friends always smoked. This was a sweeter, richer smell.

"How much further?" she asked, continuing to stare in the direction they rode. She dared not look back at him; she was having a hard enough time coping just with his touch and his scent. If she were to look around into those incredibly blue eyes or at that taunting smile, it would be her undoing. She was sure of it.

"You'll be able to see the house once we clear the narrow windbreak of trees along that next rise," Jason said. His low voice was now very close to her ear. The gentle warmth of his breath against her sensitive skin, sent yet another deep shiver down her spine, along her legs, and down to her toes. Her heartbeat quickened.

Katherine tried not to analyze why she was so nervous about having the man this close. Instead, she chose to concentrate on where they were headed—a small tree-covered hill along the far end of the pasture. As soon as they topped that low rise and the man's house was in sight, she would immediately look for possible places to hide should it prove necessary. She had become very good at hiding in the past two weeks.

"There it is," he told her as they rode through the narrow strip of trees and a huge two-storied house finally came into view. "That's Seven Oaks."

"Seven Oaks?" she asked and turned to look at him, temporarily forgetting her determination not to. Their faces were only inches apart and had he felt the urge to, he could have easily dipped his head and kissed her. That thought made her blush. She should not have such bold thoughts! After all, she was a married woman. The marriage may have been a terrible mistake, made by a foolish young girl with no notion of what love really was; but even so, she *had* made the mistake and legally she *was* still a married woman. Nor should she have such flutterings in her heart each time she looked into his intensely blue eyes.

"My mother named it," Jason explained, also aware of how close their mouths were. His gaze lingered on her lips for only a moment, then moved to the land and the house beyond. "See those big trees that surround the house? Those are Spanish oak trees."

Katherine turned away to look at the trees, already thick and green with young leaves. They were tall, so tall that they towered over the two-storied house. She couldn't keep from counting them. "But there are nine of them," she said, turning back to him questioningly.

"When my parents first built the house and decided on the name, there were only seven. Two of those trees have grown of their own accord in the years since."

"Seems to me you would rename it Nine Oaks then," she retorted, and when he chuckled at her comment, she turned away and stared toward the house once again. Her stomach twisted nervously and her insides felt giddy, as if someone had let a swarm of busy honey bees loose inside her. She attributed the odd sensations to her present condition and the fact that she had not eaten in days.

"If it really bothers you that there are actually nine oaks instead of seven, I can always cut two of them down. Which two do you think I should do away with?"

"Don't be silly," she muttered and fell silent, aware once more of the strange swirling sensations inside her that seemed to rise like the incoming tide every time that he spoke. He had such a golden voice, so deep, so rich, so—masculine, she yearned to hear it again and again. But she was certain that as soon as she had some of that stew inside her, these silly, lightheaded notions and all those odd flutterings inside her stomach would stop and she would finally return to normal.

Unable to appease her hunger just yet, Katherine turned her attention to the house. It was huge, especially for this area. Not only was the man incredibly handsome and obviously well aware of it, he must be wealthy, too. The pastures were all fenced, cross-fenced, cultivated, and stretched for as far as the eye could see in all directions. Closer in, around the house near the back, sat several smaller outbuildings and a large, angular barn one side of which was partitioned into stables. She counted twelve individual stalls, each with its own divided door opening onto a huge corral.

On the other side of the barn was another large corral, and she could tell by the slant of the roof and the low, open trough, that it was designed for the use of cattle. Several mockernut and cottonwood trees shaded the far side of both corrals and part of the small pasture beyond.

The house itself was not only huge, it was absolutely beautiful—as elegant as any Katherine had ever seen. It was a dignified colonial-style structure that stood proudly among the tall, majestic oaks. Although she did not usually pay much attention to architecture, she particularly admired the six modified Doric columns that supported the second-story gallery, then rose to meet an elaborate cornice, forming two wide galleries along the front of the house.

Most of the house appeared to be built of handmade brick, plastered and painted white. The ornate balustrades along the upper gallery had been painted charcoal black, matching the heavy wooden doors and the huge, slatted shutters, which guarded the large multi-paned windows spaced at equal distances across both floors.

A white wooden fence, which surrounded the yard on three sides of the house, was made of long, narrow planks running crosswise between waist-high fence posts. The lawn was already turning a deep, rich green, even though spring had barely begun. Deep purple irises and sunny yellow jonquils bloomed in the gardens that circled the house. A dark green hedge of English holly, clipped to stand equal in height, bordered both sides of the house and part of the area across the front. A swarm of tiny honey bees was hard at work taking the nectar from the tiny blooms deep within the foliage.

Her eyes were drawn next to the two symmetrically pruned forsythia bushes bursting with bright yellow blooms near the wide steps that led to the lower gallery. Flowering dogwoods and a glorious blanket of bluebonnets grew in the far side-yard, giving the large shaded area a fairy tale aura. Katherine smiled. She might not be too fond of the man or his boorish attitude, but she definitely liked the place where he lived. Flint would never think of looking for her in surroundings like this—they were far too grand.

Although much of the house and yard was hidden by the mammoth trees that surrounded it, the grounds did not appear gloomy. Quite the opposite. Bright splashes of sunshine filtered through the newly budded trees in hundreds of places, making it cheerful and warm. Above all else, it looked peaceful to Katherine. It was certainly a far cry from what she was used to. The house she and Flint had shared for the past few years had seemed large to her when they had first moved in, but it had not been even half this size, and although it had been new, clean, and well-furnished, it seemed drab when compared to this house.

Though Flint's house could not be considered small by any means, it had at many times seemed that way to Katherine—because of the guests who stayed with them so often, Flint's friends, whom she barely knew but was expected to make feel at home. Her husband liked having lots of people around—lots of noisy, ill-mannered people who liked to drink expensive whiskey and eat only the best foods. Leeches, all of them.

"Your home is lovely," she said with an appreciative nod, knowing she had understated the fact, but feeling he was already arrogant enough. Why should she make it worse?

Her eyes continued to take in the extreme beauty, the detailed handwork of the cornice, balustrade, and the huge door with its unusual carved designs. As she waited for his reply, she could almost visualize herself sitting in one of the woven rocker chairs on the lower veranda, enjoying the surrounding quiet. She felt oddly safe here and that was something she had not felt in quite some time. Then remembering the man at her side, the feeling quickly passed.

"Thank you," he said, "but I had little to do with the building of the house. I was only four years old at the time. About all I can really take credit for is the brass knocker on the front door that looks like a lion's head. Mom let me pick it out one day when we were in Shreveport. That's the same day she bought all the original carpets and drapes."

"You didn't mention parents before. You made it sound like this Minnie person would be the only one here. Are your parents away?"

There was such a long, cold stretch of silence, that Katherine turned back to look at him again. She could see the pain in his expression and knew, before he spoke, that both his parents were dead.

"They were killed in a hotel fire in New Orleans several years ago," he said at last.

His voice was choked with such deep emotion, Katherine wished she had never said anything. It was none of her business anyway. Why did she always have to be so curious about everything? So many times when she finally learned the answers to questions, she wished that she hadn't. Many times she would have been better off not knowing. She thought briefly back to the day she had first discovered the horrible truth about her husband.

Jason broke into her thoughts. "And since I have no brothers or sisters, I live here all alone," he continued, his voice still wistful and sad.

"But what about Minnie?"

"Minnie and her husband, Silas, live in one of the cabins out back. So does their oldest son, Mose, with his own two boys," he explained. "And although usually there are several men living in that bunkhouse out back, right now there are only two, Pete and Jack. Rede goes home every night. He lives just down the road a piece." He paused a moment, then grinned. "So you see, there are others who live at Seven Oaks, even though I live in the main house all by myself."

As they rounded the side of the house and Katherine got her first glimpse of the backyard, she was instantly delighted and again in awe. A tiny courtyard, filled with intricate little gardens and fancy wrought iron furniture, sat off to one side—in the far corner of the yard, where a side wing formed a short L. The bricked courtyard was partially shaded by one of the huge oaks and several small redbud trees just beginning to bloom. The redbuds grew right inside the gardens, lending even more color to the bright yellow jonquils and snowy pink azalea bushes that bloomed beneath the trees and throughout the courtyard. A ring of dark blue irises completely encircled a small, brick and iron ornamental pool.

A shaded veranda ran the entire length of the inner L where long wooden benches and comfortable looking woven chairs had been placed both in the shade and in the sun. Planters overflowing with lacy ferns hung from the small columns that supported the overhanging roof at regular intervals, and a dark green vine Katherine was unfamiliar with twined thickly around each of the solumns. A small Negro boy, who had been seated on one of the benches nearest the main part of the house, jumped up as soon as he noticed them, and hurried through one of the doors.

"Here we are," Jason said as he drew the horse to a stop just a few feet away from the back door. He quickly dismounted, and before she had a chance to protest, he placed both hands on her waist and lifted her easily into the air, pulling her against his strong, hard body as he slowly lowered her to the ground. His voice was deep, and his blue eyes sparkled when he spoke again.

"Go on inside and ask Minnie to find you something dry to wear. I'll be in just as soon as I turn Brandy over to Mose and explain that I'll be going out again later this afternoon."

Katherine was momentarily speechless, well aware that their bodies were pressed together and that his hands still clung to her waist. His warmth slowly penetrated her wet clothes, making her that much more aware of him. She knew she should pull away, yet she didn't. When he finally stepped back and released her, she noticed that her wet clothing had left a dark stain on the front of his faded blue shirt. She felt embarrassed and looked away.

"You'll probably find Minnie in the kitchen," he added as he swung back into the saddle and prodded the horse into motion. "Tell her I'll be along in a few minutes."

Feeling momentary outrage at his overt boldness, Katherine watched as he rode off toward the barn, his broad shoulders proud and erect. But her anger was short-lived as that odd little feeling rekindled inside her. She turned away quickly, but as she tried to take the first few steps toward the house, she found her legs unwilling to cooperate. Her already aching hipbones and lower back were now worse as a result of the uncomfortable ride, and her legs felt oddly weak. She almost tumbled backward when she tried to take the first step. It was not until she had reached the small back porch, that she was able to walk without limping, though her legs still felt as if they might buckle at any moment. Again, she was almost certain she would quickly get over her weakness, just as soon as she had something decent to eat. It was all just a temporary condition.

"Hello?" Katherine called as she stood peering in through the open door. When there was no response, she stepped inside. Although she felt awkward about entering a strange house all alone, she knew she would feel even more awkward if the man returned from the barn to find her still standing out on his back porch, gawking at the door. Suddenly, it dawned on Katherine that she did not even know the man's name, nor did he know hers, and yet she had agreed to stay and eat with him. That was not like her. That was not like her at all. But then, she was hungry and her situation was desperate. It was very important that she eat something and soon. Besides, it would be best for both of them if he didn't know her name.

"Hello?" she called out again as she entered an extremely spacious living room with a large, elaborate fireplace that took up almost all of one wall. As she looked around the huge room, she saw that the other, white plaster walls were hung with large, elaborately framed portraits, probably of family members. One portrait closely resembled the man she had just met, yet was different somehow. He seemed much friendlier in the picture. Amazing what a good artist could do.

Her gaze was drawn from the handsome portraits, to the highly polished floor where she could practically see herself in the reflection, and the narrow cove moldings that gleamed along the base and upper corner of the walls. A huge, dark blue Tartan carpet lay in the center of the floor, and the drapes that were drawn back from the long, narrow windows were the exact same shade of blue.

The furniture was as elaborate as might be expected in such a grand house. Two richly upholstered blue and gray sofas with delicately carved wooden accents were the main pieces in the room, along with paw-footed side tables and two long sofa-tables made of a rich, dark walnut. Several side chairs of similar design were arranged facing the two sofas at opposing angles, enabling a very large group to sit and visit at one time.

Katherine finally heard voices from somewhere off to her right and took several more tentative steps in that direction before calling out again. "Hello?"

Suddenly, a large, buxomy Negro woman appeared

through a swinging wooden door, wiping her hands on a small towel as her gaze swept the room. Though her excess weight made her seem ageless, having filled out the wrinkles that might have otherwise shown on her face, it was the white pepperings in the woman's frizzy, black hair that revealed she was getting on in years. The small black boy Katherine had seen earlier stood behind her, holding on to the side of her voluminous brown skirt, his eyes as wide as saucers.

As the woman's curious gaze fell on Katherine, standing in the middle of the room soaked to the skin, her brows lifted questioningly. She reached back and patted the child's curly black head reassuringly, then asked, "Who are you?"

"I'm Katherine. Katherine Mason. I—I'm supposed to—well, I've been invited to dine with—your boss."

"Mr. Jason sent you here to have dinner with him?" she asked as she folded the towel and stuffed it into a large pocket of her white apron.

From the woman's brief glance at her pitiful appearance, and from the deep frown that followed, Katherine was almost able to read the woman's mind. Clearly, she wondered why her boss would bring a woman dressed in such wet, filthy rags into such a fine house—and as a guest!

"Yes, he did," she answered quickly, making note of the name Jason. But was that his first name or last?

"Where'd he find you?" the woman asked bluntly. She reminded Katherine of Lizzie, the longtime family housekeeper who had died soon after the death of Katherine's mother. Katherine wondered if Minnie was just as bossy and opinionated as her Lizzie had been. Judging by the obstinate set of her jaw, Katherine was sure that she was.

"He found me in his pasture. I'm afraid I was trespassing and he caught me," she explained, tugging at her wet skirt.

"And he threw you in some water just 'cause you was trespassin'?" Minnie's eyes grew wide with mounting curiosity. "Land sakes, what that man won't do when he's riled."

"No, no, I was already in the water."

"Then he saved you from drowning?" she asked, suddenly intrigued.

"No, I was bathing," Katherine said hesitantly.

"With your clothes on?"

Rather than answer that one, Katherine changed the direction of the conversation entirely. "I gather you are Minnie. Mr. Jason said you might be able to locate some dry clothes for me to wear while I eat. Would that be possible?" Now that she knew there really was a Minnie and that there were also other people around, though not in the house, she was eager to get out of her wet, clinging clothes and into something dry.

"I'm sure there's somethin' you can put on," Minnie said and headed off towards another door. When she moved, the little boy at her side found himself left out in the open. He hesitated only a moment before he turned and fled from the room, disappearing into the same door he and Minnie had just entered.

"Don't mine Edmond," Minnie said with a wave of her hand. "He's just not used to seeing a white woman is all. Hasn't been many around here lately. Mr. Jason doesn't bring the women he courts out here very often. Come on, Missy. Follow me."

Katherine watched the woman's ample hips sway

from side to side, putting the wide brown skirt into lively motion as she walked through first one door and then another, until they came to the foot of a wide, curving staircase near the front entrance. Though her eyes scanned the beautiful marbled entryway and the elaborate crystal chandelier that hung from an exceptionally high ceiling, Katherine managed to hear most of what Minnie was saying.

"I've got to get back to my kitchen, but you can go on up there to the second room on the right and look into the wardrobe and find yourself somethin' to put on. It probably won't fit you right, but it will at least be clean. Meanwhile, I can wash those clothes of yours and set them out to dry—that is, if that's what you want." Minnie's nose wrinkled at the thought of anyone putting those ragged clothes back on. "But if it turns out that some of those clothes do fit you well enough, I'll see what I can do about getting Mr. Jason to let you keep them." Then she reached over and patted Katherine with genuine concern. "I'll be up with a pitcher of hot water and a big bar of soap just as soon as I get that stew off the stove."

"Thank you," Katherine said earnestly, having caught the word soap through her musings. "I could certainly use it." When Minnie nodded vigorously in undeniable agreement, Katherine laughed. "Did you say the second door?"

"Yes'm, the second door. I'll go get that water on to heat." Having said that, the woman turned and left Katherine at the foot of the stairs staring after her. Katherine felt it odd that a woman so large made so little sound when she walked. Back when she was a child, Katherine had always known whenever their

Lizzie approached, especially if she was angry about something. The whole house vibrated. Katherine smiled at the memory.

Slowly, she started the painful climb up the stairs, trailing her fingertips along the cool mahogany surface of the banister as she went. Halfway up, she paused to turn and look back on the beautiful room below. Never had she seen such grandeur. Never had she known anyone with quite as much wealth. Shaking her head, she tried not to be impressed. After all it was only money. She tried to keep in mind what her mother used to always tell her: *Money can't buy happiness, and it sure can't buy love.* Words from a very wise woman.

When Katherine reached the second door down the hall, she discovered it was closed, but unlocked. Tentatively, she pushed the heavy, wooden door open and stepped inside. The room was less elegant than the others she had seen. The furniture was darker and far more sturdy, and the curtains were made of simple broadcloth, dark brown in color, no lace, no frills. The walls were white stucco much like those below, only rougher in texture. Dark brown moldings bordered the top and the bottom of each wall, and a narrow chair-molding circled the entire room, about three feet off the floor. The rugs in this room were simple. They were multi-colored, braided throw rugs much like those her mother used to make. And although this room smelled much like the rooms below did, scented lightly with lemon oil and beeswax, there was something distinctly different about it. There was something more; something unique that stirred her senses.

Wasting no further time, Katherine quickly closed the door and headed straight for the armoire, flinging the narrow door open wide. Inside, she discovered dozens of men's shirts, all colors and fabrics, neatly folded and stacked high on the narrow shelves. Selecting a creamy yellow and white plaid, since yellow was her favorite color, Katherine quickly slipped out of her wet clothing, stuffing the sodden mass into the porcelain washbasin on top of a wooden commode. Hurriedly, she unbuttoned the shirt, briefly held the soft fabric to her face and breathed the clean, fresh scent that clung to it. What a pleasure to be able to wear clean, dry clothes again.

Standing in front of a tall, floor length mirror, in nothing more than her damp bloomers, Katherine swung the shirt around behind her and paused with it taut across her shoulders while she peered at her frail figure. She frowned at how skinny she looked and at the awful shade of green her bruises had started to turn. The bruise that drew her attention the most was the one just above her stomach. How close the blow had come. How grateful she was that there seemed to have been no permanent damage to the baby.

Quietly, she stared at her still-flat stomach and wondered when she would start to show. Probably not for a couple of months yet. Smiling, Katherine's thoughts lingered on the tiny babe growing within her, and wondered again if the child was a boy or a girl. It really did not matter to her so long as it was healthy. What a wonder motherhood was going to be. She let herself visualize the baby in her arms, but finally her thoughts returned to the present, and she realized she needed to hurry and get into the shirt if she wanted to try on some of the pants lying folded at the bottom of the chest. She also needed to find a hairbrush or a comb; she couldn't think of eating at anyone's table with her hair looking like a tangled mass of wet yarn. But what she really wanted was to wash her hair first and run a wet washcloth over her entire body. She hoped Minnie would hurry with the warm water and soap she had promised to bring her.

It was at that precise moment, while Katherine still held the shirt behind her, hurrying frantically to work one of her arms into the proper sleeve so she could try on the britches and search the room for that much needed hairbrush or comb, that the door swung open wide and in walked Jason.

Chapter Three

"How dare you!' Katherine shrieked at the top of her voice as she spun away, instantly jerking the shirt down around her shoulders to cover what she could of herself, though not quickly enough. Clutching the material to her breasts, she cried out over her shoulder. "How dare you barge in here like that while I'm dressing! Don't you have the decency to even knock? Just what do you think I am?"

"I—I," Jason stammered in surprise, his blue eyes open as wide as his mouth as he stared, half dazed, at the way her damp bloomers clung to the gentle curves of her hips and upper thighs. He hesitated only a moment before finding the words he needed to explain. "This happens to be my bedroom and I'm not in the habit of knocking before I enter my own room. And I only came up here to change shirts. This one is wet." His look of surprise gave way to obvious suspicion as his gaze moved away from her and traveled around the room for something that might have been tampered with. All he could see that seemed to have been touched was the open armoire. "What are you doing in here anyway?"

"As if you completely forgot," she accused, and braved a quick glance over her shoulder, furious to find that he had not been gentlemanly enough to turn away. Her eyes searched the room for something to cover herself or for some place to hide from his probing gaze. "Minnie sent me up here to find some dry clothes—at your request—as if you didn't remember."

"In here? I expected her to send you to my folks' room, across the hall, to try on some of Mother's dresses that should still be stored in there. I know Mother was a little smaller than you, but I figured there might be something in there you could wear," he quickly explained. Finally, he realized he was still staring at her and turned away just in time to see Minnie come bounding into the room, a broom raised high in one hand, ready to do battle, and a pitcher of water in the other. She had sloshed water all over her skirts in her hasty response to Katherine's high-pitched scream.

"What's going on up here?" Minnie demanded with a deep scowl. She glanced from Jason to Katherine, then back to Jason, as she set the large porcelain pitcher down on a nearby chest of drawers. Tapping her foot impatiently on the hardwood floor, she crossed her large arms over her ample bosom and waited for someone to say something.

Jason shrugged and shook his head as he searched for an explanation, but he was still too confused himself.

"That man burst in here while I was dressing," Katherine was quick to point out. "He didn't even bother to knock, even though the door was unmistakably closed. He just came bursting in here."

"That door's always closed," Minnie said firmly. The frown remained on her face while she hurried toward the young woman's trembling form, pulling the almond-colored comforter off the bed as she went. "And, little lady, jest what are you doin' in here in the first place, especially dressed like that?"

"What do you mean, what am I doing in here?" Katherine asked, her voice filled with indignation. Was there some sort of conspiracy against her? "*You* sent me up here to find some dry clothes to wear. And *he's* the one who suggested it in the first place."

"I sent you upstairs all right, but I didn't tell you to come to Mr. Jason's room for any reason. No one ever comes into Mr. Jason's room 'cept me. He don't like no one messin' around with his things."

"You told me to go to the second door, and that was the second door," Katherine said, pointing to the now open door, being careful not to let go of the shirt that was wrapped awkwardly around her upper body. Then, with a little less certainty, she asked, "Wasn't it?" Suddenly, it occurred to her that she might have miscounted doors. Was there one she had somehow not noticed?

"You must've misunderstood me, Missy, I told you to go to the second room on the right. This is the second room down the hallway sure enough, but this room's on the left side of the hall. I clearly remember tellin' you to go to the second room on the right."

"Oh," Katherine responded in a tiny voice. The blood rushed to her face as she glanced back at Jason, who, to her relief, now stood with his back to her, staring at the doorway, his head tilted to one side. She could imagine the smug look that had to be on his face at that very moment. Her stomach tightened. "I guess I didn't listen very carefully."

"Well, you wrap this here around you and I'll show you which room I meant for you to go to," Minnie said, the frown now gone from her face. Quickly, she helped arrange the comforter around Katherine's drawn shoulders so that she was amply covered. "Like I done told you, I don't know if any of Missus Jane's clothes will fit you, you bein' so much taller than she was and all, but it won't hurt to try some of them on."

"And if you can't squeeze into any of my mother's dresses, I have no complaints about you wearing my shirt. From what I could tell, that shirt is going to look pretty good on you." Jason taunted her over his shoulder, smiling broadly at the memory of the glorious view he had just been accidentally made privy to. Although he had caught only a glimpse before she had spun around, he had definitely liked what he saw. He felt himself responding to the fact that her body had been so perfect in every way. He wished the circumstances could have been different when he came bounding in on her. He let his imagination play with the exciting notion of her turning to eagerly accept him into her arms, that supple body eager to please him, instead of hiding from him the way she had, cowering from his gaze. It was certainly something worth working toward.

Clutching the comforter securely around her, Katherine ignored Jason's remark and quickly followed Minnie out of his room, then across the wide hallway into another room. A quick glance down the hallway before she entered the room told her that this was indeed the second door on the right from the staircase. Why couldn't she have listened more carefully? Her face flamed crimson at the thought of what Jason must have seen before she was able to pull the shirt down and turn away from his view.

Never had she felt so utterly mortified in all her life. She wondered if she would be able to manage the courage to go downstairs and eat at the same table with the man, knowing that he probably saw nearly everything about her there was to see. She was grateful she had decided not to take her bloomers off, too. At least he had not gotten an eyeful of her entire body. Again, she cringed at the thought of what he probably did see and for a brief moment she wondered what his impression was. But she quickly put aside those embarrassing thoughts and gave her attention to Minnie.

"See here?" Minnie said in a friendly voice. She had set the pitcher down again and was opening the wide double doors to the huge armoire on the far wall of the elaborately furnished bedroom. "There's still quite a few dresses in here that haven't been given to the church yet. Mister Jason, he gives them away as they are needed, knowing Missus Jane would want the garments to go to good use. That's why I feel sure that if you find one that fits, Mister Jason will let you keep it for your very own and you won't have to go puttin' those . . ." she paused, not wanting to insult the young woman. "You won't have to put that dress of yours back on until I've had a chance to mend it."

Katherine looked appreciatively at the lovely dresses and gowns that hung inside the armoire. Beautiful gowns of rich velvets, flowing silks, shining satins, and soft cashmeres in many different shades of bright, cheerful colors were gathered together at the right hand side. To the left, were more practical dresses made of cotton, wool, gingham, and lawn. The dresses on the left were far more demure in both color and style, and appeared to be more durable. Katherine reached out and ran her finger over the smooth softness of a bright blue satin gown, but it was a simple beige lawn dress that she drew out to try on first.

"I'll leave you here to try on these dresses until you find somethin' you can wear. I've gotta get back down there before my biscuits start to burn," Minnie said. "Come on down when you get yourself washed up and changed. The meal will be ready just as soon as the biscuits get done." Then, as she started out the door, she turned and glanced back at Katherine. "Oh, and you'll find a brush over there inside that pearl-topped box on that little table with the mirror, and there's slippers in that bottom drawer there. If you need any help, just holler and I'll come runnin'."

Still wrapped securely in the thick softness of the bed comforter, Katherine walked over to the bedroom door and slipped the lockbolt in place. Although she was almost certain the incident earlier had not been Jason's fault, she did not care to take any more chances. As soon as the door was secured, she returned to the armoire and let the comforter slip from her shoulders to the polished wood floor.

When she tried to get into the dress she had chosen, she found it surprisingly tight, and she had to wriggle and tug at the fabric. When she finally managed to get it over her shoulders and hips she found that she could not close the fasteners and ties. Despite all her efforts, a two-inch gap remained at the side closure, and when she looked down, she saw with dismay that the hemline stopped midway down her calves. Just how petite had Jason's mother been? She found it hard to imagine that a man so tall and broad in the shoulder could have had a mother this tiny. Obviously, his father must have been exceptionally tall.

After trying on several more dresses, Katherine realized her efforts were futile. Nothing his mother had owned was going to fit her, not even the silk dressing gown she had found. Suddenly, Katherine felt huge. At five-foot eight inches tall, she knew she was taller than most women, but never before had that fact been so distressingly evident.

With no other choice, Katherine finally reached for the yellow and white plaid shirt she had discarded. The hem of the oversized shirt came to just below her knees in front and just above her knees on the sides. The long, cuffed sleeves hung down to where only a few inches of her fingertips showed, making her feel awkward to say the least. The shirt was as large on her as his mother's dresses had been small. Frowning at the image in the mirror, she rolled the sleeves up to her elbows and adjusted the collar.

She regretted not having taken a pair of the britches in Jason's room. Too much of her legs were exposed and much more of her neckline than she cared to display. But there was nothing she could do about that now. Her attire was certainly far from appropriate, but at least it covered the essentials. It occurred to her that he'd already seen a good portion of those essentials. Mortified once again at the thought, she pressed her eyes shut and tried to put the embarrassing episode out of her mind.

When she pulled open the drawer at the base of the armoire and tried on some slippers she found there, she was relieved to discover that one pair actually fit, though snugly. At least she would not have to face him in bare feet. After vigorously brushing her tangled hair and stretching the shirt as much as she could, she finally felt presentable enough to go downstairs and face Jason.

With her stomach rumbling and churning, Katherine unbolted the door and stepped cautiously out into the hallway. The door to Jason's room was closed, but since it was always kept closed, there was no way of telling whether or not he was still inside. Drawing a deep, steadying breath, she headed for the stairway and slowly descended with as much dignity as she could muster considering how sore her feet were and how ridiculous her attire. Only the thought of finally getting something to eat kept her from turning around and running back to the bedroom.

Although she could not quite remember which way to go, the aroma of freshly baked bread and spicy beef stew led her down the correct hallway and into a large dining room. There, at one end of the long, elaborately carved dining table, was Jason, his large, shapely hands resting, fingertips pressed together, on the smooth, polished surface. She was relieved to find he did not look up when she bravely entered the room.

Lost in thought, Jason now wore a gray and black plaid shirt. The top three buttons had been left undone for comfort, allowing her a view of the wisps of dark, curling hair that covered his deeply tanned chest.

Katherine tried not to let her eyes focus on that narrow expanse of flesh as she carefully sat down in the chair at the opposite end of the table.

When Jason looked up and finally noticed her, she offered him a tentative smile. Her body responded wildly to the broad smile he offered her in return. Never had she seen such deep dimples on a man. For the first time she wondered why a man as handsome as Jason had not married. Or had he? Perhaps he was a widower. Perhaps he was divorced. Or perhaps he was still married and his wife had discovered what a terrible scoundrel he was. Maybe she'd run away from him as Katherine had fled from her husband.

"I had to settle for your shirt," she said softly, glancing down at her unconventional apparel. "Your mother's things were all too small."

"I had a feeling they would be," he said, with a deepening smile. His gaze dropped to the table for a moment to take in what the highly polished surface didn't hide from his view. Although she had buttoned it all the way to the top, the neck of the shirt was wide enough to expose the gentle curve of her collarbone. How he wished he could see more. "My, but that shirt does look good on you," he continued, "far better than it ever looked on me."

"Thank you," she stammered, not knowing whether or not to accept this as a sincerely intended compliment. She was never sure if he was taunting her or not, but this time he seemed in earnest. Folding her hands in her lap, she turned her eyes away from his penetrating gaze and waited for the food to be served. She hoped Minnie would hurry.

"You aren't used to compliments are you?" he asked

and, to himself, wondered how that could be when she was so captivatingly beautiful. Now that she had changed from that ragged dress and had brushed her long, dark hair so that it fell in smooth, damp ringlets over her slender shoulders, he realized just how truly beautiful she was. Every one of her features was perfect—her eyes, her mouth, her nose, everything.

He felt his pulse quicken as he remembered once again all that he'd seen upstairs. He could not remember a woman ever stirring his senses quite as readily. Just looking into her shining brown eyes made his head swim. Why had such a beautiful woman been allowed to roam the countryside all alone? Then, realizing she had not yet answered his question, he repeated it, knowing he would get to all his other questions soon enough. "You aren't used to anyone complimenting you are you?"

Katherine looked at him, perplexed and surprised. She had not expected a question like that and it took her a moment to consider an answer. Choosing her words carefully, she finally said, "I'm certainly not used to getting any kind of compliment from you."

"That will have to be corrected then, because a woman as attractive as you are should be told of her beauty again and again."

Startled, Katherine raised a questioning eyebrow. Leaning back in her chair, she eyed him suspiciously.

"You don't trust me, do you?" he asked. The dimples at the corners of his mouth deepened as he smiled, drawing her attention.

"I have no reason to."

Jason laughed and nodded his agreement. "I don't blame you. Most of the time, I don't trust myself. I'm far too impulsive. I have a tendency to do or say what's on my mind before I really have time to think through all the consequences. It's gotten me into deep trouble more times than I care to count. Minnie says I go around with my brain unloaded and my mouth half-cocked."

Before Katherine could consider that remark, Minnie bustled into the room, carrying a large tray of food—two steaming bowls of stew, a plate stacked high with hot biscuits, and a tall, frosted cut glass pitcher of milk. As Minnie placed one of the bowls at Katherine's place setting, then carefully poured her a tall glass of milk, Katherine felt her insides quiver in anticipation. She was suddenly so hungry, she felt weak. It took all her self-restraint to wait until Jason had been served before plunging her spoon into the creamy brown stew that filled her bowl to the brim.

She placed the first bite in her mouth and let it linger on her tongue just long enough to savor the wonderful taste of the hot food, before gulping it down. She did not hestiate to replace it with a second heaping spoonful. Never had anything tasted so good.

"There's plenty more," Jason commented, amazed at how quickly her stew was disappearing. He frowned, for he realized now that it must have been days since her last meal.

Katherine was delighted to hear there was more. She felt she could eat at least three bowls and certainly intended to try. There was no telling how long it would be before she would have the opportunity to eat again. She had no idea how much farther her brother's ranch was from here, much less how long it would take her to get there.

"Sir, could you tell me how far it is to Jefferson?" she asked when she had finally set her spoon down in order to pick up one of the three biscuits Minnie had set at her place.

"Is that where you are headed? Jefferson?"

Katherine could see no reason to keep her destination a secret from this man and answered truthfully. "Yes, I have a brother that lives there."

"And you plan to travel all that distance on foot?" he asked, unbelievingly.

"Yes, sir, I do. How far is it?"

Jason cringed at the way she kept calling him "sir." It felt like a carefully placed wedge between them. "If you promise to call me Jason, I'll gladly tell you how far Jefferson is from here."

"Okay, Jason it is," she nodded, spreading her biscuit with a spoonful of strawberry preserves.

Jason frowned when she did not offer him the use of her first name in return. He realized he did not even know her last name as yet—but he would give her more time to get used to him first. "Jefferson is only about thirty miles from here."

Only? She paused with her spoon in midair as she considered his answer. It would take her at least three more days to get to Jefferson at the rate she had traveled these last few days. Ever since she'd hit the hilly wooded area of central northeast Texas, the going had become very slow.

Jason could tell by her stunned expression that she had not thought Jefferson was quite that far, and he said sympathetically, "It's a good day's ride all right. I can imagine how long it would take to have to walk the distance."

Katherine could, too. "Are you sure it's that far?" she asked, laying her spoon down, the strawberry preserves now forgotten.

Jason nodded, wondering why he felt so apologetic. It certainly wasn't his fault Jefferson was so far away.

"Well then, the sooner I get back on my way, the better," she said, pushing her chair back from the table.

"Not until you are finished eating," Jason said firmly. "Like I've told you, there's plenty more."

"Thank you, but I'm full." It was the truth. Although she'd thought she would be able to eat several helpings, she had barely been able to finish the one. She wondered about that because her appetite had never been known to be dainty. Had her stomach become unaccustomed to food?

"But your clothes haven't possibly had time to dry," he reminded her. "Surely you don't intend leaving here with nothing but my shirt on."

Katherine had forgotten about her odd apparel and looked down at the yellow shirt with a frown. No, she couldn't very well set out for Jefferson dressed like this. It had taken all her courage just to come downstairs in the scanty outfit.

"Minnie is planning to wash out your dress, and as soon as it's dry enough, she will mend the hem and the sleeve that was so badly torn. Stay at least until she's had time to finish. While you're waiting, you can rest upstairs in one of the bedrooms. Surely a couple of hours can't hurt."

The thought of being able to lie down in a real bed for a couple of hours did sound inviting. Glancing at the clock on the fireplace mantel, she noticed that it was not yet one o'clock. If she left by three, she could still get in four to five hours of travel before it was too dark to see. Moreover, she would probably be able to cover more ground once she had rested her tired, aching body. Finally, she answered. "A short rest would be nice. Thank you."

Explaining that Minnie was busy preparing food for the hired hands, Jason showed Katherine back to the room she had changed in. As he turned back the bed covers, he saw the deep yearning look in her dark eyes. He had already noticed her slight limp and the way her arms hung heavily at her sides. She must be exhausted. He wondered how long she had traveled through the woods on foot, and why she did not walk along the main road, where it was more likely she'd be offered a ride. He decided she must be deathly afraid of strangers, which would account for her wary attitude toward him.

"Make yourself at home," he said and was startled by the way she gasped just at the sound of his voice. Why was she so nervous? Was it because they were alone in a bedroom? Probably, though it certainly didn't make him nervous. He smiled inwardly at the emotions it did arouse. "I have to go out to the barn for awhile. I've got work to do; but if you need anything, anything at all, just holler down to Minnie and she'll get it for you. Meanwhile, she'll be sewing up the tears in your dress."

"Thank you, but I doubt I'll be needing anything. Please have her bring the dress up here when she's through," Katherine requested, her eyes never straying far from the turned down bed.

"Just don't leave without saying goodbye first," he cautioned, then looked at her one last time. Noting once again how truly beautiful she was, he smiled broadly and left.

As he helped Silas and Mose unload the wagonload of lumber and supplies he had ordered, all Jason could think about was the woman now asleep in his parents' old room. So many questions remained unanswered. There was so much he wanted to know about her. He had intended to at least find out her name, but she still hadn't given him the chance to do even that.

Unable to concentrate on anything else as he worked, Jason continued to wonder about the many mysteries that lovely young woman presented. It occurred to him that he really did not want her to leave Seven Oaks just yet; he wanted to keep her there a while longer, at least long enough to solve all those mysteries that seemed to surround her. And that bothered him. He was not usually the type to care one way or the other about any woman. Oh, he'd had his share of women in his twenty-seven years—he was certainly no saint—but no woman had ever stirred his imagination quite the way that this one did.

By the time the wagon was unloaded and the supplies stored away, Jason found himself more determined than ever not to let the young woman leave. He would do whatever it took to keep her there short of hog-tying her, and even that might not be totally out of the question. As the sun sank behind the trees that lined the hills along the west pasture, he hurried back to the house intending to find some way—he wasn't sure how—of preventing her departure.

Bounding into the kitchen, he found Minnie leaning over a steaming pot, a large wooden spoon in her hand.

There was no sign of their guest anywhere.

"Has she come down yet?" he asked, hoping to sound only casually interested as he tossed his hat on a wooden peg near the door.

"Not yet," Minnie assured him, laying her spoon aside. "I took that dress on up there as soon as I finished and laid it across the bentwood just like you told me to, but I was real quiet so's not to wake her. That poor child is exhausted."

"We'll just let her sleep awhile longer then," Jason told her, knowing it would be dark soon. He felt certain she would not be quite so eager to leave once night had fallen. He would at least be assured of her company until morning, and by then, he should be able to come up with another reason for her to stay.

"I think that'll be best for her, too," Minnie nodded, suppressing a grin. She knew why Mister Jason was so eager to keep the pretty young woman there a while longer. She'd seen the way he had looked at her all through lunch. Keeping her face as straight as she could, she pointed out needlessly, "It will probably mean she'll have to spend the night here. She sure can't be headin' out of here in the dark. Wolves would eat her for sure. So, I've already got it planned for her to eat with you again. I'm cooking up two thick beefsteaks with lots of vegetables. I sure hope she wakes up in time to eat. It looks like your supper's going to be ready in about half an hour."

"I don't mind a late supper. Go ahead and feed everyone else and see to our supper last. I don't mind at all," Jason assured her. "If she doesn't wake up soon, though, one of us might have to go up there and get her up. As much as she needs her rest, she also needs her nourishment. That beefsteak will do her good."

"That's true. That poor girl is mostly skin and bones."

Jason disagreed, not from what he'd seen. Granted she was thin, but he'd hardly describe her as skin and bones. From what he'd had the pleasure of viewing—though he'd barely gotten a glimpse—she was just about right. A few more good meals and she'd be about as perfect as a woman could get. His eyes widened at the images taking shape at the back of his mind. Again, just the thought of her had stirred his insides into a beehive of activity. Heading out of the kitchen, he wondered just how long he should wait before trying to wake her. Starting upstairs, he shook his head wonderingly, partly upset, yet most intrigued. How could one little gal he knew absolutely nothing about cause so much commotion to rise up inside him so quickly? As he bounded up the stairs two at a time, he wondered if he had time to shave again.

Chapter Four

"Miss, it's time you woke up."

Slowly, Katherine forced one eye open to focus on her immediate surroundings. When she did, she discovered Jason standing beside the bed smiling down at her. What a pleasant awakening.

Her own smile spread slowly across her face in response as her eyes drifted closed again. He stood looking down at her a moment longer before speaking again. How like an angel she looked in sleep. So serene, so peaceful, so different from the way she was when she was awake—when she was keenly alert, as if she felt she had to constantly be on guard against something, skittish as a newborn colt.

He wondered about that. He had a feeling she was running away from something or someone, but could not imagine what. Who would want to harm anyone so beautiful, so full of life. Only a fool. So why was she running? Why was she so nervous? "Time to wake up. Supper is almost ready."

"Supper?" Her eyes flew open in alarm. Quickly, she

glanced around the room for a clock, blinking in sleepy confusion. When she realized there was no clock in the room, she looked toward the window and saw that the sunlight had gone. Leaning forward to get a better look out the window, she noticed that the sky was already dark, then suddenly realized that both the bedside lamp and the one on the wall near the door had been lit. "What time is it?" she asked in alarm.

"It's just past seven o'clock," he said gently.

"Seven o'clock? I've been asleep for six hours?" It was hard to believe so much time had passed that quickly. It seemed as if she had lain down only a few moments before. But the darkened window did not lie. It had to be at least seven o'clock. Lightly, she rubbed her face with the back of her hand. "Why didn't you wake me earlier?"

"I figured you needed your rest." He shrugged. "Be glad I decided to get you up now or you'd probably have missed out on supper entirely. Minnie's so busy getting the meal ready she couldn't come up here to wake you, and left on your own, I doubt you would have wakened for hours. As you can see," he said, pointing to the blue wool dress on a nearby chair, "she finished mending your dress. You'll have just enough time to slip out of my shirt and into your dress before supper gets served. Or you can come on down in my shirt. Doesn't really matter much. It'll just be me at the table and I never have cared much for eating formal." Privately, he rather liked the way his shirt looked on her.

Katherine's muddled thoughts were just starting to clear as she threw back the covers and climbed out of bed to take a better look at her dress. So sore were her muscles when she moved, she was totally unaware of the generous expanse of leg she inadvertently revealed to Jason as she slipped from the feather mattress onto the polished wood floor. Barefooted, she padded across the cool floor to the chair, took the dress, examined it closely, and was delighted to see that the repairs had been so professionally done. "Minnie did a good job. I must remember to thank her."

"You can thank her by hurrying down to supper. She says it'll be ready in about fifteen minutes," he replied. Turning to leave, he gave her bare ankles one last wistful glance. "Come on down as soon as you're ready. Nothing worse than cold beefsteak."

Katherine could think of a long list of things that were far worse than cold beefsteak, but did not feel it appropriate for a guest to argue with her host over such a trivial matter, even a reluctant guest such as she was. "I'll be right down."

This time, when Katherine stepped over to the mirror to brush her hair, after having quickly changed back into her dress and Jason's mother's slippers, she was pleased to see that the dark circles she had noticed beneath her eyes earlier had faded until they were hardly detectable. Although she still looked somewhat gaunt, the few hours of rest had done wonders for her appearance and had made quite a difference in the way she felt. True, her muscles were still sore, and her feet still ached with every step that she took, but she could tell that some of her strength had returned. She might have lost valuable traveling time, but the benefits gained were well worth it. Now that she had rested, she surely would be able to go farther in less time. As she ran the brush through her long brown hair, she smiled.

She felt more like her old self again, ready to take on the whole world if need be.

"You look lovely," Jason commented when Katherine finally appeared at the dining room door, still smiling to herself. Quickly, he pushed his chair back and stood until she had fully entered the room. Then, as she approached the table, he reached over and pulled out a chair that was much closer to his than the one she had sat in earlier.

"It's a little hard to believe I look very lovely considering the worn condition of my clothing and all, but thank you just the same," she responded, fighting a strange urge to blush. She glanced curiously at him for a moment before approaching the chair he so gallantly offered. She found it hard not to notice the fine hairs that lightly covered the back of his darkly tanned hands.

Such strong looking hands, the hands of a man who did an honest day's work. Nothing like her husband's hands. Even though her husband's hands were extremely important in his chosen profession, they were slender and lily white, and had not a single callous. You'd think they were the hands of a doctor, not the hands of a notorious killer. She shuddered, pushing the thought far to the back of her mind.

"Can you possibly be the same man who acted so rudely earlier?" she asked. "I wonder. Do I dare give you the opportunity to pull that chair right out from under me? Or shall I play it safe and move along to another seat?"

Jason laughed at her pointed remark. "I realize you have reason to doubt my character, but take a chance. I promise to behave myself, at least for tonight."

Katherine thought about that as she did indeed take a chance and slowly lowered herself into the waiting chair. It almost sounded as if he expected there would be other nights to consider. It was an intriguing thought, but she knew she had to be on her way just as soon as possible, though probably not until morning.

After Jason had seen to Katherine's chair, he paused at the doorway to tell Minnie to serve, then hurried back to his usual chair, which placed him to Katherine's right, facing her at an angle. "Before we eat, I have one request to make of you," he said, while settling himself in the small, hardwood chair. He had waited politely quite long enough for her to give him her name. He did not intend to wait a moment longer.

"Oh? And what is that?" she asked, instantly wary. No telling what sort of request a man like Jason might make. She had not missed the way the man's eyes wandered over her, much like a cat looks at a tempting morsel of fish. It was one of the reasons she still didn't trust him.

"You have carefully avoided telling me your name, and I can't keep referring to you as 'that woman' forever. What's the big secret? Surely you can tell me your name."

"We never have properly introduced ourselves, have we?" she agreed with a smile of relief. Although she still thought it would be better if he did not know her name, she refused to make a name up. "My name is no secret, not really. It's Katherine. Katherine Mason. Now will you please set me straight on your full name? I know it is Jason, but is that your first name or last?"

"First. My full name is Jason Alan Morris."

"What a coincidence. I have a young cousin whose

name is also Jason Alan—Jason Alan Sobey."

"He must be a fine man," Jason said jokingly, his dimples deepening in his lean cheeks, drawing Katherine's attention away from his pale blue eyes for a moment—but only a moment—for his eyes were his most interesting feature. "Anyone with a name like that has to be a fine man," he went on to say. "What does he do for a living?"

"He's a cattle rustler," she quipped, then waited until a look of total surprise spread over his face before continuing, "No, I'm not really sure what Jason does for a living. It's been six years since I've had any real family news. All I know is that when we were children, he admitted to me that he wanted to be a riverboat captain."

She paused a moment, remembering. She and Jason had been so full of adventurous dreams as children. He had told her about wanting to be a riverboat captain, and she had confided in him about wanting to marry a rich man and see the world. Sadly, she wondered if Jason had ever managed to find his happiness, or had his youthful dreams been shattered by the blunt edge of reality like hers had?

Jason watched the emotions play across Katherine's face for several moments before finally interrupting her thoughts. "Six years since you've had any real family news? Why is that? Or should I mind my own business?"

"My father and I had a falling out several years ago and although I did write him to see how he was getting along, he never answered the letters." She paused to swallow the lump that had risen in her throat. Her father had never bothered to as much as acknowledge her letters in any way. She had poured out her heart and soul to him, begged for his forgiveness, but he had never so much as sent her a postal card in response. If only he could bring himself to forgive her.

Blinking back the tears that had started to well up in her dark eyes, she explained, "The only family news I've had in the past six years has come from my older brother, Andrew; but he writes such short letters and never mentions Jason or any one else in the family, other than Father. Still, I think of Jason from time to time. I truly hope that he has indeed become a riverboat captain and is as happy and as carefree as ever."

At that moment, Minnie entered the room with a tray of steaming hot food and tall glasses of chilled water. "I do think I outdone myself tonight, Mister Jason. Mmmm-mmm, it sure does smell good, don't it?"

"Yes, it does," Jason said appreciatively, taking a deep whiff of the delicious aroma that came from the tray. "I can hardly wait to sink my teeth into that beefsteak. I'm as hungry as a bear."

"You's always hungry as a bear." Minnie chuckled as she served Katherine a thick, juicy beefsteak, thinly sliced potatoes in white gravy, and steaming mounds of green beans and black-eyed peas. After she had served Jason, Minnie placed her hands on her hips and announced to them both, "You two eat hearty, but save room for a big piece of my apple pie. Silas done had one slice and says it has to be one of the best I ever baked."

"I'll be sure to save room," Jason promised as he lifted his fork from the table, eager to dig right in.

"Don't you go eatin' yet, Mister Jason. You've got company at your table. You should say the blessin' first. It's only proper."

"By all means, let's be proper," Jason muttered with a slight frown, reluctantly returning his fork to the table. With a resigned sigh, he folded his hands on the table and bowed his head, glancing up just once to make sure that Katherine had done the same before he carefully recited: "Dear Lord, thank you for the many blessings you have bestowed upon us, especially for the bountiful food of which we are about to partake and may we always be openly thankful for everything you do for us. In Christ's name. Amen."

"That's better," Minnie said, nodding appreciatively. "You can eat now. Call if you need me," she said, turning to leave. Looking back over her shoulder, she cautioned them both, "And if y'all don't eat all those peas and green beans, you won't be havin' no apple pie after all." Then, with a quick twirl of her skirts, she was gone.

"I want to apologize for Minnie's behavior. She gets a little bossy sometimes, and I guess that's as much my fault as it is hers; but she does mean well," Jason said, lifting his fork once again.

"No apology is necessary," Katherine laughed, all gloomy thoughts pushed once again to the back of her mind. "We used to have a freeservant just like Minnie. She was one of the most aggravating women I have ever known, but I loved her dearly."

"Then you understand," Jason nodded.

"Enough that I intend to eat every pea on my plate," she said with a firm nod, and they both laughed.

There was little talk while they ate. There was only so

much they could say about the weather, and they did not know enough about each other to talk about anything else. It was not until they had both eaten their fill, that Katherine spoke again as she sat back from the table.

"That was very good. Maybe *too* good," she said with a slight groan, making an effort to stand.

Jason chuckled and patted his own stomach soundly. "Why don't you join me in a short walk out to the barn to check on my two new foals? It'll help us work off some of what we ate."

Katherine considered the invitation, but finally declined because her feet were still sore and she recalled that the barn was quite a distance from the house. She decided instead to sit for a while in one of the wickerwork chairs out on the back patio. There she sat quietly, listening to the breeze gently stirring the leaves and the crickets and katydids giving an evening concerto, accompanied by the occasional bellow of a cow off in the distance and the faint sound of a dog barking playfully at the bright yellow half-moon. The sounds were so peaceful, Katherine's head started to nod.

Jason went to the barn to check on his two foals, but quickly returned to join Katherine in the torchlit gardens, startling her out of her reverie with the sound of chair legs scraping against the red brick terrace. Just as he settled himself comfortably next to her, a large yellow-striped cat appeared out of nowhere and lay down quietly at his feet.

"Friend of yours?" she asked, indicating the new arrival who was now stretched contentedly across the cool patio floor with his head resting lightly on his front paws.

"That's Bart," Jason explained, bending forward and rubbing the cat lightly under its fuzzy yellow chin. Bart meowed appreciatively, rolled over on his side to offer Jason easier access, then started to purr loudly. "He just showed up in the kitchen one day, and after having had an ample taste of some of Minnie's Sunday chicken, decided to stay. Didn't you, boy?"

"Appreciates good food does he?" she asked and leaned forward to offer the cat a friendly stroke. When she did, the side of her hand grazed Jason's and an odd sensation shot through her like summer lightning, causing her to jerk her hand away.

Jason frowned, but said nothing as he gave the cat a final pat, then leaned back to stare at her quizzically.

"Lovely night, isn't it?" Katherine said, in an attempt to break the awkward silence that had fallen between them. She was well aware that he was staring at her and hoped to draw his attention to something else. "It's a little chilly out here, but aren't the stars beautiful."

Jason looked up at the starry sky. "Yes, I suppose they are. Never gave stars much thought before, except when I've needed them to find my way."

"I've never been able to do that," she told him. "But then, I rarely travel at night. I hate to admit it, but I'm pretty much afraid of the dark. I'm especially afraid to be out in the woods alone after dark."

"Afraid the boogie man's going to get you?"

"No, I'm more afraid of the boogie bears and boogie wolves," she said defensively.

Jason stared at her thoughtfully for a long moment, then asked, "There's something I've been dying to know and hoped you would tell me without me having to ask."

"What's that?" she asked cautiously.

"Just what were you doing out there in my pond this morning?"

"I think that was rather obvious," she said, suddenly flushing as she recalled the embarrassing episode. Why couldn't he leave it alone? Did he take some sort of perverse pleasure in other people's discomfort? It reminded her of her husband—rake them over the coals and watch them dance. "I was taking a bath," she said aloud.

"But why in *my* pond? What were you doing in my pasture in the first place—alone?"

Katherine debated how much she should tell him; then decided it would be best to say as little as possible. "I am on my way to my brother's ranch near Jefferson."

"On foot?" he asked, though he'd already figured that out.

"Yes, on foot. And all that walking had made me thirsty, so thirsty that when I saw your pond, I just ignored the 'no trespassing' signs. Then, when I got closer, the cool water looked so refreshing I decided to jump right in. I'm sorry I trespassed, but I was truly very hot and extremely thirsty."

"You actually drank that water?" he asked, surprised and a little put off at the thought.

"Yes, why do you ask? Surely the pond isn't poisoned, or you would never allow your cattle to drink from it."

"No, it's not poisoned," he admitted, deciding not to mention what drained into the pond after a heavy rain—it was smack in the middle of a cattle pasture and was not continuously fed by either a stream or a spring.

Rather than upset her with something that was over and done with, he changed the subject entirely, "So you are headed for your brother's ranch over near Jefferson. Is that the same brother who writes you those short letters every now and then?"

"Yes, Andrew." She spoke her brother's name with such fondness, it made Jason smile. "He bought a small ranch somewhere just outside of Jefferson a couple of years ago. I've never actually been there, but from the way he describes it, it must be a truly beautiful place. He's very, very proud of it."

"I imagine he is. Land up around Jefferson is real pretty, especially down along the river. But that's a full day's ride from here. It'll take you days to walk that."

"I have little choice," she responded, leaning her head wearily against the back of the wickerwork chair. She was not ready to be reminded of all the miles she still had to travel.

"If you're willing to wait until Saturday, you can ride over to Jefferson with me. I was planning to head over there Monday, for a big cattle auction, but I can probably get away as early as Saturday."

Katherine glanced at him in surprise, silently weighing her choices. She could strike out again on her own, first thing in the morning—on feet that had gone beyond aching and throbbed even now as she sat resting—and by stopping only to sleep, she might be able to reach Jefferson as early as Friday afternoon. Or she could wait, give her feet a chance to recover, and ride the last leg of her long journey in relative comfort. She studied Jason's face. Although at times he seemed to be kin to the devil, the man had twice kept his promise to behave himself. But how long would that last? Might he have any hidden motives in his invitation to stay?

Although she was coming to like him better, she was not really sure she trusted him yet. Then again, was it worth all the pain and effort it would take just to be able to arrive in Jefferson a day earlier? The main reason she wanted to reach Andrew's ranch was for her safety. She was probably just as safe here, if not safer. Her husband would never find her here. But then, remembering the way Jason had looked at her several times that day, she wondered if there weren't other dangers to consider.

"Are you sure I won't be putting you out by staying until Saturday?" she asked, though she realized she had already made up her mind. She would stay until Saturday. It would not only be best for her, it would also be best for the baby.

"What's one more mouth to feed?" he said with a broad smile. "Minnie's used to me taking in strays. Besides, it'll be a welcome change to have someone pretty to talk to in the evenings."

Katherine felt her pulse quicken. Did he actually think she was pretty? As thin and pale as she was now? No—she decided quickly—of course not. He was just being nice in order to convince her to stay.

"Thank you," she finally said in response to his compliment. "But I intend to help out around here during my stay. I don't want to be a burden on either you or on Minnie." What she didn't say was that she did not want to be beholden to him since there was no telling what payment he might try to extract if he thought it was due him.

"Then it's settled. You are staying. My house is your

house." Then, with a sparkle in his eye from still-vivid memories, he added, "And feel free to come into my room at any time and borrow any of my shirts you want."

Katherine pressed her eyes shut, trying to forget the embarrassing episode in his room, and then, afraid the conversation was about to veer off in the wrong direction, she quickly excused herself and went up to bed.

Still physically exhausted, Katherine slept soundly through the night and well into the following morning. It was almost eleven o'clock when the clattering wheels of a wagon jolted her rudely awake. Hurrying to the window, she glanced out to see that it was Jason, driving an empty buckboard into the main part of the barn. A curious warmth spread through her just at the sight of him, and she suddenly realized she was eager to be downstairs in case he came into the house. Despite her misgivings, she had already grown fond of the man.

With the fresh pitcher of water and new cake of scented soap that had been left for her on the commode near the bed, she hurriedly washed and dressed. Brushing her hair, she was disappointed to note that her long, dark tresses simply refused to shine as they should.

What she really needed was a long bath and a chance to wash her hair thoroughly. And that was one of the first things she intended to do when she got downstairs. She would find out where they did their bathing, then heat enough water for a long, leisurely bath and a thorough shampoo.

When Katherine went looking for Minnie, she found that the kitchen was empty. Since there was steam rising from several pots on top of the stove, she felt certain that Minnie had not gone far, and she stepped outside to look for her.

It was a beautiful morning. The sun had already climbed high into an azure sky dotted by an occasional fluffy cloud. A cool breeze rustled the leaves as Katherine strolled into the shaded area of the gardens in search of the housekeeper. As she sank into the same chair she had sat in the night before, she found her eyes drawn to the barn, where she had last seen Jason. She saw no one at all now. Other than the leaves rustling above, nothing at all stirred. But she could hear sounds coming from inside the barn, and felt certain someone was in there, probably Jason. But where was Minnie?

Slowly, she scanned the area for sight of the woman, and for the first time, really took notice of the several outbuildings that surrounded the house and barn. One of the larger buildings closest to her, had been built to match the house, right down to the black slatted shutters flanking the two narrow windows and the handmade bricks that had been carefully laid and painted white. But though very similar in design, this smaller structure was only one story high and only one-third the width of the main house. And, judging by the huge double black doors that opened onto a narrow graveled drive, she felt certain this smaller brick building had to be the carriage house. She wondered why anyone would need such a large carriage house for it could easily accommodate up to eight carriages or buggies.

All the other outbuildings were also painted white with a charcoal trim, but they were built of wood, for the most part. There seemed to be a bunkhouse; a smokehouse, with a woodshed built onto one side; an ice house; and one building that appeared to be a blacksmith's shed or a large tool house of some sort. Three of the buildings that were situated farthest from the house were tiny cottages of some sort, but only two of the identically built dwellings looked as if they were actually lived in.

Katherine wondered about the cottages. Were those the "cabins" Jason had told her Minnie, Silas, and Mose lived in? The word cabin seemed quite an understatement to Katherine. Although they were dwarfed by the size of the main house, they were clearly large enough to accommodate good-sized families. To Katherine, a cabin was something small and roughly built. These buildings were a far cry from that—each was built two stories high and each had its own fenced-in dooryard. She knew she would certainly be proud to call any one of them home.

Beyond the cabins was a neatly planted vegetable garden with green, leafy plants in various stages of growth, and beyond the garden lay a huge, grassy pasture dotted with pale pink and bright yellow wildflowers. Large, robust cattle, like those she had seen the day before, grazed lazily on the green grass in all directions. A narrow stream wound lazily through the gently rolling pastures, where, at one place near a tall stand of pine and sweetgum, it had been dammed to form a small pond. The languid pool of crystal blue water was accented by the deep green of the grass that circled it and the dark reds and pale pinks of the wildflowers that dotted its shoreline. As she gazed at the beautiful, tranquil spot, it occurred to her that it looked very much like the pond where Jason had found her the morning before.

Shuddering at the remembered humiliation, she shifted her gaze from the scene, quickly forcing her thoughts on to other things. It was then that she noticed Minnie emerging from the barn with a tall stoneware pitcher in her right hand, and a large bundle, wrapped in brown paper and tied with white string, tucked under her left arm. Though she seemed to have the pitcher well in hand, the package was starting to slip.

"Here, let me help you," Katherine said, rising and hurrying toward Minnie, who was now only a short distance away.

"Take the package," Minnie said, turning so that Katherine could remove it from under her arm. "It's something Mister Jason picked up for you in town when he went in this morning for a keg of nails. He didn't tell me for sure what's in it, but I suspect it's clothes from the mercantile. He asked if I'd take it on up to you right away."

Katherine squeezed the bulky package between her fingertips and concluded that Minnie was probably right. It certainly felt like clothing. Curious to see just what Jason might have picked out in the way of women's clothing, she began to tug on the string, but found it too strong to break with her bare hand and the knot too secure to untie.

"You'll need a pair of scissors to get into that package," Minnie said. "There's a pair in Missus Jane's sewing room. Just go on through the kitchen and into the room on the right. That's Missus Jane's sewing room. You'll find scissors in that brown leather case in the top drawer of the tallest cedar chest." She grinned as she added, "You won't have no trouble findin' the correct room this time; it's the *only* door on the right. You can even try on the clothes in there if you want. I'll see that no one disturbs you."

"I'd really like to take a bath first," Katherine started to say, knowing she'd feel better about trying on new clothes once she had a bath and a shampoo.

"Already ahead of you, Missy. I got hot water already waitin' on you, and the bathing room is that little room this side of the kitchen. You have to enter it from the outside, though. It used to be a storage room till Missus Jane had it turned into a special bathing room like the ones she'd seen in Shreveport. Before that, they had to either carry hot water up the stairs and bathe in their rooms or set a tub out in the kitchen and bathe there. While I'm at it, that door over there—at the end of that part of the house over there—is where you'll find the privy. No need to go back upstairs if the need arises," Minnie explained, realizing Jason probably had not bothered to mention such a private matter to her. "I'll go ahead and tote your water in for you while I got the time. In about half an hour, I have to serve the noon meal to the hands."

"Oh? Do they eat at the house?"

"No, outside behind the bunkhouse usually. They got a big table set up out under the trees, and I just carry the food on out there and serve it up, except durin' the winter when it gets real cold. Then they fix up a table inside the bunkhouse, and I serve their food to them in there."

"Where does Jason usually eat?"

"Depends on which meal. He usually eats breakfast alone, at the house, and the noon meal outside, with the men—but for supper, I never know if he's goin' to want to eat at the house by himself or out at the bunkhouse with the men. Tonight though, I know he's eatin' at the house, because he done told me he wants to eat with you, and told me what he wanted me to fix."

"He won't be having lunch at the house?" Katherine asked, realizing she was disappointed though she had no reason to be. She was certainly used to eating alone. Unless her husband had some special reason to rise early, or they had guests, she almost always ate her lunch alone. And there, toward the end, she had eaten more suppers alone than not.

"Not that I know of," Minnie replied. "He don't like to have to clean up just to eat. Out in the field, it don't matter if he's dirty and sweaty."

Just before Katherine followed Minnie into the house, she gave the barn one last, wistful glance, wishing that maybe, just maybe, she might catch a glimpse of Jason. But to her regret, he was nowhere to be seen. Suppertime suddenly seemed very far away.

Chapter Five

"Shoo, cat, shoo," Minnie spat as she turned to find Bart padding across her counter, his green eyes staring intently at the fat, juicy ham she had just taken out of the oven. "That's for Mister Jason's supper, not yours. And if you don't behave yourself and get down from there right this minute, you ain't even goin' to get none of the scraps. Now, shoo!"

Bart paused a few feet away from the succulent meat and sniffed deeply, turned to look back at Minnie, then sat down to study the situation further; but when he saw Minnie take a menacing step in his direction, twisted dishtowel in hand, he leaped down from the counter and, meowing loudly, scampered to safety underneath one of the chairs.

"Mister Jason and his strays," Minnie muttered to herself. "Always allowin' you homeless creatures to hang around here, doin' just about whatever you please. If I didn't go and find homes for a lot of you now and then, this place would be overrun with you scoundrels."

"Meowrrr . . ." Bart stated in his own behalf.

"Meow, yourself, you sorry yellow-haired devil. You'd be gone from here, too, if I'd had my way, what with the way you go sneakin' around this kitchen and all. But no, Mister Jason had to go and take a special likin' to you and because of that, he says you can stay. You and Rebel, that scraggly haired mutt of his. Ain't an ounce of good in either of you." She wagged her finger at the cat who was still crouched under the chair. "Too bad you ain't no female. He's always more than willing to let me find homes for the females."

She continued to grumble and shake her head as she returned to the stove to inspect her candied carrots. "At least he has enough sense to know that it's the females that bring the most trouble." Then, a smile spread slowly across her plump face at a thought that had just occurred to her. "But then, maybe he's gonna change his mind about female strays now that Missy Katherine has done straggled in. He doesn't seem to be too eager to get rid of her. No siree, none too eager at all. Oh, well, no matter; that's one female stray I won't mind if he decides to keep." She chuckled aloud at the thought. Wouldn't it be something if . . .

"What's so funny?" Jason asked as he entered the kitchen, startling her so that she dropped the heavy iron lid with a clatter that sent Bart scurrying from the room.

"N—nothing," Minnie replied, her dark eyes wide with guilt. Not only had she been thinking naughty thoughts about Missy Katherine and Mister Jason, she'd actually said some of them right out loud. She pressed her lips tightly together, hoping he hadn't heard any of what she had just said. It would be even worse if he was somehow able to read her thoughts. "What are you doin' in so early?" she asked gruffly, to cover her embarrassment. "It ain't even four o'clock yet."

"We got the loft fixed, and Mose and Pete claimed they could clean up the mess without my help, and then, Mose volunteered to ride out and check on the herds for me. Since that left me with very little to do, I decided to come on in and get an early bath."

"A bath? A real sit down bath? You ain't gonna just wash up out by the well pump?" Minnie asked, her eyebrows raised. It was unusual enough that he was allowing someone else to check on the herds for him, but to come in at this hour wanting a bath was almost too much for her to believe.

"Yes, Minnie, a real sit down bath," Jason answered, amused at the way her eyebrows arched halfway up her forehead whenever something truly caught her by surprise. If they were to rise any further, they just might meet with her hairline.

"A bath on a Tuesday?"

"Is there some law against having a bath on Tuesday?" he asked as he pulled his hat off, dipping his head sideways in order to wipe his sweaty forehead with his rolled up shirt sleeve.

"No, of course not, it's just that . . ." she paused as she searched for words that would explain her surprise without actually insulting him. After all, bathing had never been one of his favorite pastimes, not that he didn't keep himself clean. It was just that Mister Jason had never been partial to sitting down to take his bath. Then, remembering that Katherine hadn't come out of the bathing room yet, she shook her head and said, "I'll go ahead and start heating you some water, but it might be a while before you can actually take that bath. Missy Katherine is taking one right now. If I'd known you was goin' to be wantin' a bath and so early, I'd have asked her not to spend so long."

"Oh?" he said, turning to stare with keen interest at the wall between the kitchen and the bathing room. "She's in there right now?"

"Yes, and although she's been in there for hours, it just might be hours yet before she comes out. You know how white women are about their grooming."

"No, how are they? I've always wanted to know," Jason pressed, grinning at the way Minnie was starting to get flustered. As bold and outspoken as Minnie usually was, there were certain things she was embarrassed to talk about in the presence of a man.

"Oh, surely you remember how sometimes your mother would spend half a day in there washing her hair, primping, and doin' whatever else white women think is so important—especially if there was some big do that she and your father was goin' to. But Missy Katherine has been in there for four hours already; maybe I'll just tap on the door and ask her to hurry it up a little. Surely she's clean enough by now."

"She's been in there four hours?" Jason asked, his face suddenly tense. That *was* an awfully long time for anyone to take a bath. Cocking an ear in the direction of the wall, he listened for a moment. He detected no sounds of splashing water nor any other sounds. "Yes, tap on the door," he said to Minnie. "You don't necessarily have to hurry her up—I can always wash up out by the pump if she doesn't finish soon—but I would like for you to make sure she's all right. It seems strange to me that I don't hear anything."

Minnie's eyes grew wide with concern as she set her dishtowel aside and headed for the back porch. Now that Mister Jason had brought it up, she hadn't noticed any sounds for the past hour or so. That wasn't natural. Something *was* wrong. Why hadn't she noticed the silence before?

Jason was right behind her.

Bart was right behind Jason.

Rapping lightly on the door, Minnie called out, "Missy Katherine? Missy Katherine, this is Minnie. You need anything in there?"

When there was no response, she tried again, "Missy Katherine? Missy Katherine, you all right in there?"

When there was still no response, she reached down and tried the door latch only to discover that the door was bolted from the inside. Her heart pounded in her chest as she remembered how her first grandson had died—drowned in a tub of water only half as deep as the bath Missy Katherine was taking. Her face twisted with worry, she turned to Jason. "Mister Jason, she don't answer."

Jason, too, tried the latch and when he saw that it was, indeed, bolted from inside, he pounded on the door with his fist, shouting out Katherine's name. Fearing the worst when she still did not answer, he lifted his booted foot high and kicked the door in, splintering the frame with a loud crack, which sent Bart scampering back to the kitchen.

"What in the . . . ?" Katherine came awake with a start. When she realized that she had been wakened by someone kicking in the door—and that person was Jason who now stood only a few feet away—she screamed and ducked down into the water, flinging her long handled back brush directly at the intruder.

"You're okay," Jason muttered in disbelief, holding the wet, soapy brush against his chest right where it had landed. He was so stunned by the fact that nothing was wrong and that he had just burst in on her bath for no real reason, all he could do was stare speechlessly.

"I was okay—before you came bursting in here!" she cried out, blinking, and trying to come fully awake so she would be able to better handle whatever might happen next. "Just what do you think you are doing?"

"I—I thought I was—well, I thought you were—I thought I was saving you," he muttered, still staring down at her, his eyes slowly drawn from her face downward to discover that almost all of her lovely body could be seen right through the soapy water. He felt himself responding to what he saw and knew he should turn his back, but he didn't—he couldn't.

Barging in behind him, Minnie took only a moment to size up the situation. "Well, it's obvious she's all right now," she said as she yanked hard on Jason's arm until she was able to spin him around and pull him out of the room and out onto the back porch. Once she had him outside, she scolded him roundly. "And now that you've seen she's all right and that she don't need no savin' after all, you ain't got no business in there. No business at all."

Jason blinked as the words soaked in. He felt that "all right" was an understatement to describe Katherine Mason, and he stood just outside the door, craning his neck in an attempt to catch one more glimpse of her before Minnie swiftly stepped back inside and slammed the door in his face.

Finding that the door would not close all the way now that the frame had been broken, Minnie secured it by placing a small chair under the knob. Thoroughly provoked, she then turned to Katherine. "Why didn't you answer us if you was all right?" she demanded. "Didn't you hear us knockin' on that door and callin' out your name? You scared us half to death. We thought you'd done drowned."

"I'm sorry," Katherine said, still somewhat dazed from having been so abruptly awakened, and beginning to just worry about how much Jason might have seen this time. Was his barging in on her at the most inopportune moments really accidental? Three times in two days hardly seemed coincidental. "I didn't hear anyone knock," she said to Minnie.

"Well, we both did," Minnie assured her.

"I guess I didn't hear you because I had sort of drifted off to sleep. The water was so warm and felt so soothing to my sore muscles that I just couldn't stay awake. And you are right, I could have slipped into the water and drowned." Looking at the door, she shook her head in an attempt to clear away more of the cobwebs. "I can't believe I didn't hear you knock or call out my name. I really must have been out."

"And after all that sleep you had yesterday and this mornin'. You must have somethin' wrong with you. It ain't natural to be so tired all the time," Minnie said, her voice full of true concern. "Maybe I should have Mister Jason send in to town for Doc Edison so he can come out here and have a look at you."

"There's no need. I'm fine. It's just that I've been traveling on foot for several days and it has worn me out. A little more rest and I'll be fine."

"On foot? All by your lonesome? Why would a gal like you be travelin' on foot alone like that? Why would you be travelin' on foot at all? I can't imagine you not bein' offered a ride, but then some folks that travel these roads are . . ."

"I haven't exactly been traveling along the roads. I've been taking a lot of shortcuts, like the one I was taking when Jason—found me." Then, hoping to change the subject, Katherine asked, "Would you hand me my towel? This water's gone cold and I'd really like to get out now."

Minnie glanced around until she spotted the thick, yellow towel on the washstand, across the room from the porcelain tub. "You sure you don't want the doctor to come out and see to you? I don't know what your natural color is, but you look far too thin and pale to me, so pale your cheeks take on a greenish color in places. Mister Jason will pay for the doctor's callin', if that's what worries you. He's always payin' to have Doc Turner, the veterinarian, come out here and look at some of the more pitiful animals who stray in here either half-starved, or injured in some way, and he never complains about that."

Katherine frowned and wondered how she should take that comment as she stretched her hand out to accept the towel Minnie held out to her. Was the woman comparing her to a stray animal? She wanted to smile. In a way it was an appropriate comparison. "Yes, I'm absolutely sure I don't need a doctor to examine me. I'm fine."

As she stood up with her back to Minnie and hurriedly unfolded the towel so she could wrap it around her before stepping out of the tub, Minnie could not help but notice the large green and blue bruises all across her back, buttocks, and shoulders. She reached out a hand to touch one, then decided against it. Suddenly, she realized the pale green patches along the young woman's cheeks were probably bruises too. Her concern for Katherine deepened, and she asked once again, "You sure you don't want the doc to have a look at you? Mister Jason could send Silas into town for him and they'd be back here before dark."

"I'm fine," Katherine said, shaking her head lightly at Minnie's needless concern. Minnie was just as much a worrier as Lizzie had been, if not worse; but Katherine had to admit it felt good to have someone so concerned over her health for a change. Still, she did not need a doctor. All she really needed was a little more rest and a few more good, solid meals. She already felt much better than she had when she first arrived. Even her feet were no longer swollen and not nearly as sore. She was able to walk now without limping at all. "Don't worry about me so," she said firmly, but kindly.

But Minnie did worry about her. She worried about those bruises all across Katherine's frail back and wondered just how they got there. Back in the kitchen, getting supper ready, her thoughts remained on Katherine. She had taken an immediate liking to the poor girl, and it bothered her that someone might have put those horrible bruises on her. Minnie refused to believe that they had been inflicted in anything but anger. Although she realized that Katherine could have been hurt in a fall or some other sort of accident, somehow Minnie doubted it. There were too many bruises, in too many places.

No, deep inside, down deep where she instinctively found the truth more times than not, Minnie knew that someone had beaten Katherine severely, probably several days ago. And the more she thought about it, the more she came to realize that Katherine was running away—running away from whoever had done that to her. That's why she didn't travel the roads where she might be offered a ride. The girl was afraid of being found. Minnie felt such a surge of pity and compassion for the girl that she vowed to herself and her Lord God, that as long as Katherine was living with her and Mr. Jason, whoever had done such a horrible thing would never get a chance to hurt her again. Not as long as she was around to protect the poor girl.

Minnie shuddered to think of the sort of person who would do such a thing to a woman. There was no doubt in her mind that it had been done by a man. What she wondered now was who the man was and what on earth could have occurred to have led to such a terrible thing.

After what had happened that afternoon, Katherine was reluctant to go downstairs, but felt obligated to do so. Not only was she Jason's guest—which was reason enough for her to go downstairs for the evening meal—he had been kind enough to buy her two lovely dresses and a complete set of undergarments. Despite the low necklines on both the dresses, which were far lower than any she would have bought herself, she had felt it had been a sweet gesture on his part. She was somewhat distressed, however, to find, as she tried everything on, that every single garment was a perfect fit. He had known exactly what size everything should be, but then why shouldn't he? He'd seen practically all there was to see the other day in his room. Blood rushed to her face as she realized that what he had not been able to see then, he just might have seen that very afternoon. She had no way of knowing just what he might have seen before she had ducked beneath the water and covered herself.

It was the embarrassment of imagining what he *might* have seen that made it so difficult for her to go downstairs and face him now. But as she tied the mint green velvet sash and adjusted the matching collar of the lovely emerald green taffeta dress, she knew she must find the courage to go downstairs—if for no other reason than to thank him, though she knew she would not be able to make much use of two such narrow-waisted garments, at least not for long. In just a matter of weeks, her waistline would start to thicken and the two lovely dresses would no longer fit.

Sadly, Katherine stared at her trim figure in the mirror and imagined what she would look like just a few months from now. She wondered if Andrew would be able to lend her the money for the expandable clothing she would soon need to wear. And then, there were the things she would need for the baby itself once it arrived. She sighed at the thought of the burden she would be placing on her brother, for she knew it would be quite some time before she would be able to earn the money to pay him back. But as she adjusted the wide skirt over the frilly petticoats Jason had bought her, she knew that however grim the future might be, it was far better than the future she and her child would have had had she stayed with her husband. Patting her abdomen gently, she felt a surge of warmth through her being for although the babe was not yet three months in the making, Katherine already loved it with all her heart. Nothing else mattered as much.

"I was about to give up on you," Jason said when she finally entered the dining room. "Minnie's already been in here three times wanting to know if you'd come down yet."

"I'm sorry, but when I have no clock to keep an eye on, time just gets away from me." She cast her gaze downward to the dining room floor for she knew that what she spoke was only a half truth.

"That's perfectly all right. When I see results like those, I find myself unable to complain. It makes the waiting well worth it. You look absolutely beautiful." As he reached for her hand, the smile on his face revealed that he spoke the truth.

Though it was against her better judgment, Katherine allowed him to press his lips to her palm, an act that sent tantalizing shivers through every inch of her. Trying to ignore the strong physical response, she slowly but firmly withdrew from his grasp and folded her hands demurely. "Before we sit down to eat, I want to thank you for the lovely gifts. You are far too generous."

"Just seeing you in that dress is thanks enough," he declared, dropping his gaze briefly to explore the gentle curves and deep contours that he had known the dress would reveal. His words had not been spoken out of mere courtesy; she was absolutely beautiful. He had a strong urge to pull her to him and press her body firmly against his in a strong embrace. "I really wanted to get you a fancier dress, one more worthy of your beauty—but those, I was told, have to be special ordered in advance. I'd have gone ahead and ordered one anyway, if I hadn't found out that it takes at least a week to get a dress made. But if you'd be willing to stay an extra week, I could order a really fancy dress for you—one of those frilly ball gowns. Sapphire blue, I think. You'd look heavenly in sapphire blue."

"I have no need for a ball gown." She laughed at the thought of it. She had not been to a ball in years. Her husband hated dancing, though she loved it dearly, and there was no way in the world he would allow anyone else to escort her. She hadn't been to a dance of any kind since she was sixteen. It saddened her to realize how much she had missed out. "Thank you just the same," she added.

"I don't know. They have some truly grand balls in Jefferson from time to time," he said hopefully, realizing that he wanted the honor of being her escort. He'd be the envy of all the men in Jefferson for Katherine was far lovelier than any belle he'd ever seen at a ball.

"I don't doubt that they have wonderful balls in Jefferson, but I assure you I won't be attending any."

"Don't you care for dancing? I'd have thought you would. Or is it that you never learned how. If that's the problem, I'd be glad to teach you."

"No, no, I love to dance," she responded with enthusiasm. "It's just that—that I don't know anyone in Jefferson except for my brother, and he doesn't care much for dancing." She felt guilty at having lied—Andrew loved to dance—but the little white lie was easier than telling the truth in long, drawn out detail.

"So you don't know anyone in Jefferson. I go to Jefferson quite often. I'll take you."

"No, no, that won't be necessary," she said quickly, lowering her eyes to the chair Jason had just pulled out for her. Not only would she soon be in no physical condition to attend social events such as dances, it would be far safer if she kept to herself. The fewer people who saw her the better—Flint was sure to be showing her picture around as he searched for her.

"You don't care much for me do you?" he asked bluntly, having misinterpreted her silence.

"Oh no, it's not that at all." She hurried to assure him. "I like you. I like you *very* much—it's just that . . ." Although she felt the time had come to tell Jason about her husband and the real reason she dare not attend any balls in Jefferson with him, or anyone else for that matter, she was having a difficult time getting the words past her tongue. For some unexplainable reason, more than the trouble it might eventually cause him, she did not want Jason to know she was married, nor did she want him to know anything else concerning that part of her past. She clung to her secret like a frightened child.

"You are still upset about what happened out in the back pasture yesterday, aren't you?"

"No," she answered quickly, then realized that her being angry at him would be as good an excuse for her behavior as any. "Well, yes, maybe a little. You were incredibly bold toward me out there, and such boldness is hard to forgive. You had no reason to act that way to me."

"Only that I saw you as one of the most beautiful women I'd ever laid eyes on, and the situation being what it was seemed to encourage my boldness. But I agree, I never should have taken advantage of your predicament like that. I had hoped that my apology, and the dresses, would make up for some of what I said and did. What else can I do to win your approval?"

Their eyes met and held for several moments while Jason waited patiently for her answer. Just inches away from his magnetic blue eyes, Katherine found that she could not think clearly. It felt as if she were being drawn right into his being—as if the mere intensity of his gaze had cast a magical spell over her.

Opposing reactions battled within her. Part of her longed to give way to the impulse she had fought since the moment they met—the impulse to reach out and touch him, if only for a moment. Another, only slightly stronger, part of her yearned to pull her gaze free of his and change the topic of conversation entirely, change it to something less personal, something less dangerous. But, as she continued to stare into his eyes, she found that neither action was possible.

Minnie's sudden appearance in the dining room solved the dilemma. "Good," Minnie said, seeing Katherine. "She's come down. I'll bring the food on in." She turned and went back to the kitchen.

Katherine took that opportunity to turn away from Jason and sit down. "I've been looking forward to tonight's supper," she said, "ever since Minnie pulled that ham from the oven. And if that ham is only half as delicious as it smelled in the kitchen, we are in for a real treat."

"It will be," Jason assured her. "I don't know exactly what it is Minnie cooks her ham in, but no one else's can compare." He was reluctant to allow the topic of conversation to turn to one of so little interest. It frustrated him to realize how very close he might have been to finding out just how Katherine felt about him—and whether or not he had any chance with her. But the moment was gone. As he helped her scoot her chair toward the table, he vowed to try again later; it was becoming increasingly important that he know just what her feelings might be. He was more attracted to her than he'd been to any woman before. Standing next to her now—catching her womanly scent, remembering what she looked like without any clothing—made him ache to know her more intimately.

Though all through supper, he constantly watched for the chance to turn the conversation back in the desired direction, it was hours before Jason was able to do so. The opportunity finally came when she joined him to check on two foals that were having trouble nursing. As they made their way along the winding cobblestone walkway that led through the gardens to the barn, he found he could not help but mention the enticing way the moonlight shone on her hair.

Gazing up at the fat slice of moon, she paused and spoke almost reverently. "It is a beautiful moon isn't it? So stark and bright against the blackness of the night sky. Far more brilliant than all the stars that surround it. Some things are so incredibly beautiful that words are inadequate to describe them."

"I agree," he said though his thoughts were on her and not the moon overhead. He could feel his desire growing as he moved close to where she stood, her face still tilted skyward, her ivory skin bathed in the silvery light. He allowed himself a long moment of pleasure as he let his gaze travel over her. Approving of everything he saw, he quietly drank in her beauty, wishing suddenly not only to hold her but to kiss her as well. As he became more aware of his now excruciating need for her, the closer he came to reaching out and drawing her to him.

He wanted to feel the velvety smoothness of her skin, sample the honeyed sweetness along the gentle curve of her lips, run his hands through her long silken tresses. Never before had he felt such an overwhelming urge to seduce a woman, and even though she had resisted advances before, he knew at that moment that he was going to do what his body decreed. He intended to kiss her.

"I've always found the moon such a fascinating thing," she went on to say, her attention still focused on the dazzling night sky. "Lizzie used to tell me it was made of cheese, but I think not. What do you think?" It was then she turned to Jason and realized what he was about to do. There was no denying the passionate look in his eyes. The word *don't* froze on her lips, leaving them slightly parted as he came even closer, his own lips parted, eyelids heavy with the desire that had so quickly overtaken him. She was powerless to stop him, for at that moment she realized she wanted to sample his kiss as much as he did hers. But that was as far as she'd go—no more than a sample.

The kiss was far more than a sampling. It was more powerful than any kiss she had ever experienced, sending a strange, shimmering warmth through her, flooding her senses with a lingering heat, making her feel instantly lightheaded and weak in the knees. Though she had secretly longed for the touch of his lips and found the kiss to be all she imagined and more, she knew it was wrong and did her best not to give into it completely. She knew only too well the dangers ahead should she not show resistance to his kiss—and it was resistance that she must display for him right away.

Bravely she fought to still the emotions he had stirred within her as she brought her hands up and spread them against his chest in a futile effort to push him away. Her action only made him tighten his hold, pulling her closer. The more she struggled, the more demanding his kiss became, and the harder it was for Katherine to keep from being swept away by the warm tide of passion that raged through her entire being.

Although her mind warned her that she must gather together what little strength she had left and make another effort to free herself—that allowing him to kiss her in such a way was wrong, wrong, wrong—her body rebelled, and she pressed closer to him, accepting the pleasure his kiss offered, yielding to her own burning need, allowing her hungry body to explore and enjoy the passions this man had aroused in her. Her thoughts went beyond the kiss and into the wonder of what it must be like to be made love to by a man like Jason—so gentle, yet so demanding.

The kiss deepened, causing her mind to send out another alarm, but again the message went unheeded. Shame flooded through her, but still she did nothing to stop him. She felt suddenly helpless and allowed him to hold her more intimately, her breasts flattened against his strong, muscular chest, her thighs pressed firmly against his own. A burning heat settled deep at the core of her being, and at that moment she wanted him more than she had ever wanted a man—even though a part of her knew it was wrong to want him. Hot tears scalded her eyes, and she fought to get them under control. She did not want Jason to know of the anguish his kiss had caused her. It was no fault of his and she did not want to hurt him in any way. Was that why she could not pull away from him?

Though she berated herself for her actions, she timidly brought her own hands around him and lightly grasped his shoulders from behind. She knew she should be trying to push him away, but instead, she found herself responding so fiercely to his kiss, to the passion that raged inside her, that she pressed herself closer against him.

Slowly, his hands moved down her back, coming to rest on her hips. Fire coursed through her veins, sending its sensual heat to every fiber of her being—and as he brought his hand up and cupped one of her breasts, caressing the rigid tip through her dress, she moaned aloud at the sensation. It had been so long since she had been made love to, really made love to.

The pleasure of Jason's touch was drugging her senses, and Katherine knew that if she didn't act soon, there would be no going back. But then who would know? Only she would—and Jason. Suddenly, she realized how unfair it would be to Jason to let him make love to her without his knowing that she was a married woman. He needed to be told.

Allowing herself to savor one last moment, Katherine finally found the strength to push away from him. When she saw the questioning look in his eyes, the tears she had held back until now, spilled unchecked down her cheeks. With a trembling hand, she dashed them away quickly. "I'm sorry, Jason," she said, "but that never should have happened. Never. I should have stopped you immediately."

"Why?" he asked, bewildered by her tears. He had expected outrage, even condemnation, but not tears.

"It was wrong of me to allow such a thing. So wrong."

"But why? Why was that kiss so wrong? We are not children. I want you. I still want you."

A sob caught in Katherine's throat and she turned away, ready to flee before she fell at his feet in a quivering emotional heap, for she wanted him, too. Oh, how she wanted him. Hurriedly, she ran from him, but he quickly caught her, his hands gently gripping her shoulders, pulling her back against him. "Katherine, don't run away. Let me make love to you."

"I can't." Her voice was barely audible, her throat tight with emotion. "I want to. I want to very much, but I can't."

"Tell me why," he demanded quietly. His mouth was so close that his warm breath fell gently against her forehead.

Turning to face him, she found it impossible to look into his eyes; the pain she saw there struck her heart like a thunderbolt. Instead, she concentrated on a stray thread that peeped from one of his buttonholes. "There is something I haven't told you. Something I should have told you right away, but didn't, couldn't."

Tenderly, he lifted her chin, forcing her to look at him. "And what is it about your past that could be so terrible? Whatever it is, I seriously doubt it will make any difference in the way I feel about you right now."

If she was going to tell him she was no longer a

virgin, that was something he could live with. After all, he had known other women. Whatever had happened to either one of them in the past should not be of much concern now. What mattered was what they now felt for each other—and one thing was certain—he was rapidly falling in love with her. It was a wondrous revelation, for he never expected to feel so strongly about any woman. After all, he was twenty-seven years old and had yet to love any woman deeply enough to ask her to marry him. Although there had been a few serious romances, he had never felt anything as strong as what he felt for Katherine now.

"I—I am married," she finally blurted out, then wrenched herself from his grasp and fled through the torchlit gardens, so blinded by tears, so overwhelmed by shame, that she could hardly see where she ran.

"Married?" his bewildered voice trailed off into the darkness. That was the last thing he had expected her to say. What was he going to do now? The woman he had come to care about, really care about, in so short a time, was married. He shook his head, unable to believe it.

Married.

Chapter Six

Although the morning dawned clear and bright, by late afternoon the sky had turned dark and dismal, promising rain. The weather matched Katherine's mood perfectly. Unable to stand still in any one place, she turned away from the bedroom window and began pacing the floor. Her bed still offered no sleep, no dreams in which to find refuge from her troubled thoughts. She had not slept at all since she had fled into the room the night before. She had tried lying down, but could not keep her thoughts from whirling about at a dizzying pace, keeping her awake with the deep misery and utter heartbreak of her situation.

She was a married woman. A *married* woman. She had no right to fall in love with another man. Even though there was no love left in her heart for her husband, she had no right to be in love with anyone else. Divorce was impossible. Not only would Flint never allow it, she could never even ask for one. She did not want him to know where she had gone. He was never to know of the child he had helped to create—for the child's sake. She could never fall in love again, for though she no longer felt anything for her husband—only fear and disgust—she was indeed married, and would be, until death dissolved their vows.

Though Katherine had thought she had cried herself out, the tears flowed again, spilling over her cheeks. She was doomed never to love a man—or ever be loved by one again. The only consolation her life offered was the child. Regardless of anything else, she would have the child to love, and love it she would. She would have to somehow forget her feelings for Jason, though at the moment that seemed an impossible feat.

The sound of footsteps in the hall caused Katherine to stop pacing and turn toward the door expectantly. The footsteps were too heavy and strong to be Minnie's; she knew it was Jason again. He would knock, call out her name, and once again she would not answer. Then, he would try the latch and find the door still bolted. But no, this time, he merely paused outside her door, as if listening for movement, then turned and went back down the hall to his own room. He had knocked at her door three times in the last hour.

Breathing more easily when she heard his door clatter shut, Katherine went to the bed and sank slowly into the soft mattress. Leaning forward, her face in her hands, she wept bitterly. She could not bring herself to face Jason again. It was then that she decided to leave. It would be the best thing for everyone. She would write him a brief note, thanking him for his generosity, and leave quietly.

She longed to take at least one of the new dresses with her—if for no other reason than to remind her of the man who had finally proved to be so kind and gentle, so different from the man she had married. But she decided it would be best to leave everything he had bought her. She could hold the memory of his kiss next to her heart, and dream of what might have been had she been fortunate enough to meet Jason first, before she ever knew Flint, but she would take no physical reminders. She would leave with nothing more than what she had come with.

Having made her decision, Katherine changed back into her tattered blue woolen dress and the scraps of leather that were all that remained of her shoes. Searching for something to write with, she was relieved to discover a stack of pale yellow writing paper in the small night table nearest the bed. There was also a pen and a bottle of ink, but the ink had long ago dried to a dark blue powder which made the pen useless. What was she to write with? It was then that she remembered having seen a small lead pencil carelessly tossed inside the bottom drawer of the armoire.

With the pencil in hand and the thick stack of paper across her lap, Katherine began her farewell letter:

Dear Jason,

I realize this is the coward's way out, but I simply could not face you with my shame. By the time you find and read this letter, I will be gone, but before I left, I had to find a way to tell you how grateful I am for all you have done for me in these last couple of days. You have not only clothed and fed me, you have reminded me what it is like to be alive again. I will always remember you for that and I will find a way to repay you someday.

Regards,
Katherine Mason

With tears in her eyes, Katherine gently folded the letter and wrote Jason's name on the outside, then placed it on top of the dressing table where he or Minnie would be certain to find it. While straightening the bed, which was a tumble of sheets and quilts from her restless night, Katherine tried to get her emotions back under control.

Although there was so much of her life she wanted to leave behind forever, the few memories that she had of this place, and of the few days she had spent here, she intended to take with her and keep near her heart forever—especially the memories of Jason. Just the thought of his strong, masculine face and his warm yet devilish smile, made fresh tears well up in her eyes. She would cherish even the astonished look on his face when he had repeatedly barged in on her at embarrassing moments. Even if she had wanted to leave such memories behind, it would have been impossible to do so.

The knock at the door startled her. She had been so lost in thought, she had not heard anyone approaching. She stood perfectly still and waited for someone to speak.

"Missy Katherine? Missy Katherine, you all right in there?"

Minnie's voice sounded concerned, so truly concerned that Katherine decided to answer. "Yes, I'm fine."

"You been sleepin' all this time?"

"Y—yes, yes, I have."

"That ain't natural. I don't care what you say. Can I come in and see you for just a moment?"

"I—I'd rather you didn't. I'm not dressed. Besides, I'll be down as soon as I do get dressed. Shouldn't be long."

"You promise?"

"I promise," she said, casting her eyes downward, for although she would truly be down shortly, she planned to slip out the front door before anyone could see or hear her.

"Good. You done missed breakfast and the noon meal. I don't want you missin' supper, too. You may think your rest is important, but eatin' is far more important if you really want to get your strength back. And I fixed you something special for dessert. It's goin' to make your stomach jump right up and shout out a string of thank yous for every mouthful you send down to it."

"Sounds wonderful. I can hardly wait." Katherine bit her lip to hold back a sob. Minnie was so much like her old Lizzie. If only Lizzie or her mother were still alive. She certainly could use a woman's shoulder about now. And she knew that Lizzie, especially, would have been understanding. Lizzie wouldn't remind her that it had been her own foolishness that had put her in her present situation. Lizzie would sympathize with her, then try to help her find a way out of her trouble.

"Just don't take too long," Minnie called through the door. "I expect supper to be ready about six, and it's almost five now."

Was it that late?

"I won't be," Katherine replied, relieved that her voice did not crack from the emotions welling inside her. She heard Minnie's footsteps retreating down the hall, obviously satisfied that Katherine would indeed be down for supper.

Sniffling slightly, Katherine put her misery aside for the moment and returned to the bed. She carefully pulled the undersheet taut, then the oversheet, the quilt, and finally the bedcover. It was after she had plumped up the pillows and while she was folding the comforter—the one that had come from Jason's own bed—that her heart began to ache once again. Burying her face in the comforter's cool softness, she could detect his special scent, a scent she was surprised to recognize. It disturbed her to such an extent, she did not hear the footsteps falling softly outside her door. The sudden knock broke the silence of the room and startled her.

"I'm not quite dressed yet," she called out, thinking it was Minnie again.

"I'll wait. We have to talk," came the reply. It was Jason.

Katherine felt her heart leap with sudden panic. "We can talk at supper," she said quickly. "Go on down and wait for me in the dining room. I'll be down as soon as I finish."

"I'll wait right here. We can walk down together."

"That won't be necessary." She closed her eyes to the anguish she felt just from hearing his deep, determined voice. He obviously did not trust her.

"It may not be necessary, but I'll do it just the same."

"No, please, go on downstairs." She tried to keep her

tone light even though she felt her heart breaking. Sadly, she stepped over to the door and touched the smooth wooden surface at the place where his voice seemed the strongest. "It will be at least ten minutes, or maybe even fifteen, before I'm ready to come down."

There was a lengthy pause before Jason replied. "All right, I'll leave," he said. "But hurry. I am anxious to talk with you."

Katherine listened closely for his footsteps and was relieved when she heard him walk slowly toward the stairway. Quickly, she finished tidying up the room, wanting to leave it exactly as she had found it. Then, she walked back to the door, pressed her ear against it, heard nothing, and quietly slipped the bolt out of place.

"Jason?" she called out, just loudly enough for him to hear should he have returned to the hallway for some reason. She pressed her ear to the door and listened once more. Hearing nothing at all from outside, she slowly lifted the main latch and opened the door just enough to let her slip through sideways. Making as little noise as possible, she carefully pulled her skirts free of the doorway with one hand, and reached back inside to ease the door closed with the other.

"What are you doing in your old dress?"

Jason's voice came from right behind her and startled her so that she let out a high-pitched yelp. Whirling around to face him, her eyes blazed with fright.

"What are you doing out here in the hallway?" she demanded, furious at having been so easily tricked.

"Waiting to talk to you," he said simply, then reached to open the door she'd just closed. "And I'd rather talk in there, than downstairs where we are sure to be interrupted." When he noticed her fearful glance toward the bedroom, he added, "I'll leave the door open if you are worried about what I might try to do in there."

Realizing her farewell note was in full view and would be the first thing he would notice once he had entered, Katherine stepped away from the room and stated firmly, "I'd rather talk out here."

Jason stared at her a moment, then looked suspiciously toward the room. "Why are you so afraid for me to go into that room?"

"I'm not," she responded a little too quickly.

"Yes, you are. I can see it in your eyes. You don't want me to go in there. Why?" Not waiting for an answer, he stepped inside and looked around. His eyes immediately came to rest on the folded note.

Katherine's shoulders sagged helplessly as she followed him inside. It would do her no good to turn and run now; he could catch her too easily. There was no choice. She would have to stay and try to explain why she had decided to leave so abruptly. She was certain he was about to demand a reason.

Jason picked up the letter, read his name, then turned to her with a questioning look.

"It's a farewell letter. I'm leaving."

"Why? Because I kissed you? How was I supposed to know you were married?"

"You weren't." She dropped her gaze to her folded hands. "But now that you do know, surely you understand why I must leave."

Jason said nothing. Instead, he unfolded the letter and read the message inside, his face frozen as his eyes scanned her words. "No, I don't understand why you feel you must leave. I don't understand at all. I thought you had decided to stay until Saturday. The plans were all set. What did you think? That I didn't intend to follow through with my promise to take you to Jefferson? Did you think I planned to keep you here against your will? Heck, I intended not only to take you to Jefferson on Saturday like I said I would, but right to your brother's very door."

"And I appreciate it, but I cannot stay here, not now." As she raised her eyes to meet his, she found his intense gaze urging her on, forcing the truth out of her. "I dare not stay. Not feeling the way I do about you." Her hand flew immediately to her lips in an effort to still them. She could not believe she had actually spoken her private thoughts aloud. "Oh, I never should have said that."

"I'm glad you did," he replied earnestly. "It's some consolation, knowing that you do at least feel something for me."

Not knowing how to respond, Katherine stepped over to the window and stared at the dark, churning clouds that still threatened rain. Similar clouds had gathered around her heart.

"Katherine, I want to know why you are running and who it is you are running from," Jason said as he moved to stand behind her, so close she could feel the warmth of his body. "There's every chance that I can help you."

She turned to deny that she was running away, and thus disclaim the need for help, but seeing his determined expression, she knew it would do no good. She spun back around to face the window again, trying to decide how much she should tell him and how much she should still keep secret. Staring out at the stormy gray sky that hugged the earth for as far as she could see, she wondered how much he had already guessed.

"It's your husband, isn't it?" he pressed. "You are afraid of him for some reason, and I think that reason has to do with those faded bruises that practically cover your body."

"How do you know about my . . ." she started to ask, turning around to face him. Before she could finish the question, his hands caught her shoulders, holding her fast.

"I saw the bruises across your stomach and shoulders the other afternoon in my bedroom. I didn't give it much thought at the time. I figured you had fallen down while traveling over rough, unfamiliar terrain, but now I think those bruises have something to do with the reason you are running."

What was there left to keep secret? He had so much of it figured out for himself. Closing her eyes for a moment to escape his searching gaze, she took a deep breath and finally admitted, "Yes, I am running away from my husband."

"May I know why?" he asked quietly. Afraid he might be hurting her without meaning to, he eased his grip on her shoulders but did not release her as he waited for an answer.

Moved by his sensitivity, Katherine opened her eyes and looked at him for a long moment. Maybe it would be best if he did know everything. Then he could better understand why she must leave here immediately—why it would be best for all concerned if she broke her ties with everyone at Seven Oaks as quickly as possible. It involved far more than the mere fact that she was married. It was who she was married to, and what he was likely to do to anyone he found helping her, or even just giving her shelter. And it would be unfair to allow even a simple friendship to develop between her and Jason. It would be putting everyone in danger, and for what? For a few days rest and a ride to Jefferson? She felt a sudden surge of shame for ever having accepted Jason's generous offer. It was bad enough she was about to put her brother in jeopardy. She couldn't put a stranger at such risk.

"It's a long story," she began hesitantly.

"I've got all night," he replied. He stepped back and gestured for her to be seated in one of the two chairs at the window.

"I'd rather stand." She watched as he moved to lean against one of the tall, wooden bedposts, letting her know that it didn't matter to him if they stood or sat—as long as they talked.

"I guess I should start with my husband's name. I happen to be married to Flint Mason." She waited to see his reaction. He knitted his brow for a moment, as if trying to place the name. Then his eyes slowly widened in shocked recognition, and she knew that he'd figured out just who she was married to.

"That's right." She nodded. "I'm married to a gunfighter, a murderer. Only I had no idea that he was a gunfighter when I married him." She looked away from Jason to the window again, her heart so full of regrets that she felt it might burst.

"And when you found out he was a gunfighter you decided to run away?" he prompted her softly.

"No, I've known about that for almost a year now," she admitted, still unable to meet his gaze with her own.

"But when I finally did find out who he really was, he told me he was already trying to go straight for my sake—that he had already stopped wearing his gun in public—and he swore he would never use his gun against another man again."

She took a deep breath and released it slowly. "Wanting that to be the truth, I readily believed him, and for a while he was the perfect husband—very attentive and always bringing gifts home from town. Not long after that, Flint started to drink. Oh, he had always drunk some, but suddenly he began to drink heavily. Before long, hardly a night went by that he didn't fall into bed stinking drunk—that is, when he cared enough to even come home and find his bed."

A pained look came into Katherine's eyes as she relived those bitter times. "It was just a couple of months later that I learned all about how my dear husband had been seen quite often coming out of one particular saloon girl's bedroom. Juanita, I think her name was. When I confronted him with that, he flew into a rage, calling me names I don't care to repeat. He struck me several times in his fury, ordering me to stop spying on him. He knocked me down once against the dining room table, and I was foolish enough to get up so that he could knock me down again. When I refused to get up after that, he stormed out of the house and didn't come back until the next day."

"And that's when you decided to leave him."

Tears welled up in her eyes, and her gaze drifted up to the elaborately sculptured ceiling. Only vaguely aware of the beauty above her, she went on. "No, I didn't leave him then. I should have, but he came back so apologetic, and he seemed so sincerely sorry for all he had done, that I decided to give him another chance. I stayed, and faced his drunken anger again and again."

"Then, what finally made you leave?"

"One day, while he was supposedly away on one of his many business trips, I had healed up enough to go into town without raising eyebrows, and that's when I first heard other rumors concerning Flint—about how he had killed a young boy, just a few months before, in a town about forty miles away. I realized then that not only had he broken his sacred wedding vows, and had failed to be true to me as a husband, he had also gone against his promise not to use his gun anymore. He had lied to me about everything. I was furious, so furious that it made me sick to my stomach, and I wretched until I was so weak I couldn't stand up and had to be helped to a bench. Although I had known it was a possibility, that was when I really came to suspect my condition for the first time. I went straight to the doctor to have my suspicions verified, and he was quick to tell me that I was indeed with child, though not very far along."

"You are going to have a baby?" Jason asked. His gaze drifted down to her stomach and he stared at her in awe. A slow smile spread across his face as he thought about the babe that was growing there.

"Yes." Her hand went possessively to her abdomen and she responded with a slight smile of her own. "As close as the doctor could figure, the baby is due the latter part of September, or the beginning of October."

Slowly, her smile faded. "And the baby is the main reason I finally found the courage to leave Flint. I don't want this child to grow up under the influence of a man so cruel, so bloodthirsty as to kill a thirteen-year-old boy."

"Thirteen?" Jason echoed in horror.

"Yes, thirteen. By the time I got home, I had my mind made up to leave him. He wasn't due back home for days yet, and I intended to be far away before he ever knew I was gone. I had just pulled down my valise from the attic and had started to pack, when Flint rode up, home early from his trip. Of course, he demanded to know why I was packing and where I thought I was going. That's when I confronted him with what I had found out in town. I openly accused him of being a liar, a cheat, and—worst of all—a murderer.

"I was so angry at the time that I didn't realize he was already drunk, though it was still early in the afternoon. He was always more violent whenever he had been drinking. He immediately became enraged, out of control, and began to slap me around until I finally fell to the floor, dazed by the pain. But he didn't stop with that—the moment I hit the floor, he began to kick me over and over again until I thought he was going to kill the baby. Somehow, I managed to get up and make a run for the door, but he caught up with me, grabbed me by the hair, and flung me against the cabinet where he always kept a large stock of liquor. I managed to grab one of the bottles and smashed it against his head, knocking him to the floor. I didn't wait to see if he was conscious or not. I flew to his desk, stole the money I knew he kept there, then ran to the bed, closed the valise with what little there was already in it, and ran out the door. As I ran for my baby's life, I could hear him calling my name, but I never looked back. I climbed onto the horse he had left still saddled outside, and once on him, kept my eyes trained on the nearby woods."

"Why didn't you run to the neighbors for help? Or were you afraid he might harm them, too, if they helped you?"

"We had no neighbors. Flint didn't like anyone snooping into his business so we lived out in the country, miles from anyone. That's why I was so long in finding out who he was. The only people I had any contact with were his friends, who came there to visit—and they'd been warned to keep quiet about what he was really up to. I honestly thought he was just a good businessman, and I was foolish enough to believe that all his wealth came from sawmills and lumber companies. It was not until I had learned about his reputation with a gun that I also found out he was a gambler, a rake, and who knows what else. I feel lucky to have gotten out of there with my life, and more importantly, with my baby's life. Never had I seen such pure hatred in his eyes. I'm certain he would have killed me if I hadn't smashed that bottle against his head."

"Have you been to a doctor to be sure the baby is okay?" Jason asked with concern.

"No, I don't dare go into any towns just yet. Flint has too many friends who know who I am and would immediately recognize me. In fact, several of them are out looking for me right now. I feel sure he's offered a reward for my return."

"What makes you think that?"

"Because four days ago, I got off the stage at Pine

Mound to wait for the one that would take me to Jefferson the following morning. That evening, when I went down to the hotel restaurant, I saw two of Flint's good friends talking with the desk clerk—showing him what I'm almost sure was my photograph. Luckily, it wasn't the same desk clerk that had signed me in earlier. I saw him shake his head no, but I realized it was only a matter of time before one of the guests, or one of the other employees, recognized me from the photograph, so I ran up to my room, got my valise, and left town on foot. And knowing that once someone did positively identify me, which would cause them to focus their hunt in that area, I took to the back roads and the woods. I didn't dare walk along the roads or even approach any houses."

"So you haven't actually seen a doctor to be sure the baby is okay," Jason said, more to himself than to Katherine.

"No, but I'm sure the baby is all right. I've known two women who miscarried, and I haven't shown any of the signs that they did."

"Still, I would feel better if the doc had a look at you," Jason said firmly. "I'm going to send into town for Doc Edison."

"Jason, I won't be here. Remember? I'm leaving."

A sudden flash of lightning flared through the window, followed by a distant rumble of thunder. Staring first out the window, then at her tear-stained face, Jason said simply, "Not in weather like this. Not only is it about to pour, it is almost dark. You will at least stay until morning. In the meantime, I'm sending for Doc Edison."

"But what if one of Flint's friends shows my

photograph to the doctor? He'll recognize me, and that can only mean trouble for you."

"Let me worry about that," he said as he left the room.

His mind was made up; there was no point in arguing with him.

Chapter Seven

"What did the doctor say?" Jason asked as he entered the room. Katherine was lying in bed with the sheets pulled up to her chin, and Minnie was at the window, tossing the water from a small white basin out into the rainy night.

"He said the baby is just fine," Minnie answered with a quick smile. "Yessir, those was his exact words. But he told Missy here she should be takin' better care of herself, that the fall she took just might have weakened the lower . . ." She paused, embarrassed. "Well, he said the fall might have done some damage that he can't see, but that as far as he could tell, the baby was doin' just fine."

"Good. It's better to be sure about these things," Jason said, relieved. Since he wasn't the father, or even a relative, he had felt it wasn't his place to speak to the doctor directly about Katherine's condition. Forcing himself to be patient, he had seen Dr. Edison to the front door, then raced upstairs for the news. Patience was not one of his virtues, and the waiting had almost driven him mad. Had a stranger seen him pacing the floor in the library, he might have thought that he was the father. In a way, Jason wished that he were.

"I suppose you two will finally be wantin' to eat now," Minnie said hopefully as she wiped the basin and put it back on the commode. She had not understood why neither one of them would eat until after the doctor's visit, since the area being examined had nothing to do with the eating parts of the body.

"I'm really not very hungry," Katherine said, but when Minnie scowled disapprovingly, knowing full well that she had not eaten all day—and had a little one inside of her to think of—she quickly added, "but I'll be down just as soon as I've gotten dressed."

This time she meant it. She had no desire to go running off into the dark, especially in the rain, which had been coming down steadily for the last two hours.

"There's no need to get dressed," Jason said, and when Minnie glared at him, quickly added, "What I was going to say is that you could bring the food up here and serve it to her in bed. You could bring my supper up here, too, and we could pretend we were out on a picnic."

"That's a ridiculous notion," Katherine said with a laugh. "I'm not about to put Minnie to that much trouble. It'll just take me a moment to get dressed and come down."

Minnie's scowl turned to a look of amusement as she thought about having a picnic right there in a bedroom. Only her Mister Jason would think of such a thing. "It's no trouble, Missy. I don't mind, and as late as it is now, it would be senseless to go to the trouble of gettin' dressed when you'll just have to turn around and get yourself ready for bed again as soon as you've eaten."

"Fine," Jason said quickly, not giving Katherine another chance to object. "Bring everything on up here as soon as you have it ready."

"Will do," Minnie said cheerfully, hurrying out of the room. Already into the spirit of things, she planned to put all the food in a big wicker basket, just as she would if she were really packing a picnic. It would be far more fun—and easier—than carrying all that food up on trays. Although she wasn't sure what she believed about Katherine's supposed fall last week—or about the fact that she was married, but had no idea where her husband was—she did like Missy Katherine. She liked her a lot.

It did not matter to her in the least that the poor gal had somehow gotten herself with child and had decided to cover her shame with a make-believe husband—after all, the gal did not have on a wedding ring, nor had she as much as mentioned a husband until that evening. Minnie had a feeling it was the baby that was at the center of all the gal's problems, and she was glad to finally know it. Poor thing, no doubt when her father had found out, he had flown into a rage and beat her severely for sinning. But Minnie didn't care that Katherine had sinned. She still liked the gal, and could easily tell that Mister Jason liked her, too. This picnic idea might be just the thing to bring them closer together, for Saturday was only two days away.

"It's not that I really mind this idea of yours about

having a picnic in my bedroom," Katherine said softly, the crisp white sheets still pulled up to her chin, her face slightly flushed. "But there is one problem neither one of you seems to have thought of."

"Oh? And what's that?" Jason asked, drawing a chair up to the bed in preparation for the picnic supper that would be set on the quilt. After settling himself comfortably, he looked her squarely in the eye—a habit she found somewhat unnerving at times.

"It's the fact that—well, it's that I'm—I'm afraid it has to do with my present state of dress, or perhaps I should say my state of undress. You see, in order for the doctor to examine me, I had to take almost all my clothing off. Minnie put everything in the armoire."

Jason's gaze dropped to the covers with interest. "So, you are trying to tell me that you aren't fully dressed under there." He smiled, for he had already guessed that.

"Very good. That's exactly what I'm trying to tell you. I would like to be dressed in something more than my undergarments when we eat."

"I guess you'd get mad at me if I was to point out that I've already seen you in much less than what you probably have on now." He grinned at the memory of what he had seen.

"Jason! Can't you please forget that ever happened?"

"Don't really want to," he shrugged, pushing himself out of the chair and rising. "But if you are hinting for me to get out of here so you can put on my shirt, or something else, over your undergarments, I'll gladly oblige. Though I do feel it is a pitiful waste of time."

"And what do you mean by that?" she asked, pulling

the sheet all the way up to her wide brown eyes.

"Nothing much. It's just that I've already seen what you are so nobly trying to hide. That, and the fact that you will have to get ready for bed almost as soon as we've eaten, just seems to make it a waste of time. But, if it'll make you feel better, I'll get out of here long enough for you to put something else on."

"Thank you," she muttered, barely controlling her urge to duck beneath the sheets all together. She watched as he politely dipped his head in her direction, then sauntered out of the room, winking at her as he reached back and pulled the door shut. Her head spun in a whirlwind of conflicting emotions. Sometimes that man could be so sweet, so understanding, that she almost believed she was in love with him. At other times, he could be the most overbearing, exasperating human being she could ever remember having to deal with. Didn't want to forget those incidents indeed! She could feel her face burning as she stared at the closed door, the sheets still tightly clutched in her hands.

Though the door was clearly shut, and Jason was definitely aware of her intentions to make herself more decent, Katherine was not going to risk being caught in one more embarrassing situation. Keeping her eye on the door, she threw back the covers and dashed across the room for the yellow plaid shirt. Turning around—almost before she had the shirt securely in hand, she rushed back to the bed and got back under the covers to dress.

Not until she was completely shielded once more by the sheets, did she take the time to unbutton the shirt, then slip it on over her camisole and bloomers. For as long as she stayed in this house, she was going to be more careful about dressing and undressing. Never again would she be caught without all her clothes. Jason had already seen too much, far too much—though to her chagrin, she was sure he wouldn't agree. Despite her extreme embarrassment, that thought made her smile. *No, Jason would not agree with that at all.*

"You can come back in now," she called out as soon as she had the last button buttoned and the covers folded neatly about her waist.

"You sure?" he responded quickly. "I wouldn't want to barge in on you while you were indecent in any way."

With a quick glance heavenward, as if giving the powers that be a warning that she'd had just about enough, Katherine replied sweetly, "Yes, I'm sure. You can come back in whenever you're ready."

"As long as you're sure." When the door opened and Jason re-entered, his face was the picture of innocence, reflecting goodness and virtue. Only a wicked little glimmer in the corner of his eye revealed his true, less than noble thoughts. What really bothered Katherine was the fact that she was starting not to care nearly as much as she should. If he wanted to think his naughty thoughts—even if they concerned her—there was nothing she could do about it. Rather than reprimand him, she simply smiled and asked what he had accomplished around the ranch that day.

Though, in fact, he had accomplished very little—being unable to take his mind off last night's incident on the patio, and the fact that he had managed to fall in love with a married woman—Jason managed to make it sound as if he'd gotten a lot of work done that day. He told her that the corral fence had been mended in three places and several dozen calves had been rounded up for spring branding, but failed to mention that it was Pete and Jack who had rounded up the new calves, and Mose and Rede who had done most of the work on the fence.

He just couldn't get his heart into his work that day—not when his heart was so occupied elsewhere. Though he had intended to help with the fence that surrounded a small area west of the barn, he had been unable to keep his thoughts on what Mose and Rede were doing. His attention kept straying to Katherine's window, hoping to catch a glimpse of the woman who had turned his world upside down. He just wanted some sign showing that she was all right.

It had worried him that she had locked herself in early the night before, refusing to answer anyone's knock. It also worried him that he might have completely destroyed whatever friendship they had managed to develop, but in all fairness to himself, how was he supposed to have known she was married? She wore no ring. Furthermore, why would a married woman be traveling alone, and on foot? It was not until he was logging the newly branded calves into the record book, that it occurred to him she might be upset enough to try to leave without telling him—if she hadn't already left.

"I'm glad we got everything done and I decided to quit work when I did," he said, leaning back in his chair, watching her intently. "If I hadn't come upstairs when I did, you might have made good on your attempt to leave, and we never would have gotten that chance to talk. And now that I know your situation, I can better deal with it. Saturday, when we head over to Jefferson, I'll stick to the backroads. It'll take us a little longer, but we'll be less likely to run into anyone who might recognize you and cause trouble."

"Saturday? I thought I already made myself clear. I can't stay here until Saturday. I can't impose on you any longer, except maybe for tonight."

"You will stay until Saturday, at which time I plan to personally see you to your brother's door, safe and sound." The serious tone of his voice sent shivers down her spine. "I'll have it no other way. I owe you at least that much."

"You owe me? For what? If anything, I owe you."

"Okay," he shrugged. "Then you at least owe me that much."

"But I can't stay."

Jason stared at her a long moment, unable to understand why she was still so determined to leave. Slowly, he rose from his chair and walked across the room to the armoire, pulled open the double doors and turned to face her. "If I have to take all three of your dresses away in order to keep you here, I will. The doctor said you were to take better care of yourself for your baby's sake, and tramping through the woods for days on end is not what I'd call taking good care of yourself."

He had a point there. It might be in her own best interest if she left first thing in the morning, and it might even be in Jason's best interest, but if the baby was to be considered at all—as well it should be—then waiting until Saturday for a ride to her brother's ranch was really the smartest choice.

"So, what is it going to be? Do I have your word that you'll stay until Saturday at which time I will gladly take you to your brother's ranch, or do I take all your clothing away from you right now in order to make you stay?"

"All of it?" Her eyes widened as she considered just how far he might go to carry out that threat.

"If I have to, I'd even take all the clothing you have on your back right now. Every stitch."

He meant it.

"But you don't understand. If my husband finds me with you, or even discovers that you helped me in any way, he'll be angry with you, too. He might be angry enough to try to kill you."

"Let me worry about that, if and when the time ever comes."

"I don't think you understand how violent his temper is. And lately, it's gotten much worse. In the beginning, he never used physical violence on me, but now he's done even that. You've seen the proof. No telling what he'd do to you."

Jason felt a terrible rage building inside him. The thought of what she had gone through at the hand of her own husband made him wonder if he, himself, might not be capable of killing a man so brutal. "That may be so, but for now, you had better be the one during the worrying, for I'm just about ready to follow through on my threat of taking away all your clothes."

"I'll stay," she finally said, with a little more anger in her voice than she actually felt. Although she felt he should be more concerned about his own safety, she had to admire him for his fearlessness.

"Do I have your word?" he asked.

"Yes, you have my word." Sudden relief washed over her like a warm, gentle tide. Deep down, she had not wanted to leave Seven Oaks, not just yet. And if she was to be really honest with herself and look deeper still, she knew she would have to admit that she did not want to leave Seven Oaks at all.

To Katherine's relief—yet also to her disappointment—Jason remained a perfect gentleman all during their bedroom picnic, even when Minnie was gone from the room to get something she had forgotten. He talked mainly about all the rain they had gotten lately; the pasture that needed reseeding, but couldn't be tilled until it stopped raining; and about some of the neighbors' troubles and triumphs—but he pointedly refrained from asking her anything more about her past. He kept the conversation carefully impersonal, and she was grateful for that, but she was also a little perturbed that he wasn't more curious. Had the situation been reversed, she would have been bursting with dozens of questions.

What pleased her about the evening was that it gave her an opportunity to get to know Jason better. By the time they had finished eating and he had retired to his own room, she had learned several things about him that she memorized and filed away in her heart for future reference.

His favorite food was beefsteak and potatoes, which

was why Minnie had prepared it again. He claimed he could live on beefsteak and potatoes if only Minnie would allow it, and he admitted that the only reason he ever ate any green vegetables was to keep peace with Minnie.

Katherine also learned that although he rarely took time away from his work, occasionally he liked to go fishing with Mose and his two sons. He said that he wished he could do that sort of thing more often, but after his father's death, he was left with more work than he could handle. Katherine got the strong impression that Jason thrived on his work—that being master of Seven Oaks was his entire life, which made her wonder why he had never married and provided Seven Oaks with a mistress. Although Minnie did a wonderful job with the house and the cooking, she was surprised that Jason had not found a wife to take more personal care of him and his house. And as handsome as Jason was, she wondered why some woman had not maneuvered her way permanently into his life.

She sighed audibly as she settled down into the warmth of her bed. Wouldn't it have been nice if she could have married a man like Jason, instead of having been so easily fooled into marrying a man like Flint. Deciding it was pointless to ponder over things that could never be, Katherine closed her eyes and at last drifted off to sleep.

The following morning Katherine awoke early to the chatter of mockingbirds just outside her window. With no clock to tell the time, and afraid she had overslept once again, she fought the urge to go back to sleep and hurriedly tossed back the covers. As she slipped into one of the dresses Jason had bought her and ran a brush through her hair, she heard the sound of men's voices coming from outside.

When she looked out the window she saw that one of the men was Jason, talking to a tall, slender man near the barn. She was disappointed to find that he had already left the house and, judging by the previous three days, it would be late in the afternoon before she would be able to see him again—unless she took a little stroll out by the barn and just happened to run into him there.

It was certainly a lovely enough morning for a walk. Yesterday's storm clouds were gone, and in their place was a single, tiny white wisp, drifting slowly in a bright, azure sky.

Although she had not thought at all about breakfast while dressing, when she stepped into the kitchen and smelled the aroma of sausage and biscuits, she decided to accept Minnie's offer and ate heartily.

When she finally stepped into the warm spring sunshine, she caught a glimpse of Jason disappearing into the blacksmith's shed to the right of the barn, and she decided that was the direction her walk should take. Having to stay on the cobblestone paths for fear that the rain-soaked ground might ruin the only decent pair of slippers she had, Katherine slowly made her way toward the blacksmith's shed. As she neared the door, she became aware of two sets of eyes peering out at her from the darkness. Both pairs of eyes were barely doorlatch-high and disappeared before she could get close enough to see who, or what, they belonged to.

It took a moment for her eyes to adjust to the dim

light inside, but Katherine immediately sensed that Jason was not alone. Too many shadows moved about the room. When she could see well enough to make out more than shapes, she saw the little boy who had clung so possessively to Minnie's skirts the day she had arrived, and another boy, about two inches taller. Both boys stood just behind Jason, mouths closed tight and eyes opened wide.

"Good morning," Jason greeted her, grinning. He looked from one wide-eyed little boy to the other, then back to her. "I'd like for you to meet a couple of the best hired hands I have on the place. I think you've already met Edmond," he said, resting a hand on the smaller boy's head. "And this boy, on the other side, is his older brother, Samuel."

While Edmond hid himself quickly behind Jason's thigh, Samuel stepped forward and extended his right hand in greeting. "Pleased to meet ya, ma'am."

Although it was more common for a woman to offer her hand to a man than vice versa, Katherine graciously accepted his hand and shook it much like a man would. "And I am very pleased to meet you. Jason has told me what fine workers you two are, and I can certainly see that he has told me the absolute truth. My, but you both look strong as bulls."

It was not quite the truth, for the two boys were scrawny as newborn pups, but Katherine's remark won favor with both boys. The two exchanged glances and grinned. Pulling himself up to his full height, Samuel hooked his thumbs into the corners of his front pockets. "You're right about that," he agreed. "I can lift a bucket full of oats and pour them in the troughs all by myself. And Edmond can carry an armload of hay with no trouble at all. Together, we can drag the privy box all the way to the manure wagon and unload it by ourselves."

"Can you, now?" she asked, looking impressed.

"We can hammer nails real good, too. We was just about to help Mister Jason put that latch back on the side door of the barn where Bullet busted out last night."

"Have to find the hammer first," Jason pointed out as he scrambled through a large wooden box filled with tools. "Never can seem to find one when I need one."

"You want to come watch?" Samuel asked, eager to impress Katherine further.

"Why yes, I love to watch strong men at work."

"Someday, I'm going to be just as strong as Mister Jason and my pa," Samuel went on. "Did you know that Mister Jason happens to be one of the strongest men in the whole world?"

Jason looked up in surprise, and to Katherine's amazement, actually blushed as the boy continued.

"Take your shirt off for her, Mister Jason. Let her see how good your muscles are."

"I don't think the lady would really be interested in seeing my muscles," he muttered, looking toward Katherine apologetically.

"Oh, I don't know. I think I'd enjoy seeing your muscles," she said, delighted to see Jason flustered about something for a change. She found it pure joy to have the upper hand in this situation. "Why don't you take your shirt off and show me just how good your muscles really are."

"Yeah, Mister Jason, show her how that muscle in

your arm can bulge up so big." Then to Katherine, he said, "Wait until you see this. He's got my pa beat by two inches. That's the gospel. They got Grandma's sewing tape and measured once."

"You actually measured?" Katherine asked, acting more impressed with each statement that Samuel made. She could barely keep from laughing as Jason shuffled nervously, trying to get Samuel's attention so that he could change the subject.

"We did it on a bet," Jason said sheepishly. "You know how it is when fellows get together and get to talking."

"No, how is it?"

"They start bragging over the silliest things."

Katherine looked at him for a long moment, letting him squirm under her unfathomable gaze. "Well," she said finally, "are you going to show me these fine muscles of yours or not?"

Defeated, Jason started to slowly unbutton his shirt, his right brow raised in a silent warning that should the urge strike her, she had better not laugh.

"There now, make your arm bulge," Samuel said as soon as Jason had his shirt removed and tucked neatly into his waistband. "Make it bulge up real big."

Rubbing his hand over his face first, Jason finally raised his right arm up to his shoulder, and though obviously reluctant to do so, flexed his muscle for Katherine.

"Aw, you can do better than that," Samuel protested. Turning to Katherine he added, "He can, you know. He can make it bulge up much bigger than that."

Reluctantly, Jason obliged the boy and flexed harder.

"There, you see how big that muscle is? Touch it," Samuel urged. "You'll find it's as hard as a rock. Go on. Touch it. He don't mind. See? He lets me touch it whenever I want." Samuel tiptoed over to Jason, and curving his hand over the bulging muscle, he pressed down, making absolutely no impression on the sinewy mass.

"I feel like a side show," Jason muttered under his breath as Katherine slowly lifted a finger and pressed it into the hardened flesh, feeling a flutter of excitement at finally being able to touch him.

The muscle was just as hard as Samuel had claimed it to be, and, for a fleeting moment, she wished she could trail her finger up the rounded curves of his arm and across to the broad muscles that filled out his back. She wanted to know if all his body was this firm, this strong. Never had she seen a man so fit, so totally masculine.

Although Flint was lean and broad across the shoulder like Jason, he had never developed muscles like these—muscles that came from day after long day of hard work. Flint had never had much use for an honest day's work. It suddenly occurred to her that Jason was everything she had ever wanted Flint to be. Though Jason harbored a devilish streak that surfaced at the worst possible moments, he was basically a good man. Not only did he do an honest day's work, he took great pride in that fact. Jason was strong, yet caring, even when it came to someone else's boys. He was gentle when he needed to be, yet unyielding when it counted the most. The more Katherine came to know Jason, the fonder she became of him—and the more she wished she could get to know him better. It was a good thing Saturday was only two days away. The longer she stayed, the harder it would be to say goodbye.

"May I put my shirt back on now?" Jason asked, interrupting her thoughts.

"If you feel you must," Katherine said with the same sort of shrug he had given her when she'd asked if he was ever going to forget those embarrassing little incidents that had concerned her. And in just as cavalier a manner, she tilted her head and added, "Just don't do it on my account. I happen to like the way you look without your shirt." Though she said it to get back at him, it was a true enough statement. She could stand there all day, watching the rippling muscles beneath his sun-browned skin—and as for the silky dark hair that ran across his broad chest in such abundance, she had never before felt such an urge to reach out and touch anything.

Realizing that she was becoming more aroused than was good for her, Katherine looked away to where Samuel stood watching her curiously. She spoke to him in a barely controlled voice, "Well, it was certainly nice to meet you at last, but I have to be getting on back to the house. The walk did me some good, but I feel like I should do something to help Minnie since she has done so much for me. I've been idle long enough."

"I doubt she'll let you help her," Jason said as he slipped his arms back into his shirt and adjusted it over his shoulders. "First of all, she is used to doing all the housework herself, and secondly, she isn't about to let you do anything at all that might put a strain on the . . ." He paused as he realized there were too many listening ears. ". . . on the you-know-what. You can go on up there and ask if you want, and I'm sure she'll appreciate the fact that you did, but all you're going to hear is how you are supposed to be taking special care of yourself."

Samuel's eyes narrowed, for all this sounded suspiciously like grown-up talk, and he knew it was time to leave. "Come on, Edmond. Let's go see if the hammer got left in the barn."

Edmond was quick to comply and was out of the door before Samuel could completely edge his way around the grown ups. By the time Samuel turned to make sure Jason knew where they would be, all that was left of Edmond was a tiny trail of dust.

"We'll wait for you in the barn," he said, then nodded good-bye to Katherine.

"I'll be right there."

Finally alone, Jason was able to speak openly without having to worry that his words might be repeated. Looking deeply into her eyes, he stepped closer and laid his hand gently on Katherine's shoulder—an act that caused her to tremble with sensations she could barely control.

"Katherine, you've had a rough time of it these past few days, and you have a long, hard ride ahead of you on Saturday. Why don't you just take advantage of today and tomorrow, and rest all you can? If you care to read, Minnie can show you where the library is. There are all sorts of books in there. Or, if you would simply like to sit outside and nap in the sun like my mother used to do on occasion, that's fine too."

"Minnie will think I'm being lazy."

"You have a very good reason for being lazy," he said and smiled gently. "You have to remember that." Then, realizing he had an overwhelming urge to lean forward and take a kiss that was not rightfully his, he removed his hand from her shoulder and resumed fastening his shirt. "Now go, I've got work to do. We'll have plenty of time for talk later tonight."

Katherine could hardly wait.

Chapter Eight

"You sure do look pretty," Minnie said, looking up from her work as Katherine entered the kitchen, already dressed for dinner in one of the dresses Jason had bought for her. "I sure do like your hair like that. Real pretty."

"Thank you," Katherine said, glad to have someone else's opinion. After having discovered a small silver box of hairpins and tiny combs up in her room, she had spent almost an hour combing her mane of dark brown hair back from her face and up to the top of her head where she arranged it in a spectacular array of curls. She had found a pretty blue ribbon to weave in and out of the curls that matched the blue of her dress almost perfectly. She had chosen the blue dress because it was obviously Jason's favorite color—as she had noted from his own choice in clothing and from the touches of blue throughout the house. "I thought I'd do something different with it for tonight."

"Looks real nice. Mister Jason's goin' to sure be impressed," Minnie said with a knowing smile. "I doubt he's seen anyone look quite that pretty in quite some time."

"Why would you say that? A man like Jason? I'm sure he sees lots of women far more beautiful than I could ever hope to be."

After some thought, it had occurred to Katherine that the whole reason Jason had never married was because there were probably several different women he was interested in who were just as interested in him. Why should he narrow the field to just one woman when he could enjoy the company of many? This conclusion was somehow troubling to Katherine.

"Jason? Lots of women? Not that I know anything about. As far as I know, he hasn't been seein' any woman since the middle of last summer, and then it was only a couple of picnics and the Fourth of July dance with Stella Bishop, a gal from over to Circle Crossing." Minnie frowned. "And lo and behold, if she ain't already married now. I guess when she saw that there was goin' to be no real future wiht Mister Jason, she went on to greener pastures. They always do. She married Jewell Taylor, over to Daingerfield way, sometime last fall. Mister Jason didn't seem too concerned, but then I reckon he was glad it wasn't him, for he sent her a real nice wedding gift. A sterling silver jewelry box, I believe."

"I suppose Stella just wasn't the right woman for Jason. I'm sure eventually he'll find someone special and will finally settle down." But the thought of it made her heart ache. How she wished it could be her. How she wished her circumstances could be different.

"I'm beginnin' to doubt it. Heck, he didn't even do no courtin' during Christmas, when there was all those fine parties to go to. I sure do worry about that man. Here he is, twenty-seven years old and not only ain't he married yet, he don't even got any good prospects. All he does is worry about this place and work himself too hard. What good's it goin' to do if he ain't got no heir to take over when he gets too old to work it anymore? Can you tell me that? What good's all his hard work goin' to be to him then?"

While Katherine pondered the question, Minnie, herself, furnished the answer.

"It ain't goin' to do him no good at all. And once he's gone, the place will probably just go back to the State. After all, he ain't got no family left to inherit it. No children. No parents. Not even any brothers or sisters. And only one cousin that I know of, and he's a lot older than Mister Jason. That foolish man sure needs to seriously consider takin' himself a wife and startin' a family. He ain't gettin' any younger, you know. I've told him that time and time again, but he don't seem to listen."

Smiling, despite every effort not to, Katherine could just imagine how many times Minnie had spoken to Jason on this subject. It was obvious that Minnie was not one to hold her tongue when she had an opinion about something—not even something as personal as Jason's taking a wife.

"I guess there's not much more you can do but hope he eventually finds the right woman," she said finally, in a feeble effort to console Minnie, for the woman had worked herself into quite a frenzied state.

"That's all I can do. He sure won't let me invite none of the unmarried gals that live around here over for tea anymore."

"I gather you've tried?"

"Just the once. Me and Missus Jane once invited Mrs. McKinsey and that pretty young daughter of hers, Miss Shirley Faye, over one Sunday afternoon for tea as a surprise for Mister Jason, but he didn't take too kindly to the idea. He was nice enough to them while they were here, but once they was gone, he lit into me and his mother like a bantam hen protecting her young."

Katherine laughed at the thought of Jason having to entertain two women at tea. For some reason, she just couldn't picture him balancing a teacup on his knee and nibbling on ladyfingers. She was surprised that Minnie or his mother had ever thought he would enjoy such a thing. "I gather this Shirley Faye did not impress him enough to further their acquaintance?"

"I guess not. He never did pay a call on her. But that was four years ago. It's way too late now. Shirley's already married, too, and has three fine sons. She sure would have made Jason a good wife."

Realizing Minnie equated a good wife and a happy marriage with being able to produce children, Katherine remembered her own predicament and felt a twinge of regret. It had taken her six years to become pregnant, and now that she was finally going to have a baby, she was running away from her husband, refusing to be his wife any more. If only Flint had been able to change, things might have been so different. If only he could have been more like Jason, then maybe—just maybe—they might have had the happy marriage she had expected.

Putting the thought out of her mind, Katherine walked over to where Minnie was busily chopping apples. She saw that she was preparing two more pies for their supper.

"If you'll give me a knife and a board, I'll help you," she offered.

"In that pretty dress? Won't hear of it. Besides, I only have two more apples to cut up, then all I have to do is toss them into the bowl with the rest of those things, stir it all up, pour it into those crusts, and they'll be ready to bake."

"Then I'll help with something else."

"Missy, I already told you earlier this afternoon; this is my kitchen and I don't like no one else workin' in it. I can do better when I work by myself. Since it's still a couple of hours till supper, why don't you go into the parlor and rest a while. It's real quiet in there."

Remembering Jason's comment about his books, Katherine decided to find something to read instead. "If you are absolutely certain I can't be of any help to you, I think I'd like to read for a while. Jason said something about a library. Which room is that?"

Following Minnie's directions, Katherine went into the west wing of the house and found the library. She was extremely impressed with the number of books that Jason had somehow acquired in the area where books were not easy to come by. Two walls of the room were lined from floor to ceiling with books on every conceivable subject. On the far wall, facing the fireplace, was a long mahogany desk whose polished surface was also covered with books. Curiosity led her to the desk to see what those books might be.

She was not too surprised to find several books dealing with animal husbandry and land management, but she was very surprised to discover that one of the books on the desk was a slim volume of poetry. Did Jason actually read poetry? She had never known a man who read poetry. Most of Flint's friends could barely read their own "wanted" posters, much less enjoy the beauty and depth of poetry.

Opening the small book, she began to read. The first poem—about a child at play in a field—was tender and moving. It made her eager to read more. With two hours at least before supper, Katherine settled herself in a comfortable chair and read on.

"Here you are." Jason's voice brought Katherine from her reading with a start. His broad, muscular body filled the doorway. "Minnie said I would probably find you in here."

"I had to find something to do so I thought I'd read for a while. You were right. Minnie won't let me help her, and I was bored silly not having anything to do." Katherine had no idea why she felt compelled to explain her presence in the library when he'd been the one to suggest it. "I hope you don't mind, but I'm reading the book of poetry that was on your desk."

"No, I don't mind at all. Help yourself to any of these books," Jason said, gesturing widely while he stepped closer to her and drank in her beauty. Hard as it was to imagine, she seemed to grow more beautiful each day.

Her large, expressive eyes were no longer shadowed and the faded green bruise was gone from her cheek. Her face, which seemed to have filled out a little, glowed with a healthy pink. "My mother always enjoyed reading at bedtime. If you wish, feel free to carry any of these books up to your room, or even outside into the garden. You don't have to stay in here and read in these cramped chairs."

"Cramped?" She hadn't noticed, but then she was not built like Jason. Glancing at the powerful muscles rippling under his shirt—and the masculine way in which he filled out his long denim britches—she doubted that many men were built like Jason, either. "I assure you, I am quite comfortable. But I would like to take this book up with me at bedtime since you were kind enough to offer. I'll leave it here for the time being and come back for it later."

"Good, because supper is almost ready, and I'm more than ready to eat something. How about you?"

"Ready and willing," she said as she rose and laid the book on her chair.

"Ready and willing, huh?" Jason said with a chuckle, that devilish gleam in his eyes.

"To eat," she specified, her brow raised in warning. "Ready and willing 'to eat'."

"Oh."

Katherine's brow went even higher, but she made no further comment, accepting Jason's arm and allowing him to escort her from the room. He should have been scolded for such a bold insinuation, but she knew from past experience that even the harshest reprimand would do little good. It was in his nature to speak his mind. What was it he claimed Minnie said about him? He went around with his brain unloaded and his mouth half-cocked. Even if he could be coerced into an apology, the words would be hollow; his heart was in that which he had already spoken. Since any comment she might make at this point would never change that, she had decided that the best way to deal with such bold little remarks was to ignore them.

Supper that night was only slightly different from what Minnie had served the night before. Roast beef had been substituted for beefsteak—but, once again, there were creamed potatoes, peas, beans, and sourdough rolls. It was a hearty meal, which would sustain Jason and all the hard-working men at the ranch, but Katherine was starting to wish for something a little less filling. While she was Jason's guest, of course, she wouldn't make any complaint. Once at Andrew's, however, she would take a hand in preparing the meals, making sure there were plenty of green vegetables, fresh fruit, and various meats and fowl. What she particularly longed for at that moment was braised chicken and rice. Just the thought of it made her mouth water, and it occurred to her that it might be one of those cravings associated with pregnancy. She wondered what Minnie would think of adding braised chicken to the menu.

After supper, Katherine again agreed to take a walk with Jason in order to work off the heavy meal. She felt sure that this time there would be no need to worry about his behavior. Now that he knew she was married—and carrying a child—he was not as likely to try to steal kisses. She had no doubt that whatever interest he might have had in her earlier, it would be gone now.

Again, as she rose from her chair, she accepted his proffered arm, and tried her best to ignore the tingling wave of excitement that coursed through her the moment their arms met. It was best that she not think about the emotions that Jason stirred in her. Instead, she tried to concentrate on the star-filled sky and the silvery glow of the half moon that hovered just above the treetops.

Slowly, they followed the meandering cobblestone path, first to the barn, where Jason made sure the twin foals had had their supplementary feeding, then, back out to the gardens. A gentle, refreshingly cool breeze wafted around them.

The only light came from the shimmering moon which cast soft, slow-moving shadows across the garden, making it seem almost enchanted.

"If you'd care to sit for a while, I'll light one or two of the torches," he offered, not at all ready to call it a night.

"Yes, I'd like to sit for a while, but you don't have to go to the trouble of lighting the torches. It's fine just as it is."

"But I thought you were afraid of the dark. You know—afraid all those boogie bears and boogie wolves will get you."

Katherine could tell he was teasing her, but didn't particularly care. "I usually am afraid to be outside in the dark, but I feel safe enough with you here."

"That's nice to hear. I'll leave the torches alone, then," he said. She seated herself, and he joined her, pulling his chair close to hers.

"Well, who's going to be the first to remark on the beautiful night?" he asked, noticing how the moon's silvery beams enhanced her beauty, arousing emotions in him that he couldn't seem to control. He wanted so much to say that a night such as this was meant for lovers—and he wished he could be her lover. How he wished he could kiss her forbidden lips. It tore him apart to think of the privileges that belonged to her husband and could never be his. He trembled with the intensity of his desire for her. Never had he wanted a woman as much as he wanted Katherine. What a fool her husband must be not to have cherished a woman such as this.

"I guess I'll be first," she said softly. "It is a beautiful night, isn't it? I'm inclined to believe there are far more stars shining over Texas than there could possibly be anywhere else." Her upturned gaze swept the glittering heavens.

"Have you traveled much?" he asked, continuing to let his eyes wander over her, memorizing every detail.

"Not really. Other than Kansas, I've never been anywhere outside of Texas." His penetrating gaze was beginning to make Katherine uncomfortable, but when she shifted her position, his eyes followed her closely. Unable to avoid the intensity of his gaze, her heartbeat quickened.

"Kansas?"

"That's where Flint and I lived. On a small farm, out in the middle of nowhere."

"But you originally are from Texas?" His eyes were drawn to the movements of her lips as she talked. Such kissable lips.

"Yes, I grew up in a small town not too far from here. Ever hear of Gilmer?" Realizing that his eyes were riveted on her mouth, she flicked her tongue nervously over her lower lip.

"Of course. That's only about thirty miles southwest of here. Is that where your father lives?"

"Yes, he has a small ranch just outside of town. Well, it's small in comparison to Seven Oaks, but pretty big for that area. Last I heard, he had turned to farming and was growing cotton on part of his land—and doing pretty well with it."

"I gather you got that information from your brother."

"It was in his last letter, but then again, it's been six months since I got my last letter from Andrew. Papa might be back to growing corn by now. That's what Andrew says he grew for two years before he decided to try cotton." She paused as she thought again of her father. She could see him clearly, sitting behind the plow, coaxing Sadie and Buckwheat to give him their all. He was a tall man—a little too thin the last time she saw him—but still very handsome for someone his age. Though work weary, his shoulders were straight, his back strong. At age forty-two, he had still had a full head of unruly, dark brown hair that had a tendency to fall into his face while he worked. Oh, how she missed that man. Feeling the tears starting to build, she decided to change the subject to something less painful.

"I wonder if Andrew decided to raise cotton, too. He had just gotten his place cleared in time for fall planting when he wrote me, but he never did say what it was he intended to plant."

"Could be cotton," Jason agreed, distressed by the pain that had been briefly revealed in her eyes. "I understand cotton is bringing in a very high price these days, and his being so close to the docks there in Jefferson, he wouldn't have to worry about transporting it very far in order to get it to market. Tell me more about this brother of yours. Is he married or does he live alone?"

Katherine felt another moment of sadness. "He used to be married, but Jenny died only a year after the wedding. She caught some sort of fever—I'm not sure what—but she died within just a few days. As far as I know, Andrew hasn't even thought about seeing any other woman since then."

"How long ago was that?"

"Two years ago."

"Two years isn't that long," he said, his face suddenly clouded with his own deep sorrow.

Remembering that his parents had died just a few years before, Katherine wished dearly she could think of something to say that might comfort him, but no adequate words came to mind.

"It's obvious your brother's heart hasn't had time to heal yet. It'll probably do him good to have you there with him for a while. It'll help get his mind off his loneliness. And I imagine the baby will bring a little joy back into his life. No matter what the tragedy, a baby always seems to make everyone feel a little brighter."

Remembering the conversation she'd had with Minnie earlier, Katherine asked, "It's obvious from that statement, and the way you cater to Samuel and Edmond, that you love children. Why is it you've never married and started a family of your own? I think you'd make a wonderful father."

"Of course, I would," he laughed, and leaned back in his chair. "It sounds to me like Minnie's had a word or two with you."

"She did mention something about your having neglected that part of your life."

"She would." He chuckled. "That woman's been after me to take a wife ever since I can remember. She can't understand why I've allowed so much of my life to go to waste. I can't count the number of times she or

Mother tried to fix me up with some girl or another."

"And why haven't you ever married?"

His laughter stopped and his handsome face grew solemn. "Never wanted to. Never even seriously considered it until recently."

Katherine felt a sharp ache deep inside her. "So you've recently found someone who interests you enough to consider marriage? That will delight Minnie no end. Why haven't you told her?"

Jason stared at her a long moment before answering. "Because that someone is you."

"Jason, no!" she cried out softly, overwhelmed with emotion.

"You asked. I'm simply stating the facts. Ever since you came here—and even since I learned you were already married—I've found myself wondering what it would be like to have you for my wife. I think about making love to you constantly, and whenever I'm near you, I practically go out of my mind wanting you. I think, too, about the babe you are carrying, and in my mind, I see you holding it tenderly in your arms, nurturing it, and it hurts me to know I'll never be a part of that. Katherine, I know it's wrong, and I know it will probably send you running from me again, but I have to say it. I have to get how I feel out into the open."

"Jason, don't." She pressed her fingers gently against his lips to still the words she was afraid to hear, words that once said would forever torment her.

He closed his eyes at the gentle pain her touch caused him, and spoke softly against her fingertips. "I can't keep it penned up inside of me any longer. I've got to say it aloud. And I've got to say it to you. I've fallen in love with you." He took her hand from his lips and held it between his own, his eyes still closed, his face twisted in anguish. "Lord, help me. After all these years of trying and failing, I finally have fallen in love—with a married woman."

Tears filled Katherine's eyes, blinding her as she pressed her damp cheek to his hands. "I'm so sorry, Jason. I'm so very sorry. I never meant for you to fall in love with me. If there was any way to undo whatever it is I've done to bring this about, I'd undo it. It hurts me to know I've caused you all this pain. Please believe that. I care far too much for you to ever intentionally hurt you."

"Do you? Do you care for me at all?" He had to know.

Trembling from the pain that now seared her heart, Katherine nodded—her cheek still pressed to his hands. "For what little good it will do us, Jason, I love you too."

"Do you? Do you really?" There was renewed hope in his voice. "If that's so. If that's really how you feel, why don't you file for a divorce and marry me? I promise to do everything within my power to make you happy."

She was jolted to the core of her being. How could she explain so he would understand? "I—I can't get a divorce," she said, with a sob in her voice.

"Why not? If you're afraid of people around here finding out you're a divorced woman, you can file in another town, in another state, if you want—maybe in Kansas. I'll hire a good lawyer and pay for whatever you need to see it through."

"I can't. I thought I already explained that to you. I can never let Flint know where I am, and if I file for divorce, he would be given a chance to appear in court with me. He would find out where I am. Don't you see? I never want him to know where I've gone, and I particularly never want him to know about the child. The baby would bind me to him. If I ask for a divorce, he'll take my baby from me, just to punish me. I could never bear that. I can't risk losing my child. And then, if he found out that the reason I wanted a divorce was because I was in love with you, he'd probably kill you. That's the way he is. He kills people who get in his way. If he killed a thirteen-year-old boy, he'd think nothing of killing you. I couldn't bear the thought of putting you in such danger."

"I can take care of myself, and I can take care of you, too. He'd never be able to take your baby from you. I wouldn't let him."

Violent tremors shook her body as she tried to make him understand. "You don't know Flint. You don't know how brutal he is. He's a killer, and he's good at it. And he has friends who are just as ruthless. They would be only to happy to help him keep what he considers rightfully his. If it was just myself I was putting in danger, it wouldn't be so bad, but there's the child to consider. My child. I can't do anything that might put my child in danger. I'd rather die than risk my child's future. And you. I can't allow you to put yourself in such danger either." Rising shakily, she wiped her tears with the back of her wrist. When she spoke again, her voice was barely audible. "Please, Jason, please don't ask it of me. Please try to understand."

Unable to bear the pain in his eyes any longer, she turned and ran toward the house. Her mind was whirling.

"Katherine, wait!" Jason's chair clattered to the floor as he rose and pursued her.

"It's hopeless," she cried out, stumbling through the darkness, unable to see.

"Katherine, stop!" he shouted, realizing she was on the rocky pathway leading down to the cellar. "You'll fall. Please! Stop!"

It was too late—at that moment, Katherine's dark form tumbled forward and disappeared from his sight.

"Oh, my God!" he cried out as he ran toward the sunken area just in front of the cellar door. His first thought was of the huge stones that buttressed the earthen walls carved deep in the ground. "Katherine, are you all right? Katherine?"

There was no response to his words. All that could be heard was the violent pounding of his own heart.

Chapter Nine

"My baby . . ." Katherine murmured the moment she woke, even before she became fully aware that she was back in her bedroom, undressed, and under the covers. Minnie's smiling face hovered over her.

"The baby's just fine," Minnie assured her, adjusting the cool, moist cloths that were draped over Katherine's forehead and across the top of her head. "The doctor's done been here and gone, and he says the baby is just fine—but he told us you would probably wake with a terrible headache. How does your head feel?"

Katherine concentrated on her head and could come up with only one answer. "Wet."

"It doesn't hurt none?"

"Maybe a little," she conceded, for when she tried to raise her head from the pillow, a dull ache throbbed in her temple.

"Well, the doc left some powders to give you the moment you woke up. I'll get them ready."

While Minnie stirred the medicine into a glass of

water, Katherine lifted her head, despite the pain, to peer into the small dressing alcove. When she realized that Minnie was the only other person in the room, she fell back on the pillow, disappointed not to find Jason.

"He's downstairs, gettin' himself good and drunk," Minnie said candidly, in response to Katherine's unspoken question. "When he found out you was all right—that all you had wrong was that bump on your head—I guess he decided it called for a celebration, 'cause he went off to the library to have a good stiff drink. But he done had more than one stiff drink. Last time I checked, he'd done celebrated himself into a stupor. I think your fall frightened him far more than he was willin' to admit, 'cause he's not much of a drinkin' man. I don't know if you've quite caught on to it yet, but I do believe that man is in love with you."

All the heartache of their last conversation came rushing back to Katherine. She sobbed loudly, and the tears flowed down her cheeks unchecked.

"There, there, now. No cause to be cryin' like that," Minnie soothed. "I already told you, the baby's fine and you're goin' to be fine, too. Just keep that cold cloth on your forehead for a while and drink this. The doctor said it would ease the pain and would help you to sleep."

Katherine eyed the drink warily. She had never liked taking medicine. "What is this?"

"Just the powder the doc give me." Seeing Katherine's expression of distaste, Minnie chuckled. "Maybe you should hold your nose while you drink it. That will help kill the taste."

"Do I have to drink it?"

"Missy Katherine . . ." Minnie's voice held a warning note. "Yes, you have to take your medicine. Why, you're worse than Jason. Now open up."

Reluctantly, Katherine pinched her nose and swallowed the medicine. "Ugh!' she said, as Minnie waited until the last drop was gone.

"There now. You should be able to sleep without any trouble," Minnie said, plumping the pillows. "All you really did was to hit your head on a rock, but hard enough that it knocked you out for a while. A injury like that might not be serious, but it could cause enough pain to keep you from sleeping. And don't you go gettin' out of bed without someone nearby. The doc doubts you'll have any dizzy spells, but just to be on the safe side, he said for me to be with you when you first get up tomorrow. I'll be up right after I get all the men fed. You just lay there in that bed until then."

"But what if I need to . . ." Katherine blushed faintly.

"Ring that bell at your bedside real hard, and I'll come runnin' to help you with the chamber pot," Minnie put in quickly. "We don't want you takin' any more falls."

When Minnie had turned out the lamps and gone downstairs, Katherine's thoughts turned once again to Jason and his open declaration of love. The throb in her head was nothing compared to the ache in her heart, and she hoped the medicine would take effect quickly, for she simply did not want to think about any of that now. Eventually, she began to feel drowsy, and finally she slept.

True to her word, Minnie came bustling into the

bedroom bright and early the next morning to help Katherine get out of bed. When it was clear that she wasn't at all dizzy, Katherine quickly dressed and went to find Jason. She was going to ask him to take her to Jefferson a day early—even if it meant they would arrive late in the evening—but when she saw what a terrible mood he was in, she did not broach the subject. She quickly decided she could wait one more day, though she dreaded having to spend another evening with Jason, knowing the depth of his feeling for her. Being alone with him on the long ride to Jefferson was going to be difficult enough. How she dreaded saying good-bye, even though she knew it was for the best.

That night, Jason stayed out in the fields until after dark, and by the time he had washed and changed, dinner had been delayed an hour. Katherine was in the parlor reading another book of poetry, when Jason finally came to tell her it was time to eat. Although he was freshly shaved and dressed in a bright blue plaid shirt, Katherine could see the deep lines of fatigue in his face, and she knew it was because of her.

"Jason, I—I." The words wouldn't come.

"We'll talk about it after dinner," he said, his voice ominously low.

Katherine went through the motions of eating without really tasting her food. Sitting at the table with Jason was torture, knowing this wonderful man wanted to marry her, yet it could never be.

"I'm finished," Jason suddenly announced, though his plate was still half full. "I'm ready to talk." When she made no response, he asked, "Outside, or in the parlor?"

Knowing it was another beautiful starry night,

Katherine chose the parlor; whatever he had to say, she needed to keep a clear head and did not want to be influenced by her surroundings.

After they entered the parlor, Jason went to a small cabinet and pulled open the doors. "Care for something to drink?"

"No," she said simply, then seated herself in the closest chair. She was trembling and wasn't sure how much longer she could remain standing.

"Well, I do," Jason muttered, opening a bottle, then setting it aside and turning to face her. "You are leaving tomorrow."

Though it was a simple statement of fact, Katherine responded, "Yes, I am."

"Before you leave here, I want us to settle something."

"What?" Her stomach twisted into a tight knot when she saw the deadly serious look in his eyes.

"My first thought was to keep after you until you gave in and got a divorce—but I've decided not to pressure you any more."

"I appreciate that." She felt some of the tension ease, but still kept alert.

"But I do want to discuss our future." Noting her questioning glance, he continued, "Yes, our future. I simply can't turn my back and pretend you never entered my life. In the few short days since we met, I have grown to love you deeply. But I have resigned myself to the fact that we cannot be married—at least not right away. What I do want to know is this . . ."

He paused for a moment, his eyes boring into her as if trying to read her thoughts. "Would it be all right if I called on you at your brother's farm? I realize it sounds very improper, what with you being married and all, but I do want to continue seeing you. We wouldn't have to do anything very public. Maybe have a picnic on occasion, or take a ride through the country. Or simply sit at your brother's and talk. Just—please, Katherine, don't shut me out of your life."

Not wanting his loving, hopeful gaze to influence her decision, Katherine looked away while she considered his words. She saw no real harm in letting him call on her—and she knew she didn't want to live her life without ever seeing him again, either. Finally, she turned back to him and said softly, "I'd like that."

Jason threw his head back as if a great weight had been lifted from his shoulders. "I was so afraid you would say no—that you might think a clean break would be best."

"No, Jason, I've been thinking about us, too. Although we can't be married, nor can we show how we feel for each other openly, I hated the thought of never being able to see you again. Yes, please—whenever you are in Jefferson, do stop by to see me. Andrew will understand, and I won't hesitate to tell him how we feel for each other. He never did like Flint; he was much like Papa that way, but I know Andrew will like you—at least until he finds out he might have to share certain honors with you." When Jason looked confused, she asked laughingly, "How does Uncle Jason sound to you?"

A broad smile lit up his face as he moved across the room and knelt before her. Taking her hand in his, he said with obvious delight, "Uncle Jason sounds wonderful to me. Do I have your permission to spoil my nephew or niece with gifts?"

"Of course," she laughed with him, then suddenly became very solemn. "But I want to make something clear from the start. If, one day, you find someone who will make you a good wife, and you decide that you want to get married and have children of your own, I want you to know I'll understand." Her insides ached at the thought of it, but it was true. It would hurt her terribly, but she would definitely understand.

"There can be no other woman for me," he said firmly.

"You may think that now, but I want to leave that option open for you. It wouldn't be right to try to bind you to me for the rest of your life."

"Too late, I'm already bound to you," he said, bringing her hand to his lips for a gentle kiss. "And I hope that some day circumstances will change so that we can be married."

"Jason, I've already told you. I can't risk letting Flint know where I am, or that he's fathered this child. For the child's sake most of all."

"Eventually, the child will grow up, and if he has the same strength of character his mother has, he can be told of his parentage. When he's an adult, he'll be able to understand the reasons it had to be kept a secret. Once that's done, there would be no real reason for you to refuse to get a divorce." Jason's voice was calm and matter-of-fact. "I will wait for that day." In the back of his mind, he also knew that there was always the chance that Flint would one day meet his match and be killed, thus making Katherine a widow, free to marry again. But he didn't want to mention that to her for fear that she might consider him cold and calloused even to think of such a possibility.

A long discussion about the various prospects the future might hold for the two of them made the thought of leaving the next morning a little easier to bear. It was a relief for them both to know that when they next parted, it would not be a final good-bye.

When Minnie arrived in Katherine's room at the break of day, she carried a small, leather valise with strict orders to see that Katherine was wearing one of the dresses Jason had bought her and that the other was neatly packed in the valise, along with his yellow plaid shirt. Katherine voiced no objections, and when Minnie hugged her good-bye, both women wept.

"You take good care of yourself and that young'n, you hear me?" Minnie said in a choked voice. "I don't get over Jefferson way very much so's I can check on you, but if you're ever this way again, Missy, you stop in and pay us a visit."

"I will," Katherine vowed, sniffling. "I promise." Though she could not yet imagine what excuse she might have to come back this way, she knew she would think of something, for when she left Seven Oaks, she was determined it would not be forever.

"Well, I'd better get you and this here bag on down there. Mister Jason and Mister Rede are about ready to head out."

"Mister Rede? Is Rede going with us?" she asked, not knowing if she was relieved or disappointed that she would not be alone with Jason.

"Mister Rede always rides with Mister Jason whenever he goes to an auction, just in case Jason buys any cattle and can't find a drover to bring them on back. To tell you the truth, I think Mister Rede's got him a gal over in Jefferson, because he never misses a chance to make the trip with Mister Jason.

Suddenly worried, Katherine wondered how Jason would explain his taking the back roads to Rede without raising his suspicions. She had carefully avoided all the men on the ranch over the past few days. Now, not only would Rede be getting a good look at her, he might start thinking she had something to hide. It made her more than a little nervous, especially when she remembered that Rede was the one who didn't live on the ranch. He'd be the most likely to run into any of the men who might still be out looking for her. Since there was no way to avoid the situation, she followed Minnie downstairs to meet the man.

Her only hope, as she stepped out onto the back porch, was that Rede might be trusted to keep his mouth shut out of loyalty to Jason. The more she thought about it, the less troubled she felt, for she doubted that Jason would allow Rede to go with them if he couldn't be trusted. Besides, the only thing Rede could really tell Flint or his friends was that she had stayed at Seven Oaks for several days before going on to Jefferson. Maybe she could pretend she was going to catch a riverboat from there. It might help prevent Flint from searching too hard in the Jefferson area and send him off in another direction. She decided to do just that.

"A riverboat, huh?" Rede asked in his usual drawl as he rode alongside the carriage. Though his eyes were fixed on the road ahead, his attention seemed increasingly drawn to Katherine. "How far you plan on going?"

"I—I don't really know," she stammered, for she had no idea where the riverboat went after it left Shreveport. "I guess I'll stop and see some friends in Shreveport for a few days before going on. Traveling by boat always makes me a little queasy."

"Me, too. And I'll tell you what. You'll never get me on another one of those boats as long as I live," he said, with a grimace.

Jason had immediately understood why Katherine had made up the story about the riverboat—and he could have put in a comment or two to back up her claim—but he was absorbed in a childhood memory of his own first ride on a riverboat.

"You know, Jason," Rede said, breaking into his reminiscences. "You never did say why a lady as pretty as Katherine would want to stop by and visit the likes of you. Is she some sort of kin I don't know about?"

"No, just a good friend," Jason replied, honestly enough.

"Of the family," Katherine put in quickly.

"Oh? Did you know his parents?"

"I used to see them from time to time," she responded swiftly, remembering the portraits that hung in Jason's living room.

"Nice folks," Rede commented, and then, as if testing her, he asked, "Who do you think he looks more like, his mother or his father?"

"As I recall, he favors his mother, though he does have his father's strong jawline." She spoke without hesitation, glad she had examined the portraits at length, looking for similarities.

"Yeah, I guess they share the same jaw," Rede conceded. Then, to Katherine's relief, he fell silent.

And although his narrowed green eyes kept cutting back to her face, he did not speak directly to her again until they were almost to Jefferson.

"Excuse me, ma'am, but you mentioned catching a riverboat earlier. Were you planning on catching a boat this afternoon? If you were, you may be disappointed. It doesn't look like we're going to get there in time to make it—not with Jason taking the long way around like he did. But then, I don't blame him; I'd want to enjoy your fine company for as long as possible, too, if I was him."

"No, I don't have plans to catch any of the boats today. I'm going to take a room for the night and get the first boat out tomorrow." She gave him a friendly smile, but inside, she had an uneasy feeling he was still testing her.

"That won't be until tomorrow afternoon. There are no boats on Sunday morning anymore. I guess they think you ought to be in church instead of going somewhere on a boat." He continued to study her face closely.

"Then I'll just have to wait until tomorrow afternoon."

"That means you'll be having to eat Sunday dinner all by yourself. What a shame. A pretty lady like you."

Realizing what Rede was leading up to, Jason quickly interjected, "No, she won't be dining alone. She's already accepted my invitation to join me at the Excelsior."

"I see," Rede said in a low, meaningful voice, as if he truly did see far more than met the eye. Katherine felt her stomach knot, and even though Rede said nothing more about it, she could tell he was speculating about their relationship. He could not seem to keep his eyes off her at all after that.

Finally, Jefferson came into view, and Jason sent Rede on ahead to book rooms for all of them at the Excelsior Hotel. When Katherine looked at him with a frown of protest, he held his palm up, gesturing silently to assure her he knew what he was doing.

As soon as Rede was out of earshot, Jason turned to her and explained, "It's getting pretty late. By the time we find out just where your brother lives and ride out there, it will be after dark—hardly the time to be paying a surprise visit on anyone, even your brother. I figure it would be better to check into the hotel and find out just where your brother's farm is, then drive out there tomorrow about noon. That way, you will be rested and he'll have time to prepare a place for you."

Katherine could see his logic, and because it also would mean a delay in their having to say good-bye for a while, she agreed, taking his suggestion to keep her head down and not look at anyone directly when they entered the hotel and went to their rooms. With Rede having gotten the keys in advance, it was possible that they wouldn't have to speak with anyone at all.

It went exactly as Jason had planned. Rede was waiting for them outside the Excelsior, his attention diverted from Katherine by a pretty young woman selling flowers. As soon as they drove up, he handed the two room keys to Jason, then went off to take care of the carriage. As they entered the lobby and walked up to their rooms, Katherine kept her head down, her hair drawn forward, concealing part of her face. To her relief, they passed no one on the way to their rooms.

"I'll have to say good-bye to you here," Jason said as

he opened the door and stepped aside for her to enter. "I don't want to chance Rede coming back and finding me in your room. I think he already has too many ideas about us."

Katherine nodded, though she felt sharp disappointment. She was not ready to be left alone.

"Besides," Jason continued, "I need to start asking around to see if I can find out just where your brother's farm is. I'll have dinner sent up around seven so you won't have to go downstairs to eat. I'll also stop by and check on you before I go to bed. I'll let you know then, about what time we should leave here tomorrow."

"Could you please have a bath sent up as well?" she asked, gesturing to her dusty garments.

"Sure, I should have thought of that." He frowned at his own lack of sensitivity. "See you in a little while."

Katherine did not close the door until she could no longer hear his footsteps.

With each knock at the door, Katherine was both hopeful and fearful—hopeful it might be Jason, afraid it was someone else who knew her. But each time, it was one of the hotel staff: once to bring up her valise, once with the hot water for her bath, and once to see what she wanted for dinner. By the time that Jason actually knocked at the door, she had given up hope but not fear. She did not get up from the chair where she sat staring into an empty fireplace.

"Who is it?" she asked, trying to disguise her voice.

"Me, Jason."

She flew to the door.

"Jason! I was so worried."

"Did you actually miss me that much, or are you just eager to hear the news about your brother?"

"Both," she stated honestly, her eyes going to the many packages he carried.

"I'm sorry it took me so long, but all anyone wants to talk about these days is the Rothchild trial. Everyone seems to have an opinion about whether or not he killed that girl. I had a hard time directing the conversation to anything else." Glancing down the long corridor in both directions, he finally asked, "No one's around. May I come in?"

"Yes, of course," she said, stepping back quickly so he could slip in before someone appeared in the hallway.

"Did you find out where my brother's farm is?" she asked eagerly as soon as she'd bolted the door.

"Katherine, you'd better sit down," Jason said gently as he laid the packages on a table.

"Why? What's wrong? It's my brother, isn't it?"

"Well, yes, in a way," Jason hedged, unsure of how she would take this latest development. "Please, sit down and I'll tell you everything I found out."

Katherine sat, and waited for Jason to join her, before voicing her concern once again.

"Is Andrew dead? Is that what you have to tell me?"

"No, nothing like that," he assured her quickly. "The man I talked to said he'd seen your brother just three months ago, and he was the picture of health—all happy and excited about his decision to move to Arizona."

"His what?" Katherine asked in disbelief.

"That's right. It seems that your brother decided to sell his land here and head west to homestead a larger place. After having heard about how much land there was in Arizona for the taking, he and two of his friends left Jefferson together about three months ago. The man I talked to sold them one of the wagons they took with them, but he couldn't remember just where in Arizona they were headed or if they'd even decided on that yet."

"But why didn't he tell me?" Katherine asked, still not ready to believe any of this. "Why didn't he write and tell me he was planning to do any of this?"

"I can't answer that one. My guess is he planned to write you about it once he found a place and was settled in. All I know is he sold the land to somebody named Brown, bought up all the supplies he thought he'd need, and left shortly afterward."

"What am I going to do now? Where am I going to go?" Katherine asked, the tears welling up in her eyes. "I certainly can't go to Papa's. That will be one of the first places Flint will look for me. But there's no other place to go. What am I going to do now?"

"You are going back to Seven Oaks with me," Jason said firmly. It was a decision he had already made.

"I can't do that," she protested, though her reasons for protesting eluded her at the moment. "I have to find out where it is my brother went, and go there. But how? I don't have the money to travel that far."

"And what's wrong with going back to Seven Oaks for a little while?" he asked. "If it's the idea of living under the same roof with me, you won't have to. You can have one of the cabins out back. It wouldn't take much to fix it up, and you'd not only have a place of your own for as long as you want, you'll have plenty of room for the baby once it arrives. And look at all the space the boy will have to grow up in."

"Boy?" she asked, momentarily sidetracked. "What makes you think it will be a boy?"

"I don't really know. Just a hunch, I guess. And what better place for a boy to grow up than out in the country, on a ranch? And even if it's a girl, she'd still need lots of room to grow and play. There's plenty of that at Seven Oaks. He—or she—could have his own pony to ride, his own trees to climb, his own yard to chase a ball in." His blue eyes sparkled with enthusiasm.

"I couldn't accept all that from you," she said with a firm shake of her auburn curls. "Besides, if Flint was to ever find out . . ."

"I know, I know. He'll try to kill me. You've mentioned that before. That's just something I'll have to live with. And if it bothers you to think of yourself as some sort of kept woman—and I suspect it might—you can help with the housework to pay for your room and board. Minnie is pretty stubborn when it comes to her kitchen, but she's getting old now, and whether or not she'll admit it, she could use a little help around the house. You could help by doing some of the household chores that aren't directly related to the kitchen. She'll never give up those. Of course, you'll need to limit your physical activity until after the baby is born, but even now, there are things you could do to help that won't be too much of a strain. The older Minnie gets, the more help she is going to need. And don't ask why I don't simply fire her and replace her with someone younger. I would never want to replace Minnie."

"I wasn't going to. I already know you would never

try to replace Minnie. You couldn't, even if you wanted to."

Jason held his breath. He could tell she was seriously considering his offer, for she had stopped crying and was deep in thought. He pressed on. "You could start small, and gradually take over more and more of her chores, and she'd never have to face up to the prospect of becoming useless in her old age. Her slowing down wouldn't be so apparent, even to herself, with you there taking up the slack."

Katherine smiled at the way he made it sound like a favor to Minnie. "You make me feel selfish for saying no," she said softly.

"Then don't say no. It'll mean we can see each other every day." His blue eyes pleaded with her to say yes.

"But what will your friends think?"

"Hang my friends. If they are really friends, they'll believe that I hired someone to help Minnie with the housework. Of course, I'll have to pay you a wage so I won't be lying."

"No, please. It's enough that you're giving me a place to stay."

"You wouldn't want me to lie about it would you? Let me warn you, I'm a terrible liar. No, it would be best if I paid you a wage of some sort. If you feel guilty about taking it, then spend it on the baby. Surely you can't object to a little extra money to spend on your own child."

"Jason, you are far too kind." Her brown eyes glistened with the depth of her feeling for him. She was still hesitant about agreeing to the arrangement, even though it was what she really wanted.

"Just don't let it get around. I don't want my men to start thinking I'm some sort of pushover," he said, grinning. Then, remembering his purchases, he brought them over to her chair. "And wait till you see the two new dresses I bought you. They've got these pleats in the waistline so that when you start to grow, they reshape themselves to fit. The woman at the store told me they can be used right up to the day the baby arrives. I also bought a nightdress with a similar design. Although I like the idea of you sleeping in my shirt, it won't be long before you'll be popping the buttons right off. This one will fit you no matter how big the baby gets."

Katherine was speechless. All she could do was sniffle, and dab at the tears that rolled down her cheeks. Never had she been so relieved. Never had she felt such deep joy.

"And look here," he said eagerly, as he pulled the lid off the largest box. "A toy chime. All the kid has to do is roll it across the floor like this." He got down on his knees and demonstrated. "I found it at Sedberry's Drug Store. It was the only one they had. Hear how it makes real music? Kind of like a music box. He'll love it."

"I'm sure he will," she said, laughing through her tears at his enthusiasm.

"And this isn't all I bought. I couldn't carry it all, so I arranged to have some of it delivered. Since I had to stop at several stores before I found out anything about your brother—storekeepers being the best ones to ask—I bought blankets, diapers, sleeping shirts, caps, booties, and even a small cradle with little lambs carved into it. Cutest thing you ever saw." His face fell suddenly, as a thought struck him. "I hope you don't mind. It never occurred to me until just now that maybe you'd want to pick out the cradle yourself. But if you don't like it, we can send it back and get another. I guess I figured you wouldn't want to be seen in any of the stores, so I'd just as well go ahead and buy it. It just now occurred to me that you could choose it by mail order."

"I'm sure it will be fine, but you shouldn't have done all this," she said, and though she shook her head in protest, her face held a radiant smile.

"You told me I could spoil the child," he reminded her.

"But not all of this is for the baby. What about those dresses? And the nightdress?"

"Those are for the baby, too. Surely he would want his mother properly dressed at all times, and in something that would give him lots of room to move around in." He smiled mischievously.

"I see," she said, her voice soft with love, as she gazed, totally adoring, into his shining blue eyes.

And what she saw there, at that moment, amazed her.

Chapter Ten

Rede was full of questions when he found out that Jason planned to pass up one of the largest auctions to be held in all of East Texas that spring in order to take Katherine back to Seven Oaks. The answers he received didn't seem to satisfy him, and he acted almost angry at the news. He simmered down a bit, however, when Jason told him he would not be expected to ride back with them and could stay on in Jefferson a few days, as he had planned, and at Jason's expense.

The story given to Rede was that Katherine had received a message from the people she was planning to visit, informing her that sudden illness in the family would make it impossible for them to have visitors for an indefinite period of time. It sounded flimsy, even to them, but it was the best they could come up with on such short notice.

Though Rede raised his eyebrow skeptically, he did not actually say he doubted their story, nor did he openly express disapproval. Even without his openly voicing his opinion, Katherine could sense that it would be a while before Rede would come to accept her—if ever. But Rede's sour attitude really didn't bother her that much, for she was far too happy with the way things were turning out for her in every other way.

Minnie's reaction to Katherine's return was quite the opposite from Rede's. She asked no questions whatsoever. She simply welcomed her back with open arms and hurried to get her bags. She didn't even ask any questions about all the packages and boxes that also had to be carried up to Katherine's room.

It was not until breakfast on the morning following their return, that they finally told Minnie why Katherine had returned. It was a far different story from what they'd told Rede—and far closer to the truth—since Minnie already knew about the baby and that Katherine was running away from something. Additionally, Katherine felt that she could trust Minnie to keep whatever they told her strictly to herself. At Jason's suggestion, however, she did give her permission to tell Silas. There were no secrets between Minnie and Silas, and Jason had learned long ago that both could be equally trusted.

"You didn't have to give me no excuses. I'm just glad you are back," Minnie said after she had been filled in on most of the reasons for Katherine's return.

Like Rede, she guessed that she hadn't heard the whole story—but what she believed they were trying so hard to not tell her was that they had finally discovered they were in love. And, as Minnie knew often happened with young lovers, they were still embarrassed. "It's a shame that your brother just up and left like that," she said, "not letting you know he was leavin' or anything, but I must admit I do like the results of his havin' done so. It'll be nice havin' you around here while that baby's buddin' inside you, though I can hardly wait for him to be born so I can hold him in my own arms."

"You, too?" Katherine asked. "And what makes *you* think this baby is going to be a boy?"

"Just a feelin' I got." She shrugged, then smiled secretively as she reached over and laid her hand gently on Katherine's abdomen. "Oh, it's a boy all right."

"I agree," Jason put in quickly, raising a forkful of ham to his mouth. "A fine, strapping boy to help out with some of the chores around here. He'll probably be a little ornery, like his mother, but there's always a chance he'll outgrow such behavior."

Katherine glowered at him from under lowered eyelids, eliciting nothing but a chuckle in response.

Minnie grinned at more than the humorous barb. What pleased her was his implying that Katherine would be staying at Seven Oaks for some time to come. It sure did sound to her like this arrangement was far more permanent than they had let on so far. What she did wonder though, was why they didn't just go ahead and get married. It would certainly be best for that child. Surely they both realized they were in love with each other by now.

Katherine had to stay in the upstairs bedroom until Jason could find the time to have some furniture moved from the main house to the empty cabin. On the way back from Jefferson, he had promised her an old bedroom suite that was stored in the attic, and a few odds and ends that he claimed he didn't need. He had been quick to explain, however, that it would at least be Tuesday afternoon before he could spare the manpower to do the moving, because on Monday he was going into Daingerfield on personal business, which would mean extra work for the other men. He could not actually promise Tuesday, either, unless the men got through with their chores early.

In the meantime, Katherine planned to go down each morning to open the windows and give the house a good airing. It had been closed up for years and had a damp, musty smell. There were also layers of dust to be swept out, and the walls needed a thorough scrubbing. As she started to work on Monday morning, she had a feeling it would take at least until Wednesday to get the place clean enough to move furniture in.

The morning quickly turned into afternoon before Katherine finally had all the floors swept and mopped. When they were finally as clean as she could get them, she was disappointed to see how dull they were, and realized she would have to hand rub them with beeswax to restore the original gloss. She decided that while she was at it, she would wax the wooden moldings and the staircase, too. If this was to be her home for a while, she wanted it to be something she could be proud of.

With that project in mind, Katherine headed toward the main house to see if Minnie could spare any beeswax or perhaps some lemon oil. With Jason away for the entire day, she felt she might as well keep busy until he returned. Not only would it mean that she would be able to move in that much sooner, it would also help keep her from missing him as much.

Because the beautiful spring day had been unusually

warm, Katherine had pinned up her long hair before setting to work. As she swept and scrubbed, it had gradually come loose in several places, and long tendrils of brown hair now curled freely down her neck and at the sides of her face. Much of the dust she had swept from the floors had settled on her dress, face and arms. Perspiration streaked her forehead and soaked her gray muslin dress between her breasts and under her arms. But she gave little thought to her appearance, for Jason was not due back for hours, and Minnie had seen her look far worse on the day that she'd first arrived.

"Minnie?" she called out, tramping heavily up the back steps in an attempt to shake loose some of the dust before entering the kitchen.

"Oh, my," Minnie said as she hurried to the door. When she caught sight of her, she frowned and crossed her arms accusingly. "You've been working mighty hard out there haven't you? I hope you aren't overdoing it. You do remember what the doc said, don't you?"

"Yes, of course I do. And I assure you, I do stop and rest every now and then, but you have to realize that I'm very eager to get my house in order. I'm especially anxious to uncrate that cradle Jason bought and decorate the baby's room. You can understand that, can't you?"

"Sure I can, and just as soon as I get this roast on to cook, I'll be down to help you for a while."

"You might not want to, when you hear what I'm planning to do next." Katherine laughed, though she knew it wouldn't matter to Minnie in the least. "If you have some beeswax or lemon oil to spare, I intend to do something about that dull floor."

"I've got plenty, but are you sure you should be doin' that kind of work, what with the baby and all?"

"I'll be just fine. And I seriously doubt you coddled yourself when you were carrying a child, either," Katherine quickly pointed out.

Minnie thought about that and finally nodded, "All right, I'll give you the wax and the oil if you'll at least take the time to come in and eat a proper lunch. It's after two o'clock and you ain't eaten since breakfast. I was just starting to pack you a lunch with the intention of bringing it to you."

"Good, I'm famished," Katherine said, surprised to hear it was quite that late. "But since I'm so filthy, why don't you bring it out into the garden and I'll eat there."

Giving Katherine's clothing a quick glance, Minnie wrinkled her nose and agreed it was a good idea.

While Katherine waited in the garden for Minnie to bring her lunch out, she sat down in one of the wrought iron chairs and tilted her head back. Finding it far more relaxing than she had expected, she closed her eyes, and let the gentle breeze cool her overheated skin. As usual, her thoughts drifted to Jason and the wonderfully generous heart that was hidden beneath his brash, devil-may-care exterior. Her peaceful musings were suddenly interrupted by the clatter of a buggy approaching the house from the main road.

Her eyes flew open, and her heartbeat quickened as she glanced toward the sound. Her first thought was that it might be Jason returning early, and she certainly did not want him to catch her looking the way she did. Quickly, she jumped to her feet and focused on the moving buggy, ready to take flight toward the house.

But as she strained to see, she realized it was not Jason at all, but a lady and her driver.

"Uh-oh," she heard someone say, and turned to find Minnie standing halfway between her and the house, scowling at the new arrival. She was clearly annoyed.

"What is it?" Katherine asked as she hurried to Minnie's side.

"Mrs. Dankin," she said in a none too reverent tone, then hurried toward the wrought iron table with Katherine's lunch basket.

"And who is Mrs. Dankin?" Katherine asked, following closely behind.

"The Reverend Fagan's sister who just recently came here from back east somewhere. I'll warn you now, she's a real busybody, that woman. Always puttin' her nose into everybody else's business, and if that isn't bad enough, she always claims she does it in the name of the Almighty. Right now, she's dead set on saving Jason's soul. If she hadn't already spotted you—which I'm almost sure she has, since she has the eyes of a hawk and the ears of a cat—I'd tell you to hurry and get yourself out of sight to avoid having to meet her and put up with her nosy questions. Just be careful what you say; she can twist almost anything to suit her purposes. And if you give her any fuel for gossip, she'll have it spread all over Morris County by nightfall."

Katherine could feel her stomach tighten with nervous tension as she watched Minnie turn and stomp back to the house, muttering something about having to find a special tray. Not knowing what to do in this kind of situation, Katherine simply sat back down and waited for whatever was about to happen, the lunch on the table now completely forgotten.

Although the woman did look in her direction several times as she moved from the ornate buggy to the door that opened into the living room, Katherine just nodded politely. She hoped fervently that the woman would take care of whatever business she'd come for and leave without bothering to stop and speak with her. But she doubted she'd be that lucky. She had known busybodies before.

Just as the woman was preparing to knock, Minnie appeared in the doorway, wearing a little white cap instead of her usual red kerchief. In her hand was a small silver tray. Katherine couldn't hear what was said from so far away, but watched as the visitor placed a small white card on the tray and turned to leave. At first, it looked as if Mrs. Dankin was not going to make a trip to the garden since she headed straight for her carriage. But she stopped at the buggy just briefly, to retrieve her fan, then turned and walked quickly in Katherine's direction.

"Uh-oh," Katherine said under her breath, echoing Minnie's sentiments. Out of the corner of her eye, she could see Minnie, also, hurrying toward the garden, as if hoping to intercept the visitor. And then, to her horror, she noticed that Jason's carriage was now turning into the drive. She felt trapped—and then angry—at what she knew was about to happen. Since she could not rush away now without being rude to Mrs. Dankin, she would be forced to remain where she was until Jason joined them—and she did not want him to see her looking as if she'd fallen into a coal bin.

"Hello, my dear," Mrs. Dankin said, waving her fan at Katherine.

"Hello," Katherine responded politely, rising reluctantly to greet the woman. "Please, excuse my appearance, but I'm afraid you've caught me at a bad time. I've been working pretty hard today, cleaning out Jason's spare cottage." She nodded in the direction of the cabin.

As Jason's carriage came to a stop a short distance away, both women turned to watch him alight and hurry toward them. Some of Katherine's anger melted just at the sight of him. Though drsesed much as usual, in a casual shirt and denim pants, he looked especially handsome to her. She winced as he came closer, mortified at her own unattractive appearance.

"Good afternoon, Mrs. Dankin," he said, offering her one of his more dazzling smiles. Graciously, he took the gloved hand she extended. "So good of you to pay us a visit."

A few yards away, Minnie was still chugging toward them, the silver tray clasped in one hand and Mrs. Dankin's visiting card in the other. When she finally came up beside them, she slapped the card on the tray and presented it to Jason. "Mister Jason," she announced formally, and unnecessarily, "Mrs. Dankin is here to pay a short call on you, sir."

Coughing to keep from laughing, Jason recalled Mrs. Dankin's previous visit during which she had scolded Minnie severely for not knowing the proper way to present a visitor. With a straight face, he reached for the card, glanced at it briefly, then tucked it away in his shirt pocket. It had been Mrs. Dankin's use of the word *barbaric* that had most offended Minnie—though, at the time, she'd had no idea of its meaning. It had taken Jason quite a while to explain the strange customs of people back east and to finally soothe her ruffled feathers. "Thank you, Minnie," he said ceremoniously. "I shall receive her here. Would you please make some lemonade and serve it out here in the garden?"

"There's some already made," Minnie said, lifting the lid of the basket and pulling out a small stoneware pitcher. "I'll just have to go back to the house and get a couple more glasses. There's also some cinnamon teacakes in here," she added, rummaging around in the basket, "if I can just find them. They might be mushed up a little, but they'll still taste just as good."

"Wonderful, I would enjoy something sweet with my lemonade." Then to his guest, he smiled and said "I assume you will stay for a glass of lemonade and a teacake? Mushed or not, Minnie's teacakes are by far the best around."

"Of course," said Mrs. Dankin with a tight, little smile, glaring at Minnie whose manners she still considered barbaric.

"Then please, have a seat," he said graciously, gesturing toward the chairs. "Make yourself comfortable. I gather you've already met Katherine?"

"No, we were just about to introduce ourselves," Mrs. Dankin replied, quickly shifting her attention back to Katherine, who was busy trying to restore her tousled hair. She had already wiped some of the dirt and perspiration from her face and neck.

When Katherine realized that all eyes were on her once again, she dropped the strand of hair she was trying to tuck back into place, and slowly lowered her arms, smiling awkwardly as she clasped her hands demurely at her waist.

"I must tell you my curiosity is most aroused," Mrs.

Dankin said, returning the awkward smile.

"Well, let me have the honor of introducing the two of you," Jason said, gesturing once again for them to be seated. When both women remained standing, he shifted his weight from one foot to the other, and continued, "Katherine, I would like to introduce you to Mrs. Elizabeth Dankin, a member of the Good Faith Baptist Church. It's a new church—one I just recently started to attend—thanks to the kind invitation Mrs. Dankin extended a couple of months ago."

"Yes," Mrs. Dankin interjected, her eyes darting quickly from Katherine to Jason as she fanned her flushed cheeks. "And when we didn't see you at services yesterday, I decided I'd better ride out here and find out what happened. I thought perhaps you had fallen ill or injured yourself, but I guess I was wrong."

"No, I feel just fine. In fact, I can't remember ever feeling better," he acknowledged, and turned to gaze lovingly at Katherine. "Maybe I should finish my introductions, and that will explain why I didn't make it to your brother's services yesterday."

Katherine felt her insides knot as she waited to hear what Jason was going to say about her to Mrs. Dankin. She didn't trust his suddenly mischievous smile or the devilish gleam that had come into his blue eyes. What really worried her was what Mrs. Dankin's reaction would be. Despite the innocent reasons for Katherine's being at Seven Oaks, she *was* a married woman, living in the same house with an unmarried man. Even as gifted as Jason could be with words, would he be able to make Mrs. Dankin understand?

"Mrs. Dankin, I would like for you to be one of the first to meet Katherine," he said, paused for effect, then quietly added, "My beautiful wife."

The stoneware pitcher fell from Minnie's hand and smashed on the cobblestones, but Katherine was too stunned to notice. She stared, speechless, at Jason.

"Your *wife?*" Mrs. Dankin asked, her fan frozen in midair.

"Yes, my wife, Mrs. Jason Morris—Katherine to her friends. We were married on Saturday." He gazed at Katherine with husbandly pride and gave her a wink only she could see.

Mrs. Dankin smiled, then frowned, then smiled again, rather uncertainly. "I didn't even know you were engaged," she said reproachfully. "Why didn't you tell anyone?"

"I did let a few people know, but to tell you the truth, I was so afraid she might change her mind and call the whole thing off, I decided to keep it fairly secret. It's still hard for me to believe she actually said 'yes' and married me."

Katherine's head was whirling. What had happened to the Jason who claimed to be such a terrible liar? Where had this silver-tongued devil come from? Not only had he manufactured the wildest story she'd ever heard, he actually had Mrs. Dankin swallowing it!

"Why wouldn't she want to marry a handsome man such as yourself?" Mrs. Dankin asked boldly, then raised a gloved hand to her cheek and stared quizzically at Katherine's disheveled appearance.

"She doesn't usually look like that," Jason explained with a chuckle. "When she discovered that we no longer have servants' quarters in the main house, she decided to fix up the vacant cabin so there will be a place for her lady's maid to stay when she arrives at the end of the week."

"Lady's maid?" Mrs. Dankin repeated with obvious interest. "I gather you are from back east?"

Katherine had no idea what to say and turned to Jason for help. After all, this was his story, not hers.

"Katherine's from St. Louis," he said without hesitation, "but has been visiting relatives in Jefferson for the past few months. I originally met her over a year ago—when she came to Jefferson to attend the wedding of her cousin, who is also a friend of mine. But I didn't have the chance to call on her until she came back to Jefferson a few months ago."

"You surely don't waste any time, do you, Mr. Morris? A courtship of only a few months, and already you've made her your bride?"

"Didn't want to risk her getting away from me," he laughed and reached over to pat Katherine's hand affectionately. "I've waited far too long to find someone like her. There isn't anything on this earth I wouldn't do to make certain I don't lose her."

Katherine looked around to see Minnie's reaction to this extraordinary conversation, and found her kneeling beside the shattered pitcher with a few of the broken pieces held gingerly in her hands. Her face was expressionless, but Katherine could see the muscles at the back of her jaw working nervously.

"I hope you realize what a truly lucky woman you are," Mrs. Dankin said to Katherine. "You are married to an amazing man."

The time had come to speak, and Katherine hoped her voice wouldn't fail her. "I certainly can't argue that. Jason is truly an astonishing man—always so full of fun and surprises."

"Speaking of surprises," Jason put in before she could say anything more, "I took your ring into town, like you asked me to, and had it sized down to better fit your finger. The jeweler couldn't believe your fingers are as small as I told him, so it may still be a little large."

To Katherine's amazement, Jason reached into his shirt pocket and pulled out a tiny black velvet sack, which he handed to her. "Hurry and get that thing back on your finger where it belongs. I don't care for the idea of my wife going around without her wedding ring."

Slowly, Katherine loosened the drawstring closure and looked inside. To her further amazement, there was indeed a small, gold wedding ring at the bottom of the sack. Gingerly, she drew the ring out and carefully slipped it onto the third finger of her left hand.

"Is it still too large?" he asked as soon as she had it on.

"No, it's fine as it is," she mumbled, gazing at him in wonder.

"Good. Oh, and I also brought you back several other things from town. I know you said you didn't need anything, but I couldn't resist buying something for my beautiful new bride. I'd really like for you to try them on the very first chance you get."

"I'll have to take a bath first," she responded, playing nervously with the new addition to her left hand.

"That's fine, but I'd like to be there when you try them on. I want to see the expression on your face."

Despite her shocked surprise at everything Jason had done, Katherine felt herself wanting to laugh at the way his last remark had flustered Mrs. Dankin.

"Oh, my, how late it is getting to be," she sputtered. "It looks like I'll have to pass on the lemonade. I really must be going. I have other calls to make."

"I'll walk you to your carriage," Jason said, not making any move to dissuade her. "And please do, call again. Maybe next time Katherine will be better prepared to receive guests."

"Yes, I'm sure she will be. I'm so eager to get to know her better. It is such a relief to finally meet someone else from back east. I can hardly wait to present her to my brother. You will bring her to church on Sunday, won't you?"

"Of course. I'm looking forward to the chance to show off my beautiful new bride," he replied quickly, though he knew that by Sunday he would come up with an excuse. He would not risk taking her to church until there was no longer any danger from Flint Mason. "Won't everyone be surprised?"

Mrs. Dankin's reply did not quite reach Katherine's ears as she and Jason slowly walked to the waiting carriage. Katherine was not inclined to accompany them. Instead, she waited until they were almost to the drive, then turned to Minnie with a bewildered shrug. What on earth had come over Jason?

Minnie's only response was a silent shrug of her own.

Chapter Eleven

"It looks like you were just about to have lunch," Jason commented when he returned after Mrs. Dankin's carriage had driven off. Poking around in the lunch basket, he said, "I was so eager to get back here and show you everything I'd bought, I didn't stop to eat. Mind if I join you?"

"Just like that?" Katherine asked, dumfounded. "No discussion about any of the things you just told Mrs. Dankin, or about how you happened to have this ring?" Katherine couldn't believe his casual manner.

"Oh, you would like to discuss that?" he asked innocently. "I didn't realize."

"Yes, I most certainly would." Her voice rose with exasperation. "Why on earth did you tell Mrs. Dankin that we were married?"

"Just seemed like the thing to do at the time." He shrugged, then turned to Minnie who was listening to every word while she continued to clean up the pieces of broken pitcher. "When you go back in to make more lemonade, would you bring another plate and some more food? I'm starved."

"Not until you answer her question," Minnie said with a firm shake of her head, rising slowly to face him. "I, also, want to know why you told Mrs. Dankin all them lies, and I ain't leavin' this here spot until you do some fancy explainin'."

"Maybe Mrs. Dankin is right about you," Jason said with a chuckle, knowing how that would rile her. "Maybe you are a little too big for your bloomers."

"Yes, and maybe you are tryin' to avoid answerin' her question," Minnie said, scowling and standing her ground. "What got into you, young man, tellin' such a wild tale to that lady?"

"What makes you think it was a wild tale? What makes you think Katherine and I weren't married while we were in Jefferson?"

Minnie's eyebrows lifted slowly and she turned to look questioningly at Katherine.

"I'd have told you, if we had gotten married," Katherine responded quickly, then added, "Besides, I'm already married. I told you that."

"But I thought you just made that up because of the baby," Minnie said, finally coming to believe that Katherine was indeed already married.

"No," Jason interjected, "but that's the reason I told Mrs. Dankin she was married to me, and that's the reason I bought the ring." When neither woman seemed to know what he was talking about, he added, "The baby. I knew that eventually someone would come out here, for one reason or another, and see Katherine. And, within a short time, it will be very obvious to everyone that she is going to have a baby.

That sort of thing can't be hidden forever, even with the cleverest of clothes. With no ring on her finger, I knew people would start to talk, and I couldn't stand the thought of anyone saying anything disrespectful about Katherine."

He shrugged lightly. "So with that in mind, I bought the ring. Then, when I found Mrs. Dankin already here—before Katherine had a chance to move into the cabin—I realized that even a wedding ring wasn't going to prevent a lot of ugly talk. It had to be obvious to her that Katherine was living in the main house. Where else could she be staying if the cabin is still vacant?"

He gestured toward the cottage's open doors and windows through which it was easy to see there was no furniture. "And since Mrs. Dankin already knew, from earlier visits, that there are no longer any servants' quarters in the main house, she would have quickly deduced that we were living by ourselves in my house. As innocent as our arrangement actually is, Mrs. Dankin would have read evil into it, and Katherine would suffer."

"And what happens when I do move into the cottage?" Katherine asked. "Won't that seem a rather strange thing for a wife to do?"

"Yes, it would—and I know how much you were looking forward to moving into there and making it your home—but I guess you'll just have to give up that notion now and continue to live in the main house."

"But what about the baby?" Minnie demanded. "That room she's in now is a big room, but it's not big enough to hold all the furniture that's already in there and the baby's things, too. She needs a room right next to hers, for the baby, and there just ain't one. What are you going to do, knock a hole in the wall to the next room?"

Jason frowned. He had not thought about that problem. "I guess I'll just have to trade rooms with her. Then she can turn that small sitting room adjoining my bedroom into a nursery. It gets full morning sun and is certainly big enough for a child's bed and several other pieces of furniture."

"I can't permit you to give up your own bedroom," Katherine put in quickly. "I'll find a way to fit the baby's things into the bedroom I'm already using. Besides, the baby doesn't have any furniture except for the cradle."

"You haven't seen everything I bought today." Jason chuckled. "What's in the buggy over there is only a part of it. I sort of took it upon myself to order a few more things for the baby's room. Of course, that's when I thought you'd be living in the cabin. Look, the whole reason you have to give up the cabin and stay in the main house, is because of what I said to Mrs. Dankin. I can at least give up the larger bedroom in order to make it more convenient for you. I realize my furniture isn't exactly what a lady would choose for her bedroom, but you can add a few flowers, a pink bedspread, and maybe some lace curtains to make it more feminine. We could trade furniture, too, but that would raise too many questions since I'd have to bring in some of the men to help with the move. I think it would be best if we let them believe we got married, too. Minnie need be the only one who knows the truth. And of course, Silas."

"But what about Rede? He'll tell everyone the truth the minute he gets back," Katherine pointed out.

"How does he know for sure what the truth is? How can he be absolutely sure we didn't take the time to get married before we came on back here?"

"He'll know."

"He may suspect, but he can never be sure," Jason reassured her.

"He'll want to know why we didn't tell him Sunday morning if we were married on Saturday night."

"I won't tell him we were married Saturday night. He doesn't know Mrs. Dankin, so I doubt they'll ever have the opportunity to compare stories. If he asks, I'll tell him we were married on Sunday, shortly after we spoke with him. If he wants to know why I didn't tell him ahead of time, I'll simply say that he didn't seem to approve of you, and I wasn't in the mood for a lecture."

"I don't know. It just seems wrong."

"Maybe so, but it sure simplifies things. It explains your living with me in the only way that most people will understand and be happy with. And after the baby is born, it will make life a little easier for him."

Minnie stood by, quietly listening to Jason's many reasons for continuing the pretense that they were man and wife, but something was bothering her. Finally realizing what it was, she asked, "But what about Missy's real husband? Don't he figure into this any at all? After all, it is his child you'll be pretending to be father to."

"No," Katherine said quickly, suddenly angry and fearful at being reminded of Flint. "He's not ever to know that he even has a child. I ran away without telling him I was pregnant, and I'm going to try my best to keep him from ever finding out."

"Is he why you were all covered with bruises when you came here?" Minnie asked softly.

Katherine looked away in shame, but answered truthfully. "Yes."

"Then he don't deserve to know," Minnie said firmly, and turned to leave. "I'll go make the lemonade and bring out some more ham and bread. There's already enough potato salad for the two of you. After I bring the food out, I'll go ahead and get started moving Mister Jason's things out of his bedroom."

As Katherine had predicted, when Rede returned the next morning, he was more than a little surprised to hear from the other hands that Jason had gone and gotten himself married. He immediately sought Jason out in the barn to ask a few questions to which Jason gave the prepared response.

"I guess there's nothing for me to do then, but go on up there and offer the new missus my congratulations," Rede said resignedly when he realized that Jason was not going to deny the marriage. "I just think it was an awfully quick decision. How much do you really know about Katherine?"

"Enough to know that I love her," Jason responded truthfully.

Shaking his head, Rede walked out of the barn and headed toward the house. Having already spotted Katherine hanging sheets out on the clothesline when he had first ridden up, he headed straight for her. Not wanting Katherine to have to face Rede by herself, Jason hurriedly closed Bullet's stall gate and ran to catch up with him.

When Katherine noticed the two men approaching, she stopped her work and waited with growing apprehension. The dreaded moment had arrived. Rede was back, and had obviously already learned of the supposed marriage. If he did believe they had gotten married, it was clear by his expression that he was not at all pleased.

"Hello," she greeted them cheerily. "Where are you two off to in such a hurry?"

"I just wanted to come up here and offer you my congratulations," Rede said, rather aloofly, regarding her with narrowed eyes. "I hear that you somehow persuaded old Jason here to marry you just before you two left Jefferson. Quite an accomplishment. I can't count the number of ladies that have tried to do just that with absolutely no luck. I guess you have the magic touch."

"That she does," Jason said with a smile and leaned over to place a brief kiss on her cheek. Her heartbeat quickened at the touch of his lips. Ever since the announcement of their marriage, he'd been displaying little intimate signs of affection, for appearances' sake—but each time he touched her, no matter how briefly, it drove her to distraction. She was starting to wish it could somehow be true, that somehow she really could become Mrs. Jason Morris.

As Rede continued to stare brazenly at her, Katherine felt sudden shivers travel up her spine. She tried to think of something clever to say to help win him over, but her mind was a perfect blank.

"Well, I got work to catch up on," Rede finally said, reaching up to tip the brim of his hat. "Good mornin' to you, Mrs. *Morris.*" The way in which he deliberately emphasized the last name made her even more anxious, and her heart began to pound. Did he somehow know who she really was?

With the news having spread that the boss had been married, Katherine could not escape formal introductions to everyone she had previously tried so hard to avoid. By the end of the week, she had begun to feel as if she actually belonged at Seven Oaks.

Silas and Mose took to her quickly, and when Katherine's new furniture arrived on Thursday, they carried it up to what they thought was the married couple's bedroom. Gradually, the room began to look less masculine as Jason's austere bedroom furniture was replaced by the more elaborate pieces he'd originally purchased for the cabin.

Pete and Jack also helped her, though they were not quite as willing to go inside the main house as Mose and Silas. But whenever they noticed the new missus hanging the laundry outside, they took turns helping her carry the heavy basket from one end of the yard to the other. Thus far, hanging the laundry out to dry was the only real work Minnie would allow Katherine to do.

Even little Edmond had come to accept Katherine, and although he was still very shy, he seemed to enjoy having her around. Only Rede caused her any discomfort, although he did his best to avoid her whenever he could.

Katherine knew that something had to be done to gain Rede's friendship, though she could not imagine what that could be. Then, one day in the second week of her supposed marriage, the opportunity finally presented itself when Rede was asked to replace several damaged boards in the laundry room floor.

It was an extremely hot day for late March, and Katherine could see, when she came in with the morning's laundry, that Rede had worked up quite a sweat—and probably quite a thirst. She hurried into the kitchen, poured a tall glass of lemonade, then served it to him with one of her brightest smiles.

"Thanks," he muttered briefly, stopping his work just long enough to gulp the cold drink.

"You looked thirsty," she said simply while trying to work up the courage to say what was really on her mind. Finally, she took a deep breath and plunged forward. "You don't like me, do you, Rede?"

"What's not to like?" he replied. "You are prettier than any woman I ever saw, you've got all the proper manners, and you seem to make Jason happy."

Although his words were polite enough, the set of his jaw told her there was something he was holding back. She had to find out what that was.

"But you don't like me."

"Let's just say I don't trust you. I don't trust any woman who comes walking unannounced into a man's life one day, and somehow has him asking to marry her just a few days later. You weren't here a full week before you managed to get Jason to marry you."

"It was just one of those things," she tried to explain.

"So I've heard," he said gruffly, then reached for the board he had cut and fitted it into place.

Katherine felt her stomach knot. "What have you heard?"

"More than I cared to hear."

"Please, tell me."

"I can't spend all day sitting here jawing with you. I got work to do," he said with finality, hammering a nail into the board with vengeance.

Later that night, when Katherine recounted the conversation to Jason, he shrugged it off as meaningless. "Katherine, Rede hasn't heard what you think he's heard, or he would have come to me with it."

"How can you be sure of that?"

"I think he'd love the chance to discredit you. No, all he has against you is the fact that he thinks you are a conniving, manipulative woman, but then, Rede thinks all women are conniving. That's one reason he's almost thirty-four years old and has never gotten married. He loves to charm the ladies, but whenever one of them starts pressing for a commitment, Rede takes off like a whipped pup. Just don't take what he says so seriously. Eventually, he'll grow to like you. It's just going to take him a while."

Katherine hoped Jason was right, but a deep fear gnawed at her that Rede had somehow found out who she really was.

Katherine's worst fears gradually receded as days passed and Rede did nothing more than avoid her.

When the fear did recur, it was always late at night as she lay awake in Jason's room, alone, but wishing she wasn't.

In the weeks following their return from Jefferson, Jason had made no overt advances toward her. He seemed content with the little gestures of affection he displayed whenever anyone else was around, and occasionally, when they were alone, he would press a tender kiss to her forehead, presumably without really thinking about it. It was becoming a habit with him, a habit Katherine had no inclination to break.

They had fallen into a comfortable but loving friendship, and Katherine found herself looking forward eagerly to each evening which they spent together. Being with Jason was the highlight of every day, and it was getting to the point where she actually dreaded bedtime, when they would have to say good night and go to separate bedrooms.

It was at those times that Katherine wished most fervently that they could really be husband and wife, so they could share far more than they did. As wrong as she knew such thoughts were, she ached with a woman's needs and longed to know what it would be like to have Jason lying in bed beside her, loving her as only a husband should.

During the day, she was able to keep her thoughts in clearer perspective and her emotions under control, but the nighttime seemed to defeat her. Maybe it was the fact that they were usually apart during the day, but always together at night, that made it so hard to put Jason out of her mind and get to sleep.

One night her need for him had grown so strong, her

desire so intense that she got out of bed and padded across the hall to his door. Once there, however, she found herself unable to actually reach for the door handle and open it. She stood there in the cold, dark hallway for several minutes, shame fighting desire. Although she felt that Jason would understand her needs and would not think any less of her if she were to enter his bedroom, she finally turned away for his sake.

"I think it is a fine cause for a celebration," Jason said, uncorking a bottle of champagne. "It's our one-month anniversary. I think that's plenty of reason to celebrate." He poured two glasses of wine.

"But we aren't really married," she reminded him as she curled up on the sofa, tucking her feet under her skirt. Having finished their evening meal, they had retired to the parlor, as usual, to talk and enjoy each other's company.

"Are you trying to ruin my party?" he asked with a mock frown. "Here, I've brought wine up from the cellar for an anniversary toast and have a special present for my lovely wife, and she wants to put a damper on it all."

"A present? Why didn't you say so?" she laughed, and accepted the champagne with no further hesitation. "What shall we toast?"

"Eleven more glorious months, at which time we can celebrate our one-year anniversary," he suggested, raising his glass and grinning. "I love any reason to celebrate."

"Then to eleven more months," she agreed, and in

the spirit of things, she quickly drained the glass dry, choking a bit on the bubbles. "Now, where is my present?"

"Ah, such is love," he frowned again, and reaching behind the sofa, brought out a large package tied with colorful string. "Sometimes I believe that if you had really married me, it would have been solely for my money."

As soon as he handed her the gift, he quickly refilled their glasses and suggested another toast. "To the wonderful act of giving presents. I love buying them, and you certainly have become more willing to accept them over the past few weeks."

Stopping in her struggle to untie the package, Katherine lifted her wineglass and again drained it quickly, not wishing to ignore his toast, but, at the same time, eager to see what was inside the box.

It was true, she had become more receptive to his gift-giving. At first, it had made her feel awkward to accept so many gifts from him, but when she realized that he truly enjoyed giving her things, and could easily afford it, she had come to look forward to his presents. Sometimes they were something as grand as Miss Ruby Sutton, her newly acquired lady's maid—whom he claimed to have hired in order to appease Mrs. Dankin—and sometimes the gift was as silly as a toy trumpet. He claimed it was for the baby, but he'd played with the trumpet for hours before putting it aside. Whatever the gifts, she had come to enjoy receiving them. If he was so very determined to spoil her, who was she to try to stop him?

Hurriedly, she worked at the unyielding knot until

she yelped out in frustration. "Sometimes I think you tie these things just so I can't get into them. Hand me your pocket knife."

"The lady grows impatient?"

"Yes, the lady grows impatient."

"Then permit me to cut the string for you," he said, opening the knife that he'd already drawn from his pocket. As he leaned over her to cut the string, his shoulder brushed hers. It felt so good to Katherine that she leaned back against him without really thinking about what she was doing, and, in a reflex action, Jason kissed the top of her head.

"There, now, open it," he muttered, his voice suddenly husky. He coughed and knelt beside her so that he could see her expression when she pulled the lid off the box. "And don't you dare tell me you don't like it."

The box was filled with black silk, and she gasped in surprise as she drew it out and discovered a diaphanous nightdress. She held it up for a better look.

Never had she seen a garment so daring. The neckline plunged so low, it would surely reveal her navel, and the inserts of black lace sewn into the silk at strategic places would do little to conceal her other attributes.

As she examined it more closely, she noticed that the seams at the sides had been sewn only from the lacy armholes down to about where her waist would be. Her entire leg and part of her hip would be exposed whenever she sat, though she doubted the gown had been designed for sitting. It was truly the most beautiful, provocative gown she had ever seen.

"Jason, whatever possessed you to buy something like this? You should be ashamed of yourself. You are truly destined for the devil himself!" Though her words were harsh, she said them with little conviction, for she could hardly wait to see how the nightgown would look on her. Knowing her reprimand had not sounded too convincing anyway, she found she couldn't keep from laughing, for she knew he had bought it to shock her and it had certainly done that. "Such flimsy material. Positively useless."

"Oh, I don't know. Looks like it would be rather cool on a hot night. It won't be long until summer gets here, and the nights can sometimes get pretty dern hot. And with those slits going way up the sides like that, I figure it will offer you plenty of room when the baby starts to grow."

"How very considerate you are," she agreed and pulled the slit apart to reveal just how much room she would truly have. "Now that you mention it, yes, I can see how very useful this gown will be. Come July and August, I'll probably be thanking you again and again for having had the foresight to buy it."

"Ah, then it's time for another toast. To my wonderful foresight and undying generosity," and he hurried over to pour them more wine.

After they had finished the champagne, Jason began to search the cabinet for another bottle, but Katherine suggested he not bother, for she was already feeling a bit tipsy.

"But I'm still thirsty. And I'm hungry again. I wonder if Minnie left anything in the icebox worth eating. Let's sneak out there and see. Minnie doesn't have to know we were in her kitchen."

"No, I think not. I'm still full from all that dinner."

"You're not even a teensy weensy bit hungry?" he asked, hoping to persuade her to stay a while longer. "I sure could go for a big slice of cheese and a fat slice of bread. I tell you what, you go see what there is in the kitchen to eat, and I'll go down to the cellar and get another bottle of wine."

"No, I've already had too much of both. In fact, the wine has started to make me sleepy. I think I'll just go on up to bed and let you gorge yourself alone."

"Killjoy," he muttered, frowning as she gathered up her package and left the room. Katherine's legs were unsteady as she made her way up the staircase, and she realized she had been right not to have any more wine. Stopping occasionally to lean against the railing, she slowly made her way to her room. After a brief struggle with the door, she found her way inside, dropped the package on her new chaise longue, and quickly began to undress.

Her first thought had been to put on her usual nightdress and go straight to bed, but the lure of the new gown with its fancy inset lace and dangerously low neckline made her turn to the box and slip the silky garment over her head. The soft material felt sinfully good as it drifted down around her, cool and crisp against her skin. She had never worn anything so alluring, so absolutely wicked, in all her life—though she had fantasized about it many times.

Stumbling across the room to the mirror, she gazed at the vision before her and giggled at how terribly revealing the gown really was. The lace had indeed been carefully placed, for it ran directly over her nipples, revealing just enough of the dark rosy circles beneath to tease the imagination. Another swath of lace started at the side of her waist and angled downward to just below her abdomen. To her embarrassment, yet amazement, it cleverly revealed almost half an inch of her dark, curling hair. Although she knew that men rarely designed women's clothing, she had a strong feeling that some man had had a hand in designing this garment.

Wondering if she dare sleep in it, fearing Ruby, her new maid, might come in and discover her in it the next morning, Katherine continued to stand in front of the mirror and gape at herself. Suddenly, she wished Jason could see her, but then reprimanded herself for such a shameful thought. Finally deciding to wear the gown for a few minutes longer, Katherine sashayed across the room in a provocative manner and lay down on top of the covers. Feeling terribly sexy in all that black silk, she plumped up the pillows, leaned back, and pretended to be vamping some handsome man, someone exactly like Jason. But the bed felt too comfortable and the wine too relaxing, and she soon fell sound asleep, still in the gown. As usual, her dreams were of Jason.

Disgruntled that Katherine had retired so early when he was still eager to share her company, Jason went down to the cellar for a second bottle of wine. Having found enough cheese to appease his appetite, he drank toast after toast all by himself until the bottle was nearly empty and he, too, began to feel drowsy. With nothing to keep him downstairs any longer, he eventually abandoned the bottle, though not yet empty, and began what seemed to be an unusually long climb to the second floor. In his wine-induced stupor, he made his way to his bedroom door, pushed it open, and had closed it behind him before he realized he no longer slept in that room.

The sound of the door closing awakened Katherine just enough to realize that Jason now stood in the middle of her room, unmoving, staring at her in surprise.

"Jason? What do you want?" she asked groggily, shaking her head, trying to clear her wine-fogged brain.

"I—I forgot I switched rooms. I'm sorry," he said, though inwardly he wasn't sorry at all as he viewed her in the daring black gown.

Pulling herself into a sitting position, she glanced down and realized what had captured his attention so thoroughly. She felt it strange that she did not feel embarrassed. Instead, she laughed at the stunned expression on his face. "Does it look anything like you thought it would when you bought it?"

Jason's sense of decency demanded that he turn his head and leave the room immediately, but the desire to stay was too strong. Slowly, he moved towards the bed.

"You are beautiful. You are the most beautiful woman I have ever known. God, how I wish you were really my wife."

Katherine stared into the blue depths of his passion-filled eyes, gauging her own wild reaction to his open, blazing desire. She smiled knowingly up at him. "I know. I wish that you could truly be my husband—more than I have ever wished for anything in my life."

"It's just not fair, is it? I love you more than I ever

dreamed possible, yet I can't have you."

"Yes, you can," she said quietly and held her arms out to him, her eyes shining with love. "I may be married to someone else, but that's only in the eyes of the law. Flint broke our wedding vows long ago. They no longer exist for me. Nor does the man I married. In my heart, I belong to you."

Chapter Twelve

Jason needed no further encouragement. His fingers went immediately to his shirt, and in a matter of seconds, he had the many buttons undone and the shirt tail tugged out, allowing Katherine a tantalizing view of his tanned chest and the dark hair that curled across it, then tapered downward, disappearing beneath his waistband. She watched with growing interest as he hurriedly pulled the shirt all the way off and reached down to unfasten his britches. When he finally joined her in bed, all his clothes were strewn across the floor, and he was completely, magnificently naked.

"Katherine," he breathed softly, pressing his lips to hers in a long and passionate kiss.

Katherine was filled with rapture. Inwardly, she had longed for this moment since the day they had met, though it had taken her a long time to realize it. Now that she knew it was what she wanted, really wanted, she could hardly believe it was happening. The thought of what was about to be shared between them was still somewhat frightening, yet, at the same time, too wonderful for words.

Hesitantly at first, she held him close, reveling only in how splendid it felt to have his body next to hers. Then, with trembling hands, she gently explored the taut skin along his powerful back. Muscles that had grown solid and strong from years of hard, honest work, rippled beneath her fingertips. So overwhelmed was she by the feel of him—so overpowered by the magic of his lips as they hungrily devoured hers—she was only vaguely aware that he had pushed the lower part of her gown aside. Taking full advantage of the deep slit along the side of the garment, his hands now roamed freely over the cool skin of her exposed thigh and hip.

It was not until his hand moved up over the gown to cup one of her breasts that she felt the true raging fire of his touch. Even through the silken fabric, the sensations were almost too much to bear. Shafts of sheer, white-hot pleasure shot through her, setting her instantly aflame. How she wished the garment did not lie between them. How she wanted to feel his glorious touch directly against her skin.

As if sensing her need, Jason slowly worked the gown upward until her firm round breast was finally bared to his touch. Aching with his own ever-increasing need, he fought the urge to conquer quickly and—ever so gently, ever so slowly—he explored the softness of her breast, caressing its fullness with the curve of his hand as his thumb stroked the tip until it grew rigid.

Katherine's smoldering passions ignited in frenzied desire, her body aching to draw him closer, to pull him right into her heart. Soon, the silk nightgown was drawn over her head and tossed to the floor.

With their bodies now naked and pressed intimately together, the kiss deepened, and their tentative explorations of each other became more frantic, their need more pressing. Willingly, Katherine gave in to the swirling sea of sensations that quickly engulfed her, drowning her in an exquisite floodtide of turbulent emotions. It was all she could do not to cry out from the sheer joy and rapture that flowed from her heart through her body.

There was no turning back; Katherine had no wish to. Lost now to her own passion, she became more and more aroused with each place he touched, with each place he kissed, until she ached with a boundless need to be fulfilled. His sweet taste and familiar scent only served to excite her further. Her heated blood raced through her body, making her feel more vibrant, more alive than she had ever felt before. Never before had she felt such blazing excitement. Her pulse pounded with its force, throbbing in every part of her body. As her senses whirled in a wondrous state of delirium—intoxicating her, heightening her passion—she yielded eagerly, instinctively, to his masterful touch.

As her desire rose to consume every inch of her flesh, Katherine arched her body to meet his, pressing herself closer to him. She was on fire, wild with a burning need. Her hands pressed into his back with all the strength she possessed. She needed to somehow bring him closer, make him a part of her, so much a part of her that the heartbreaking fact they would never be able to marry would no longer matter.

Aroused to near madness, Katherine soared ever upward while Jason's hands continued to work their magic first on one breast, then on the other. She wondered how much more of this bittersweet torment she could take. Surely not much. There had to be a limit.

Yet still, their passions mounted, their kisses became more and more demanding, their needs more and more pressing. Eager to share with Jason that which she had denied herself for so long, Katherine tugged at his shoulders, hoping to make him understand that the time had come. She pressed against him with all her might; her breasts flattened against his chest, her mouth more insistent at his lips. She ached with the sweet agony of her own wild passion, her insides blazing with need. Desperately, she sought to pull him into the flames.

But Jason was not yet ready to end the slow, sweet climb. Slowly, masterfully, his lips drew away from hers and made a nipping, teasing trail down the ivory column of her throat, then across the tempting curve of her collarbone. Understanding his intention, Katherine quivered with anticipation and arched her back higher while his lips moved hungrily closer to her breast. When he paused to nip lightly at the sensitive skin encircling the rosy peak, she thrust her breasts out as far as she could to remind him of his destination, and the moment his mouth finally closed on the straining bud, she moaned and reached out, pressing him closer, urging him on. But Jason needed no urging.

Unable to bear much more of the exquisite agony, Katherine clutched again at his shoulders and prayed he would take her soon. With every stroke of his skillful hand, on her breasts, with each caress of his hungry tongue, she urgently wanted to give him more, so much more. He already had her heart—he'd had that from the beginning—now it was time for him to take the rest of her.

"Jason," she whispered huskily. "Jason, make me yours. Make me yours forever."

Slowly, he rose and looked down at her naked beauty once more. He watched her swelling breasts strain forward with the fire that blazed inside her, and he knew that the time was right. Eager to feel her warmth pressed against him again, he took only a moment longer to gaze at her beauty, then lowered himself to her once more.

Flames of pleasure seared every fiber of her being as he finally moved to claim her. At last, Jason was a part of her. It was an exquisite, almost indescribable feeling, a rapture beyond any she had believed possible—and it continued to build.

Katherine's breathing, shallow and gasping, grew stronger and more rapid as she reached higher and higher for the pinnacle—until finally, in a glorious burst of ecstasy, she cried out his name. Jason responded with a deep, shuddering groan that racked his entire body again and again. Never had lovemaking been so all-consuming; never had it meant so much to either of them.

Fulfilled at last, they both fell back into the softness of the pillows, their bodies still entwined, their energy spent, languorous in the aftermath of love.

"Jason, I want you to know just how much I do love you," Katherine said softly, breaking the peaceful silence that surrounded them.

"And I love you. I just wish there was some way for us to legally be married. I want you to really be my wife.

I want to know you are mine forever."

"As far as I'm concerned, I already am yours forever. Our love was sealed just a few minutes ago, here, in this bed. I've made my commitment to you, in my heart, where it truly counts. You know it, and God knows it. We might not be able to make it truly valid in the eyes of man, because I'm still legally wed to Flint, a mistake I can't do anything about. But as far as my own heart is concerned, I'm as bound to you now as if we'd taken our sacred vows in front of a church full of witnesses."

"And I am bound to you, my love. Forever."

"Forever," Katherine murmured, as she snuggled into the crook of his arm and pressed her cheek against his warm chest. Quietly, she listened to the gentle heartbeat of the man she loved. The man who also loved her. He was a man like no other. Never had she known such happiness. Never had she felt so complete. As she closed her eyes, she could sense that this time it would be different for her. This time it would be the way it was supposed to be, because Jason truly loved her.

Even after Katherine had fallen into a deep, peaceful sleep, Jason made no attempt to leave her. The two lovers remained in each other's arms for the rest of the night—united at last.

When Ruby entered the bedroom early the following day with Katherine's morning cup of hot chocolate, she found Jason still asleep in Katherine's bed. She did not say anything, but she simply proceeded with her usual routine of opening the drapes and wetting a cloth for Katherine to wash her face.

Although it had surprised her to find Jason lying in Katherine's bed, naked from the waist up and probably from the waist down as well, she was glad of it. She felt it strange that in this day and age a man and wife should have separate bedrooms. It was not the natural order of things. Should she ever marry—and there was always the chance that someday she might, for she was still young enough if ever the right man came along—she would definitely not ask for her own private bedroom. No, a marriage meant sharing, especially the bed. Jason had every right to be there. Ruby just hoped it would prove to be a permanent arrangement.

"Good morning, Mr. Morris, sir. Would you be caring for a cup of chocolate this morning?" she asked, while trying not to stare at the handsome expanse of broad chest.

Jason looked around at the clothing strewn everywhere, none within his reach, and frowned. He had meant to be gone before Ruby came in. He looked apologetically at Katherine who had gathered the covers around her and was blinking at the suddenly bright, sun-filled room.

"No, Ruby, I don't care for chocolate. I'm a coffee drinker," Jason quickly answered. "And Minnie will have my coffee already poured by the time I get dressed and downstairs. No need for you to bother."

"No bother at all, sir. If ever I can be of assistance, just let me know. I've not enough to do to keep me busy anyway." Then to Katherine she added, "If there's nothing else I can do for you at the moment, ma'am, I'll leave you to your privacy."

"Thank you, Ruby," Katherine said, nodding her head in dismissal. Having noted the calm way in which

Ruby had handled the situation compared to the way Jason fidgeted beneath the covers until she was gone, she wanted to laugh.

"I'm sorry, Katherine," he said. "I had meant to be out of here before Ruby came in with your morning chocolate. I usually wake up long before sunrise."

"Well, judging by all this bright light, sunrise was hours ago," Katherine pointed out.

"I know, and I'm sorry."

"Will you quit apologizing? What's done is done. There's nothing we can do to change it. Besides, Ruby thinks we are legally married, as does everyone else, except for Minnie and Silas." Suddenly, she frowned, for Ruby just might mention to Minnie what she had seen. What would Minnie think of her? Although Katherine did not regret what she and Jason had done, she did want Minnie to understand. Flinging back the covers, she hurried to get dressed. She wanted to tell Minnie before Ruby did, and try to explain to her how much she loved Jason and how, in her heart, where it counted the most, she truly belonged to him.

The moment Katherine entered the kitchen and found Minnie punching a huge mound of dough with both her fists, she realized that Minnie already knew. Though barely twenty minutes had passed since Ruby had discovered them, Minnie already knew.

"Ruby told you, didn't she?"

"That you and Mr. Jason spent the night together in your bed? No. She didn't have to. When Mr. Jason didn't come down for breakfast at his usual time, I figured he just overslept because of all that wine he had—after all, I found two empty bottles—so I went on up to wake him. But of course, he wasn't in his room, and his bed wasn't even slept in. My next thought was to see if you had any idea where he was since you was the last to talk to him. I know I should have knocked first, but it just never occurred to me that there was any reason to."

"Then you saw us?"

Minnie nodded, her face drawn in a deep frown as she continued to pound the dough.

"It's not what you think."

"It's not?" she asked skeptically.

"Well, it is, but it's not. Please, let me explain it to you."

"You don't have to explain nothin' to me. It ain't none of my business, anyway, what you two do."

"Maybe so, but I want to explain it to you, anyway. I want to try and make you understand the reasons behind what has happened. I want you to know just how much I have grown to love Jason."

In order to be sure that Minnie truly did understand, Katherine told her everything about her past life. She left nothing out, because she wanted Minnie to know just why she could no longer love Flint—and why she was too terrified to risk getting a divorce.

"Flint used lies and deceit to get me to marry him, and he used more lies and deceit, after we were married, in order to keep me. He is not the man I promised to love, honor, and obey. I don't think that man ever truly existed. Our entire marriage was a farce. I want you to understand that."

"You didn't have to explain nothin' to me," Minnie said again when Katherine seemed to have finished.

She had kept quiet while Katherine had her say, letting her speak her piece totally uninterrupted. "I told you that. I'm not about to judge you for what you done. I'm in no position to judge anyone, anyway. If you say you love Jason, that's what matters most."

"I do love him, and in my heart, I'm truly bound to him forever. Last night, we not only expressed our love, we made a sacred commitment. Our vows may not be legal in the eyes of the law, but as far as I'm concerned, Jason *is* my husband and I *am* his wife."

"And if the day ever comes when we can make it legal, we will," Jason said, as he came to stand behind Katherine, startling them both, for neither one had heard him enter the kitchen.

"See that you do," Minnie said sternly, though she couldn't suppress a smile. Shaking her head at the strange situation, she muttered, "That poor child has suffered enough broken promises."

"Well," Jason assured her, "that's one promise that won't be broken."

In September, by the time the baby was due to arrive, Jason had not only come to truly think of Katherine as his own beloved wife, he had also come to consider himself the father of her baby, and he was doing all that he could to see that the child would want for nothing.

All summer long, he had been unable to go into town without returning with something new for the nursery. By August, the small room adjoining their bedroom was overflowing with the latest in baby furniture and every toy imaginable. Eventually, Jason had to find another place to store some of the things, especially the toys the baby would not be able to play with until he was older. But he wanted to store them where the child would be able to get to them if he wanted to. And it would be best if the room was downstairs, since that's where everyone tended to be during the day.

That's when he decided to dismantle the sewing room. Knowing that Minnie was the only one who used the room, he had everything moved out to her cabin, despite her protests that those things had belonged to his mother and he should not be so quick to give them away. But Jason had other plans for the room, and he knew that his mother would not have objected to Minnie having her things.

Once the room was empty, he decided against wallpaper and had the small room stripped and plastered, and painted a cheery shade of yellow. And rather than lay dust-catching carpet that might be unhealthy for his son to crawl on, he decided to leave the wood floors bare and highly polished. He wanted his son's playroom to be the best room in the entire house.

Once the room was ready, he immediately moved in many of the toys he had already purchased, filling the shelves that ran along one wall and a large wooden toy chest. Then, he went out and bought still more toys, games, and a large stuffed pillow-horse for the boy to wrestle with when he started to walk.

As the expected date of the baby's arrival grew closer, he and Katherine spent more and more time in the room, sometimes working to improve it in various ways, sometimes simply daydreaming about what it was going to be like to have a child at play in there. Then finally, late one night in early September,

Katherine realized she was having more than her usual back pain, and by morning, the child had been born.

"It's a boy. A fine, healthy baby boy," Minnie told her mistress as she bent to wipe Katherine's sweating brow.

"It's a boy, all right," Doc Edison agreed, adding with a grimace, "with a very powerful set of lungs, as you can hear."

"He just wants everyone to know he's finally here." Minnie chuckled and looked fondly at the screaming, wriggling mass of blue, purple, and pink.

"I want to see," Katherine said, trying to lift her head to catch a glimpse of her son.

"Not yet," the doctor said. "We've still got work to do. When we're all finished, you can see your son."

"What work?" Katherine demanded. As far as she was concerned, the ordeal was over.

"You just push when I tell you," he said simply, then looked towards Minnie. "You ready with the water?"

"Ready and eager. Hand him here," Minnie said and left Katherine to see to the baby.

"What are you doing to him?" Katherine tried once again to lift her head from the pillow, but she was just too tired, too physically drained, and her head fell back before she could see what was going on.

"Just givin' him his first bath, Missy. We want him to look his best for his momma."

"Lie back down, Mrs. Morris," the doctor said, distracting her from what Minnie was doing. "In a minute, I'm going to tell you to push hard, and I want you to do just that."

"Why? Are there twins?" she asked, astonished at

the thought.

Minnie chuckled at Katherine's naiveté. "No," she said, "one is all you're gettin' this time. Just do what the doctor says."

The loud, insistent pounding on the bedroom door stopped Katherine from asking more questions.

"What idiot bolted this door?" It was Jason. He'd heard the baby's cry and wanted to be let in.

"I bolted the door, Mister Jason," Minnie shouted across the room. "We've got enough to do in here without worryin' about an overanxious father gettin' in the way. You can't come in here just yet. You'll have to be patient for a few more minutes."

"Come on, I want to see the baby," he demanded. "I want to see it now."

"In a minute."

"Damn," he muttered, then shouted, "At least tell me if it's a boy or a girl." He pounded on the door again, louder this time. "Do I have a son or a daughter?"

Minnie smiled at Katherine. "I think that privilege belongs to you. You tell him what a fine boy he has—just do it before he breaks that door down."

"The door will hold," Katherine said with a slow smile. "Let him wait. I want to see his face when he finds out he does indeed have a son."

The pounding on the door grew louder still. "Dammit, are you going to tell me or not?"

"Jason, darling, you'll just have to be patient," Katherine called out at last.

"Don't you 'darling' me. Let me in." Then came a loud heavy thud followed by a muttered oath of pain.

"He's trying to knock that door down; you'd better

tell him before he hurts himself," Minnie warned, her eyes twinkling with amusement.

Katherine relented. "Jason, watch your temper. You certainly aren't setting a very good example for your son."

"Dammit, I said let me in," he cried out, still pounding. Then there was silence. "Did you say *son?*"

"Yes, I said *son,*" Katherine replied, beaming with pride.

"And if you'll just hold your horses a minute, you'll be able to see that boy," Minnie shouted, working as fast as she could to cleanse all traces of blood from the baby. She knew that Jason was courageous about everything but the sight of blood.

When she was finished, Minnie bundled the now rosy-pink babe in a soft lamb's wool blanket and held him up for Katherine to see. The baby had finally stopped crying and now lay quiet.

"He's beautiful. Hand him to me," she said eagerly, blinking back the happy tears that had sprung to her eyes.

"You can hold him just as soon as you're finished," the doctor interjected. "Push."

Katherine frowned. The last thing she wanted to do was push again, but in order to have her baby in her arms, she grimaced and pushed with all the strength she had left.

"Now you are finished," the doctor announced. "Let her have her baby."

"What about me?" Jason called through the door. "When do I get to see my son?"

"Just as soon as I get things cleaned up in here,"

Minnie promised him, and gently lowered the baby into Katherine's waiting arms. She looked only briefly at the sight of a new mother holding her son for the first time, then hurried to the door and slid the bolt back.

"You can come in now," she said sweetly as she swung the door open.

"About time," he muttered and quickly glanced around for the son that everyone seemed so eager to keep from him. He was barely two steps inside the door when his gaze fell on the soft bundle nestled in Katherine's arms. His pulse quickened as he stepped closer and was finally able to see the baby's face. So tiny, so very tiny.

"Jason, I'd like for you to meet Jeffrey Alan Morris, your son," Katherine said, drawing the blanket back so that Jason could get a better look.

"Hi, Jeffrey," Jason said, his eyes sparkling with joy and wonder. Touching his fingertip to one tiny fist, he smiled with a tenderness that brought tears to Minnie and Katherine's eyes. Gently, he pulled back two little fingers and laughed softly. "Look at that. Look at how perfect he is."

"Want to hold him?" Katherine asked.

"Who? Me? Hold him?" Jason's blue eyes grew wide with concern. "No, not me. I might hurt him."

"Nonsense," Minnie said with a laugh, and bent over to help transfer the baby to Jason.

Jason's breath caught in his throat as Minnie gently lowered the baby into his cradled arms. He gazed down at his son in wide-eyed amazement, then looked up at Minnie with a concerned frown. "What do I do if he starts to cry or something?"

"You simply hand him back to his momma so he can be properly comforted." Minnie laughed, unable to believe that Jason could be so unsure of himself with a baby. Now that she thought back on it, he had refused to hold either Samuel or Edmond until they were almost six months old.

When the baby continued to lie quietly and peacefully in his father's arms, Jason slowly relaxed and found he was able to breathe again. Not knowing what else to do, he again reached for one of his son's tiny fists and slipped his finger into the baby's grip.

"How'd it go in here?" he asked Katherine, though his eyes remained on his son. "Are you all right?"

"Never been better," she said, content to lie back and watch the two men in her life get acquainted.

He looked up to see if what she said was the truth and could easily tell that it was. Her dark hair hung in damp curls, and her beautiful face was far too pale to suit him, but her glowing smile and sparkling brown eyes told him that she truly was happy.

"That may well be," the doctor interrupted, and Jason looked up with a start. He'd forgotten all about the doctor. "But you need lots of rest, young lady. Little Jeffrey does too. Minnie, put the baby in the cradle next to the bed while Jason walks me to the door."

"I'll be right back," Jason assured Katherine, frowning as Minnie lifted the child from his arms.

"No, you won't," Minnie told him. "The doc's right. Missy needs her rest, and to tell you the truth, you look like you could use some, too."

"Rest? I can't rest," he said energetically. "I've got work to do. I've been thinking. That boy is going to need a tree swing before you know it. Every boy needs a tree swing. I'd better get right on it."

Katherine and Minnie both laughed. It was no use trying to explain to Jason that it would be quite some time before little Jeffrey would be able to use a tree swing.

Chapter Thirteen

May, 1880

"He looks more and more like you every day," Jason commented, as he and Katherine sat in the garden watching Jeffrey chase after a yellow butterfly. As he spoke, he leaned forward on the small ironwork bench, ready to move should little Jeffrey actually catch the butterfly and decide to see what flavor yellow might be. Jeffrey was quick to taste anything that came into his hands these days.

"Do you really think so?" Katherine asked. "In a way, I think he looks more like my father." Her expression grew wistful, though her eyes never left her son as his pudgy little legs carried him in erratic circles through the garden.

Watching Katherine's smile fade into such a doleful expression, Jason leaned over and kissed her. His heart went out to her. "Why don't you go see your father?"

"He wouldn't want me to." Her response was the same as always. She leaned forward and plucked a single rose from a nearby bush. As she breathed in its delicate fragrance, she remembered how roses had been her mother's favorite flower and how their house had always been filled with them. Slowly, she lowered the flower, playing idly with its stem while she continued to watch her son and think about her father.

"I can't believe that."

"He told me never to come back." She frowned at the bitter memory and lifted her gaze from Jeffrey to Jason.

"It was said in a moment of anger. You said things, too, that you didn't really mean. Katherine, the poor man's a grandfather and doesn't even know it. Though I know you don't mean to be selfish, I think it's a little inconsiderate of you not to take Jeffrey over to see him."

Katherine's frown grew deeper. "Do you? Do you really?"

"Yes, Katherine, I do," he responded honestly. "The man deserves a chance to know his own grandson. One look at Jeffrey and it would melt any barriers between you."

Katherine turned to watch as Jeffrey toddled back toward them, having finally given up on the butterfly. Her heart ached as she looked at his tiny cherub face, aglow with a smile that so resembled her father's. Not yet two years old, and already he had traits she could easily recognize. It was the almond shape of his hazel-green eyes and the high arch of his light brown eyebrows that reminded her most of her father. As she gazed down at her son, she did wish her father could see Jeffrey—even just once—to know someone so much like him existed, his very own grandson. "Okay," she said, "I'll do it. If you'll go with me, I'll take Jeffrey over to meet Papa."

"Of course, I'll go," Jason said and reached out to caress her cheek. He realized how much courage it had taken her to come to that decision and he was proud of her. "It's not as if you're simply going into town. It's a full day's ride over there. I wouldn't dare let you travel that far alone. Besides, I'm eager to meet the man, myself. I'd kinda like to thank him for a job well done."

Katherine looked at him questioningly, but when she realized he meant her, she smiled. "I wonder what he's going to think of you."

"More than he thought of Flint, I hope." Jason grinned.

Katherine chuckled at that thought, but then, her face grew tense. "I wonder how he's going to react when I suddenly show up on his doorstep?"

"I think he'll be pleased. After all, it's been almost eight years. He probably thinks of you often, and I imagine by now he fully regrets the things he said to you."

"Not Papa. He doesn't ever say things he doesn't mean, not even in anger. What he said to me that day was what was truly in his heart." A tear came to her eye but she blinked it back.

"Maybe so, at that particular moment—but people change, and the way they feel about things changes, too. Katherine, I wouldn't suggest that you go to see him if I thought he was going to turn you away in anger, or refuse to speak to you. I love you too much to lead you into anything I thought might hurt you. I really expect him to hear you out. There won't be any door slammed in your face."

"Oh, I hope not. I don't think I could stand the pain a second time. Oh, Jason, what if he does?"

Jason took a deep breath, and tried not to show any trace of worry. "He won't. You have to believe that. Not when he sees what a fine grandson you've brought him."

"No, I don't want him to accept me back because of Jeffrey. I want him to accept me back because he has forgiven me," she said adamantly. "I want to face him alone at first. I've got to know his true feelings about *me.*"

"Then, that's how it will be," Jason agreed, then lunged to catch Jeffrey before the boy could yank Rebel's tail again. The poor dog did not have the same good sense that Bart did. The moment that Jeffrey had learned to walk, the cat had headed for higher ground, and stayed there.

After having finally gotten Katherine to agree to go to Gilmer and face her father again, Jason did not want to give her the chance to change her mind. Although it was already Thursday, which would give them only one day to pack, he planned their trip for Saturday morning. He would have stayed at the ranch that weekend, to supervise the first cutting of hay, but he decided to let Mose and Rede handle it by themselves this time. Katherine's needs were far more important, and she needed her father.

The roads that led from Seven Oaks to Gilmer were not as good as the roads to Daingerfield or Jefferson, which made the going a little slower. Although they left Seven Oaks early—just before dawn—it was almost two in the afternoon before they reached Gilmer, and nearly three o'clock before they emerged from a long wooded stretch two miles beyond, and at last reached the many acres of cleared land that belonged to Katherine's father.

As they made their way along the northern edge of the vast area of grassy pasture land, broken only by small clusters of water oak, pine, cottonwoods and two narrow fencelines, they looked ahead for Katherine's father's house. And there, finally, in the middle of a huge clearing, up on the highest of the surrounding hills, sitting among spreading pecan trees, was the house where Katherine was raised.

Though the outbuildings were about what he was used to seeing, the house itself was larger and more elaborate than Jason had expected. Built of rough wood and gray mortar, it was a practical yet beautiful structure with several solid wood posts supporting an open veranda that ran the full width of the long, sprawling house. As they drew closer to the house, Jason noticed it was built in the shape of a U and, eventually he realized it covered every bit as much area as his own house did, only it did not have a second story. Everything was on one floor, which he imagined proved very convenient at times.

The large dooryard that had been formed by a narrow waist-high, split-rail fence was kept neat and green, yet there were hardly any flowers—only a few well-kept rose bushes, near the far side of the house, and a sprinkling of wildflowers across the front.

Very few shrubs grew around the house, as they did at Seven Oaks, yet when Jason, Katherine, and Jeffrey rode around to the backyard, at Katherine's insistence, they found a large ornamental pool and several red rock and gray mortar walkways leading to different areas of the house. It was a perfect place for a garden, yet there was none. Clearly, there was no woman living here, and whatever touches Katherine's mother, or even Katherine, might have once lent the place, were no longer evident.

As he brought the carriage to a halt, Jason glanced down at Katherine's pensive expression and could see the conflicting emotions within her. A curious mix of hope, fear, and sadness was displayed on her beautiful face as she gazed out at her surroundings. He looked out, too, noticing the deep, green pastures that ran as far as the eye could see, to the west and to the north of the house. It delighted Jason to see that Brangus, the same crossbreed cattle he was raising, grazed peacefully along the rolling hills. It meant there would be at least one thing he and her father had in common, and could talk about should the conversation lag—if a conversation could be started at all. He tried not to worry about that just yet.

On the east side of the house, just ahead to their left, and dipping down onto the south side, lay acre upon acre of freshly tilled soil with tiny green plants peeping out of the ground in perfectly even rows. From where they were, it was hard to tell, but he thought it might be corn. Evidently, Katherine's father had not taken to raising cotton, after all. There was an advantage to corn. If corn did not find a market, the crop could at least be fed to the cattle.

As Jason leaned over and looped the reins around the canopy post, he noticed that Jeffrey had spotted a squirrel playing with a pecan that must have been on the ground since the fall. With the tiny animal squarely in sight, Jeffrey was trying to pull loose from his mother, eager to climb down and give chase.

"Oh, no you don't," Jason said firmly and reached over to take his son into his arms. Then to Katherine, he lowered his voice and asked, "Will he be in the house or in the barn, or out in the pasture somewhere at this time of day?"

"I don't know. Saturday used to be his day to ride with the rest of the men into town, but he was always back by noon. I guess we should try the house first."

Quickly, Jason shifted Jeffrey to his left arm and climbed down to help Katherine out of the carriage. He could tell by the tension in her hand that she was terrified by the anticipated confrontation, and he could not blame her.

"Be brave," he said softly. "Whatever happens, remember that Jeffrey and I love you."

Katherine smiled up at him as she gathered her skirts and turned to face the house. Jason had spoken the truth. No matter how her father received her, she would still have Jason and her son. Though it would hurt terribly to be rejected by her father again, she would still have her own family, and that was important.

"Wish me luck," she said as she stepped away from Jason. As previously agreed upon, Jason and Jeffrey waited near the carriage while Katherine went to face her father alone. Each step she took brought her that much closer to the inevitable, and, by the time she reached the back door, her heart was pounding so violently she could hardly hear her own knock.

An eternity passed and the door did not open. Her

stomach knotted. What if he wasn't home? What if he had gone somewhere for the entire weekend? Worried now that they had made the long trip for nothing, she knocked again, louder.

Finally, she heard something stirring inside.

"I'm coming, I'm coming." It was her father's voice. Her heart leaped to her throat as she waited for him. Finally, the door opened, and she was, once again, face to face with her father. The little speech she had practiced left her completely.

All she could say was, "Papa."

"Katie?" he asked, his pale blue eyes wide with disbelief. Slowly, he reached up and raked an unsteady hand through his now thinning hair. "Katie, is that you?"

"Yes, Papa," is all she could answer. The time had come. Would he slam the door in her face or welcome her into his arms?

There was no hesitation in Brandon Warren's actions. With a loud cry of joy, he bounded out onto the back veranda, swept his daughter into his arms and swung her around and around, hugging her close as if she were still a child. "Katie, my Katie. It's really you! It really is you. Come home at last."

"Is it, Papa? Is it still my home?" she asked in a weak voice, trembling with the emotions that flooded through her.

"Oh, Katie, dear Katie, it's always been your home. You don't know how much I've regretted my last words to you, almost from the instant they were out of my mouth. I had let my anger and my jealousy overrule my good sense. I couldn't think straight. I was so afraid of losing the last person I had to love, yet I drove you away with my anger. Can you ever forgive me?" Tears filled his soft blue eyes and streamed, unchecked, down his face.

"Forgive you?" Katherine wept along with him. "I've come to ask you to forgive me."

"Ah, Katie, I've missed you. I've missed you so," he said, then broke down completely in loud, bitter sobs. Brandon Warren wept aloud until his shoulders shook.

"Papa, Papa, don't cry." She hugged him closer.

"You don't know how very much I've worried about you," he finally managed to say, his voice strained as he held her tighter and pressed her cheek into his shoulder. "I know that whatever life you've been forced to lead, whatever horror you've suffered, has all been my fault."

"Then I must thank you," she told him plainly, drawing away so he could look into her eyes and see the truth in their dark brown depths. "For I have a very good life."

When Brandon looked down at his daughter, clearly skeptical, she took him by the arm, "Come see, Papa. Come meet my husband and my son. Come meet your very own grandson."

Confusion, then curiosity, then sheer delight swept across Brandon's face as he looked in the direction she led him to find a man, a total stranger, holding a small child out in the yard. And alongside the man was a fancy black and red carriage—the carriage that must have brought his Katie to him.

"I'm a grandfather?" He wanted to be reassured.

"You most certainly are. Come, meet Jeffrey. He's quite a character. Much like his grandfather, I'd say."

When Jason saw that the time had come for them all

to meet, he reached up and dashed away the tears that had welled up in his own eyes, then hiked Jeffrey further up on his hip, and headed toward father and daughter.

They met halfway, all too emotional to speak, except Jeffrey, who looked the tall, gray-haired man over, then turned to Jason and asked, "Gran'papa?"

Jason simply nodded. The man was indeed his grandpapa.

Smiling brightly, Jeffrey turned back to his grandfather and waved his little hand in greeting, then hid behind it, suddenly embarrassed.

"Can I hold him?" Brandon asked eagerly, looking first to Katherine and then to Jason.

Jason smiled and held Jeffrey out for Katherine's father, watching the pleasure on the man's weathered face as he spoke to his grandson. It was not until Brandon and Jeffrey had become well acquainted, that Katherine turned her father's attention back to Jason, the man she so dearly loved.

"Father, I'd like for you to meet my husband, Jason. Jason Alan Morris."

Brandon's glowing smile darkened as he looked over at the man who now extended his hand. "Husband?"

"Yes, Father, my husband. We've been married for nearly two years. I guess you're wondering what happened to Flint." She, herself, wondered what she was going to tell her father, for she did not want to lie to him, but wasn't sure he would be able to accept the truth.

"No, I don't have to wonder about Flint. I know all about him. I'm afraid he comes by here quite regularly, hoping to find you."

Katherine's eyes flew to Jason's, her heart suddenly stone cold. "He still comes here?" Her eyes swept the area as if she expected to find him nearby, watching her.

Brandon's nostrils flared slightly as he responded to his daughter's question. "Yes, he comes by here every few months or so, making threats, trying to find out where you are."

Suddenly, Katherine started to tremble and her hand went to her throat where a terrible pain had become the focus of the fear that went through her on hearing Flint's name. The immediate turnabout in her emotional chemistry was almost too much to bear, and she had to fight an overwhelming dizziness in order to remain on her feet. "Oh, Jason, he *does* still look for me! He hasn't given up. He'll never give up. He still wants to find and claim what he thinks is his."

"Then it's true. You haven't divorced Flint." Brandon had to know. His gaze again went to Jason.

"Let's go inside, sir, and I'll tell you all about it," Jason said. "Katherine, why don't you see if there's somewhere you can put Jeffrey down for a nap. He's bound to be exhausted by that long trip." What he failed to say aloud was that things were about to be revealed that Jeffrey best not hear, even at so young an age. But Katherine fully understood and did as he suggested. She took the child by the arm and hurried him into the west wing of the house, to her old room, where she put him down for a nap. She felt a sudden tug on her heart when she discovered the room had not changed. It seemed a bit smaller, but she knew that was not possible. It was the same.

Because it was a strange place and Jeffrey had never

slept anywhere but Seven Oaks, she had to sit at the child's side until he fell asleep. By the time she was able to leave her bedroom and join her father and Jason in the living room, they had already discussed what had happened between her and Flint, and Jason was explaining what Katherine's life was like now.

Not knowing what her father might say about her unlawful relationship with Jason, she tried to enter the room without being noticed. But both men saw her and immediately rose as she entered.

She waited, watching apprehensively as Brandon's very solemn expression slowly changed to an adoring smile. He held out his arms to her, and once she was beside him, he embrace her lovingly.

"I like this new husband of yours," he said firmly. "He's the sort of man I wanted you to marry all along."

Katherine gazed up at him in amazement. He was going to accept Jason as her husband. Though he knew the truth about their relationship, he fully intended to accept their marriage as real. She hugged him tightly. "I love you, Papa. I want you to know just how much I do love you."

"You don't know how good that is to hear, Katie. For so many years now, I've feared that you hated me. And you'd have had every right. The awful things I said in anger. Once I'd had the time to calm down, I regretted every word."

"Then, why didn't you answer my letters?" she asked, desperately needing to believe him but still very wary. "If you truly felt that way, why didn't you at least answer my letters?"

"What letters? I never received any letters from you. If I had, I would've done more than answer them. I'd have gotten on the next train out, and come to see you in person. In fact, I tried to find you once, after having read something about Flint being up around Dodge City. I took a little trip up there in the hope of finding you and apologizing, but by the time I got there, Flint was long gone and most people didn't even know he had a wife."

"You never got my letters? But I wrote so many." Then the truth dawned on her. "Flint must have destroyed them. Because I rarely got the chance to go into town, I always gave them to Flint to post for me." She suddenly felt very foolish. Why should Flint have mailed them? He hated her father almost as much as her father hated him. It made her ache to know she could have gone home at any time and yet had no way of knowing it. It gave her even more reason to hate Flint.

"Well, that's all in the past now, isn't it?" Jason said lightly, smiling affectionately at Katherine. "You two have finally resolved your differences and are a family again."

"And I find I have a new family." Brandon laughed. "Family I never even dreamed of. That's a fine son you two have."

Katherine waited anxiously to see if Jason was going to tell her father the truth about Jeffrey's parentage. When he simply accepted the compliment, relief washed over her. Even though she didn't feel her father would hold it against the child, she felt it was better that he not know the truth at this time—especially with Flint coming by so often to try to find out where she had gone. A dreadful fear shot through her again at the thought of Flint still searching for her after all this time—nearly two years. She had hoped he would have given up by now. Clenching her fists, she prayed fervently that he would not choose this weekend to come by and question her father. The thought of it turned her blood to ice water, and for the rest of their stay with her father, she kept a watchful eye on the road.

It was the thought of Flint riding in unannounced plus the fact that her father looked as if he had not had a decent meal in quite some time, that kept Katherine indoors more often than not. Immediately, she took over the kitchen, running Walt Porterfield completely out of the house. Walt was the chief cook for her father and his four other ranchhands. He was the only other person on the ranch the afternoon that she arrived, and he was glad to surrender the kitchen for the weekend.

By the time they were ready to leave, early on Monday morning, Katherine had managed to catch up on the past eight years of her father's life; Jason and Brandon had established what was to become a lasting friendship, and Jeffrey had a new stick-horse to play with—whittled for him by Billy, one of the old-timers who had worked on the ranch since before Katherine was born.

It was a tearful goodbye, but full of hope and promises. At first, Brandon had thought it best that he not be told just where they lived, but in the end, he felt that he had to know and promised to come visit them in the fall, around Thanksgiving, if possible. Katherine promised to have Minnie prepare a huge turkey with all the trimmings.

Feeling that he, too, should get into the spirit of things, Jason promised to help Brandon eat the turkey.

When all he received for his generous offer was an assortment of noticeable frowns, he made another suggestion. "How about I promise to take very good care of your daughter?"

"And my grandson." Brandon put in, giving Jeffrey a final hug before handing him over. "I expect them both to be in the best of health when I arrive." Then, he stepped back to let them go, not daring to voice the fear that dwelled inside him—the fear of what Flint Mason might do if he found out where Katherine had gone and that she was living as another man's wife. He vowed to himself that no matter what Flint might threaten, he would never learn of Katherine's whereabouts from him. He'd die before he allowed Flint to cause Katherine further unhappiness.

As the carriage pulled out of the graveled drive and headed back to Seven Oaks, Katherine snuggled close to her husband, tears shimmering in her dark eyes and a smile of pure contentment on her face. She had finally been reunited with her father. Any gap that had separated them in the past was now completely bridged.

"How can I ever thank you for making me come back to Gilmer?" she asked, pressing her cheek lovingly against Jason's muscular arm.

"Oh, I'll think of something," he quipped with a devilish grin. Then, with sudden vigor, he snapped the reins high over the horses' backs and shouted, "Get up, you two hayburners. I find I'm suddenly in a real big hurry to get home!"

Chapter Fourteen

Summer, 1883

"But why is it spelled with an *e* like that, when it's said with an *a?*" ten-year-old Edmond demanded to know, growing more frustrated with the English language each day. Though it had been his idea for Katherine to teach him how to read, he had not expected it to be quite so hard. Although often frustrated, he was dead serious about learning and determined to figure out all the reasons why certain words differed so much from others. Samuel, on the other hand, came to the early morning lessons mainly to get out of doing some of his least favorite chores. He couldn't have cared less why a word that started with an *e* sounded like it started with an *a*.

"I don't really know why the word is spelled *e-i-g-h-t* but reads like it begins with a long *a,*" Katherine said, shrugging her shoulders. As a child, she had often wondered the same thing.

"One-two-three-four-five-six-seven-*eight,*" Jeffrey

chimed in, wanting to put what he had learned to use. He grinned up at his mother, his big hazel-green eyes twinkling beneath wayward curls of dark brown hair.

"Very good, Jeffrey," Katherine said, putting her book aside and lifting her four-year-old son onto her lap. Slipping an arm around his pudgy waist, she looked over at Edmond's scowling face, and felt her heart go out to the child who wanted so badly to learn to read and write.

"I guess that's enough for today," she said to Edmond and Samuel. "You two still have a few chores that have to get done before lunch." Then, turning to Jeffrey, she reminded, "And you, young man, have all these toys to put away before you can go with me into town."

Jeffrey looked around the cluttered playroom and frowned. "What toys?"

"The ones you pulled off the shelves while I helped Edmond and Samuel with their reading. That's what toys. And if you don't get them picked up and put away, you are not going outside to play, and you are certainly not going into town with me later this afternoon."

Jeffrey frowned again as he climbed down from his mother's lap and reluctantly began to gather up some of the smaller toys. After depositing one load in the toy chest, he turned and looked around the room, unable to detect much improvement. Toy soldiers, tops, pieces of his train set, picture books, penny banks, toy tools, toy guns, wooden boats, balls of all sizes, and plush pillow-animals were scattered everywhere. His little frown burrowed deeper. "It'll take forever."

"Then you'd better get a move on," Katherine told him, placing her lesson books back on the shelf and clearing the small table of the writing tablets and pencils that Edmond and Samuel had left behind. After she had pushed the three small ladder-back chairs up to the table and was turning to leave, she glanced back over her shoulder at her unhappy son. "I'm going to help Minnie in the kitchen for a little while. Come tell me when you're finished, so I can come see how well you've done."

She chuckled to herself at the grim expression on Jeffrey's face as she left the room. She wondered if the child would ever learn that when you mess up, you have to clean up. But then, if Jason had his way, they'd have a special maid just to pick up after little Jeffrey. Ruby already did too much of that, anyway. It was all Katherine could do to keep the two of them from spoiling Jeffrey rotten.

Jeffrey might only be four years old—nearly five as he would be quick to point out—but the boy already had his own horse, his own hunting knife (though it was stored on a high shelf for now), and his own real leather boots. All had been purchased by an overly indulgent father. But Katherine really couldn't complain, for it was also Jason who had taught Jeffrey how to tell at a glance the difference between a poisonous snake and a non-poisonous one, how to tie a knot that wouldn't slip, and it was Jason who had shown him how to fall off a horse so that it wouldn't hurt as much. These were the things only a father could show a boy, things Katherine, herself, never knew.

"I gather Jeffrcy's cleanin' up his room," Minnie said, without looking up from her bowl of thick brown cake batter. It was the loud, clatter of toys being dropped haphazardly into the toy chest, and slung onto shelves, that had tipped Minnie off. No one could ever accuse Jeffrey of being an ovcrly quiet child.

"Reluctantly, but he's doing it." Katherine smiled. Knowing Minnie was not about to let her help prepare the cake—for cakes and pies were Minnie's specialties—Katherine went over to the sink, slipped on a white linen apron that hung nearby, and began to wash and peel the fruit she planned to use in the punch. "Does Jason suspect anything?"

"About the party? No, I don't think so," Minnie replied. "He does know today's August 14, his birthday, and that I'm going to fix him a fancy chocolate cake. But he don't know that you've invited all the neighbors over to help him celebrate, and he sure don't know about his fancy new saddle."

"Thirty-two years old. It's hard to imagine. He still looks the same to me as he did at twenty-seven. He hasn't aged a bit since the day we met." It was true. Jason was every bit as handsome and every bit as virile, as he had been on the day that he'd found her trespassing on his property, over five years ago. It still sent a strong current of excitement through her just to visualize his strong, roguishly handsome face, and to know that the face, and the good-hearted man behind it, belonged to her. Because of Jason Morris, her happiness knew no limits.

"You keep him young," Minnie said sincerely. "And if you must know, you don't look like you'll be no twenty-nine on your next birthday either."

Katherine groaned. "Don't remind me," she said. Just yesterday she had noticed a faint sprinkling of silver in her otherwise dark mane of hair.

"What time you headin' into town to pick up his saddle?"

"Right after lunch. He thinks I'm going in to order a few fall dresses like you suggested the other evening after dinner." Katherine laughed conspiratorially. "Little does he know that most of the money he gave me for my new wardrobe will go toward paying off that new saddle. I may have to wear all last year's clothing this fall, but it'll be worth it to see his face when he sets eyes on that fancy new hand-tooled saddle with its sterling silver horn and all the sterling silver loops and rings. Finest thing a man ever rode on."

"He'll be real proud," Minnie agreed with a firm nod of her head, but she knew the moment Jason learned that the saddle was not completely paid for, he would see to it the balance was taken care of and that his wife also had her new fall clothes. "How you plan on gettin' that saddle on the place without him seein' it?"

"That's where you come in," Katherine told her.

"I thought so," Minnie muttered good naturedly.

"When I return from town, I'll drive up very slowly. Watch for me, and the moment you spot the buckboard turning into the drive, you clang the emergency bell and get Jason to come inside."

"I'll tell him there's a snake in the house again," Minnie quickly decided. "That always gets his full attention, 'cause he knows I don't take the time to decide if it's a poisonous snake or not."

While Jason was chasing an imaginary snake, Katherine would drive the buckboard into the carriage house out of his sight. From there, Mose would see that the saddle found its way to the main house in time for the party.

Katherine waited until after lunch to leave for town. Even though Jeffrey had managed to get his playroom picked up in time to go with her, he decided at the last minute to stay home and play pirate with his new wooden sword.

Katherine realized it was just as well, for every day around three o'clock, he would start to get cranky for his nap, and the bed in the wagon was not very comfortable. She agreed to let him stay behind if he promised not to get carried away and skewer Bart or Rebel. To be on the safe side, she asked Ruby to keep an eye on him and the pets.

It was a beautiful afternoon. The sun shone brightly in a pale blue, cloud-dotted sky, and although the temperature must have been over ninety, a pleasant breeze cooled her as she sat beneath the canvas awning of the buckboard. The prospect of surprising Jason with both the new saddle and the party, prompted her to sing softly to herself as she drove the wagon along the narrow, tree-lined road that led into Daingerfield. When she remembered her last trip into town, she was grateful for the shower they had had the afternoon before. The rain had settled the dust and made traveling on the small dirt road much more comfortable.

Because the road, as she got closer into town, had been recently leveled and the ruts filled in with fresh gravel, Katherine was able to make record time, and she was in Daingerfield, ready to enter the leather shop by one-thirty.

"Just finishing up on it," Mr. Mars said when he saw her enter the shop. "I'll have it ready to load for you in about thirty minutes. There are just a few more pieces of hardware to attach. I'd have done this yesterday, but some of these pieces didn't arrive until this morning."

"Thirty minutes will be fine," Katherine said with only a little disappointment. "I have a few other things I need to do while I'm in town. I'll be back around two."

"I'll have it ready," he promised, then bent once again to the stirrup he was working on, his punch already in position.

Since most of the things Katherine needed could be bought at Creel's Mercantile, she decided to make that her next stop, and have those purchases loaded into her wagon. From there, she would stop by the post office to see if any mail had come in since Silas's last trip to town, and finally, she wanted to pay deputy Zeb Fielden a visit.

As usual, Daingerfield was a beehive of activity as people went about their daily business in this small, but prosperous, East Texas town that boasted a busy railroad terminal, crowded stockyards, noisy saloons, elaborate restaurants, a new chair factory, two newspapers, two large hotels, and various other establishments that lined the main thoroughfare and branched off into side streets.

"Good afternoon," Sheriff Ragland said, looking up from his steaming coffee mug to find Katherine standing just inside his doorway. Katherine had hurried through her errands and had entered the sheriff's office less than an hour after having left the leather shop.

"Looking for Zeb?" he asked as he set the mug down in the only clear spot on his paper-strewn desk. "You just missed him. He just a few minutes ago stepped over to the Star Restaurant to get himself a late lunch."

"He's just now having lunch? Why, it's after two o'clock," Katherine said, surprised.

"We've been pretty busy around here. Some pretty rough characters rode in to town last night and have been whooping it up over to the Palace Saloon something awful. A real rowdy bunch. Already had to help settle two card disputes, among other things, this morning alone."

The sheriff tilted his head to one side and looked at her speculatively, "Best you steer clear of that place. In fact, I strongly suggest you walk on the other side of the street until that group has cleared out of town. They've already accosted poor Mrs. Haught for no reason other than she looks so pretty. She did nothing to provoke them, either. She was simply walking along the boardwalk, minding her own business, when one of those characters jumped out and pulled her right into the saloon, then forced a kiss on her. If Jim had been in town, there'd have been real trouble. He'd have probably killed them. You know what a temper Jim Haught has when it comes to his wife. In fact, we've decided not to even mention it to him, at least not until after that whole bunch has moved out."

Katherine nodded that she understood. Big Jim, as

he was affectionately known by the locals, was a big, burly fellow who had been in many a tussle over just a stray glance cast accidentally in his wife's direction. If Big Jim knew a man had actually forced a kiss on his wife, he'd probably go berserk. "What if he finds out before they leave town?"

"We're hoping that doesn't happen."

"Can't you order these men to leave town?"

"Best I can do is put them in jail if they openly break some law, which they haven't. Kissing another man's wife isn't against the law in this town, nor is arguing over cards—though some of the threats they've made to Greg Connor, who owns the Palace Saloon, have come close. Right now, we're just biding our time, keeping a close watch on them."

"Then I'll be sure and avoid the walkway in front of the Palace. Thank you for the warning," she said, before turning to leave. When she stepped outside, she frowned at the thought of having to walk all the way across the street when the Star Restaurant was only a few doors down, just the other side of the Palace. But not wanting to chance any trouble, she lifted her dark, calico skirts several inches and started across. It also annoyed her to realize that she would have to cross back, further down, to get to her destination.

When she finally arrived at the Star Restaurant, she found Zeb Fielden sitting at a table near the front window, busily cutting into a thick slice of roast beef, his heavy black mustache drawn low over his lips while he concentrated on the task before him.

"May I join you for a moment?" she asked when it became apparent he was not going to look up until he had the entire slice of meat cut down to manageable pieces.

"Mrs. Morris," Zeb said with surprise, as he scraped his chair back in order to rise and greet her. "Yes, please sit down. Have you eaten?"

"Yes, hours ago," Katherine said, as he pulled out a chair for her.

"Well, what can I do for you?" he asked when he was once again seated, fork in hand.

"It's about that business my husband is having you check on," she said in a low voice, not wanting anyone in the restaurant to overhear her. "Have you learned anything we should know about?"

"Nothing new, I'm afraid," Zeb told her apologetically, his slate gray eyes avoiding her steady, probing gaze.

"Nothing at all?" Her hands curled into fists from the frustration she felt.

"Not since I heard he was back in Dodge City," he said in a very low voice. "I've been keeping my eyes and ears open, but I haven't heard or seen anything about him in over a month. I guess that injury put him out of commission for a while—though not very much, if he was able to ride out of Dodge City on horseback just a few days later."

Katherine's expression was grim. "I guess he's over his injury then."

"Evidently it was only a flesh wound. Just enough to make him lose a lot of blood and need a doctor's attention." Zeb wished he had more to tell her. He really did, because Jason Morris was one of Zeb Fielden's closest and most trusted friends from the time that they had been schoolboys together.

When Jason had finally gone to Zeb for help in finding out more about Flint Mason, he had known Zeb would not ask any questions and would not mention the curious request to anyone else. He had been certain Zeb would do what he could and keep quiet about it because Jason would do the same for him.

It was shortly after Jason had approached him, that Zeb found out Flint was back living in Kansas, though he periodically came to Texas. And it was Zeb who learned of Flint's injury, only days after it had happened, and that there was yet another notch Flint could add to his gun—if he was a man who kept records.

Though Flint had been shot in the left shoulder, his opponent had been shot clean through the heart, which was the spot most gunfighters aimed for. Flint had killed yet again—and again it had been called self-defense, for the other man had supposedly drawn first. As usual, there were witnesses to back up Flint's story, leaving him as free as ever to roam and kill.

Though Katherine and Jason had not put their thoughts into words, they both secretly hoped that Flint would meet his match one day. Katherine felt guilty about harboring such thoughts—even against someone as evil as Flint—but it was the only way that she and Jason could ever be legally married. No one had yet to question the legitimacy of their marriage, and keeping it that way was important to them both. Even so, there had been some whispered speculation on the early arrival of their son, but to their relief, no one seemed to doubt that Jeffrey was truly Jason's flesh and blood.

Many people remarked on how much the child resembled his father, often pointing out traits the two had in common. And the birth certificate, which was filed at the courthouse, clearly stated that Jason Morris was Jeffrey's father. But if anyone had chosen to make a search for a marriage certificate bearing the names of Jason and Katherine, they would find none—not in the Morris County courthouse nor in any other. Jason, particularly, wanted that piece of paper. He desperately wanted to make their marriage legal, no matter how belatedly. It was a point of honor with him—Katherine's honor as much as his own, and so he continued to bide his time and keep his eyes and ears open for any mention of Flint's death.

"I'm really sorry I don't have more recent news." Zeb apologized again. Although Jason had never disclosed his reasons for wanting so much information on Flint Mason, Zeb had sensed it had something to do with his beautiful wife.

Zeb had formed certain suspicions early on—and they came very close to the truth—but he knew it was none of his business. He was merely doing a favor for a friend. "I've got to contact the sheriff in Dodge City this afternoon about some of the fellows that have been causing trouble over at the Palace. Seems some of them are from up around that area, and I'd like to know just who we're dealing with. When I get him on the wire, I'll ask if there's been any update on Flint. I'll tell you anything I can find out at the party tonight."

The party. Glancing up at the gilt-framed clock on

the wall, Katherine saw that it was almost three o'clock. She had to hurry back to Mr. Mar's leather shop, get the saddle loaded, and be on her way. There were still lots of preparations to see to, and she'd want to take a bath and redo her hair at some point during the afternoon.

"We'd appreciate anything you can find out," she said, in parting. "Jason is eager to know if Flint's still anywhere around Dodge City or not. So, I'll see you this evening, and remember, it's a surprise. Don't you dare show up before seven."

"I'll be waiting out by the road with everyone else," Zeb assured her with a broad smile that lifted his mustache high.

Realizing how late it was, Katherine was more disgruntled than ever at having to cross the street again in order to avoid passing the Palace Saloon on her way to the leather shop. Lifting her skirts again to avoid the dust of the street—yet careful not to let any of her ankle show—she waited for a break in the traffic, then hurried across.

"Kat!" She heard someone call out, just before she reached the other side. Her heart turned to stone and her feet froze just inches from the raised boardwalk. She felt all the blood drain out of her, and suddenly her legs were weak. Flint was the only one to ever call her Kat—Flint, and a few of his closest friends. No one else.

Terror stricken, Katherine wondered what she should do. Although she had not heard enough of the voice to tell if it was Flint or not, she decided to take no chances. Closing her eyes, she prayed that this once,

"Kat" would prove to be someone else's nickname. Then, she quickly stepped up on the boardwalk without as much as turning around.

"Kat! Kat Mason!" she heard, and now there was no doubt. Though she felt sure it was not Flint's voice, whoever it was had come from her past, and meant to get her attention. She felt another icy prickle of fear, but never paused, hurrying along the boardwalk as quickly as she dared without attracting attention. Deeply afraid of whoever it was catching up with her and proclaiming her true identity to all the people of Daingerfield, she moved toward the nearest alley, intending to slip behind the stores and swiftly get to the buckboard which was parked on the far side of town.

"Kat! Come back here!" she heard behind her.

It was not until she was well into the dark shadows of the alley between Sutcliffe's Dress Shop and the Perry Freight House that she found the courage to look back. There, stumbling across the main thoroughfare, his bleary eyes riveted on her, was Patrick Walls. He was a very close friend of Flint's—one of his cockier, crueler sidekicks who had stayed at their house often enough to recognize her without any difficulty. She must not let him get a second close look at her.

Driven by panic, she lifted her skirts higher, and ran as hard as she could through the back alleys, grateful she did not meet anyone who might wonder about her flight. Finally, she emerged on the far side of town, within sight of her buckboard. Afraid now to take the time to get the saddle, she hurriedly untied the tether strap, secured it to the horse's harness, climbed onto the seat, and slapped the reins hard against the horse's back. As she headed swiftly out of town, it took all the restraint she had not to drive the animal into a dead run, which she knew would surely serve to raise suspicion.

By the time Katherine reached the house, she had thought of all the worst that could happen. She realized it was only a matter of time before Flint would know that she was somewhere in the vicinity of Daingerfield. Patrick was certain to tell him just how and where he'd seen her, and he would try to get that information to him as quickly as possible. What if Flint was one of the men inside the saloon? They hadn't heard of his whereabouts in over a month. He could be anywhere. And even if he wasn't there with Patrick right now, Patrick would know where to find him.

Icy fingers clutched at her heart. Flint would immediately come looking for her, asking questions of the people who lived in Daingerfield, most of whom were well acquainted with her by now. Once he found out just where she lived, he would also learn about Jason. He would be furious to find out that they had been living as man and wife all these years. He would kill Jason. She had no doubt about that. Flint wouldn't rest until he saw Jason lying dead at his feet—and it was all her fault. She never should have agreed to stay. Deep down, she had always known it would come to this. Despite all Jason's arguments to the contrary, she had known how it would end. Yet, she had selfishly stayed, had pretended to be Jason's wife in spite of the danger.

As she reached the main gate at last, she almost

overturned the buckboard in her haste to reach Jason. In her mind's eye, she could see Flint already hot on her trail. Jason needed to know right away. He needed to be warned so that he could take measures to protect himself.

With tears streaming down her face, she called out his name, even before she had come to a stop. When he did not immediately appear, she started to become hysterical. "Jason, where are you?"

"Missy Katherine? What's the matter with you?" Minnie stepped out onto the back porch, alarmed by the screaming.

"Where's Jason? I have to talk to him," she said, barely able to make out Minnie's worried face through her tears. "I have to warn him."

"We sent him over to Craig Monk's, to borrow his spray pump. Ours conveniently broke down just as Silas was about to spray the orchard. We figured it would be a good way to get Mister Jason out of here for a while so you could get the saddle unloaded and up to the house." Minnie stepped further out on the porch to get a better look at the wagon. All she could see were a few parcels wrapped in brown paper and a small wooden crate. "Where is the saddle?" she asked.

"I didn't get it. I couldn't get it," Katherine said impatiently, then turned back toward the wagon. "I've got to find Jason. I've got to warn him. Flint will try to kill him. I know he will."

"Who's Flint?" Minnie called out in confusion as Katherine climbed back into the buckboard and jerked up the reins. Then, Minnie remembered. It had been five years since she'd heard the whole story, but she remembered that Flint was the name of the man Katherine had been desperately running from—the man who had brought her such cold-hearted misery. Minnie felt a shiver of apprehension as she watched Katherine ride off, wheels clattering, toward the Monk ranch.

"Silas," she called out at the top of her lungs while her eyes quickly scanned the area for sight of her husband. "Silas, get your rifle. Looks like we've got us some trouble comin'."

By the time Katherine returned, alone, Minnie had the entire ranch up in arms. Though no one knew why, they all had their rifles and handguns loaded and ready. Minnie had not taken the time to give them details, only that someone named Flint was coming who meant trouble for Jason. Then, she'd rushed off and hitched up one of the buggies, and the next thing they knew, she was headed toward town.

"Where's Jason?" Silas asked, hurrying toward Katherine who stood wringing her hands.

"Jason's on his way into town," she said, her voice barely audible. "I tried to stop him, but he wouldn't listen. All he has with him is his rifle. He wouldn't even take the time to stop by here and get his handgun." She tried to hold back the tears that had started again.

"Minnie's on her way into town too," Silas supplied. "She's gone to get the sheriff." His grizzled white eyebrows were drawn together with worry. "Is she in danger, too?"

"Not as long as she stays out of it," Katherine said, looking off in the direction of town with such an anguished expression that Silas began praying loudly for the safe return of both his Minnie and Jason.

When Pete, Jack—and the new hand, Robert Bryant—noticed Katherine had returned, they came bounding out of the barn to see what they could do to help. As soon as they learned that Jason had gone into town, by himself, to face whatever trouble he was in, they all wanted to mount up and go in after him. Katherine talked them out of it. Jason had said he wanted to handle this alone, and she would respect that decision. She ordered all the hands back to work, promising to keep them informed the moment she heard anything. And later, when Rede learned of the trouble, on his return from mending the north fence-line, he, too, wanted to ride in and help Jason. It had taken even more persuasion on Katherine's part to keep him at the ranch.

Katherine expected it to be hours before she heard anything from either Jason or Minnie, but it was only forty-five minutes later that a disgruntled Minnie came riding back into the yard. Katherine was outside in an instant, wanting to know what had happened to bring her back so soon and in such a state of distress.

"Mister Jason passed me on the road and ordered me to come back home," she said, her lips pursed in anger and her eyes dark with fear. "He's going into town to face that man alone. I thought I'd just follow behind anyway, but when he realized what I was up to, he turned back around and swore he'd fire me on the spot if I didn't turn this here buggy around right that minute. I still considered followin' him, but then, he also threatened to fire Silas and Mose, too. In all my days, I never saw him get so angry about me disobeyin' one of his orders. What could I do?"

"You did the right thing," Katherine assured her.

Minnie climbed down from the buggy and let Silas take it on to the carriage house while she stood watch beside Katherine.

"What we goin' to do about the party? Mister Jason's friends should be arrivin' in less than an hour."

"Not much we can do. We'll serve the cake and punch, and try to explain that the surprise was on us—that Jason will not be home for his own party."

"That's true enough, I reckon. This sure is goin' to be a long evenin' to bear."

As Minnie had predicted, the first guests arrived sharply at seven, in a large group that had waited on the road, out of sight, until the appointed time. Although they had been disappointed to discover that Jason wasn't there, it didn't seem to put a damper on anyone's spirits, and Katherine did her best to hide her inner turmoil as she discharged her duties as hostess.

When it got to be nine o'clock, and there was still no sign of Jason, many of the guests began taking their leave. By the time Jason rode in at nine-twenty, there were only a few well-wishers left to greet him.

Katherine had never been so happy to see anyone in all her life when Jason entered the parlor, his brow lifted in question. She flew to him, wrapping her arms about him, hugging him tight. Grateful for his safe return, she closed her eyes and bit down on her lower lip to keep from crying.

"What's going on here?" he asked, holding on to her and looking around the room. The answer was immediately obvious as the few remaining guests rushed to his side to wish him a happy birthday.

"Too bad you missed your own party," Craig Monk put in with a hearty laugh. "You'd have certainly enjoyed it. Next time you go rushing off into town, you should let your wife know more about it so she can tell you if there's something more important going on at home. Can't say it looks too good for the birthday boy not to be at his own party."

"I hope someone thought to save me some cake," Jason said, quickly smiling to hide his inner turmoil. His eyes went to Katherine, relaying a silent message that they would talk just as soon as everyone had left.

"No cake that I know of," Craig replied, with a shake of his head. "I think Eric Ewan got the last piece just a few minutes ago. There might be some punch left, but you'll have to hurry to get any. I'd join you in a birthday toast, but we were just about to leave. Tommy and I have to bundle the wheat we cut today and get it up in the loft before it rains."

Although it was only a few minutes later that the last of the guests made their way out the door, it seemed like an eternity to Katherine. She had to know if the danger was over or just about to begin.

"Tell me what happened in town," she said breathlessly, just as soon as the door had closed.

"Nothing."

"Nothing?" she repeated incredulously. "Jason, something had to happen. What did you do?" Her eyes searched his face.

"Nothing. Didn't have to. Jim Haught had already done it for me."

"Jim Haught?" she asked, then remembered that

someone at the saloon had forced a kiss on his wife earlier that day.

"Seems Patrick Walls got a little fresh with Jim's wife early this morning," Jason explained. "Jim got wind of it and came into town looking for the fellow who did it."

"Patrick?" she asked, taken aback.

"Yes. Seems Jim's good friend, Micah Taylor, was in the saloon when Patrick pulled Jeanne inside and started to force himself on her. Though Zeb says it never got any further than a kiss, because the sheriff was there almost instantly to rescue her, Micah rode right out to find Jim and tell him what had happened. Jim was furious and rushed into town to right the wrong done his wife, even if it meant taking on that whole gang. But as luck would have it, Patrick had left the saloon and was crossing the street all alone when Jim and Micah rode up, and Jim was able to take him on without any interference from the others. Zeb says it all happened shortly after you had been in to talk with him at the restaurant. You barely missed seeing it for yourself. In fact, Zeb was still eating when he heard all the ruckus."

"Did anyone get killed?" Katherine asked, and prayed that if anyone had, it was Patrick.

"No, Patrick Walls is now lying unconscious in Doc Edison's office, and the doc doesn't know yet if the man's going to live or not. Seems Jim pounced on him like a madman and damn near beat him to death. It took four men to pull him off."

"Oh, no!" Katherine said, sickened by the thought of what it must have been like. "Did they arrest Jim?"

"Mostly for his own protection. Patrick's buddies didn't take too kindly to what Jim had done, and there were some pretty bad threats made against Jim's life. Zeb and Sheriff Ragland were afraid the men just might try to carry out some of those threats, so they put Jim in jail where they could protect him better. As far as the charges go, there are two witnesses willing to say Jim was provoked into fighting, though I suspect it was Jim that did most of the provoking. In any case, Patrick's friends can't dispute it since they were still in the saloon when the fight started."

"Was Flint one of those men?"

"No, Zeb's pretty sure of that," he said and pulled her close. He felt such a strong urge to protect her from any further hurt. His heart ached at the fear he saw in her dark eyes.

"I wonder if Patrick was able to get a wire off to Flint before Jim got to him." Grateful for Jason's strength, Katherine pressed her cheek against his chest and closed her eyes.

"No. I don't think he really had time to, but I looked into that, anyway. The only wire sent to Dodge City this afternoon was from Zeb, when he checked up on Patrick Wall's reputation and the rest of the men."

"Then Flint can't know."

"Not yet, anyway. But I have to warn you that when word about Patrick reaches Flint, he might decide to come down here and find out for himself just what happened to his friend. Outlaws can be a loyal bunch. For the next few weeks, I think it would be best if you stayed away from town entirely."

Katherine had already reached the same conclusion.

"Will Zeb let you know if he does show up?"

"He said he would ride out himself, if necessary."

"Then about all we can do is sit and wait," Katherine said, her expression grim as she drew away just enough to look up into his eyes.

"There's not much else we can do. Just sit, and wait."

Chapter Fifteen

The hot, dry days of August slowly cooled into September, and to Katherine's growing frustration, Zeb Fielden was not able to ascertain Flint Mason's whereabouts. Still, she was glad to know that Flint had not, as yet, shown up in Daingerfield to check on the incident concerning Patrick Walls.

Patrick had lain unconscious in Doc Edison's office for almost two weeks before he had finally shown any real signs of improvement. But after he did come to and could eat a decent meal and take his medicine on a regular schedule, he got his strength back very rapidly and was able to ride out of town by the fifth day of September—before either Zeb or Jason was able to get permission from the doctor to see him.

They had both wanted to ask him a few questions about Flint. Jason was never able to find out if Patrick's memory of having seen Katherine might have been erased by the traumatic events that followed. He hoped that might be so.

Patrick had left town in a hurry, but had sworn to the

doctor he would be back for vengeance. Though he left of his own accord, and even before the doctor felt that he should, he vowed to return one day soon in order to pay his "last respects" to Big Jim Haught—the man who had attacked him so violently and had permanently scarred his face.

Because of the threat, Jim Haught was not released from jail until five days after Patrick and his friends had left town, and only after a report had been verified that the entire group had been seen in the small town of Tishomingo, well into the vast Indian Territory that began seventy-five miles to the north. It was surmised that the group was probably on its way further north, to Tulsey Town, or west, to Fort Sill. Either way, it appeared they were headed back to Kansas.

At the suggestion of Sheriff Ragland, Jim had lain low after his release, sticking mostly to his farm several miles outside of town. At his wife's insistence, he was taking no risks. There was always the chance that the men would decide to backtrack and pay him a surprise visit. Because of that, he continued to be alert for any sign of trouble on his place for weeks. But when the end of September drew near, and there was no sign of trouble, Jim came to the conclusion that the threats had been empty ones, made by a man who had no intention of carrying them out.

But Katherine was not as easily convinced and she continued to avoid going into town for any reason. She intended to stay away until there was a confirmed report concerning Flint's whereabouts. She knew there was still a good chance that Patrick would find Flint and tell him about having seen her on the streets of Daingerfield, and she didn't want to be around should

Flint come riding in looking for her.

On the morning following Jason's birthday, she sent Mose into town to pick up Jason's saddle, with apologies to Mr. Mars, and the following week, she sent Minnie to pick out a couple of ready-made fall dresses. Though the dresses did not fit as well as they would have had she been able to go into town herself, Minnie was able to make the necessary alterations. Even so, there seemed to be little need for new dresses since Katherine continued to stay at home and out of sight.

For the first few weeks, her nerves were raw, and she was unable to sleep or eat properly. Then, slowly, she learned to cope with the situation, and found some solace in long, hard work. But the thought of what might happen if Flint did find out that Patrick had seen her was never very far from her mind. Try as she might to push the thoughts away, they continued to haunt her dreams and intruded on many of her waking hours.

Jason continued to try to reassure her, especially after so much time had elapsed. He tried to explain that if Patrick was indeed able to remember having seen her and had informed Flint of her whereabouts, Flint would have been there by this time. Even so, Katherine noticed that Jason had started to carry his handgun, along with his rifle, everywhere he went—especially if his destination was town. Though he might not actually strap the handgun on, he always had it within reach, either on the floor of the buckboard or looped around his saddle horn.

By October, when there was still no word of Flint, Jason began to wonder if he might not have already met his fate in some desolate place where his body would not be discovered. He became more hopeful when it was reported, again and again, that Patrick Walls had been spotted throughout southern Kansas, but never with Flint. The possibility of his being dead was a good one, and Jason was starting to seriously consider going to Kansas to see what he could find out, when one day, Zeb Fielden showed up at his door, hat in hand, eyes wide with uncertainty.

"Got a minute?" Zeb asked as he slapped his hat back on his head and breathed a sigh of relief, very glad it was Jason who had answered the door and not his wife.

"Sure, what's up?" Noticing that Zeb kept glancing nervously into the house, Jason quickly stepped outside and pulled the door closed behind him. Katherine had just gone upstairs to tuck Jeffrey in for his nap, but could return at any moment—and Jason could tell that whatever Zeb had to say, he wanted to say it in private.

"I got a telegram today from Fort Sill. Seems Patrick Walls and seven other men are headed back south. Though the telegram did name four of the other seven men, three were left unidentified, and, remembering how you said this Flint Mason was a good friend of this Wall fellow, it just could be that one of those men is Flint. I thought I better come out here and warn you right away."

"I appreciate it. How long since they were seen at Fort Sill?" Jason's eyes narrowed as he considered the many ramifications Patrick's return could have, especially if Flint was riding with him.

"They left there this morning, and even though they have traveled by horse thus far, there's always a chance they could board a train and be down here as early as tomorrow morning. Even if they continue on horseback, they could still be here by the end of the week, if they rode hard. We've already warned Jim Haught, and asked him and his family to move into the Morris House Hotel temporarily, so we can keep an eye on him. That way, if they are headed for Daingerfield—and that's exactly where I think they are headed—we should be able to keep Jim from getting himself killed."

"I realize you'll be needed in town once they do show up, so I don't expect you to come riding out here to let us know if Flint really is one of the group; but if you could send out a rider, I'd gladly pay the expense. Even if Flint's not among them, I want to know it as soon as you do."

Zeb looked his friend in the eye for a moment, then took a long, deep breath. "Look, I know it's not really any of my business why you want to know where this Flint guy is, and what he's been up to, but if there's any danger to you or your wife, it might help me cope with the situation better if I knew about it."

"I'm sorry, Zeb, but it's something I just can't talk about. Not even with you."

"Can you at least tell me if you or your wife would be in any danger should he show up here?"

Jason considered the request a legitimate one and answered truthfully, "Yes, if Flint should show up in this area, and if he was to learn that Katherine was here, there would be danger to both of us."

Zeb nodded as he thought about the reasons behind that. Either Katherine was this man's sister, or some other close relative, who had run off against his or the family's wishes—or Mason loved her, as any man would love so beautiful a woman, and she had scorned him in some way. Wondering which theory was right,

Zeb had no way of knowing it was actually a combination of the two.

"I gather he doesn't know where she is," he finally said, though he did not expect a response. "Maybe we can keep it that way."

"I sure hope so," Jason said earnestly, his jaw rigid with the emotions he was trying to control. "I love her more than I ever dreamed possible. I couldn't bear it if anything was to happen to her or my son."

"We'll just have to make sure nothing does," Zeb said with conviction, now aware that the boy could be in danger, too. To ease the tension, he forced a lighter tone into his voice, pushed his hat back, and chuckled. "With the two of us protecting them, what chance has this Flint guy got, anyway?"

"Not a chance in hell," Jason responded with a grateful smile. He relaxed a little and slapped Zeb on the back in a show of friendship. "Not a snowball's chance in hell."

Two weeks passed, and to everyone's bafflement, there was no sign of Patrick Walls nor any of the men that had been seen with him back in August. Big Jim got restless at having to stay in town, and with the fall harvest coming up, he refused to remain at the hotel any longer. They could not afford to lose the income the harvest would bring. Though he ordered his wife, Jeanne, and their two children to stay on in town, he returned to his house, several miles west of town, and resumed caring for his farm alone.

Zeb and Sheriff Ragland alternated making trips twice daily out to Jim's house to check on him, but one morning Zeb arrived too late. He had noticed smoke even before he was fully out of town, and had forced his horse into a dead run. He thought he heard distant gunshots over the thundering beat of his horse's hooves, yet couldn't be sure. By the time he finally topped the hill in front of Jim's house, the damage had been done.

Although the house still stood exactly as always, the barn was a smoldering pile of blackened rubble. Zeb paused on the hilltop, rifle drawn, and watched for any sign of life. Other than the slight bending of the tall pines in the cool autumn wind, Zeb could see no movement at all from his vantage point. But not willing to risk riding into an ambush, he rode on to the next ranch to round up several volunteers. He made sure every hand was properly armed before returning to Jim's place to investigate.

As he had feared, the fire had been set to force Jim into the open, and he discovered him lying on the ground just behind his house, shot through the stomach and the right thigh, up high near his hip. Though such wounds would have killed a lesser man, Jim was still alive—but barely. He had managed to drag himself several yards toward the house before he had fallen unconscious. There was a wide trail of blood leading away from where his rifle lay in the reddish-brown dirt, and a small pool of his blood had formed in the place where he had collapsed. Zeb immediately dispatched a rider to send the doctor out and inform the sheriff.

Meanwhile, the other men helped get Jim back inside the house—not an easy task considering Jim's size—and Zeb, in search of clues, walked over to the charred, smoking mass that had been Jim's barn. As he studied the ground, he noticed several sets of horse prints coming in from the north and circling the barn, then leading away, off to the northwest. And, as he came closer to where the oversized barn door had once stood, Zeb noticed a large dark blotch in the dirt, in the middle of an indentation that was roughly the size of a man. He realized it was more blood. Someone had been shot and fallen to the ground, but who? Several sets of boot prints told him it had taken at least three men to get the injured man back on his horse.

Evidently, Jim had managed to get off one good shot before he had been gunned down. Eager for more details, Zeb hurried inside to see if Jim could be roused enough to give him any details. While he was inside, he heard riders enter the yard and his first thought was that Patrick Walls and his friends had returned.

Drawing his pistol, and motioning for the others to do the same, Zeb eased up to the nearest window and peered through the lace curtains. He was vastly relieved to see Jason, Pete, Jack, Robert, and Rede climbing down from their horses.

"Zeb? Where are you?" Jason called out, having already recognized the roan horse and the black leather saddle.

"In here," Zeb shouted back as he headed for the front door.

"Where's Jim?"

"He's in here, too. He's been shot. It's bad. I've just sent a man into town to get the doc and the sheriff."

"Saw the smoke all the way from Seven Oaks and knew something had happened," Jason explained as he entered the house. Nodding in the direction of the blackened rubble outside, he asked, "Patrick?"

"That's my guess. I haven't been able to get much out of Jim as yet. I do know one of them is injured."

"Are you going after them?"

"Not alone. I saw at least six, maybe eight, sets of tracks out there, and my guess is there were others that held back and acted as lookouts. That's a few too many for me to take on by myself. But as soon as the sheriff gets here with whatever posse he can round up, we'll take out after them."

"I'm riding along," Jason said. It was a statement, not a request.

Within an hour, Doc Edison, Sheriff Ragland, and eleven other men rode up into the dooryard. All were ready and eager to run down the men who had tried to murder Big Jim. After a quick assignment of duties, the men took off in two separate groups, the sheriff in charge of one and Zeb in charge of the other. Jason chose to ride with Zeb's group, even though they were not the ones who would follow the tracks leading away from the barn. Instead, Zeb's group headed due west for Boggy Creek and followed it north, knowing that many an outlaw had headed into that wet marshland to hide his trail, and it would be the most likely place this band of outlaws would go.

It was just after the sun had settled behind the treetops that Zeb finally decided to turn back. They hadn't come across a single sign of a horse having traveled through that area in the past forty-eight hours, and only hoped that the sheriff had had better luck. It was not until they were almost back to Jim's house, that Jason spotted a gray curl of smoke, just a shade lighter than the slowly darkening sky. Any later, and the smoke might have gone unnoticed.

"Looks like it's coming from the old Turner place," Zeb observed when Jason pointed it out to him.

"That place has been abandoned for over a year now," Jason said. Everyone knew that after Elizabeth Turner's husband had died of the fever, she had gone back east, never bothering to sell her house or even rent it out. The house had stood empty, the grounds rapidly deteriorating ever since.

"And one of us should have thought of it. It's the perfect place to hide out. They could have rounded on the creek side and followed that little rivulet that runs right up behind the house and we'd never have seen the tracks."

"Apparently, that's what they did. What do we do now? Should the nine of us go ahead and storm the place, or do we wait and send someone to locate the others and bring them here?"

Zeb thought about it for a moment. "Even if it is Patrick Walls and his gang, I doubt that they plan to go anywhere until daylight. We'll head on over and keep a watch on the place while Cody rides out to see if he can find the sheriff."

Without further delay, Cody Sutter was off in the direction they felt the sheriff would most likely be, and the rest of them rode slowly and carefully in the opposite direction, toward the Turner place.

Although they had fully expected to run into a lookout of some sort, and had kept a close watch out for one, they managed to get within sight of the house without being discovered. From their vantage point on top of a small rise to the southeast of the house, they could see a faint, flickering light in one of the back rooms—the same room from whose chimney the curling wisp of smoke came. It seemed that Patrick and his men had limited themselves to just a small fire to ward off the chill of approaching night.

Though there were no horses in sight, Jason and Zeb both were aware that any number of animals could be housed in the large barn on the far side of the house—or might have been taken right into the house itself. The men wished they knew exactly where the horses were so they could make their plans accordingly. Eventually, they heard a whinny from the barn and were relieved to know that if they did decide to storm the house, the outlaws would not be able to ride off without having to make a run for it out in the open.

It was just before midnight when the sheriff and his small band of men arrived to take over, and, being a man who had never been known for his patience, he decided to sneak up on the house and take them by surprise. But the surprise was on them, for when they burst through the front and back doors at precisely the same time, they found only one man inside. The wounded man had been left behind to fend for himself and lay bandaged in torn, dirty linen, beside a dwindling fire, very near death.

With extreme caution, Jason and Zeb entered the room together, with pistols drawn. There was a rifle beside the man, within easy reach.

"Easy does it," the sheriff said, right on their heels.

The three recognized the man at the exact same moment. Patrick Walls.

Jason's first thought was that it was mighty strange

for the man's supposedly loyal gang, who had ridden all this way to help avenge a wrong done him, to have so quickly deserted him—left him to die all alone. A prickle of apprehension traveled up his spine. He had a horrible feeling they had been set up. Keeping his gun drawn, he turned and headed outside to see if his suspicions were true. All he was able to discover was that several horses had been housed inside the barn. Only one remained. A quick trip into the surrounding woods, with Pete and Rede at his side, brought no further discoveries, but they decided to wait in the shadows, out of sight, until they could be absolutely sure they had not been led into a trap.

As it turned out, Patrick had indeed been left behind to die, and before he did, he answered a few of the sheriff's questions, though reluctantly. Yes, he had gone to Jim's house with the intention of getting even with him and, yes, Jim had been the one to put the bullet in his chest. And although he refused to reveal the identities of those who had been with him, he had shaken his head *no* when Zeb had asked point blank if Flint Mason had been one of the gang.

"Do you have any idea where Flint is?" Zeb pressed him.

Again, Patrick had shaken his head and then tried to force a laugh, though it came out as a barely audible gasp. "Flint don't want no part . . ." But before he could finish the sentence, his body tensed with a last, sharp pain, then relaxed in death.

Jason returned just minutes afterward, upset to find that the man had died before he could ask him a few questions of his own. Questions like: Where was Flint?

Was he even alive? Would he be likely to come down here to try to find out about Patrick's death, or would the other men explain it to him as a clear case of self-defense on Jim's part? He had so many questions that Patrick Walls might have been able to answer. Never had Jason felt so frustrated. He didn't even know if Patrick had ever told Flint about having seen Katherine. He prayed that he had not, but knew he could not rely on prayer alone.

Less than a week later, Jason decided to make the trip to Kansas to see what he could find out on his own. He was in the process of packing when Zeb finally heard some solid information concerning Flint. When Zeb had wired the marshall at Dodge City to find out if there were any next of kin who might want to claim Patrick's belongings, he asked about Flint once again. It had become a habit with him. This time, the marshall wired back that Flint was in Dodge City at that very moment, and had checked into the Dodge House early in the afternoon.

Within a week, on the final Monday in October, Zeb had further news, and again approached Jason privately, catching him at the very end of the day, as he rode the northern fence-line, near the main road, in search of any breaks in the wire or split posts that needed replacing.

"What brings you out this way?" Jason asked, having spotted Zeb at about the same time Zeb had spotted him.

"I've got more news concerning Flint," he said simply. His mustache twitched as he waited for Jason to ride closer. "This time, I think it's what you've been waiting to hear."

Jason's heart thudded wildly as he pulled Brandy to a halt. "What is the news?"

"He's dead."

"How do you know?" Jason asked, incredulous.

"Got a message from the sheriff in Cimarron. Seems I've been asking so many questions about the man over the past few months, he felt I might know of any next of kin. Record shows he has a wife somewhere, a wife that would be entitled to the money they found on him and to some land it seems he owned just up the Arkansas River a ways. Record states his wife's name is Katherine and there is no record of her death or of a divorce."

Jason knew there was no point in lying to Zeb and decided to tell him the truth. "You've got it figured right. Katherine is Flint's wife."

Zeb showed no sign of surprise nor did he display his feelings on the matter in any way whatever. "You mean Katherine *was* Flint's wife," he pointed out. He paused only a moment before asking, "What do I tell the sheriff in Cimarron? Will Katherine be wanting to lay claim to the money and the land? I don't really know how much land is involved, but they found quite a considerable sum of money on him, and there were two expensive rings—one a man's and one a woman's."

"That will be for Katherine to decide, though I doubt she'll want any of it," Jason said. "Meet me at the house and we'll tell her the news together, and you can ask her then what she wants to do about the money and the land."

Minutes later, they arrived at the house, though

from different directions, and walked through the back door together in search of Katherine. When they found her in the living room frowning over a basket of mending, Jason closed the door and let Zeb tell her everything he had told him earlier.

"How was he killed?" she asked, her voice drained of all emotion. She set her darning aside and stared up at them both with unnaturally large eyes.

"Sheriff said he was shot just outside of Cimarron. Must have been a gunfight because there was another man's body lying nearby." He decided to spare her the details—that Flint had been shot in the back and then again, in the face. To Zeb, it sounded more like an ambush, but if it had been ambush, why hadn't the money been taken. With no answer for that one, he decided to keep his opinions to himself.

It seemed appropriate to Katherine that Flint had been killed in a gunfight, but still—though she never would have believed it—she felt a strange tug at her heart when she stopped to consider the tragic circumstances of his death. It bothered her that she should care at all. Why should she grieve for what had never been?

"Ma'am," Zeb went on to say. "The sheriff told me Flint Mason had a wife, a wife named Katherine, who is entitled to claim the money that was on him at the time, his jewelry, and some land he owned there in Kansas."

Katherine felt her stomach knot as his words sank in—a wife named Katherine. Her eyes widened as she realized that she had been found out.

"Don't get me wrong. I'm not here to judge you. I

just want to know what to tell the sheriff in Cimarron," Zeb said, then smiled reassuringly.

Katherine looked to Jason, who then knelt at her feet and spoke softly. "If you feel the money and the land should be Jeffrey's, I'll understand."

"No, I don't want the land or the money. Give it to some charity," she said firmly. "But I would like for the jewelry to be sent here. I want to make absolutely sure that the dead man they found was Flint. It's always possible that someone else's body could have been mistaken for his, but there would be no way I could mistake his jewelry—especially not the fancy emerald ring he always wore on his left hand."

"Then I'll have them both sent right away," Zeb assured her. "I'll send word the moment they arrive."

As Jason walked Zeb out to his horse, the full effect of what she had just learned hit Katherine squarely. And, to her utter confusion—for she had no love left for the man—tears welled up in her eyes and streamed down her cheeks. Rising quickly, she turned and fled upstairs. In order not to awaken Jeffrey, she did not go into her own room, but ran in the opposite direction, into one of the guest rooms.

Still unable to discern why, she wept bitterly. Never had she struggled so to understand her own feelings. Though she could not help but feel an odd sense of remorse, an undeniable sadness, she also felt relieved—greatly relieved. The many emotions that clashed inside her were so complex, so completely opposed to one another that they drained her and left her too weak to stand.

Hours passed before Katherine emerged from the darkened room, the strange sadness finally purged from her heart. As she stepped out into the lighted hallway, a smile brightened her face, for she was fully aware that at last, at very long last, she and Jason could make their marriage a legal one. But better than that, she knew she would no longer have to live in fear that Flint would someday track her down.

She was free at last.

Chapter Sixteen

"Jason, what are you doing sitting out here in the cold without your coat?" Katherine came up to where he was sitting in the garden. When she had not been able to find him anywhere in the house, she had grabbed her shawl and headed out the door, almost certain she would find him either out at the barn or sitting alone in the garden.

Jason looked up in surprise. He'd been so deep in thought that he had not heard her soft footsteps on the cobblestone walkway. "I—I guess I hadn't noticed how cold it was starting to get," he said, gesturing for her to take a seat alongside him. "It wasn't this cold when I first came out."

"How long ago was that?" she asked, wondering why his handsome face wore such a forlorn expression. She had expected to find him happy over the prospect of finally being able to make their marriage legal.

"Since right after Zeb left. I went back inside to find you and discovered that you had taken to the guest room and had closed the door behind you."

"But why didn't you come in?" As she spoke, she lifted his arm and tucked herself beneath it. Snuggling close, she looked up at his strong face and knew something was wrong. Something was very wrong. She had a feeling it had to do with Flint's death.

"I didn't want to intrude on your privacy. I figured you needed to be alone after having learned such traumatic news, otherwise you wouldn't have gone off like that and shut yourself up in one of the guest rooms." He brought his other arm around to hold her close.

"Thank you for that. I did need to be alone for a while. I needed to sort through my feelings and get myself back on an even keel."

"What sort of feelings did you have to sort through?" he asked, hesitantly.

He looked down at her with such loving tenderness, such unmistakable devotion, that it warmed her heart and made her forget the chill of the evening. She smiled contentedly, nestled in the arms of the man she loved.

"I had to sort through a combination of different feelings," she answered honestly. "Relief. Regret. Maybe even a little pity. I discovered that after I'd finally learned he was dead, shot to death in much the same manner he'd killed so many, I felt a strange sort of gratification—for it seemed appropriate to me that he should die in a gunfight. At the same time though, I felt deeply sorry for him—that he couldn't have been the man he had pretended to be around me for so many years. But most of what I felt initially was relief—and I felt so guilty for that."

She paused and thought for a moment, then leaned away just enough to look into his eyes. There was just enough moonlight to allow her to see how very concerned and how deeply worried he still was. Worried about her? Her heart ached with the need to reassure him. "But in the end, after I'd sorted through all the other emotions that had clouded my heart, I found I was left with only my joy—because at last, at very long last, you and I can be married. We can truly be husband and wife. All I want to know now, is when?"

Jason studied her face a long moment. Eventually a relieved smile spread across his face and his tense features softened. He sighed as he pulled her closer and pressed his warm lips to her temple. "Whenever you say, Katherine. Whenever you say. Yesterday will not be soon enough for me."

"But you have the final cutting of the hay to see to, and then there's the fall branding next week," she reminded him.

"The calves won't mind if I forego the fall branding, and my men can see to the final cutting and binding of the hay," he pointed out quickly.

"No, Jason, we've waited this long, another two weeks won't hurt anything," she tried to explain, remembering how just yesterday the subject of fall branding had seemed very important to everyone. "Go ahead and get all your work done and out of the way. I don't want anything distracting you while we're away."

"Away?" Jason asked, then realized that, of course, they would have to go someplace where nobody knew them. It would certainly raise many a righteous eyebrow if they went to the local justice of the peace and asked to be married, when they were supposed to already have been man and wife for almost six years now. "Where do you want to go?"

"I was thinking maybe Shreveport. It's far enough away to be able to get married without anyone around here knowing, and yet close enough that it won't take forever to get there. Besides, there's a lot of things for us to see and do while we stay there on our honeymoon."

"Honeymoon?" he said, and he grinned devilishly, his dimples deepening with his own wicked thoughts. "I can already think of plenty for us to do to keep ourselves busy during our honeymoon, and we don't have to leave our hotel room even once to do them."

Katherine laughed lightly and snuggled back under his arm. She pressed her cheek against his chest and wondered how he could radiate such warmth when it was so cold outside. She decided it was because he had such a big and generous heart. "What about nourishment?" she asked. "We'll have to venture out of our room at some point to find sustenance. We'll need something to keep up our strength."

"I can have something sent up to the room," he quickly reminded her. "If we play our cards right, we won't have to leave our room for weeks."

"Weeks?"

"Of course, weeks. I've decided we're going to do this up right. We're going to take at least two weeks for our honeymoon, though we'll have to tell everyone it's a business trip. They might not quite understand a honeymoon after nearly six years of marriage. And we'd better go ahead and get our plans underway, because I'll want to leave just as soon as possible."

"Plans?"

"Yes. First of all, I want you to go into town and order yourself a really beautiful dress to be married in. I don't care how much it costs. And while you're there, find yourself a very alluring nightgown for our wedding night." His eyes sparkled at that last thought. "In fact, buy a new nightgown for every night of our honeymoon."

"I think that would be a little extravagant," she pointed out, suppressing a smile.

"Okay, buy however many you think you'll need, but keep in mind that a few of them might get torn by a very impatient husband, which usually renders them useless if you want to wear them again."

"I'll try to buy some without too many ties," she assured him with a laugh, remembering how frustrated he became whenever there were a lot of ties or stubborn buttons involved. "But keep in mind that if I special order a fancy new dress, it'll take at least a week to have it made—maybe more."

Jason frowned a moment, then finally consented, "Okay. I guess I'll have to be patient, though I don't really want to. You order the fanciest dress ever made and the most seductive nightgown ever dreamed of, and I'll go ahead and oversee the fall branding and the final cutting of hay. That'll give me plenty of time to get everything squared away around here and see to it that we get the best rooms held in advance for us at the Emerald Hotel." He thought a moment about what date they should plan to leave, then finally decided. "We can probably leave here in about two weeks—let's plan for Friday, November second."

"I'm glad you've decided to be levelheaded about this—to take enough time to see that it's done right, and I do so want this to be just right. Even a small wedding like ours will take a little time and a little planning."

"And more than a little practice," he murmured, bending forward to nuzzle her soft brown hair and nibble the edge of her earlobe.

"Practice?" she asked, drawing back, pretending confusion.

"Yes, if you want to get something right, you must be willing to practice it," he replied. Jason's voice was solemn, but his eyes twinkled with mischief.

"You want to practice exchanging our wedding vows?" she asked, with a straight face.

"Not especially. I was thinking more along the lines of our wedding night."

"If you ask me, you don't need any practice in that area whatever. You've already got that down just right," she assured him, clasping his neck to draw his lips down to hers. "Take my word for it. That's one art you've already mastered."

"Think so?" he asked, smiling mischievously. His mouth closed on hers in an extremely demanding kiss. He had every intention of proving just how right she was. "Do you really think so?" he asked again, his words muffled by continuous kisses.

"Umm-hmm," she replied, overcome by the warm, tingling sensations that Jason always aroused in her.

When he finally released her, she was lost in a pleasurable dreamy fog.

"Is Jeffrey in bed?" he asked, his soft voice tense with desire.

"Yes, he's been in bed for hours," she assured him, with a coy wink and an enchanting smile, for she had already guessed what his next words would be.

"Then shouldn't we be in bed, too?"

"Before we've had our dinner?" she asked, then leaned forward to nibble playfully at his lower lip.

"Dinner's already ruined," Jason announced in a low growl. "Minnie told me so hours ago, and I told her to go on to her cabin, that we'd make do with something ourselves."

"Oh, then maybe I'd better get in there and cook you something," she suggested sweetly. The warmth of her breath fell gently across his mouth as she ran the tip of her tongue lightly over the sensitive inner edge of his lower lip. She felt a wonderful satisfaction in the shuddering reaction it caused.

"You've already got something cooking," he assured her. "Out here."

"Then, by all means, let's go on to bed," she said, and was not at all surprised when he swept her up into his arms and quickly carried her inside.

"What's your hurry?" she teased, as he bounded up the stairs, taking them two at a time. "Afraid you're going to drop me if you don't hurry? Getting weak in your old age?"

Jason simply growled and narrowed his passion-filled eyes. Deciding that the beast needed soothing, Katherine reached up and kissed him gently on the corner of his mouth. She was rewarded with another, throatier growl that sent delicious shivers of anticipation racing through her.

When they reached their bedroom, Katherine took one arm from his neck to reach down and open the door. But before she could turn the knob, he had swiftly kicked the door open.

"My, my. The man grows impatient. You really could have waited for me to open it," she admonished. Her eyes were bright with loving mischief as he pushed the door closed with his back. The room was cloaked in semidarkness, lit only by the soft glow of a small oil lamp near the door.

"No I couldn't have waited for you to open the door," he said, his hungry eyes devouring her beautiful body. Dumping her unceremoniously on the bed, he crawled on top of her. Quickly, he straddled her hips and placed his strong hands on her shoulders. His lips hovered just inches above hers.

Katherine's pulse quickened as she waited for his next move, for she knew from experience that whatever it was, it would be exquisite. But when all Jason did was stare down at her for a long, endless moment, she grew impatient and reached up to kiss him. That was enough to break whatever spell had come over him. Once again, he growled, as if in deep pain, and pressed himself down against the length of her body, enfolding her in his arms. To her delight, he returned her teasing kiss tenfold.

A moment later, their clothing was off and their naked bodies were entwined. Passions soaring, they lost themselves in another hungry kiss. Jason and

Katherine's lovemaking had always been extremely pleasurable, but knowing they would finally be able to make their marriage legal—that the threat of her dark past would no longer be lingering over them—this night was special. Because of what they had learned tonight, they would not only be man and wife in their hearts, but in the eyes of the law as well.

Katherine tingled just to think of it, as Jasŏn's hard, strongly muscled frame pressed intimately against her and his mouth worked its usual magic. His need for her was urgent and his breath came in ragged gasps.

While Katherine's sensitive fingers roamed over the wide rippling muscles along his back and hips, Jason's hand came forward to caress one of her straining breasts. Tenderly, he stroked and caressed, lightly teasing the rosebud tip until Katherine gasped with the pleasure he brought her.

After a moment, his mouth gave up its loving assault on her lips, and began to trail little kisses downward, until it closed on the tiny peak that his fingertips had just made so rigid. Deftly, his tongue teased the sensitive tip with short, tantalizing strokes until her head tossed wildly on the pillow and her body arched higher and higher. She cried out his name, and his lips moved to her other breast.

Such sweet, sweet ecstasy. Katherine was not sure how much more of the delicious torment she could bear nor was she able to coax him to stop long enough to bring her the relief she sought. She pulled gently at his shoulders, but his mouth continued its sensual onslaught. Her body shook with a blazing desire that mounted within her, until she thought she would burst.

A delicious ache, somewhere low inside her, suddenly reached an unbearable intensity, and her body cried out in immediate release from the sensual anguish.

"Now, Jason. Love me now," she moaned, barely aware that she had spoken at all.

Drawing deeply, one last time, on first one breast, and then the other, he finally moved to fulfill her. With long, lithe movements, he brought their wildest longings, their deepest needs to the ultimate climax. When release came at last for Katherine, it was so wondrous, so earthshaking, she cried aloud with pleasure. Seconds later, Jason shuddered and groaned with the same intensity.

Sated at last, a wonderfully pleasant languor stole over them, and they settled back into the rumpled bed, their love aglow, their happiness once again complete.

Neither spoke. Neither wanted to break the sensual calm that always followed passion's violent storm. Snuggling happily against him, Katherine's heart overflowed with joy and glorious contentment. Smiling to herself, she realized that only Jason could bring her such unparalleled happiness.

No one else.

At Jason's continued insistence, and despite her own belief that she already had several gowns lovely enough to be married in, Katherine left early the following Saturday morning to go into town and order a very special wedding dress.

With Ruby away visiting her mother, and Jason busy with the final cutting of the hay, Katherine made the trip by herself. Eager to get her business done and return home by mid-afternoon, she left Seven Oaks just after daybreak, heading first for Sutcliffe's Dress Shop.

Though physically she was all alone, she held Jason so close in her heart, it seemed more than enough company. Even the chill in the autumn air could not dispel the happiness she felt as she drove her carriage toward town. Several ideas of how she should have her dress designed ran through her mind as she drew closer to Daingerfield. Finally, she reached the main thoroughfare and found a good spot to leave her carriage, several blocks away from the dress shop.

As usual, Daingerfield was thronged with people who regularly chose Saturday to take care of their errands in town. Though the hour was early and a light morning mist still hung in the air, the sidewalks were already crowded with shoppers, food peddlers, newspaper boys, farmers, cowpokes, and local businessmen. And, on the graveled main street that divided the town in two, clattering buggies, fancy carriages, and overloaded carts fought for the right of way.

A shrill blast could be heard in the distance announcing an incoming train, and horses whinnied nervously but continued to hurry under their drivers' stern commands. People and dogs rushed to and fro, and Katherine had to stop more than once to avoid a collision.

"Good morning," she responded several times to the many familiar faces she met on her short walk to the dress shop. Being able to recognize so many friendly faces made her feel an integral part of the small town she had come to know and love—the town where Jason had grown up and gone to school—a town that had happily accepted her as Jason's wife.

Smiling pleasantly, she stepped up on the wide-planked boardwalk just in front of Sutcliffe's Dress Shop, glancing only briefly at the pretty calico dress displayed in the wide, multi-paned window.

A tinkling bell announced her entrance and she was immediately greeted by the smiling proprietor, Nancy Sutcliffe.

"And what may I do for you this morning?" Mrs. Sutcliffe asked, sweeping gracefully forward to offer Katherine her assistance. As might be expected, Mrs. Sutcliffe was fashionably attired in a simple but elegant blue twilled dress, gathered just below the bustline into narrow, Watteau pleats.

Noticing another customer already at the counter, Katherine nodded politely toward the other woman. "Go ahead and wait on Mrs. Nelms—I'm in no hurry. I want to browse through your books for a while, anyway."

"Of course. Be my guest," Mrs. Sutcliffe said, and stepped aside to let Katherine find her own way to the small sitting area in the back where pattern books and catalogs could be viewed at leisure.

Sutcliffe's Dress Shop had a reputation for catering to its customers, and Katherine was served a fresh cup of coffee and a small sugared teacake as she browsed through the first of many pattern books. She was pleased to see that so many patterns had been added since the last time she had looked for a dress. She wanted her wedding dress to be in the latest fashion.

Soon, she had her selection made and sat back in the high-backed, richly upholstered chair to await Mrs. Sutcliffe or one of her two assistants. Her eye scanned the many bolts of material that lined the far wall, mentally discarding all bright colors and anything of pure white.

By the time Mrs. Sutcliffe was free to wait on her, Katherine had her choice made—a shimmering moiré silk the color of rich cream, which would look perfect trimmed with narrow satin ribbon and delicate ecru lace inset with tiny pearls. As soon as she had her order placed, sketches were drawn to be sure they fully understood what she wanted, and before she knew it, she was on her way, content with the choices she had made in both her wedding dress and her frilly new negligee.

It was barely past twelve when she stepped inside Creel's Mercantile to finish the rest of her shopping. She had considered stopping at the Star Restaurant for a quick sandwich, but then decided she was not really hungry and quickly vetoed the idea in favor of finishing her errands. She was eager to get back home to Jason.

A faint scent of cinnamon and leather filled the large store as she hurriedly made her way down the crowded aisles, pointing out what she wanted to buy to the gangly young man who assisted her. Soon, the wire basket he carried was full and he was forced to return to the counter for another. She wanted to be sure to get everything she needed today, because she hoped to start packing for Shreveport early the following week. And before she was finished, the young man had filled three heaping baskets.

"Will that be all?" William Creel asked, preparing to tally her bill. His hazel eyes sparkled at such a large purchase.

"As far as I know, that is it," she replied, taking a last look around to be sure she wasn't forgetting something.

"Tony," Mr. Creel said to the gangly young man, "you've done a good job helping Mrs. Morris so far. Now, will you please see that all these things get safely to her carriage? Get Andy to help you." He double-checked the total and had her sign the bill at the bottom.

Within minutes, all the items had been either boxed or bound with paper and string, then carefully loaded into the arms of the two waiting boys.

"Which way, ma'am?" Tony asked when they had stepped outside onto the boardwalk. As he paused for her answer, Andy bumped into him, and both loads almost went flying.

"It's the black and red Stanhope in front of Chambers Chair Factory," she replied, sorry that the boys had to go so far with such heavy loads. "Go on ahead," she added, "and put them in the back. I'll be along shortly." Before letting them go, she quickly placed a penny in each boy's shirt pocket to be sure they were well rewarded for their services. She watched the two of them carefully make their way along the sidewalk for a moment, then quickly turned around to go to the post office just down the street.

A few moments later, she was back out on the boardwalk with the handwritten note the postmaster had given her along with their regular mail. It was from Zeb, asking that either she or Jason stop by the sheriff's office the next chance they got. With nothing else demanding her attention, she turned and headed for the sheriff's office.

"Katherine, that was quick," Zeb said, as he put aside the rifle he was cleaning and rose to greet her. "I just left a message at the post office less than an hour ago for you to stop by. I guess you already got it."

"Yes, and I'm very curious," she told him candidly.

"Flint's jewelry arrived on the train this morning." Stepping back, he pulled open the top drawer of his desk. Inside, was a small box wrapped in several layers of brown paper that Zeb had already torn open. As he lifted the lid and held the box out to her, he said, "There are two rings here. One's a man's ring, and the other is a woman's. According to the report, he was wearing the man's ring and had the woman's tucked away in his wallet."

A vague feeling of melancholy swept over her as she looked at Flint's fancy emerald ring, and there beside it, the wedding band she had been so careful to leave behind. Somehow, it bothered her to think that he had carried the tiny gold ring with him all those years.

"Do you recognize either of those rings?" Zeb wanted to know.

"Both of them," she said with a faint nod, as the significance of the rings hit her squarely. In her hands, was proof positive that Flint was dead, for he would never have parted with either ring willingly. "They both belonged to Flint."

"That makes it official then," Zeb said, stepping over

to place the lid carefully back on the box. "I'll need your signature verifying that you received these items. Then you're free to take them and go."

Katherine's eyes widened in alarm. "I don't want my name connected with Flint in any way. Keep the rings. I just wanted to be certain he was the man that was killed."

"Of course, you wouldn't want to sign for them. I'm sorry. I didn't think," Zeb said quickly. "I can sign for them if you'd like."

"No, keep them. I don't want them. I really don't." She set the box down on his desk and took a small step backward to prove it.

"I can't keep them," Zeb protested, scratching his head over the dilemma. "It wouldn't be right."

"Then give them away, or sell them and put the money to good use. I really don't want them."

Seeing that she was serious, Zeb agreed to keep them in his desk for a while. In a month or so, if she still felt the same way, he'd sell them to the local jeweler and give the money to a needy family. Katherine thought it was a good idea, realizing that would be right around Christmas, and she left the rings in Zeb's capable hands.

Still disturbed by the fact that Flint had carried her wedding ring with him all those years, Katherine slowly made her way back toward her carriage, barely aware of the polite nods and friendly smiles directed at her by passersby. Her thoughts were locked in the dark, cheerless realms of the past.

It was not until someone actually bumped into her that her thoughts resurfaced to what was going on around her. When she looked up to apologize, her heart suddenly froze. Somehow, through all her sad musings, she had called the demon himself back to life!

Frantically, she tried to blink the vision away, but she couldn't. Standing there before her—staring down at her with a rage so intense it made her knees buckle—was none other than Flint Mason, who, to her dismay and utter shock, was very much alive.

Chapter Seventeen

"You are supposed to be dead," Katherine gasped, when she was able to find her voice. She trembled from head to foot, and the blood had drained from her face, leaving her weak and pale, as if she were truly staring at a ghost.

"I assure you, Kat, I am very much alive," Flint said. His green eyes bored into her with such intense anger, she put her hand protectively to her throat and took a step back. "And after six years of searching for you, I've finally found you." He put out his hand to touch her face, but she took another step back out of his reach.

"Flint, no," she stammered, continuing to slowly back away. Frantically, she looked around for a means of escape. But there was no place to run, no place to hide. The horrible thought that any attempt to flee might provoke him into openly revealing her secret—telling the whole world around her that he was her real husband—held her to the spot. Her next words came out in a voice so small and strained, she wasn't sure he could hear her. "Flint, we need to talk."

"So talk," he said tersely, with a jerk of his head that caused his jet black hair to fall forward and sweep sideways across his forehead. Never taking his eyes from her, he folded his arms defiantly across his starched black shirt, and waited for her to either speak again or make a run for it.

"Not here," she replied in a strident whisper, then turned to nod politely at someone who had just greeted her in passing. If they stayed there much longer, someone was bound to become curious about the tall, arrogantly handsome stranger she had stopped to talk to.

"Where?" he asked in an obligingly low voice, though he refused to actually whisper, for he felt he had nothing to hide. It angered him to realize that she, on the other hand, did have something to hide, and it was obvious that it had something to do with him.

"I don't know, just not here. Not where everyone can hear us." Her eyes pleaded with him not to make a scene.

"Then I'll follow you out of town," he said matter-of-factly, though his eyes continued to bore fiercely into hers, warning her not to try anything foolish. "We can talk once we're all alone."

"No!" she responded instinctively, but then, when she realized it was the only way, she took a long, steadying breath and finally agreed. "Okay, follow me out of town. I know a spot a few miles out where we can be alone."

"Good," he said, and a flicker of something more than anger flashed from the jade depths of his eyes.

"To talk," she quickly asserted. "Nothing more."

"We'll see," he said, and he smiled with cheeky self-assurance, for he had no intention of just talking. He'd spent six long years looking for his wife and had finally found her. He had dreamed of this moment for far too long, and was not about to let it go by with just talk—not when Katherine was even more beautiful than she had been six years ago. Though it was hard for him to believe, she was twice the beauty he had married. Her long, brown hair was combed differently—worn now in elegant curls on top of her head—but it was still just as thick and luxuriant as ever, and her eyes were every bit as fiery and full of life as he remembered, maybe even more so.

He was relieved to know he had not broken her spirit during those last few months before she ran away. And yet, there was something different about her, something he could not quite put his finger on. Maybe it had something to do with the fancy blue outfit she wore, for she had taken on a far more womanly figure, filling out the curves of her fitted jacket beautifully. But he knew the difference in her was more than her outward appearance. It was in the way she carried herself, the way she held her head—so proud, so tall, so very determined.

On the way out of town, Flint had a chance to reflect on the way his beautiful wife had looked the last time he had seen her. Though he only remembered bits and pieces of their last encounter, what he could remember had haunted him all these years. At last, he would have the chance to apologize to her, to try to make her understand, to show her that he had finally changed. Once he had explained the situation as it had been then, he was sure he would be able to convince her to give him a second chance. That's all he asked for—a second chance.

Katherine, too, had the opportunity to think back to that horrible day six years ago, to the way he had turned on her, striking her again and again until she had feared for the very life of the baby then growing inside her—her own Jeffrey's life. She shuddered, realizing that Flint could easily turn violent again, and she glanced back over her shoulder to try to determine if he had been drinking. He seemed to be sober. That was the only thing she could see to her advantage.

"Isn't this far enough?" he called out to her, impatient to speak with her, to hold her in his arms again.

"No. I want to get off the main road. I don't want anyone to see us together," she said adamantly. She had no way of knowing how deeply her words had stung him, that they'd struck him like a slap in the face. "There's a road just up ahead that leads to a small, wooded pond where we can talk in private. No one will see us there." She hoped that would also prove to be to her advantage. It was certainly a risk, for if he should turn violent again, she would want someone around to come to her aid, and there would be no one there to help her. She already knew she was no match for his strength. She tried not to think about it. "No one will be able to accidentally overhear us."

"Fine," he told her. Gritting his teeth, he fought to control the anger that was building inside him at her refusal to be seen in his company. He knew he must not let her see that side of him. He must show her he had changed.

Eventually, Katherine pulled her carriage to a halt in

a solitary patch of sunshine near a small tree-shaded pond. She shivered with more than the crisp autumn air as she realized that the hour of reckoning had arrived. Hoping he would not sense her fear, she held her shoulders back, her head erect, and turned to her seat to face him squarely. Flint admired her for her outward show of courage, for it was only the way she clutched the side of the carriage, her knuckles turning dead white, that revealed her inner turmoil.

"Katherine, you are more beautiful than ever," he said what was foremost on his mind, then quickly slung his leg over his jet black horse and slid easily to the ground. He winced only briefly at the resulting pain in his left leg.

"Don't say that," she snapped angrily. Her heart grew instantly hard with the hate she had harbored over the years. "I don't want to hear such things from you. Keep your pretty words for your saloon trollops."

"I can't help saying what's in my heart," he said as he reached for a low-hanging tree limb and quickly looped his reins around it. He tried not to flinch at her cruel words while he made his way closer to the carriage. "But if it bothers you to know that I still find you as attractive as I ever did, then I won't mention it again. Climb on down here, so we can have that talk."

"I can talk just fine from here," she said firmly. She took several deep breaths through gritted teeth and tried to decide exactly what she should say to him that would let him know how very angry she felt at that moment. Her first inclination was to simply order him straight to hell. That would be short and certainly to the point. But her fear of a violent reaction prevented her from saying anything so drastic.

"Katherine, climb down. I'm not going to hurt you," he said in a low, even voice, still struggling to control his hair-trigger temper. There were too many emotions battling inside him at that particular moment to let him put up with much more of her obstinance. "Okay, if you don't want to climb down here, I guess I'll have to climb up there with you."

Before she could voice a protest, he did just that, swinging with an agile grace onto the seat beside her.

"Get out of my carriage," she demanded in a shrill voice, risking his further anger. As she expected, her words did very little good for he made no move to obey. She quickly moved as far away from him as the narrow seat would allow.

"I'll get out after we've had our talk," he promised, and leaned back in the plush seat to make himself more comfortable. Running his hand over the smooth red Australian leather interior, he nodded his approval. "Nice little buggy you have here." Then he brought his gaze up to meet hers and tried not to become lost in her dazzling beauty until they had finished their talk. "And to think, I've worried myself sick all these years over what might have become of you. Looks like you've managed to do pretty good for yourself. Or does this thing belong to your employer?"

"What employer?" she asked, confused.

"Surely you are working somewhere. How else would you get your hands on the kind of money it takes to dress the way you do," he said, reaching out to stroke her soft cashmere skirt. "Nice. Real nice. I'm proud of you to have managed to do so good on your own. You can't know the sleepless nights I've suffered wondering if you were getting along."

Katherine realized he had not yet discovered she was living as Jason's wife. She wondered if there was any hope of keeping it that way. "Yes, I am doing just fine without you, and I want to keep it that way."

Her words cut through to his heart, but he had expected her to be angry with him. She had every right to be. Though he could not actually remember striking her in that last encounter, he was almost certain he had. When he had finally come to, he found the room was a mess: furniture overturned, curtains pulled down into a crumpled heap, and broken dishes scattered everywhere. And when he moved to get up, he discovered his knuckles were bruised from the force of the blows he must have delivered to her.

He had known immediately that he had lost control of himself again, though he had been too drunk to actually remember. His thoughts were too hazy to ever piece it all together, though he did recall his feeling of anger, and he could remember calling out her name. The rest was a blank.

As soon as he'd been able to sit up amid all the litter, he realized that Katherine had finally fought back. He discovered a deep, bloody gash on the side of his head, and, on the floor next to him, he found a shattered whisky bottle, also stained with his blood.

Even before he had stumbled out into the yard, he knew he would find both his horse and his wife long gone. Before she left, she had taken just enough time to pack a bag and grab the extra cash he always kept in his desk. Heartsick, he had immediately ridden out after her, but she'd had too much of a head start, probably hours, and had been crafty enough to take to a nearby stream in order to cover her tracks. Once she'd reached the deeper part of the stream, where the current was swifter and more constant, it was as if she had vanished into thin air. There was no sign of her to be found, and he was never able to locate where she eventually came out of the water.

It was a week before he'd discovered that she'd headed south, though that was what he had expected her to do. A group of his friends had quickly organized to help him look for her, and had managed to locate the livery stable where she had sold the horse. They also found a few railroad employees on the southern route who were able to identify her from her picture. And there the trail ended. The last thing he'd been able to learn was that she had supposedly boarded a steamship at Jefferson, yet no other port could verify her having actually arrived anywhere.

He did not receive Pat Wall's letter until he'd returned home to recuperate from the injuries he'd received in the ambush just outside Dodge City where he'd been beaten bloody and robbed. It was a short letter, written in a feminine hand, for Pat could not write and he'd no doubt had one of his lady friends pen the letter for him. The letter had stated simply enough that Pat thought he'd caught sight of Katherine in Daingerfield, Texas, and that it might be worth the train fare to see if it really had been her. In the same letter, Pat had also said that he was riding back down there with his men later that month, and if Flint had changed his mind about being a part of the gang and would like to ride along with them, he was more than welcome. But the date on the letter had been September 5th, and it had been nearly the end of October before Flint had gone home to check his mail.

"And just where is it you work?" he asked, drawing his thoughts away from the events that had led to his tracking her down in Daingerfield.

"That's none of your business," she said bluntly, then afraid she was about to give him cause to strike her, she climbed out on the far side of the carriage and walked several feet away. Even as she looked out over the small pond, she never fully turned her back on him. Although the trees had just started to turn, she was in no mood to notice the vivid colors. All she was aware of at that moment was that he had wasted no time in climbing down after her.

"Katherine, it is my business. I'm your husband." He reached out to take her hand, but she jerked it away. The lean muscles in his jaw tensed with annoyance.

"No, you're not my husband. Not anymore. You were supposed to be dead. I am supposed to be a widow," she hissed. Her eyes narrowed with the hate she felt for him. "And as far as I'm concerned you *are* dead."

"I hate to disappoint you, Kat, but I am alive and I am your husband." He grabbed her upper arms and pulled her roughly against him. "I don't know where you got the idea I was dead, but as you can see, I'm not." And then to prove it, he bent his head and kissed her firmly, though he had to struggle to keep her from jerking away.

Fighting with all her strength, Katherine was finally able to pull her mouth free of his. Still in his grasp, she no longer cared if she incited him to strike her or not. She'd rather be beaten than kissed again by the likes of him.

"Don't you ever do that to me again," she said in an

ominous tone.

Her heart pounded fiercely as she turned her head away from him and waited for what he would do next. She was astonished when all he did was release her and step back.

"I'm sorry. I'm not here to scare or hurt you. I'm here to apologize for everything I've already done to you. Though I honestly don't remember everything that happened that last day, I do know what I'm capable of when I'm drunk, and I want to tell you how sorry I am."

"Save your words. I've heard them all before," she told him, rubbing the bruised flesh on her upper arms where he had manhandled her. "I'm through with you. You are no longer a part of my life."

"But I am. I'm still your husband and I intend to stay your husband. Please, Katherine, just listen to me. Let me explain what the situation was back then."

"Spare me your lies. I've heard enough of them," she said firmly, again showing a false bravado as she stared him in the eye. She stood tall and erect, but inside, she quivered like a frightened child. "Legally, you may still be my husband, but I'll never again be your wife."

"Katherine, listen to me," he commanded, and again grasped her arms. "That's all I ask of you for now—just listen to me."

Katherine continued to look him in the eye as she thought over her present situation. She really had little choice but to oblige him. "Okay, speak your piece, then go."

Relieved, Flint exhaled sharply and relaxed his grip on her arms, though he did not let go of her fully. "I've come here to tell you how much I still love you, and to explain to you how very sorry I am for what I must have done to you that last day. I never wanted to hurt you. Surely you know that."

"All I know is that you did hurt me. Time, and time again, you hurt me." Her eyes narrowed with defiance, but her lower lip trembled with the painful memories of what it had been like.

"I know," he said softly and for the first time in her life, Katherine was able to see a certain vulnerability in his almond-shaped eyes. Suddenly, she realized just how much Jeffrey looked like Flint, and the thought that her son had Flint's blood horrified her.

"Katherine, I know I hurt you and I hate myself for that. I want you to know that I have not taken a single drink since the day you left me. Not one."

Katherine didn't know why, but she believed him. Though he had done nothing but lie to her in the past, she nevertheless believed him. But then, it really didn't matter that he was no longer drinking, because she no longer cared what he did. She hated him. "That still doesn't erase what you did," she said.

"Then give me the opportunity to make it up to you. Give me that. Please, as my wife, you owe me that much."

"I owe you nothing," she spat angrily, and stared at him a long moment before adding in a voice filled with contempt, "I hate you. Get out of my life. Go back to Kansas. Leave me alone."

"Katherine, please don't be like that. I love you."

"Love? Was it love that caused you to lie to me about who you were? Was it love that caused you to make all those false promises to change—to give up gunfighting? And was it love that made you take your husbandly pleasures in another woman's bed? Tell me, what sort of love is it that drove you to get stinking drunk, time and time again, and beat me until I barely had the strength to stand, much less run away?"

Flint cringed at the raw hate he saw blazing in her eyes. "I've changed, Kat. How can I get you to see that I've changed? How can I convince you how much I do love you?"

"Even if you could, it wouldn't matter. I quit loving you a long time ago," she said numbly.

"That's not true," he argued and pulled her against his lean body once again. The feel of her soft body against his drove him insane with desire for her, desire that had gone denied for six long years. "The feelings you once had for me are not the kind that die easily."

"They did not die easily," she told him and tried to wrench herself free of his grasp for fear that he intended to kiss her again—which was exactly his intention. In the next moment, his mouth came down on hers with such force she had to gasp for breath.

At first, the pressure of his lips was harsh and painful—and, oddly enough, that pleased her. She wanted to physically feel the deep disgust she had for him. Then abruptly, the kiss changed. Flint turned more gentle, his kiss became more seductively persuasive—and to her horror—she felt herself responding much as she used to. It was as if he had cast his black magic over her and caused her to lose her reason. But she hadn't lost all her sense; deep within her, a small voice urged her to pry herself loose before it was too late.

In a frantic effort to obey that voice, she pressed her hands against his chest and tried her best to push him away. But her action only made the situation worse, for he tightened his hold around her and drew her closer still. Again, her body wanted to betray her, and she almost gave way to a sudden impulse to allow him to work his evil magic over her. She ceased her struggles momentarily. A low moan came from her throat and she found herself actually wanting to lean against him, to allow him the pleasure he sought—but no! She hated him. What was wrong with her?

With the strength of a madwoman, she shoved him hard and managed to break away. With tears streaming down her face, she climbed into the carriage and grabbed up the reins, but before she could get the carriage turned around to face the road out, he was beside her, yanking the reins out of her hands.

"Katherine, don't you see? Don't you see what that kiss meant? What it proved? You do still love me. There is still a chance for us. Please, give us that chance."

"No! I don't love you! I hate you! I despise you! I love Jason!" She gasped at the realization of what she'd revealed. Damn her own foolish anger.

"Jason?" he thundered. "Who the hell is Jason?"

"Jason is my husband," she replied, without stopping to think that he wasn't really her husband, not legally anyway.

"I'm your husband, you little fool!" he shouted, his green eyes blazing with sudden fury.

"No you aren't. You're dead," she spat out defiantly. "There are papers to prove it."

"Dammit, I'm alive!" Before she was able to evade his grasp, he had her pulled against him again, twisting her arm until she winced. "I am alive, and I'm still your husband."

"No you aren't. Jason is my husband. I love him, not

you." It didn't matter how hard he twisted her arm, she had to get the words out. She only hoped that the truth would hurt him as much as he was hurting her. Shutting out the pain caused by the vice-like grip on her arm, she continued to rail at him in a voice hoarse with anger. "Jason is my husband, and I'm proud to say he has been twice the husband you ever were."

Katherine was unprepared for the abrupt way in which he let go of her. Off balance, she fell to her knees on the carriage floor. She was even more unprepared for what happened next, for only a second later, Flint dropped to his knees beside her, and, with tears in his eyes, he begged for her forgiveness.

"Flint, there is just too much to forgive," she said feeling suddenly weak, emotionally drained. It took several minutes for her to gather the strength to get back up on the seat and smooth out her skirts. "I am in love with another man. I have lived as his wife for nearly six years. I have finally found happiness. Please don't destroy that for me. Please, just go away and leave me alone."

"I can't," he tried to explain, his voice trembling from the bitter anguish her words caused him. "I love you too much."

"Please don't say that." She wanted to speak those words in anger, but there was simply not enough emotional strength left in her to do so. She felt nothing but numbness.

Slowly, Flint climbed down from the carriage. He knew that this was not the time to continue pleading his case. Katherine was too stunned by his sudden return to be able to think clearly just yet. Though he was consumed by jealousy at her declaration of love for another man, he felt it would be to his own advantage if they both had a cooling-off period. It would also give him time to find out about this Jason she was so fond of.

"Katherine, I do love you, and nothing you can say or do will make me stop loving me. And nothing you can say or do will change the fact that you are still my wife."

"Leave me alone," she pleaded. "Go back to Kansas and never come back."

"I'm not going back without you," he said adamantly. "I'm staying at the Morris House Hotel. I want you to think about what I've said—how I still love you. Think about the way you responded to my kiss, however briefly, and you'll realize that you still love me, too—that you never stopped loving me. I don't know what you feel for this Jason you spoke about, but it can't be love when you've shown such a willing response to me. We'll talk again tomorrow."

"But I do love Jason," she quickly affirmed. The strange moment of weakness she had shown during that kiss had nothing to do with the love she felt for Jason. It was the power of her love for Jason that had finally given her the strength to resist. "I do love Jason," she repeated. "I love him more than I ever loved you."

Flint's green eyes flared with a jealousy so intense, Katherine was afraid to say more. Suddenly, she feared for Jason. What had driven her to say all those things? Not only had she admitted she was living as Jason's wife, she had thrown it in the face of a man with a reputation for using deadly force to eliminate enemies. Her eyes went involuntarily to the rifle slung over his saddle. Though, at present, he was not wearing a side arm, he was never without a weapon of some kind. God! What sort of a fool was she?

"We'll talk tomorrow," he repeated, his voice cold and cryptic. His jaw was set grimly. For a long moment, he simply stood and stared up at her—his gaze penetrating and unwavering—as if he were trying to see through to her very core. Then, without another word, he strode to his horse, mounted quickly, and rode back to town.

Chapter Eighteen

Jason, Jason, what have I done?

Katherine drove the horse as hard as she could, though it seemed as if she were traveling at a snail's pace. The more she thought about it, the harder her heart pounded. The frantic beating of every pulse in her body muffled the clattering sound of the carriage as it bounded along the narrow, rutted roadway. She strained to lean forward, as if that might help the carriage move faster. She had to warn Jason. It would not take Flint long to find out just who Jason was and where he lived. Jason had to be prepared. He had to know.

This was quite different from the last time she'd ridden to warn Jason of danger; this time she had actually *seen* Flint. And not only had she seen him, she had spoken with him. She had foolishly told him about Jason. She had openly admitted her love for another man—thrown fuel on the fire. God help her, but she had felt a deep satisfaction in seeing the raw pain she had managed to cause Flint Mason—to know she'd returned some of the pain he had dealt her. But now, she realized the damage her moment of triumph had caused. Flint would come looking for Jason. She had no doubt about that. She had seen the hate in Flint's eyes.

"Jason!" she shouted with relief when she drew the carriage to a crashing halt in front of the barn, where he was helping Mose and Rede haul the heavy bundles of hay up into the loft. Now that she'd found him in time to warn him about Flint, she felt like crying with joy.

"Katherine? What is it?" Jason's face was full of concern as he hurried toward her.

"He's here. I saw him. He spoke to me. God help us both. I told him," she said. Her words tumbled out hysterically as she scrambled out of the carriage to meet him. "He knows."

"Who knows what?" He was totally bewildered until he realized there was only one person who could cause her such agitation. "You saw Flint? He's alive?"

She nodded. She had indeed seen Flint and he was very much alive.

"Where?"

"In town," she told him, gulping deeply, unable to breathe. Suddenly, for the first time since the final months of her pregnancy with Jeffrey, Katherine felt as if she might faint.

Her eyes were so wide with fear and her face so white, that Jason reached out and pulled her into his arms to comfort her. His own heart had plummeted into the depths of despair. Not only would they be unable to marry, Katherine's worst fears had now come to pass. Flint had finally found her. Though Jason knew he would do whatever it took to protect her from the man, he now wondered if he would be able to do enough. In that moment, he realized he would kill Flint if it became necessary. Katherine was all that was important. Katherine and Jeffrey.

Suddenly, Katherine burst into tears, sobbing helplessly against his shoulder, making him want to hold her closer. Aware that both Mose and Rede had stopped what they were doing to watch Katherine's emotional outburst, he quickly led her toward the house. "There, there now. Everything is going to be all right. We're going to see this through together. Everything is going to be all right."

"No, it isn't," she tried to explain, still having to fight for each breath she took. "He knows about you. He knows about us."

"It would have been hard to keep it a secret from him once he'd found you." Though Jason managed to keep his voice calm and reassuring, he felt his own fears suddenly escalating. He knew he mustn't let his fear get the upper hand, for then he would lose all reason. He had to keep a cool head, had to stay calm. As he escorted her into the living room, away from curious stares, he had to know just how serious things were.

"Does Flint know about Jeffrey?"

Katherine shook her head. "No, I don't think he even knows I have a son, much less that it's *his* son." Her eyes widened at the thought of his finding out. "We must hide Jeffrey. We must send him away. We can send him to my father's."

"What good is that going to do? Flint's bound to find out from others that we have a son. Sending Jeffrey away now will just draw attention to him," Jason pointed out, trying to think the problem through rationally. "Actually, there's no way he can find out he's the real father. Jeffrey is small for his age. He doesn't look five. You've said that yourself. Unless Flint goes to the courthouse and demands to see the boy's birth certificate, there's no reason for him to know Jeffrey's age, and what cause would he have for doing that?"

Katherine desperately hoped that would prove true. No one had ever before questioned Jeffrey's parentage. Maybe Flint wouldn't either. Her thoughts returned to the danger Jason was in. "Flint will come looking for you. Just as soon as he finds out more about who you are and where he can find you, he'll come looking for you."

"He won't have to," Jason said, and knew she wasn't going to like what he planned to do. "I'm going to go find him first."

"No!"

"Katherine, I have to. I can't sit here and wait for him to come looking for me. I have to show him I'm not afraid of him. I'm going to saddle up and leave immediately. Maybe there's some way to reason with him." He wondered if Flint might have a price. Men like him often did. If so, there might be a way to buy the man's cooperation. And whatever the price, he'd find a way to pay it.

"But there's no reasoning with Flint," she argued, clutching his arm with both hands. She had to convince him to stay at the ranch, where he would at least have the other men to help protect him. "All you'll be doing is saving him the time and trouble of coming after you."

Jason pulled Katherine close and kissed her deeply before he turned to leave. She continued to plead with him—even as he walked into the next room, pulled his rifle out of the wall rack, and broke open the breech to see if both chambers were loaded. He offered her an encouraging smile as he snapped the rifle shut, gathered up his handgun and holster, then headed out the door. "I'll stop by and get Zeb first. Flint won't try to pull anything shady with the law standing by. Lock the doors and windows. I'll try to be back before dark."

"Jason, Zeb, what brings you two in here?" Thad Cohen asked, looking up from the registration desk as the two tall men walked across the Morris House lobby.

"We're looking for Flint Mason," Zeb told him right out. "What room is he in?"

Thad pushed his spectacles higher up on his nose and studied the register. "There's a Franklin Mason in room nine, but I don't see any Flint Mason."

Zeb looked questioningly at Jason, for he couldn't remember what Flint's given name was. Jason nodded that it was the same man. "Room nine?"

"Yeah, but he's not up there right now," Thad put in quickly. "He hasn't been in here in quite a while. He stowed his gear in his room early on this afternoon, then lit right out again."

"Thanks," Zeb told him, and was turning to question Jason when Thad interrupted.

"I think I saw him go into the Redbird Saloon just a little while ago. You might try there first."

"Thanks, again," Zeb said, giving Thad an appreciative nod. "We'll do that. And if he happens to come back in here, do us a favor and send someone around to find us and tell us—but don't tell him we're looking for him."

"Will do," Thad said with an affirmative nod. "Anything to help the sheriff's office."

Zeb followed Jason to the front door of the hotel. They both paused briefly to stare at the small saloon directly across the street, where Thad seemed to think Flint had gone.

"Do you want me to go on over and see if he's really in there?" Zeb asked.

"No, we'll go together," Jason said firmly and started across the street.

"Do you know if he's alone?" Zeb wanted an idea of what to expect.

"He was alone when Katherine spoke to him," Jason told him. "But I have no way of knowing if anyone rode in with him. He just might have a friend or two along with him, but then again, he might not. I have no way of knowing."

"I guess we're about to find that out," Zeb said as he and Jason walked up to the Redbird Saloon. Smiling and tipping his hat at a small group of ladies who were hurrying past the saloon, Zeb tried to appear casual as he reached down and adjusted his holster.

Jason did the same. Then, with a brief look at Zeb, he pushed the door open with his left hand, keeping his right hand close to his pistol.

Already familiar with the layout of the small room, Jason and Zeb's eyes first swept the bar to the left, where the bartender was standing alone, polishing glasses. Then they looked off to the right, where the only four men who were in the saloon sat at a gaming table near the back.

Jason was the first to recognize Flint, from two sketches Zeb had obtained, and it irritated him to find that the man was far better looking in person. But then, there had to have been some reason for Katherine to have fallen for him as hard as she had.

By now, Zeb had also spotted the man, though Flint had not as yet looked up from his cards to notice the attention directed his way. Jason walked further into the room so that he was standing a few feet behind Flint. Zeb followed slowly. When they got close enough to hear what the four men at the table were talking about, Jason was not too surprised to find that he was the topic of conversation.

"You say he's got a big ranch out west of town?" Flint asked casually, as he arranged his five cards to better suit him.

"Yeah, the largest spread around these parts, a few miles out on Sycamore, off towards Sandy Bottom Creek," replied the man who had just dealt the cards. His attention, too, was focused on his cards, though by the look on his face, it was easy to guess he held a poor hand.

"Glad to hear he's doing so good for himself," Flint continued. "Has he gone and gotten himself married yet?" He stared down at the two kings side by side in his hand—right next to a lovely pair of eights. Nothing in his expression revealed what he held.

Jason did not wait for the response concerning his current marital status. With his eyes planted on Flint, he slowly lowered his hand until it hovered just inches from his gun. Then, in a commanding voice, he simply called out the man's name.

"Flint Mason."

The muscles in Flint's back tensed as he slowly lowered his cards face down on the table. He never turned around to see who had spoken as he brought his hands away from the table. "You can't be speaking to me. The name's Frank. Frank Mason. You must have me confused with someone else."

"I don't have you confused with anyone. I want you to step outside so we can talk in private."

"I'm not even wearing my gun," Flint quickly pointed out. "How can I draw against you when I don't even have on a gun? Why don't you just go on and leave us to our card game."

"I'm not here to draw against you. I just want to talk to you. There are a few things we need to get straight."

Slowly, Flint turned around to face Zeb and Jason, his green eyes narrowed with wariness as he tried to decide which of the two had spoken to him.

"You coming or not?" Jason asked gruffly.

One of the other three men at the table scratched his head in confusion. "I thought you said he was an old friend of yours. It sure don't look that way to me. I thought you said you knew Jason Morris."

"Let's just say we have mutual acquaintances," Flint said, his suspicions about the man's identity now confirmed. Slowly, he smiled at his own clever comment, but the coolness of his jaded gaze never changed. He continued to return Jason's stare even as he nodded toward Zeb, asking, "Who's your friend there? What's the matter? Afraid to face me alone?"

Not allowing the taunt to unnerve him, Jason simply replied, "Are you coming with us or not?"

Shrugging, as he continued to study the man who had managed to win his wife's heart, Flint slowly pushed his chair back. "Where to, gentlemen?"

"How about my office?" Zeb suggested.

For the first time, Flint gaze Zeb more than a cursory glance, and his eyes immediately lighted on the shiny deputy's badge pinned to his gray woolen shirt. "No, I don't think so. I have a strong aversion to sheriff's offices."

"No doubt," Zeb replied with a snort.

"How about we go over to the hotel across the street? I have a room there where we can talk over our business in complete privacy."

"I think not . . ." Zeb started to say, only to be cut short by Jason.

"Fine. We'll go there."

Since no one seemed to care much for the idea of walking ahead of the others, the three of them crossed the street together and entered the hotel side by side. It was not until they reached the narrow staircase, where only one man could pass at a time, that Zeb took the lead and headed up first.

If Flint wondered how the deputy knew to stop in front of room nine, he didn't let on. Instead, he quickly unlocked the door and stepped back.

Again, Zeb moved to go first, but this time he found his way blocked by a black-sleeved arm.

"Not you. You stay out here," Flint said in a low, menacing voice.

"Like hell I will," Zeb said and tried to push the arm aside.

"I don't care much for lawmen. What Jason and I have to say to one another is private."

"I don't give a damn how private it is. I'm not about to let you lure Jason into your room alone where you probably have a gun loaded and waiting."

"As long as he keeps that gun in his holster, he's safe. You have my word." Flint's expression was grim. He did not want Zeb to enter his room.

"Great. The word of a gunfighter," Zeb retorted, his nostrils flaring in disgust. "Get your arm out of my way."

Jason's eyes went from Flint's steely gaze to Zeb's. "That's all right, Zeb. I'll go in alone."

"Like hell you will. That man's not to be trusted. We'll go in together or you won't go in at all."

"No, Zeb. I'll go alone," he said and patted his friend's back reassuringly. "I understand your concern, but I think I'll be able to handle this myself from here."

"Jason, it's too much of a risk," Zeb tried to explain, but realized Jason had turned his attention to what was inside the room and was no longer listening. Knowing there was no point in arguing with Jason when he got that stubborn set to his jaw, Zeb finally stepped back and said, "Okay, go in there alone, but don't think I'm going anywhere. I'll be right out here if you need me, and if I hear anything suspicious going on in there, I'm coming in."

"I appreciate that," Jason said, his gaze meeting Zeb's only briefly before he stepped inside the room. "This shouldn't take long."

It was not until Flint had closed the door in Zeb's concerned face, that either one of the two men spoke again.

"Sit if you want," Flint said and gestured to the only chair in the sparsely furnished room.

Other than the obligatory bed and washstand, there was only the chair and a clothes tree. It was on the clothes tree that Jason finally spotted Flint's gun, a handsome nickel-plated Colt .45. Jason couldn't help but wonder how many men had met their fate at the wrong end of that revolver's long, polished barrel.

"This is not a friendly visit," Jason said coldly, declining to sit. His eyes moved away from the gun and looked back at Flint.

"I didn't think it was," Flint shot back, and tilted his head slightly to size up the tall, muscular man who now stood before him—a good two inches taller than his own six feet. If Jason's size and obvious strength intimidated Flint, he didn't show it. "At least Katherine has kept her good taste. I had you figured to be much older and even a bit on the homely side. And you don't look as stupid as I figured you to be, either. I think you already know I'm still married to Katherine. I think you already know your marriage to her is a farce."

"Legally, yes." Jason gave him that much. "But in our hearts we are married. We love each other very much."

"That may be good enough for you, but it still doesn't change the fact that legally she's still my wife."

"But emotionally, she is mine," Jason came back quickly.

"Not all together." A slow smile worked its way across Flint's lean face as he remembered his encounter with Katherine earlier that afternoon. "She has already proven to me that she still cares."

"That's a crock if I've ever heard one," Jason said with a snort, then narrowed his blue eyes and added, "I'm not one to play games, so you can quit trying to plant any doubts in my mind. Katherine and I love each other, and we are very happy together."

"That may be, though I doubt it. She still loves me and she can be just as happy with me," Flint said tauntingly. "All it took was one kiss to make her swoon in my arms again."

"I'll remind you, I don't play those games," Jason told him, his expression grim.

"Oh? Then, why are you here?"

"To tell you to leave Katherine alone." Any thought of offering this man money to stay away from Katherine was gone. He'd rather burn in hell than to reward this man in any fashion.

"Just like that? You want me to simply turn my back on my wife and leave town? I'm afraid I can't oblige you. I'm not going anywhere unless Katherine goes with me. She's my wife. I love her and I intend to make her see that."

"Don't give me that garbage," Jason snorted. "She's already told me all about how badly you treated her. She also told me all the lies you fed her to keep her in the dark about who you really were."

"Necessary lies," Flint put in. His jaw hardened with the jealous anger that now consumed him. "The only reason she told you all that was to fool you into believing she no longer loved me—so you'd think you were the only one she cared for. Well, I've got news for you, she showed me this afternoon that she still cares for me. If I'd taken that kiss any further while we were out there all alone—which was at her request by the way—I could have proven just how married she still is to me."

Though the words stung, Jason was sure they were lies. He trusted Katherine, believed in her love. "Talk out your fantasies if you like, but don't expect me to swallow them. Face up to the truth like a man. Find someone else to push around; make someone else's life a living hell. Katherine is through with you."

"I think I've heard about enough out of you," Flint said, his nostrils flaring as he headed for the door.

"Yes, you talk big for a man who is actually nothing more than a drunk and a murderer. Tell me, does it make you feel big to slap women around? To kick them until they can't stand up?"

"That's a lie. I never kicked Katherine!" Flint said angrily, though in fact he couldn't remember.

"I saw the bruises. She was still covered with them when I met her. There wasn't a place on her body that wasn't marked by your violence. Let me warn you. If you try to hurt her again—if you so much as raise your hand to strike her—I'll kill you." His tone was deadly serious. "Why don't you just face up to the truth and give her a divorce. Why hang on to someone who hates you?"

"The truth is that she still loves me. I saw that this afternoon, and I intend to do everything within my power to make her see it, too. No, there'll be no divorce. And once I've announced to this little town that I'm Katherine's real husband, you two won't be able to live so happily out there in that big house I hear you got."

"Yes, that's really going to help you win back her heart isn't it?" Fear gripped Jason but he tried not to show it. "Yes, shame her in front of all her friends. That should do it all right."

"You don't think I'm going to sit back and let you two go on pretending you're married, do you?" Then another thought occurred to him. "Do you two have any children?"

"Yes, we do. A son. Jeffrey. He's four."

A surge of jealousy hit Flint like a blow. Not only was Katherine living as this man's wife, she had given him a son—something she had managed to deprive him of. Wanting desperately to lash out at this man, Flint turned his steely gaze on Jason and said in low, bitter tones, "But your marriage to Katherine isn't legal. That makes that son of yours a bastard, doesn't it?"

Jason could not believe the rage that swept through him at that moment. He had to get out of that room or risk killing the man right where he stood. Though he felt that Flint deserved to be killed, he was not ready to face the consequences. Katherine needed him to be with her—not in some stinking jail, awaiting trial. Wanting to allay any suspicion Flint might have about Jeffrey—and wanting to strike back at the same time—Jason sneered, "At least I was able to give her a son. That's more than you can say."

"You gave her a *bastard* son," Flint reminded him, brandishing the word like a weapon. "Your son is a bastard. You hear me? A bastard? And when I take Katherine away with me, she's going to want to take that bastard son with her. Fine. I can put up with that as long as I get Katherine."

That was it. That was all Jason could take. With one powerful blow, he sent Flint crashing against the wall. Flint's expression registered shock rather than pain—and it was pain that Jason wanted to see on the man's face. But before he could lunge at the man again, he heard the splintering crack of the door being kicked open. Zeb was instantly at his side, grabbing his arm, holding him back. "Come on. Let's get out of here.

Trash like him isn't worth thc effort."

Flint got to his feet with a look of such venom, that Zeb drew his pistol.

Jason could feel Zeb's pressure on his arm, encouraging him to leave, but he still had something to say. "You claim you love Katherine. If that's the truth—if that's really the truth—then let her be. In her heart, your marriage was over six years ago, and our marriage is what's right for her, legal or not. She has a good life here. She has a family. You'll destroy her if you try to take that away from her."

"She'll survive the loss," Flint said stonily.

"If you try to destroy our happiness by telling everyone about your marriage, she will hate you. She'll never be able to face her friends again. Don't do that to her."

"She can come away with me and make new friends," Flint replied carelessly.

"She's happy here. Destroy that happiness, and she'll never forgive you."

"I can't let you two go on pretending to be man and wife. She happens to be *my* wife. If she sleeps with any man, it should be me."

"Who she sleeps with is her own choice."

"Then you won't mind if she decides to sleep with me?" Flint flung the question at him like a knife, and it hit its mark with such force that Zeb had to hold Jason back from making another lunge.

"Like I said, who she sleeps with is her own choice," Jason said, shaking himself free of Zeb's restraining hand.

"And who she decides to live with will be her own choice, too," Flint said with a new glint in his hard eyes, for he was starting to see this as an interesting challenge. "Okay, I won't reveal that she's my wife to anybody just yet. I don't really care if anyone else knows or not. After all, you know. Deputy there, knows. And best of all, Katherine knows. No, I don't think I'll tell anybody about Katherine's dark secret just yet. But in return, I want to be able to see her with no interference from you. Be a man of your word and let her make her own choice between the two of us."

"If Katherine tells me she wants to see you, I won't stand in the way," Jason said confidently, for he felt sure Katherine was not going to want to see Flint at all.

"Oh, she'll want to see me all right," Flint said with a cocky smile. "And in the end, she'll make the right choice."

"She already has," Jason told him and returned the insincere smile.

"Just keep in mind that you said the choice would be hers. When she tells you she wants to leave you to come live with me again, don't you try to stop her. I'll play it fair if you will."

Jason stared at him in disgust. It was clear Flint saw this as a game of some sort, but if it was a way to get Flint out of her life for good and without bloodshed, then he would play the game, too. "And when you finally discover that Katherine loves me and is happy here—and that nothing you can do will make her care for you again—you'll let her get a divorce, and you'll get out of her life forever."

"It'll never come to that," Flint said with a snide laugh.

"But you promise," Jason prodded. "With Zeb here as witness, you promise to give Katherine the divorce that she wants."

"She won't want it when I get through."

"But you promise."

"Yes, I promise." But in his heart, Flint knew it was a lie. He would never give Katherine a divorce. He'd rather die than give up any real claim to the only woman he ever loved.

Chapter Nineteen

At first, Katherine was appalled that Jason had taken Flint's word about something so important when the man was notorious for his cunning, cold-hearted lies—especially where she was concerned. But after thinking it over, she realized it was a better solution than shooting it out, which she had worried about from the beginning and still feared.

"It shouldn't take him long to discover that everything we've told him is the truth—that we really do love each other," Jason said reasonably. "And if by some chance, he turns out to be a man of his word, he'll soon be granting you that divorce and we can go ahead with our plans to make our marriage legal. It'll just have to be delayed a while."

The whole thing sounded a little too easy to Katherine. She knew Flint was not a man to give up easily when his mind was set. "And what if he doesn't honor his word? What if he again refuses to listen to what I have to say about us, and then refuses to give me a divorce because he doesn't believe me?"

"Then we're right back where we started," Jason told her solemnly. "And I'll have to confront him."

"You mean in a gunfight?" She could feel her stomach knotting.

"If it comes to that, yes," Jason said, then seeing the horror in her eyes, he tried to reassure her. "But it won't come to that. Eventually, Flint will get tired of trying to win you back and will want to get on to something else. The way you've described him to me all these years, he's not one to let any one thing hold his attention too long."

Katherine closed her eyes and prayed that it would be true—that Flint would indeed grow tired of his pursuit of her and would finally decide to leave her alone. Whether or not he ever gave her the divorce didn't matter, as long as he left them alone to live their lives in peace. It was really the best she dared hope for.

Flint wasted no time in his quest to win Katherine back. That very next morning he appeared at their front door dressed in a carefully pressed frock coat and square-cuffed, close-fitting trousers. Though both Jason and Katherine had come down to see who was calling at such an early hour, it was Minnie who opened the door.

At first, when he gave her his name, she refused to let him enter. But at Katherine and Jason's insistence, she eventually opened the door wide enough to let him pass through into the entrance hall. When he stepped inside and remarked what a lovely house it was, Minnie scowled and muttered disapprovingly, then moved to walk beside Katherine as she led the way into the main salon.

"You look beautiful," Flint said to Katherine, ignoring Minnie's audible *humph*. His eyes quickly swept over the pretty pale blue ruffled dress she wore, lingering briefly on the creamy swell of bosom the moderately low neckline revealed. "But then, you always look beautiful."

"No, she don't," Minnie interjected boldly. "She looks terrible. She looks like she ain't had no sleep in days. She ain't got hardly no color at all in her face and that's all your fault."

"Hmmm. If she looks so terrible now," Flint said jokingly, "I sure do look forward to seeing her when she looks her best." He bestowed a grudging half smile on Minnie. Despite her aggressive manner, he decided he liked the woman. He especially liked the way she hovered over Katherine like a mother hen. It showed she cared, and Katherine needed someone who cared about her. Smiling more broadly at Minnie, he spoke in a friendly yet grandiloquent manner that was somewhat of character for him, "Now, if you don't mind, madam, I'd like to speak with Katherine alone."

Minnie bristled at his presumptuous attitude. "Well, I do mind. I happen to mind very much, and don't you *madam* me, you—you green-eyed, lily-livered, side-windin' snake. I know who you are and you ain't foolin' me one bit with your fine hoity-toity show of manners."

Flint's brows rose quizzically as he turned to look at Katherine, then Jason. "Someone needs to tell her how it's all right for me to pay a private call on Katherine if I want. Otherwise, I might be forced to reveal a few of the real but hidden facts to her."

"What real facts?" Undaunted, Minnie folded her arms across her ample bosom. "That you're a coward who likes to beat on helpless women? That you ain't good enough for her to even wipe her feet on? That your marriage was made on lies and deceit right from the start?"

"Well informed, aren't you?" Flint commented, with an admiring nod. "Do you also know that Jason and I made a bargain, and that I am more than welcome to come visit Katherine in exchange for not causing a big stir in town with an announcement that she's really married to me?"

"I wouldn't go so far as to say 'welcome'," Jason spoke up, swallowing the bitterness rising inside him. His arm tightened protectively around Katherine's shoulder. "But, yes—he does have permission to visit Katherine as long as he behaves himself."

"Hey, no one said I had to behave myself," Flint put in with a suggesting chuckle that made Jason want to smash his face again. He was pleased to see that the blow he'd landed the day before left a dark bruise on Flint's jaw.

Flint knew he was pushing Jason to the breaking point, but he was furious at the way the man wrapped his arm around *his* wife's shoulders. Meeting Jason's icy stare with one of his own, he continued. "Whether or not I behave myself will be totally up to Katherine. Now, if you two will please get out of here and leave us alone, I'll see just how Katherine would like me to behave."

"I ain't made no bargain with you," Minnie interjected, her lips set in a grim line. "And I ain't leavin' this room."

"Very well then, maybe we'd just better find some other room to talk in. A bedroom would suit me fine." His eyes grew as wide as Minnie's as she reacted to the shocking suggestion.

"Come on, Minnie," Jason urged, taking her arm. "It shouldn't take Katherine long to hear him out, and then he can be on his way." It took all the restraint that Jason could muster not to grab Flint by his fancy lapels and toss him right out of the house—but he had to think of Katherine. If he caused any trouble now, Flint would head straight to town and spread his story with glee.

Minnie shot Flint one last look of warning before allowing Jason to lead her out of the room. Even then, she refused to stray very far from the closed door, and she became furious at Jason's apparent unconcern as he calmly went up the stairs and into his bedroom.

"Who was that woman?" Flint asked as soon as he and Katherine were alone.

"Minnie—Jason's housekeeper," she replied, finding it hard not to smile at Minnie's expression as she'd been pulled from the room.

"Jason's housekeeper? You mean you don't consider her your housekeeper, too? That's interesting."

Katherine sighed heavily at the obvious insinuation. "If you must know, I really don't think of Minnie as a housekeeper at all. Minnie is more like part of the family—*our* family."

"Speaking of family, where is this boy I've heard so much about? Where's little Jeffrey?"

Katherine felt her stomach tighten. "He's out at the barn, playing with all the calves that have been rounded up for fall branding."

"All by himself? A four-year-old?"

"Ruby, my personal maid, is with him—in addition to half a dozen ranchhands." She hoped she'd gotten the point across about the number of men on the place. She wondered if it would be a bit much to mention that each hand was armed.

"Does the boy look much like you?" Flint went on, not caring in the least how many ranchhands were about. His interest was focused on Katherine's son. He sincerely hoped the child resembled her, for he wouldn't care to raise a boy who looked like another man. It would be a constant reminder of his wife's unfaithfulness.

"No, he looks more like Jason," she told him with a confident smile. "He's a truly handsome young man."

Deep resentment flared up in Flint, and he felt like stripping the smile right off her face by reminding her of the child's illegitimacy. He realized, however, that would alienate her further. He was there to win her heart back—not to lash out at her for betraying their marriage vows. For in all honesty, he had to admit that he'd been the first one to stray. He felt a sharp wave of self-loathing as he thought of the many trips he'd made into town to visit Juanita. As he tried to recall why he had acted so foolishly—when Juanita was not half as desirable as Katherine—all he could remember was a feeling that he was no longer worthy to go to Katherine's bed. He pushed aside the memory of the dead thirteen-year-old boy.

"I'd like to meet your son," Flint said as he stepped closer to her. "Maybe I'll get a chance before I have to leave."

"Which I hope is soon," Katherine said bluntly. "Why are you here, anyway? What is it you have to say to me that you feel must be said in such total privacy?"

When he reached for the hand that was held tensely at her left side, she jerked it away and hid it behind her back. Not easily daunted, he reached behind her—his shoulder brushing her breast—and brought her hand back, to clasp in his own.

"I'm here to woo you back," he said simply. "I've already discovered that you and Jason have very few secrets from each other, so I imagine he's already told you about the bargain we made."

"We don't keep *any* secrets from each other," she corrected, though that was no longer true. She had not told Jason of Flint's brash kiss, nor of her brief response to that kiss before she had pushed him away. It was the only part of their confrontation that she had omitted telling him. "And he didn't exactly call it a bargain—but he did tell me what you both agreed to. Tell me, do you plan to keep your part of this—'bargain'?"

"As long as he keeps to his half and let's me see you without giving me any trouble," Flint said, and offered her an alarmingly seductive smile.

"And then you'll give me the divorce without any resistance?"

"You won't want it," he told her and firmly believed it. "If you'll just give me a chance, a real chance, you'll see that you still love me. Jason's already said that if I prove to be your choice, you can go with me. He won't do anything to try and hold you back. He said it was also your choice who you went to bed with, and I plan to see to it that it's me. I remember how good the two of us are in bed. You're a real tigress when your passions are aroused."

Katherine wanted to strike him but she resisted, though she did manage to jerk her hand free of his grasp. "And how do you hope to get me into your bed when I despise you?"

"You can't keep lying to yourself forever, Kat. Right now, you're still mad at me for the way I treated you there at the last—and I don't blame you. But as soon as you come to see that I've truly changed, your anger will melt, and your love for me will once again flower and grow."

"How very poetic you've become," she muttered with revulsion. "No wonder you're such a big man with the ladies. Was it flowery words like those that got you into Juanita's bed? Or does it take such an effort to get a saloon whore to do your bidding?"

Flint's mouth fell open with surprise at her venomous words. "My lovely wife has a sharp tongue on her these days." A smile spread across his handsome face as he leaned closer until she was able to feel his mint-scented breath on her cheek. "It's nice to discover she's still every bit the tigress I remember. A real wildcat. My very own wild *Kat.*"

Remembering how she had come to get her nickname, Katherine blushed to the roots of her hair. She was temporarily speechless.

"Yes, though we had other problems in our marriage, Kat, sex wasn't one of them, was it?" He trailed his finger lightly across the sensitive skin behind her ear. He was glad to find that it still brought forth an involuntary shiver from her. "Ah, yes, the blood of a wildcat still flows through your veins."

"Get away from me," she told him as she shot him a hateful glare and pulled away in shocked, angry confusion. Her mind was whirling just from his lascivious allusions. She had to get away from him or he'd somehow have her back under his evil spell. "I don't want you to touch me."

"Oh, yes, you do. You love to be touched. You love to be fondled," he reminded her, and took a step forward as she took another step back. This continued until he had her backed up against the fabric-covered wall.

"Flint, I warn you; don't you dare touch me."

"Or you'll do what?" he goaded her, trailing his finger along the sensitive skin of her throat and then downward, until it brought gooseflesh to the ivory skin that swelled just above her low, rounded neckline. He knew her body well enough to imagine the response her breasts had made to his touch. It occurred to him that her breasts had grown larger, rounder, probably from bearing a child. Childbearing seemed to bring out all the best in a woman's body. He was eager to glimpse the change that had occurred in Katherine. He had to find a way to be truly alone with her. Suddenly, he realized he was playing it all wrong. He needed to regain her trust until he could get her alone, truly alone. Then, he could seduce her at will. If he tried to seduce her here, she'd cry out, and that housekeeper would come bounding in to rescue her.

"I'm sorry, Kat, I just wanted you to see that you do still feel something for me," he said, quickly turning and walking away, wanting to sit down before her eyes discovered the tangible evidence of his desire. "Please, come sit down. Tell me more about your son. I'm ready to behave myself."

To Katherine's relief, Flint made no further unwelcome advances for the remainder of his two-hour stay. He talked only briefly of himself, but was eager to know everything that had happened to her over the past six years. It worried her that he showed so much interest in Jeffrey. Had he somehow found out Jeffrey was actually his son? Did he have a reason to suspect? "But, no," she told herself. She was just looking for trouble. Flint was merely playing on a mother's pride in her son.

"Well, I think it's about time I left, unless you plan to ask me to lunch." He paused to give her the opportunity to make just such an offer, but when she didn't respond, he made his farewell. "I'm happy at the way our visit went. I enjoyed it. I'll come back tomorrow so we can talk some more."

"No, don't," she responded quickly, shrinking from the thought of having to go through two such torturous hours again.

"The bargain was . . ." he started to remind her, his brow raised in warning.

"Not tomorrow. I have plans for tomorrow that I can't get out of. It can't be tomorrow. I won't even be home." It was true enough. She had promised to meet with a small group of ladies from the church to help make a community quilt for Jim Haught who would be laid up in bed for the next couple of months.

"Okay, the next day. I'll be here around ten. Maybe you can show me around this place. You know how interested I am in wealth."

"And I know what you will and won't do to get your own greedy little hands on money," she retorted with a meaningful glance.

"I know what I will do, but what is it I won't do in order to get money?" he asked, intrigued by her statement.

"An honest day's work for one thing," she replied, delighted at the chance to make that comment. Then, it occurred to her to offer him money to leave her alone. "You know, Jason does have a lot of money—more than you'll ever see in your lifetime. I'll bet he'd be willing to pay you to leave me alone."

Flint saw the flicker of hope in her eyes and that hurt him. "No, I don't think he would. He might be willing to die trying to force me to leave, but I don't think he would stoop to trying to pay me off."

His words took her by surprise. It was as if he had admitted there were admirable qualities in Jason that even he could see. The smile that brightened her face then was the first sincere smile she had offered him since he had forced his way back into her life. "Yes, Frank, I think maybe you are right."

The fact that she had called him Frank again did not go unnoticed by Flint. She had said his name the way she used to—before she'd learned his true identity. Though she seemed unaware she had said it, he felt a renewed surge of hope. "I know I'm right about Jason. I may not like it very much, and I may not like him very much, but I have to admit the man's got his pride and he knows how to hold on to it. But then, you've always had good taste in men."

Though she raised her eyes heavenward, she did not take the smile from her lips. "Haven't I, though?" she agreed as she walked him to the door. It seemed strange that he could be so pleasant when he truly wanted to.

Why did he go to such lengths to be so annoying most of the time?

"Ah, yes, a woman of good taste," he told her again. And then, with a wicked gleam in his eye, he thought about kissing her with such passion it would leave her breathless and yearning. But he decided to wait. It was not yet time to draw for that final card. He would bide his time until the stakes were just right. "Good day, Kat."

Then he was gone, and Katherine turned away to go and find Jason.

"Well look what the dog just drug in," Zeb said while he watched Flint close the distance between them. He leaned back in his chair with his feet planted on the top of his desk and eyed Flint through the steam that drifted up from the coffee mug he held cupped in his hands.

"I had a feeling you'd be glad to see me," Flint said with a sardonic grin. "I've come by to ask the sheriff a few questions. Where is he?"

"Gone on his afternoon rounds. It might be half an hour before he's finished. I'd offer you a chair so you could sit and wait, but I'm sure you have better things to do—like slap around several helpless women or shoot it out with a few thirteen-year-old boys in the street."

"That wasn't my fault," Flint said angrily. As he noted the look of scornful disbelief on the young deputy's face, he felt his own lips tighten. "The boy drew on me with no warning. It was dark. I had no way of knowing who he was or how old he was. I had to kill or be killed."

"Speaking of being killed, how is it that you're still alive? The sheriff up in Cimarron told me you were dead—shot in both the back and the face. He even shipped me these to prove it was you." Zeb's curiosity had gotten the best of him as he pulled open the top drawer of his desk and lifted out the box that held the two rings. As he lifted the lid and revealed the contents, he watched Flint's eyes closely. The man's questioning look had changed to one of total surprise.

"My rings. You say the sheriff got them off a dead man in Cimarron?" A grateful smile spread slowly across Flint's eyes. "He certainly didn't get very far, did he?"

"From where?"

"What do you care?" Flint snapped, not about to give the deputy his life story.

Zeb shrugged his shoulders indifferently and resumed sipping his coffee.

"Where's the money?" Flint asked after he had searched the box and found nothing else but a thick square of cotton. He eyed Zeb suspiciously. "There should have been close to two thousand dollars on that man, too."

"What do you care?" Zeb fired back, smiling at his own riposte.

Slipping his ring back on his finger, Flint stared down into Zeb's eyes with such a look of cold anger that Zeb wished he hadn't thoughtfully left his holster hanging on a wall peg near the door. He was also a good six feet from his rifle.

"I'll just have to wire that sheriff myself," Flint told him, barely controlling his rage. "And if I find out he did send that money along with my rings—and if it turns out you decided to take it for yourself—there's going to be hell to pay. I won that money fair."

"I can just imagine how fair the game was," Zeb taunted, for he had just glanced out the window, and, spotting the sheriff headed their way, he knew Flint would be outnumbered should he become violent or produce a gun. "No doubt that game was just as fair as some of the gunfights you've been in. Self-defense, I'll bet."

"I've never provoked but one gunfight in my life, and even then, the other man drew first," Flint informed him, though he wasn't sure why he bothered. "And as you can clearly see, if you just strain your eyes and look, I don't even wear my gun anymore. Unless someone makes a clear threat on my life, I keep my gun in my room."

"What's going on here?" Sheriff Ragland asked, when he entered the office to find the two men staring each other down, hate equally evident in both men's eyes.

"This 'gentleman' is here to see you," Zeb replied, his lip curling in disgust. "And now that you're back, I think I'll head on out to check on Jim Haught. Even though Patrick Walls is dead, there's no telling what one of his buddies might decide to do, and as long as Jim is laid up, we need to continue keeping a very close watch." He had meant it more as a barb than a warning, but was disappointed to see that Flint clearly didn't know what he was talking about.

"Patrick Wall is dead?" he asked, his gaze now directed to the sheriff.

"Why, did you know him?" the sheriff asked, unaware of Flint's identity.

"Sort of. We used to be good friends a long time ago. I haven't seen him in several years, though. How'd he die?"

"He and some of his friends tried to ambush a local man out at his farm," the sheriff replied, "but the man got a shot off before they could gun him down. Even so, Walls tried to make a run for it, but eventually bled to death."

"Live by the gun; die by the gun," Zeb put in, but his remark went ignored by the sheriff and brought only a raised brow from Flint.

"You wouldn't happen to know if there's any next of kin, would you?" the sheriff asked. "We done buried the body, but we've still got his horse, his saddle, and some of his personal belongings, and don't know anybody to notify to come get them."

"He's got a sister who lives in Dodge City. Her name is Gina. If you'd like, I could take it all up there to her. I have a feeling I'm going to have to make a trip up in that direction, anyway."

"I know a few people who will be glad to hear that," Zeb couldn't resist commenting.

The sheriff frowned at Zeb's rude behavior, but decided to hold his questions until after the man had left. "Tell me her last name, and I'll wire up there and make the arrangements to send his things to her. It might be that she'd be just as happy if we went ahead and sold the horse to the local livery, then sent her the money rather than shipping the animal at her expense."

"Knowing her, she would. She doesn't have much use for a horse. Tell you what—I'll stop back here when I know for sure if I'm going to have to make the trip north or not. If that's what it takes to get my money back, then I'll be leaving right away."

"I should know sometime this afternoon," the sheriff assured him and walked with him outside. "Can I have your name, so I can tell her just who would be bringing Walls' belongings to her?"

"Just tell her 'Frank.' She'll know who I am."

When the sheriff returned to his office he immediately wanted to know why Zeb was so leery of the stranger, and when he found out who Frank really was, he had his doubts about entrusting Patrick Walls' belongings to him. But then, when he considered the honor-among-thieves code, he realized it was probably all right. He would leave the decision to Walls' sister.

As Katherine walked outside with Minnie close behind, carrying a large basket filled with colorful scraps of material, she noticed a strange horse tied up near the blacksmith's shed.

"Whose horse is that?" she asked, quickly searching the grounds for sight of a stranger.

"Don't rightly know," Minnie answered. "I didn't hear nobody ride up, and Mister Jason didn't say nothin' about no one supposed to come by while he's gone to town."

Katherine had a sinking feeling. Though she specifically remembered having told Flint that she wouldn't be home to accept his call, she knew—even before she could see him standing in the doorway to the barn—that the tall, sleek animal belonged to him.

"Go ahead and put the scraps into the carriage," she told Minnie. "I think I know who our guest is, and I'll see to it that he is quickly on his way."

"Flint?" Minnie wanted to know.

"Unless I miss my guess."

"I'll go with you," Minnie said with a determined scowl. "Between the two of us, we ought to be able to send that no account snake on his way."

Katherine didn't want to take the time to argue with Minnie, for she suddenly remembered that Ruby was taking Jeffrey down to see the calves again. Panic swept over her as she hurried toward the barn. Minnie could barely keep up.

"What are you doing here?" she addressed him in a low voice so that no one else in the barn would hear. "I thought I made it perfectly clear that I wouldn't be home today."

"I know," Flint replied, "but there's been a change in plans."

"Not in my plans. I was just about to leave."

"No, in mine. As it turns out, I'm going to have to go back up to Kansas for a few days and then make a trip over to Louisiana. I won't be back here for at least a week. I just wanted to stop by and explain why I won't be able to visit you tomorrow, like we planned. I figured even if you'd already left, I could leave the message with the mother hen there"—he nodded toward Minnie who stood right behind Katherine—"or to your . . . 'husband'." The word stuck in his craw, but because there were other people in the barn who might overhear them, he decided not to cause trouble. As long as Katherine had a secret to keep, he had some control over her.

"So, why are you down here by the barn? Why didn't you come to the house to deliver your message?" she asked suspiciously.

"When I rode up, I noticed your son headed towards the barn. I was just curious to get a look at him is all." Then, indicating the boy who was peering between two planks of the large pen that held over three dozen baby calves, he smiled and shook his head with admiration. "That's a fine looking boy you have. I'm pleased to see how much he looks like you. I don't think he looks like Jason at all."

Katherine bristled at the thought that he might be digging for proof of the boy's true identity. "I appreciate the compliment, but I still believe he looks more like Jason."

Just then, Jeffrey looked up to find his mother's eyes on him and he quickly drew his head back from the planking. Eyes wide with youthful guilt, he hurried to her side to explain. "I wasn't going to climb in there, Momma. I was just petting them. I wasn't about to climb in there with them again. Not after you told me not to. You can ask Miss Sutton. She isn't going to let me climb in there again."

"I know you weren't going to," Katherine quickly assured him, but when she looked around for Ruby, she found that the woman had not been keeping a close eye on the boy at all. Her attention seemed to be focused on what Rede was doing in the far corner of the pen. Lately, it seemed that Ruby's attention was drawn more and more to Rede.

"Then I'm not in trouble?" Jeffrey asked, breathing a quick sigh of relief.

"No, you're not in trouble. I just came down here to tell you good-bye. I'm leaving now. Give me a hug." She bent down and embraced her son protectively. It was not until she released him that the boy seemed to notice Flint.

"Who are you?" he asked straight out, tilting his head and staring up at the tall stranger.

"I'm a friend of your mother," he told him, his eyes trained on the boy's animated features. He knelt down to the child's level and extended his hand. "And I'd like to be your friend, too," he said. "The name's Frank. Frank Mason."

Pleased at the grown-up gesture, Jeffrey smiled and shook Flint's hand firmly. "Pleased to meet you, Mr. Mason. My name's Jeffrey Morris."

Wanting to separate the two before Flint came to suspect the truth, Katherine turned to leave, knowing Flint would follow. She was glad that Minnie stayed behind to keep the boy from following, too.

It was not until she had led him well away from the barn that she slowed down enough for him to catch up with her—just so she could tell him good-bye and suggest he be on his way.

"I plan to be back around the middle of next week," he started to explain when he had her attention.

"Don't hurry on my account," she replied coldly. "I have gotten along six years without you. I could gladly do without you for six more."

"Well, I can't do without you for even six days. It'll be pure torture. But I'll be out to see you just as soon as I get back." He reached out and gently touched his finger to the tip of her beautiful nose. Her eyes widened and her lips parted to rebuke him, but no words came from her mouth.

Knowing he had better leave quickly before he did something he might regret to those captivatingly parted lips, he strode past her waiting carriage and swiftly mounted his horse. He paused just long enough to look back at her and smile. With a light-hearted lilt to his voice, he called to her, "Try not to miss me too much while I'm gone."

Chapter Twenty

"Mother, can I go fishing with Edmond and Samuel? They're headed over to Mr. Ewan's pond and said if it was all right with you, I could go along with them."

"I'm not too sure, Jeffrey. Will you promise to be very careful and not get in the way of the hooks?" Katherine wanted him to think she had to consider the matter further, even though she'd already decided it would be fine.

"Yes, Mother, I'll be careful," Jeffrey promised, his hazel-green eyes wide with eagerness. "I'll be real careful."

Katherine looked out through the back door and noticed Edmond and Samuel. The two boys stood just beyond the porch, patiently waiting for Jeffrey to come out with an answer. Keeping her expression stern, she walked out on the porch and asked, "You two will watch out for him, won't you?"

"Yes, ma'am," they assured her in unison. Even though there was at least six years' difference between them and Jeffrey, they liked to have the little boy's company whenever they had some time off to play or go fishing. "Pa and Mister Jason have both taught us to always be careful when we go fishing," Edmond said.

"And you'll be sure to be back in plenty of time for supper?" she went on to ask. She didn't want to seem too easy. It was bad enough Jeffrey had one overly permissive parent.

"I'm not about to miss out on my supper," Edmond assured her with a large, toothy grin. "We're just going to be gone a couple of hours. Might even bring you back a mess of fish for Grandma to fry up for tomorrow's supper."

"Well, since you've promised to be careful and to come home well before dark, I guess Jeffrey can go," Katherine finally said, quickly adding, with a firm shake of her finger in Jeffrey's direction, "But I warn you, young man, if either Samuel or Edmond come back and tell me that you didn't mind them, you won't be going again."

"Yippee," Jeffrey shouted and leaped off the porch, landing right beside his two friends. "I can go."

Not wanting to give Katherine time to reconsider, the three boys raced toward the blacksmith's shed where they kept their fishing poles and worm can. Within minutes, they were trotting off happily toward the neighbor's pond.

Katherine stood watching as her son's little denim-clad legs worked twice as hard to keep up with the older, longer-legged boys. She wondered if he were trying to grow up too fast, but knew that could not be helped. It was in a boy's nature. The corners of her mouth turned down with a mother's unhappiness, but she tried her best to put her melancholy aside. She knew that she had to let him have growing room, and she knew Jeffrey was safe enough with Edmond and Samuel, but still, she felt apprehensive.

To distract herself, she returned to her darning, and as she hoped, soon lost her motherly worries in the tedious handwork.

The rest of the afternoon passed uneventfully. Flint was still away on his business trip, which she guessed was connected with getting his money back from the sheriff at Cimarron. From everything Zeb had told them the afternoon following Flint's last visit, there was at least two thousand dollars involved, and Flint had seemed eager to lay claim to it. She wondered about how that money—if it really was Flint's—had come to be on another man's body, along with his rings and wallet. But, with Flint away, there was no way for her to find out and she tried not to let it bother her. She was too happy over the simple fact that Flint was gone.

It was not until the afternoon shadows lengthened and the boys didn't return as promised, that Katherine grew apprehensive again. When Jason returned from helping Craig Monk repair a section of fence dividing their two ranches, Katherine sent him right out again to bring the boys back home. She was furious that they had stayed so late when she had specifically asked them not to, and she intended to punish all three of them for making her worry.

While she paced up and down in the living room, the dining room, and the kitchen, she kept an eye out for the boys and Jason. As was her nature, she had conjured up all sorts of catastrophes, so that by the time she saw them coming, she was angry enough to take a whip to all three of the boys, but also so relieved, she wanted to hug them all close. As she lifted her maroon woolen skirt and hurried outside, she planned to do just that—though she knew her embracing Edmond and Samuel would scare them half to death.

Not until she realized the man who rode slowly behind the three boys was not Jason did her relief turn to anger again. But this time, her anger was directed at the man she now assumed responsible for the children's tardiness. Fear and anger clutched at her heart as she flew to confront the last man she had ever wanted to see in the company of her son.

"What are you doing here?" she cried out as she ran up to the group in the middle of the yard. She barely noticed the chilling wind which had picked up from the north and tugged sharply at her hair and long, woolen skirt.

"Been fishing." Flint shrugged, then reached back to pull up a stringer with nine large white perch attached. "And just look how good we did."

"*We* did?" she repeated aghast, staring first into his smug and smiling face and then at the three wide-eyed little boys. Her gaze rested only briefly on her son's apprehensive look before going boldly back to meet Flint's.

"Yes, we. All of us seemed to have pretty good luck this afternoon," he said and smiled proudly down at the boys. "Edmond did the best. He caught three. Samuel and Jeffrey each caught two, but then so did I. Actually, Jeffrey also caught three, but that last one was pretty small, so we decided to toss him back and let him do a little growing up. We'll go back and catch him again next spring when he should be a little closer to cooking size."

Forgetting that he was in serious trouble for having come in so late, Jeffrey couldn't resist bragging. "Edmond may have caught more for the stringer, but I caught that biggest one, there at the bottom."

"That he did," Flint was quick to agree as he untied the stringer from his saddle and handed it down to the boys. "You should be right proud of your son. He's quite a fisherman. Why don't you three put your poles down and take these fish on in to that bossy cook of yours so she can clean them. She'll want to get them in the icebox right away."

Katherine held her anger until the boys were in the house, well out of earshot. "How is it you happened to be with them on their fishing trip?" she demanded, planting her fists on her hips. "I thought you were away on some sort of important business."

"I was. It went better than I expected, though. I got back in town around noon and was just on my way out to tell you my big news when I happened to notice the boys tramping through the woods, over near the main road, and decided to see what they were up to. Besides, I've been wanting the opportunity to get to know your son a little better. Who knows, one day he may be my son."

Not exactly sure what he had meant by that remark, Katherine could feel the blood drain out of her face. Her heart froze with the dread fear that he was becoming suspicious of who Jeffrey's real father was and was hinting for proof. Had he noticed a resemblance? Had he somehow learned the boy's real age? Knowing how quick Jeffrey was to brag about being five, her stomach knotted more tightly and she felt her knees buckling. She needed something to lean on, but there was nothing within reach. It became difficult for her to even breathe. She knew she should try to say something that would turn his attention away from the boy—something that would change any notions he might have—but her mind was a blank except for her fear.

Just then, they heard the distant pounding of horse's hooves—and to Flint's dismay, but Katherine's relief—they could see Jason hurrying in their direction. Riding hard and at breakneck speed, he left a thick trail of reddish-brown dust rising behind him.

"Katherine, I couldn't find the boys anywhere," he said in a panic-stricken voice, giving Flint only a moment's glance as he pulled up beside her. His horse pranced beneath him and pawed nervously at the ground, as if sensing his master's distress. "I need to get the men together to help search for them. It's almost dark and there's a storm brewing to the north. And there's no telling where they've wandered off to."

"They're inside," Katherine reassured him, then wondering how Jason had missed them, she looked curiously up at Flint and narrowed her eyes accusingly. The brisk wind blew her dark hair across her face, but she pushed it away impatiently. "How is it Jason didn't run into you? If you followed the path that leads directly from Ewan's pond, he would have had to pass you."

"We didn't exactly come straight back," Flint admitted, and noticed the intense anger that response brought to Katherine's eyes. He quickly sought to explain. "While we were fishing, the boys got to telling me about a fort they built out in the woods over there."

He nodded toward a dense growth of trees that extended several acres onto the Ewan place. "And when I told them about a fort I'd built when I was a boy, they wanted me to see theirs. We took a quick trip over so I could get a look at it. Have you seen it? It's real impressive. Those are three very clever young boys."

"What were you doing fishing with the boys?" Jason thundered. "What the hell right do you have spending time with my son?"

"No right, really—but after I helped him dig for their worms, they invited me to come along, so I did. I didn't see anything very wrong in that."

"Stay away from my boy," Jason ordered, leaning forward in the saddle. "It's bad enough having you badger my wife the way you do. You stay away from my son."

"Badgering? *Your* wife?" Flint responded angrily. The hand that gripped his reins turned white around the knuckles as he looked down at Katherine. "I don't consider paying a friendly visit on *my* wife as badgering her."

"When she no longer wants to be your wife and you continue to force your company on her, that's badgering," Jason flung back at him, gripped by a rage so great he desperately wanted to climb down and drag Flint from his horse. Nothing would please him more than beating Flint Mason to a bloody pulp.

"Lower your voices. Both of you," Katherine admonished. Her face turned pale as she spoke. Again, she had to toss her long hair out of her face. "Do you want everyone to hear you?" Looking up at Flint, she put her hands firmly on her hips again and stared him boldly in the eye, unaware of what an alluring picture she made with the wind whipping her dress against her shapely body, revealing every curve and contour. "I think it would be best for all concerned if you would leave now."

"I'll leave if you promise to be available tomorrow morning to show me around this place, like you promised to do last week."

"Only with Minnie as an escort," she put in quickly.

Though he'd hoped to have the chance to be alone with her, he decided not to press it this time. Tempers were already too hot, especially Katherine's. "Of course, with Minnie as an escort. I wouldn't expect you to go unchaperoned quite so soon. You are too circumspect and far too much of a lady to allow that." He felt that was a very gallant thing to say and hoped it won him a little of her favor. "I guess my news can wait until then. I'll see you in the morning around ten."

Tipping his hat lightly in her direction, he offered her a quick smile and spurred his horse into a gallop.

"I can't stay as long as I'd like," Flint told Katherine as they stepped off the back porch to walk toward the barn, which they had decided was to be their first stop on Flint's tour of Seven Oaks. Though Jason had yet to be seen, Minnie was right behind them, obviously delighted with her role as chaperone.

"It shouldn't take very long to show you around here," Katherine put in quickly, and tried to suppress a sigh of relief, for she wasn't sure how much more of his nerve-racking company she could take.

"As a matter of fact"—Minnie interrupted in a voice so loud and commanding, both Katherine and Flint turned around. Smiling broadly at how easily she had gained their attention, she waved her arm in a wide arc around the property—"You can pretty well see the whole place from right here. There's the barn dead ahead and next to it is the bunkhouse. That slanted buildin' to the right doubles as the blacksmith shop and tool shed. Over yonder's the carriage house."

Flint opened his mouth to break in, but there was no interrupting Minnie once she got started. "And that wooden buildin' over there is the smokehouse and woodshed. The little one down there used to be the privy, but it's been turned into a manure shed now that we got indoor facilities." She made that last comment with added emphasis because she was so proud of the additions Jason had made in the bathing room. They were the first ones she knew of to have a commode that actually flushed. She hoped Flint would take note of how well Jason could, and did, provide for Katherine. "And those three that looks so much alike are workers' houses. The middle one belongs to me and Silas. And that just about takes care of anything you would want to see. You can go on and leave now if you want."

Katherine couldn't help but chuckle softly at how Minnie had tried to handle Flint. Unable to hide her grin, she looked at him and asked, "Any questions?"

"Mind if we get a closer look at some of the work buildings? I want to get a better idea about what I'll need to get my own place stocked right." He waited for that to sink in.

"Your own place?" Katherine responded immediately. Her hands clutched at the folds of the drab gray dress she had decided to wear in an effort to make herself less appealing. "What place?"

"That's the news I wanted to tell you yesterday, but you were a little too angry to listen. I bought the old Turner place. It needs a lot of work—the equipment that hasn't been stolen while the house has been sitting vacant is in pretty bad shape and will probably have to be replaced—but before long, I'll have it all in good working order."

"You bought the Turner place?" Katherine wanted to cry out with the anger that had so quickly consumed her. How dare he try to make himself a permanent part of her life by buying a place so near to theirs! "Why would you do something like that? You're not a rancher. You don't know the first thing about running a ranch."

"Maybe not, but I've already hired a foreman who does. And I did it to show you that I can be just as respectable, and work just as hard as Jason Morris."

"Humph," Minnie snorted. "Takes more than ownin' your own ranch to be respectable."

Flint ignored the remark. "The place has been allowed to sit until it's been overrun by goat weeds and underbrush; and what equipment that's left hasn't been taken care of. But with a lot of hard work, I'll have it looking real nice in no time. It'll be a place you can be proud of."

Katherine did not like the way he said that. "Why should I care what your ranch looks like?"

"Because someday it just might be your home," he told her. His eyes gazed deeply into hers as he tried to read her thoughts. "But if you decide you'd rather the two of us go away from here and make a brand new start, I'll gladly sell that ranch. I can buy another place wherever you like. All I want is to make you happy and make up for all the wrong I've done you in the past."

"Where'd you get the money to buy your own ranch?" she asked, suddenly suspicious. Although Flint had never been without money, what money he did have was usually ill-gotten and rarely lasted long. The two thousand would have been a start, but not enough to buy a ranch as large as the Turner place, no matter how run down it was.

"I got my money back from the sheriff in Cimarron and then went directly to our neighbor, Zack Clifton, and asked if he would care to buy my house and the land around it since his place surrounds ours on three sides, anyway. Because his daughter was about to be married and he felt it would make a fine wedding gift, he went to the bank that very afternoon and got the money for me. Then, having already asked Sheriff Ragland where I could find the widow Turner, I boarded a train for Louisiana and made the deal with her. I now own the place outright and have just enough money left over to get it pretty well stocked. I may have to forgo a few of the niceties until I get the place on its feet and making good money, but I should have what I need to run the place."

Katherine raised a trembling hand to her face. He was serious. He had indeed bought the Turner place and intended to run it as his own ranch. Suddenly, she felt ill.

"It doesn't bother you that Patrick Walls died in that house?" she asked, hoping still to discourage him.

"Why should it?"

"Patrick was your friend."

"Pat's only friend was himself. I hadn't even laid eyes on the man in almost five years. I told you, I've been trying to change, and one of the first things I did was cut myself off from men like Patrick Walls. I'm sorry the man is dead, but I don't see why it should keep me from wanting to live in that house. Pat was doomed to die young. He was careless and too much of a hothead."

Katherine wished she could think of something else to say that would show him how foolish it was for him to think he could run a ranch, foreman or no foreman—something that would dissuade him from such a horribly permanent decision. "Running a ranch is a lot of work—very hard work. I don't think you realize what you've let yourself in for."

"I've thought about it very carefully. I think it's the only way I can prove to you just how much I've changed. And once I'm accepted as a respectable part of this community, it'll be easier on you to make your decision to come back to me. You can simply tell everyone that you and Jason have gotten a divorce, and after a proper amount of time, come move in with me—your real husband—and we can be happy again."

"Why would anyone ever come to accept a man like Flint Mason as a respectable citizen?" she asked angrily. The more time she had to think about it, the more rage she felt.

"Very few people know who I am—or rather, who I was. Only you, Jason, mother hen there"—he nodded at Minnie who bristled at the remark—"the sheriff, and his deputy know that much about me. As far as everyone else is concerned, I'm Frank Mason now. Flint Mason is gone forever."

"Even if you did somehow fool the people around here into believing you were respectable, you wouldn't be considered so for very long if I was to divorce Jason because of you," she pointed out in an attempt to show him how many holes his plan had.

"Then we can go away and start over somewhere else. I can sell this place and buy another, anywhere you want to go."

"I want to stay here," she told him flatly. What would it take to make him see that?

"Then we can stay here and face these people together. I can face anything with you by my side."

"I meant that I want to stay here, at Seven Oaks. I love Jason."

At that remark, Minnie thrust her chin forward and, looking Flint directly in the eye, she boldly spoke her piece. "And the sooner you get that through your thick skull, Mister Flint Mason, the better it'll be for everybody."

Flint raised a brow at Minnie's insulting words, but chose to ignore her. Instead, he continued to address Katherine. "You only think you love Jason. I've already seen that you still want me as much as you ever did. It's only that stubborn streak in you that refuses to let you see what's really in your heart. Given a little time, I think you'll finally come to terms with what you really do feel."

"Flint, you're only fooling yourself with such a speech," Katherine told him. "Nothing you can say or do will change the way I feel about Jason."

"We'll see," Flint said, clearly undaunted by her words. "Once I've finally proved to you how much I've changed and how very much I still love you, you'll eventually start to give in to your true feelings. You'll want to be mine again."

"He don't listen to you," Minnie observed, her dark face drawn in a tight frown. "Why do you bother sayin' anything to him at all when he don't bother to listen?"

Katherine shook her head and felt a wave of frustration wash over her. She wanted to grab him by the shoulders and shake him as hard as she could to get through to him. She felt like pulling at his ear and screaming into it at the top of her lungs, but she knew even that would do no good. Heaving a sharp sigh, she wondered just what it would take to make him understand.

"Even though I'll be busy getting my own place in order for a while, I'll still find time to visit you," Flint promised, unaware that his words only served to further provoke her. "And once I get it looking real nice, I'll come get you and take you over to see it. Maybe then, you'll realize how serious I am about winning you back."

What he was careful not to say was that if the ranch did not win her over, he would take more drastic measures. If he had to strap his gun back on to get what was rightfully his, he would do it. But first, he would try getting what he wanted without using force. He would stretch his patience to the limit.

"The ranch will prove to you how much I love you, Katherine. And when you see what a different man I've become, you'll be willing to love me again—just as much as you used to."

He smiled with such cheeky self-assurance, that Katherine felt like slapping the smug expression right off his arrogant face. But rather than continue a hopeless argument with a deaf man, she hurried toward the barn so that she could get the ridiculous tour over with and send him on his way. She wanted to get him out of her sight as quickly as she could; but even more important, she wanted to be out of his sight. The way he kept looking at her was unnerving. It was as if he remembered what she looked like without her clothes, and the thought of that made her want to scream.

As it turned out, Flint's purchasing the Turner place was a temporary blessing. It kept him far busier than he had expected, and as a result, he had much less time to spend with Katherine. His new foreman, Ben Truitt, was a real worker who was dead-set on getting the ranch operational as quickly as possible, and that left little spare time for either of them. Even after Flint took on an extra hand, the foreman simply found that much more to be done. Flint was still unable to get much free time, and his desire to show Katherine a fine "working" ranch made him toil that much harder.

Katherine hoped it would take forever to get the ranch in shape. But all too soon—though thankfully it came after Christmas—Flint came by to announce that he was ready to show her his ranch. It seemed hard to believe that he had managed to get the place ready in so short a time, but Flint insisted that everything was in apple-pie order.

Reluctantly, she agreed to have Jason drive her over the very next week, but Flint was adamant that she not bring Jason and offered to call for her himself. Realizing the two men would probably end up getting into a fight anyway, she agreed to leave Jason behind; but unwilling to be alone with Flint—though he claimed to have a foreman and two ranch hands on the place now—she decided to have Silas drive her over. She promised to come that following Monday, weather permitting, and even though she knew she would regret it, she agreed to stay for lunch.

Jason took the news in stride. Although he did not like the idea of Katherine being lured over to Flint's house, he held his temper and did nothing to try to stop her. He had already decided to be a man of his word and truly let her make her own decision where Flint was concerned. And though the situation bothered the hell out of him, he had enough faith in Katherine that when she came into the barn to tell him she was ready to leave, he simply asked her to be careful.

As he watched her climb resignedly into the carriage, wearing one of her plainer dresses, he felt certain she'd be able to handle Flint. Even if the situation got out of control and Flint became violent, he was confident that Silas would defend Katherine's honor. He had seen to it that Silas was armed with a rifle.

Katherine did not want to go. The look on Jason's face as they pulled away from the barn was still clear in her mind when they arrived, less than thirty minutes later, at Flint's ranch. She hated the thought of Jason having to suffer for even a few hours and was determined to get back to him as quickly as possible.

Not wanting to wait for Flint to appear and formally greet her, Katherine immediately climbed down from the carriage, glanced around at the freshly painted barn and outbuildings, then headed for the small wood-framed house. She was vaguely aware that he'd painted all the shutters and trim bright yellow—her favorite color.

Because of her determination to see Flint's place,

hurry through their lunch, and be on her way home in as short a time as possible, Katherine marched swiftly up the steps and knocked impatiently at the door. How she hated having to be here with Flint when she knew how it tormented Jason. But when she thought of the alternative—Flint and Jason coming face to face in a shootout—she knew she had to see her part of the bargain through.

She had to do whatever it took to appease Flint until he either grew tired of trying to win her back or came to see how hopeless his efforts were. Flint had a well earned reputation as one of the best gunfighters around and Jason had no experience whatever at drawing against another man. Jason could be killed. Just the thought of Jason being gunned down sent panic racing through her. Resolutely, she thrust her fear aside and prayed that the next few hours would pass quickly.

Chapter Twenty-One

Although the sun shone brightly in a gray winter sky, the temperature was cold enough to permit a cozy fire in the massive stone fireplace, and to Katherine's dismay, Flint had placed a small table set for two near the crackling flames. She noticed that he had also drawn the curtains against the light from outside.

Amber shadows danced across the room, warm and inviting. Had she been dining with Jason, she might have considered the setting very romantic, but as it was, she felt threatened and was glad she had thought to weave a large hat pin into the seam of her dress where it would be handy should she need it. Though she would tolerate what she could for Jason's sake, there were limits to what she would allow Flint to get away with.

Katherine was on the alert in case he should try to get too intimate with her again, and was more than a little surprised when the most he did was to reach across the table to briefly hold her hand. He had not once tried to touch her during their earlier, short tour of the ranch, nor had he made any suggestive comments.

He made no threatening moves at all. Though Silas had been served a lunch in the bunkhouse with the ranchhands, leaving the two of them entirely alone, Flint did not once try to pull her close and kiss her. He remained a perfect gentleman, so much so, it made her doubly uneasy. She had fully expected to do battle and had warned Silas that should she scream, he was to come running; but she was in no way prepared for Flint's restrained courtly charm. She did not know how to react and found herself reduced to a blithering idiot throughout much of the meal, unable to concentrate on most of what was said, but determined to keep talking without knowing why.

Even when they had finished the delicious braised chicken and rice, he did nothing more than offer his hand to escort her to the only two chairs in the living room. On her arrival, Katherine had noticed that the house was very sparsely furnished and she didn't recognize any of the furniture. Flint had not brought back any of the pieces from Kansas and evidently, Mrs. Turner had taken most of her belongings with her.

"I'm sorry I don't have a nice upholstered divan to offer you a seat on, but I've had to spend so much money getting this place stocked, repaired, and the equipment replaced, that I don't have enough money left to purchase the furniture I want. Come spring though, Ben says we'll be able to produce enough extra hay and alfalfa to have some to sell at the market—enough to allow me to buy a brand new living room suite." He frowned as a sudden thought occurred to him. "I sold most of my furniture with the house to get a better price, but I paid good money to have that hutch and dining table you liked so much sent down here, yet it still hasn't arrived. I need to have the sheriff look into that."

He looked somewhat sheepish as another thought crossed his mind. "I sold your clothes, too, while I was gone. After seeing how much your body has changed over these past few years, I figured they wouldn't fit you any longer, and since I've yet to see you wear the same dress twice, I realized you didn't really need your old clothes, anyway. I'm sure Jason will let you take your clothes with you when you leave. He sure won't have any use for them."

"I have no plans to go anywhere," she reminded him.

"Not yet, but when you do," he responded with that arrogant smile.

Rather than get into the same old argument, Katherine decided to change the subject. She would offer him a few more minutes of conversation, then quickly take her leave. She was ready to go home. "You were right to sell my clothes. I've put on too much weight to ever hope to wear them again and it would have been a shame just to throw them away. They were made of such good material."

"That they were. I never scrimped when it came to you. You meant far too much to me."

That was not the direction in which she wanted to steer the conversation. She tried again. "You were right about another thing. I'm impressed with all you've done with this place in so short a time. How many head of cattle did you say you bought?"

"Bought sixty, but judging by the huge bellies on many of them, I should have ninety head or more by next spring. I could have bought more cattle, but that dirty dog who ambushed me somehow managed to spend several hundred of my dollars before he got himself killed. Either that, or the sheriff up there helped himself to a hefty profit."

"I've always wanted to ask you about that. Why did that dead man have your things?"

"I was robbed. Ambushed really. Just outside of Dodge. I had been real lucky up until that point. I'd won over two thousand dollars in a poker game and was headed back home with my winnings when I passed a man pretending to have a broken down wagon. When I stopped to see if he needed any help, he jumped me. He hit me in the left leg with a rifle butt hard enough to knock me to my knees, then slammed the rifle into the back of my head. When I came to, my wallet and jewelry were gone. So was my horse—and there I was, hardly able to walk. Eventually, I got a ride into Cimarron with an old farmer. Then, after the doctor saw to me and said I was strong enough to travel, I got a ride out to the house with a friend. That's when I found the letter from Patrick Walls, telling me he thought he'd seen you down here."

He smiled as he thought back. "Evidently, Mark Clifton had brought my mail by the house and left it so I could find it when I returned. He'd done that for me before. I'm glad he did, because right there on top of the stack was that letter from Pat."

Katherine had never felt anger toward a dead man before, but she did now. Patrick had remembered seeing her after all, and had found a way to tell Flint before he got himself shot. Bitterly, she wished Jim Haught had managed to kill him that first time, and felt only a twinge of guilt at the thought.

"So it was Patrick's letter that brought you to Gilmer," she commented.

"Yes, I thought you knew that. As soon as I read how he thought he'd seen you here—even though the letter was already weeks old and my leg still hurt—I was out the door within an hour."

If only that letter had managed to get lost, Katherine thought morosely. Everyone would still believe that Flint was dead, and she and Jason would be blissfully ignorant of the fact that her marriage to Flint was still binding. She and Jason would now be living happily in the mistaken belief that they were finally, legally married. She wanted to cry out in her misery, but somehow she kept her voice calm and rose to leave.

"It's getting late. I have to get back. Jeffrey hates it when I'm not there to put him down for his nap."

"I wish I'd had a mother who took the time to care as much as you do for Jeffrey," he said with open admiration. "You're real devoted to that son of yours, aren't you?"

"He means the world to me," she answered honestly.

"Then he's important to me, too," he told her and made no attempt to persuade her to stay. Instead, he walked her outside to her carriage where Silas sat waiting.

All the way home, she was bothered by Flint's remark about Jeffrey. She didn't want her son to be important to Flint for whatever reason. What she wanted was for him to stay far away from the boy, and she knew she would do whatever it took to keep the two apart.

But Flint had different ideas. He wanted to get to know Jeffrey better, but remembering Jason's warning to stay away from the boy, he knew he'd have to find a way to spend time with him without letting either Jason or Katherine know what he was up to.

With that thought in mind, he made several trips into the woods bordering Seven Oaks to check the fort for any sign of the boys. One day, he came upon the three of them playing together.

"Well, if it isn't my young fishing partners," he said as he stepped forward out of the dense shadows.

All three boys looked up in surprise, but any concern they might have had vanished when they recognized their unexpected visitor.

"What are you doing out here?" Edmond was the first to speak.

"Figured I'd do a little fishing over at the pond, but now that I've found the three of you here, I think I'll just stick around and talk with you fellows a while. What are you up to over there?" he asked and nodded toward where they were digging a hole at the side of the fort.

"Making an escape trap," Edmond informed him since it was his idea. "When we get finished digging the hole up under the wall, we're going to put us a door over it and then cover it with vines so that you can't really see it."

Jeffrey nodded as he brought a grimy arm up to wipe away some of the dust that had settled on his freckled face. Though he was obviously tired from all the hard work, he found the energy to smile brightly and explain, "Then, if anyone ever tries to take over the fort, we can sneak out through here and get clean away."

Though Flint had his doubts about the tiny log-and-plank fort ever being attacked, he thought the idea clever, and applauded the boys for executing it with such enthusiasm. "That's pretty smart. I don't suppose you could use any help."

"Can always use another man digging," Samuel put in quickly, for the shovel work was the least-liked aspect of the entire project. "You can use my shovel for a while."

Flint took the shovel and started to dig, making much faster progress alone than the boys had been able to manage together. Soon, they decided the hole was deep enough, and they were ready to fit on the door they had built out of scrap lumber.

When they were finished, the boys tried it out and were so pleased they decided Flint should be allowed to use their fort whenever he wanted to.

"Let's make this our secret place to meet," Flint suggested immediately, hoping to find a way to keep the boys from mentioning him to either Jason or Katherine. "We won't tell anyone else where this place is or who comes here. It'll be our secret."

The boys liked the idea of having a secret place, and even though Mose already knew where his sons' fort was, they decided to pretend that no one at all knew. And because of their shared secret, Flint was finally able to get to know Jeffrey and make friends with the boy without Katherine and Jason being aware of what he was up to.

In his determination to win the boy's affections, Flint started to bring special items to the fort to help make their visits more fun. He built small pieces of furniture for them, mounted large wooden cannons out front, and even had a special flag made for them to fly overhead whenever they were there. If the boys thought it strange that a grownup wanted to join in their fun, they never mentioned it, and he was quickly accepted as one of them.

Finally, a day arrived in late January when Jeffrey came to the fort without the other two. Samuel and Edmond were being punished for forgetting to close a gate, which had allowed three horses to get loose into the main pasture. Since Samuel and Edmond were not available to play at all that day, Jeffrey had been cautioned to go only as far as the garden, but because he knew his friend, Frank, was going to be at the fort, he had deliberately slipped away unnoticed.

With the other boys absent, Flint was finally able to ask Jeffrey direct questions without worrying that Edmond would interrupt to answer them first. Finally able to probe the boy's hopes and dreams, Flint was surprised to learn of Jeffrey's deep desire to be a Texas Ranger when he grew up.

"But you know they don't make very much money," Flint pointed out, which was true. Texas Rangers were sometimes the poorest paid men around, considering the hard work and long hours they put in.

"I know, but I don't need to make a lot of money. Father already has plenty. If I ever need any money, I could get it from him."

That was true enough, Flint thought. "And you really want to be a Texas Ranger? Do you know how to shoot a gun?"

"I shot Father's rifle once," he said proudly. "And I could shoot a pistol, too, if I ever got the chance."

"Let's just see," Flint said, kneeling to crawl out the child-size door to the fort. "I've got a pistol out in my saddlebag. Let's just see how good you can shoot."

Jeffrey's bright blue eyes widened with excitement. "You'll really let me shoot your pistol?"

"Sure, I trust you," Flint said and signaled for the boy to follow him out. "But we'll have to get further away from your house to do it. Shooting the pistol this close would bring everyone a running, and we don't want them to find out about our secret hiding place."

Jeffrey agreed, and minutes later, Flint had helped the boy up on to the back of his horse and they were headed away from Seven Oaks. Then, when he felt certain they were far enough away from any houses to be noticed, he helped the boy dismount and quickly set up a few practice targets. He was amazed at how close the boy came to hitting the large pine cones placed on top of a fallen log several yards away.

"You're a pretty good shot for a four-year-old," Flint said with open admiration.

"I'm five," Jeffrey corrected, and then, as was his nature, he went on to embroider the truth. "I'm nearly six."

Flint frowned. "When's your birthday?"

"September. And when it's September again, I'll be six."

Flint did some quick arithmetic and realized that if the boy was telling the truth, he had been conceived before Katherine had left him. If the boy was telling the truth . . . ? Carefully, he studied the child and began to discover things he hadn't noticed before: The spattering of freckles; he remembered having freckles when he was a young boy. And though the boy's eyes were not as vivid a green, they were shaped very much like his own. And his hair was dark, and wavy at the temple, like his. Anger flared inside of Flint when he realized what Katherine had tried to do. She wanted to keep his own son a secret from him.

"I think it's about time for us to go back now," Flint said, eager to confront Katherine with his discovery.

"Not yet. Let me shoot your pistol again. Please. just one more time. A Texas Ranger needs lots of practice."

"Okay. One more time. Then we've got to get back before someone misses you," Flint cautioned and watched with a new fascination as the boy lifted the heavy revolver with both his small hands and fired again at the largest pine cone. This time he hit it—though barely—and Flint felt a sudden rush of pride tinged with a certain sadness—something that made his heart ache. Not taking the time to try to figure out just what it was that bothered him, he praised the boy's aim while he eased the revolver out of his hand, then lifted him quickly onto the saddle.

Flint returned to the little fort quickly and let the boy down with orders to get on home before his mother started looking for him, knowing it would take Jeffrey at least ten minutes to reach the house even if he ran. Meanwhile, Flint cut back to the main road and rode as hard as he could until he reached the main dooryard at Seven Oaks.

Katherine was already outside calling Jeffrey's name when she noticed Flint ride up. With one last glance around for her wayward son, she turned and headed for where Flint had dismounted, wondering just why he was there. He was not supposed to return for another visit until the following morning.

"What do you want?" she asked, not about to mince words when she wanted to get on with locating her son.

"I want to talk to you," he said, his face rigid with the fury that raged within him. "In private."

"As soon as I find Jeffrey. He's run off and it's time for his nap," she said evenly, trying to hide the nervousness she felt at the tone of his voice.

"He's on his way," he informed her. "And he's the one I want to talk to you about."

She continued to face him bravely, but her blood had turned to ice water. "What about my son?"

"In private. Somewhere no one can interrupt us."

Katherine tried to think of a place where no one would be likely to find them. She realized that she wanted privacy in this particular conversation as much as he did. If he'd finally become suspicious about the boy's parentage, she certainly didn't want Jeffrey to overhear anything.

"In that first cabin there," she said, with a nod toward the cottage where she had originally planned to live but which now served as Ruby's quarters. With Ruby gone off to visit her mother, the house would be a safe place for them to talk. "Go on and wait for me. I'll come as son as I've found Jeffrey and have put him down for his nap."

"Don't take too long," he warned and turned to stalk off toward the small house. His long, determined strides made her shiver with apprehension. He was clearly angry about something and she could make a fair guess as to what.

Katherine was gripped by panic as she continued her search for her son. Fear had constricted her throat and made it hard to call out his name. How she wished Jason were home, but he had left for town right after lunch. She would have to face this alone.

Finally spotting Jeffrey in the far pasture, she ran to the dooryard fence and shouted as best she could for him to hurry. Evidently, Jeffrey had heard the strain in her voice, for he started to run as fast as his legs would carry him across the faded field of winter grass.

His blue eyes were wide with guilt and he was too out of breath to speak when he finally reached his mother.

"Where have you been?" she demanded, angrily grabbing his shoulder.

Taking several quick breaths, he pointed back toward the woods and said simply, "The fort."

"Alone?" she asked, her voice stern.

His eyes grew wider as he considered how he should answer that without getting himself into further trouble. "Samuel and Edmond couldn't play."

"Were you alone?" she asked again.

Jeffrey swallowed hard and glanced only briefly at his mother's furious face before looking down at his feet. "No, ma'am. A friend was there."

"Who? Who was this friend?"

How she hoped he would say Timothy Monk or Sammy Ewan, or any of the other young children who lived close by, but her worst fears were confirmed when he finally answered in a voice so faint she had to bend to hear it. "Frank."

She did not have to ask Frank's last name.

"Jeffrey Morris, you know better than to run off without telling me where you're going, and you know I always want to be told who you are with. Get on up to your room and take your nap. We'll discuss this further when your father gets home."

By the time Jeffrey had disappeared through the back door, Katherine's hands were trembling. Flint had spent the afternoon with her son and apparently had learned something to make him suspect the truth. Her heart pounded violently as she walked toward Ruby's cottage. She wondered if there was still a way to convince him the child wasn't his.

When she entered the small house, she found him sitting at the bottom of the staircase that led up to the bedrooms above. His head was buried in his hands. For a brief moment, her heart went out to him.

The noise of the door closing behind her brought him to attention. He rose and waited until she stood before him.

"He's my son, isn't he?"

Katherine fought the urge to admit the truth. "Who? Jeffrey? Of course not!"

"Yes, he is. He turned five last September, which means you were pregnant with him before you left me—about three months pregnant before you ever met Jason."

"Where'd you get the idea Jeffrey's five?" she asked, and prayed that somehow she could convince him by trying to look as if that was the silliest thing she had ever heard.

"He told me himself. I've been seeing him without your permission in order to get to know him better, and this afternoon, he told me how old he really is."

"Boys sometimes try to make themselves out to be older than they really are," she said, trying to make it sound like a childish prank. She caught a glimpse of herself in the hallway mirror and saw that her face was deathly pale.

"I can ride into town and take a look at his birth certificate." Flint's voice was cold. "The date of his birth should be a matter of public record."

Realizing defeat, she walked over to the staircase and sank down on the bottom step. Though there were plenty of chairs in the adjoining room, she was afraid she wouldn't be able to walk that far without collapsing. Tears filled her eyes when she looked back up into his angry face. "You may have fathered him, but he is Jason's son."

Flint was seized by a towering, uncontrollable rage. He slammed his fist down on a nearby table, so violently, a ceramic vase tumbled over and crashed to the floor. Katherine screamed at the shattering sound.

"You have no right to try to keep my own son from me!" he shouted. "My own flesh and blood."

She could not respond with more than a dazed blink, for in all honesty, she knew he had a right to be angry.

"How many times have I told you that I wanted a

child—that I wanted a son of my own? How could you do this to me? How?" When he sensed she was not going to answer that question, he thought of another. "At least tell me this, did you know when you ran off that you were carrying my child?"

"It was mostly because of my pregnancy that I ran away in the first place," she admitted, ready to tell the truth and hoping to make him understand. "You were getting more and more violent with each day that passed. You were drunk almost all the time, and you know as well as I do, that whenever you drank a lot you had no control whatsoever over your temper. I was afraid for the baby's life. And if I hadn't found the strength to hit you over the head that last day, you might have destroyed Jeffrey while he was still inside me."

Flint stood perfectly still as he listened. Blood started to seep along the edge of his raw knuckles, but he ignored it.

"Flint, I realized that if I stayed and the baby should live to be born, you might turn against him in a moment of drunken rage. It was no longer safe to be around you. You made that clear. But I had already decided to run away before you began beating me. That's why I was packing when you came home. I had been in town and learned how you had lied to me again about having given up gunfighting—that you had killed a thirteen-year-old boy in a gunfight on one of your trips to Dodge City just months before. I knew I had to get out of there and never come back. I was determined that my child was not going to grow up under the influence of someone like you. I still am."

Flint closed his eyes for a long moment and when he reopened them, they were blurry with unshed tears. "You heard about that boy? Did you also hear that it wasn't my fault?"

"Don't try to tell me how it was a fair fight. No gunfight with a thirteen-year-old boy can be fair."

"It was dark!" he shouted, his green eyes wide with remembered pain. "I had no idea he was a boy. It was late at night. I heard my name and turned just in time to see someone draw on me from the shadows. I drew my revolver and fired in a purely reflex action. I had no way of knowing it was a boy. It was too dark and he moved too quick. There was just no way for me to know he was a boy."

Realizing he spoke the truth, Katherine sat in silence for a moment and thought about what it must have been like when he discovered he had killed someone so young. Though she knew her words were inadequate, she said them anyway, "I'm sorry, I had been under the impression it was a face to face shootout."

"I would never knowingly draw on a boy," he went on to say, pleading for her understanding. "And when I walked over to get a look at who had drawn on me and saw it was only a child, I went to pieces. That's why I started drinking so heavily. I wanted to drink away the image of that youthful face staring up at me in death. And it worked, too. As long as I was good and drunk, I could forget." Tears began to stream unchecked from his eyes as he continued. "It was only when I was sober that the image would come back to haunt me. And that's also why I turned to Juanita. I no longer felt worthy enough to go to your bed. A saloon whore was all I deserved. Me—a child killer."

Katherine wept, too, and rose to comfort him. "But if you had no way of knowing it was a boy who had drawn on you, why couldn't you see that his death was not your fault?"

"If I hadn't been wearing my gun, if I had followed through on the promise I had made to you to stop wearing it, that boy would still be alive. I might be dead, but he'd be alive. No matter how I looked at it, I could see I was to blame. It could have been prevented."

Katherine could find no words to ease his pain, but she took him in her arms and held him close. "Poor Flint," she said, "the pain you must have lived with."

"It was nothing like the pain I felt when I realized you had left me. I nearly went out of my mind. I did everything I could think of to find out where you had gone. And when you didn't go to your father's and I found out your brother had left Jefferson, destination unknown, I couldn't imagine what had happened to you. I worried that you had somehow gotten yourself killed or had found a way back east to work as someone's maid in order to get by—or worse. I hated myself for what I had done to you."

Katherine closed her eyes and tried to regain control of her churning emotions. How she had misjudged this man. Though it didn't diminish her love for Jason, she now felt a tender compassion for Flint. It hurt to speak of that which had to be said, but as she pulled away from him, she knew she must say it. She must not be distracted from the real issue at hand.

"I'm sorry. I really am, but what has been done is

done. Jeffrey believes Jason is his real father and telling him any different now would devastate the child. He would never be able to understand. Please, Frank, don't make trouble by telling him you are his real father."

"But I am his real father. He should know that."

"Maybe in time, but not now. He's too young to understand. Please, I beg you; don't tell him. Don't try to claim him as your son. It will only hurt him."

Flint thought for a long moment before he spoke again. There was one clear advantage to keeping the secret for a while. "Okay, it's enough that I know—at least for now. But I intend to continue seeing him and spending time with him so that when you finally decide to come back to me, Jeffrey will be glad to think of me as his father."

"It would be better if you stayed out of his life all together. What if he should find out who you really are?"

"You mean his father, or a notorious gunfighter?" Flint asked angrily.

"Both. I don't want Jeffrey exposed to that kind of shock, especially at such an impressionable age."

"When are you going to see that I've changed? Jeffrey is never going to know about my past reputation. There's no reason for him to find out." He tried to reason with her but found it useless. Then, in a firm voice, he warned, "I am going to see my son with or without your permission. It would be better for the boy to know he had your permission because I don't want to make a sneak out of my own son. But I will see him, or I will go to him right now with the truth."

Katherine felt her anger rising again. "Don't do this to the boy. You're the wrong sort of influence. You're a gunfighter—a killer at heart."

"You know that's not true," he shouted and grabbed her by the shoulders, squeezing his fingers into her soft flesh until she winced with the pain.

Though she knew she was taking a great risk, she decided to fuel his anger to prove to him that the old Flint still lay hidden inside.

"Yes, you are. You're a killer and you know it. You claimed to have changed, but no one changes that much. You may not have intended to kill that boy, but you'll always be a gunfighter at heart. There's no way for you to leave that part of your life completely behind you. And one day, when it catches up with you, you'll get involved in gunfighting again, and eventually, you'll find yourself up against a man you can't handle. One day, you'll come across someone who will be able to outshoot you. He'll be faster and more accurate. You're getting older. You have to be slowing down. Maybe that's the real reason you've quit wearing your gun—you know that you're slowing down and that your days as a gunman are numbered."

Flint did not react in the way she had expected. Instead of slamming his fist into her face, he pulled her quickly into his arms and tried to reassure her. "You've got it all wrong. And all I want to do is spend some time with my son. I promise not to tell him I'm his father—not until you say he's old enough. And I never want him to know I was once a gunfighter. I never wanted to be one in the first place. Just please don't try to keep me from my son any longer."

Katherine felt her anger slip away and felt ashamed of herself for all she had said. As his arms closed around her she felt herself drawn to his strength, and that startled her. Quickly, she pulled away. "Just see that you keep both those promises."

"I will. I don't want to ruin any chances we have of being a family one day."

Katherine felt sorry for him; no matter what she said or did, he held on to his false hopes. "I will allow you to be a part of the boy's life as long as he thinks of you only as a friend, but don't fool yourself into believing that you'll become part of my life again, too. I love Jason and my place is with him—and Jeffrey's place is with me."

She expected another angry outburst and was surprised once again when, after a long moment of silence, he smiled down at her and said, "I love you, Katherine. I always will."

Then to prove it, he bent over and kissed her lightly. He did not try to pull her against him, or make the kiss an intimate one. He simply kissed her sweetly, then stepped back. "Explain to Jeffrey that it's all right for him to see me. I want him to be able to come over and visit my ranch—this Friday, if that's all right with you. I'll come get him about ten and will have him back safe and sound in time for his nap at three."

Katherine was too stunned by his congenial manner to answer right away. It was not until he had walked to the door and pulled it open that she voiced her agreement, "Friday at ten."

For a brief moment, as she watched his face brighten at the prospect of being with his son, she wished she could go along and see what Flint was like around

Jeffrey. She sensed that he was fun-loving and gentle around the boy, a different Flint than even she had ever seen. But she quickly put the thought aside and attempted to convince herself that the real reason she wanted to go along was to protect her son, though she was no longer sure from what.

Chapter Twenty-Two

The more time Flint spent with his son, the more he came to admire and eventually respect his rival, Jason Morris. Flint found the child to be well informed about so many things and, at the tender age of five, Jeffrey already had an amazingly clear sense of right and wrong. Though Flint continued to be very jealous of the extremely close relationship between Jason and Jeffrey, he had to admit—if he was to be at all honest—that the man had done a good job of helping raise Jeffrey thus far. Jason was so obviously a good influence on the boy that Flint did nothing to try to alienate Jeffrey from him. He tried instead to establish his own place in his son's heart.

Though grudgingly, Flint could not help but admire certain traits in his rival. And he honestly hoped that Jason would not be too devastated when he won Katherine back and the time came to take Jeffrey as well. Flint knew from experience the unbearable pain of losing a loved one and he could well imagine how painful it would be for Jason to lose two people he loved so dearly.

Maybe they could work something out so that Jason could continue to see the boy on occasion as he grew up. It would certainly be to Jeffrey's advantage and might help make Jason's bitter loss a little easier to bear. But then Flint wondered why he should feel such guilt about Jason. After all, the man had known he was getting involved with a married woman from the very beginning. He probably deserved whatever heartache befell him. Still, Flint found it hard to wish such pain on a man who had cared so much for his son—an honest, straightforward man like Jason Morris.

"So, how do you like it?" Flint asked Jeffrey as he brought his thoughts back to what was happening around him. He smiled as he looked down into his son's frowning face. Such a handsome boy.

"It's a little too hot," Jeffrey told him honestly as he dropped his spoon back into the stew and reached for his water glass with both hands. "I think I'll let it cool a little while longer."

"I thought you said you liked your stew good and hot." He chuckled at the way the boy gulped his water.

"Not that good and hot," the boy finally said when he placed his empty glass back on the table. Then, eyeing the chocolate cake that waited on the sideboard, he suggested, "Why don't we go ahead and have dessert while we're waiting for our stew to cool."

"Do you think your parents would approve of that?" Flint asked as if he were considering the suggestion.

Jeffrey frowned and answered truthfully, "No. Mother would be furious."

"Then, I think it would be best for us to wait for the stew to cool and when we're finished with that, we'll think about having a big piece of that cake."

"Can we go back out and shoot your pistol again, after we get through eating?" Jeffrey asked as he leaned forward and blew across the steaming surface of his bowl.

"If that's what you want to do," Flint told him.

"I'm getting better at it, aren't I?"

"Well, you do keep your eyes open now while you shoot. That's a definite improvement."

"Think I'll ever be good enough to be a Texas Ranger?" the boy asked pensively, resting his cheek on his hand.

"Jeffrey, I believe you will be whatever you set out to be," he told him and meant it. Never had he seen a boy with such glowing determination. Never had he known one so young to give the future so much thought, much less strive so hard as Jeffrey did toward a set goal. He smiled proudly down at his son. Five years old and already dedicated.

Jeffrey frowned as he thought about what Flint had said. "You know, Mother doesn't much care for the idea of me being a Texas Ranger. She hates guns, 'specially handguns."

"I imagine she does. Most women do. They just see the danger." He felt a twinge of guilt, for he knew he had probably helped to shape her low opinion of guns—especially handguns. "Any gun deserves a lot of respect."

Jeffrey nodded in agreement. "That's what my father says, too."

"Smart man, your father," Flint said and meant it. Jason was indeed a smart man. Flint had to give him credit for that. And he had to give Katherine credit for having found a man like Jason to help her raise her son. She had made a good choice. "What does he say about you wanting to be a Texas Ranger?"

"He says that as long as I want to be one for the right reasons it's okay with him."

"And do you want to be a ranger for the right reasons?"

Jeffrey raised his head and nodded affirmatively. "Sure. I want to bring all the outlaws and gunfighters to justice. I'll kill them if I have to, but I want to be one of those rangers who always brings his man in alive."

Flint could see hero worship in the young boy's eyes and felt it was good to have such high standards on which to form his ideals. When he thought back to some of his own early heroes, he shook his head. It was surprising that he hadn't joined the cavalry, for that was his boyhood dream. He frowned when he remembered what had shattered his dreams and pointed his destiny in an entirely different direction.

"But would you really kill a man if you had to?" Flint leaned forward to hear the boy's answer.

"If it was him or me, I'd have to. That's why I want to practice. I want to be able to take an outlaw should he decide to draw on me."

Good answer, Flint thought and smiled down at the boy. It was comforting to know there was no bloodlust behind his desire to learn how to handle his revolver.

"When you're a little older and your arms are stronger, I'll show you how to draw and fire to protect yourself. You'll have to be fast and very accurate if you plan to stay alive in the profession you've chosen."

Jeffrey's eyes grew wide with excitement. "You know how to draw and fire? Do you really? My father doesn't. He can shoot and light a match at a hundred paces with his rifle, but he doesn't know how to draw and fire a handgun. How old do I have to be before you can show me?"

"Eight," he decided for no particular reason other than it was far enough into the future, yet close enough to give the boy hope.

"I can hardly wait to be eight." Jeffrey sighed heavily, letting his mind wander over the many prospects the future might hold.

"It'll come soon enough." Flint just hoped he'd be around to see it—with Katherine by his side.

Katherine had known it was too good to be true. Flint's turning so much of his attention toward Jeffrey had at first worried her, but after a while she had grown to believe it was harmless. Flint had seemed to be doing his best to be a good influence on the boy and had not once hinted to the child that he was his real father. Best of all, it had given Flint less time to pursue her, because there was only so much leisure time a rancher could enjoy, even in the winter months. Oddly, it had all seemed to be working out just fine for everyone—until today.

When Jeffrey had innocently mentioned that Flint was showing him how to shoot a handgun and even setting up practice targets, Katherine was furious—too furious to wait for Jason to come back from his meeting in town. How dare he! How dare Flint try to mold her child into a gunman—into a smooth-shooting, fast-drawing gunfighter like himself! She was livid with rage.

"Flint? Flint Mason, where are you?" she shouted out in his dooryard, even though she was aware his foreman and both his ranchhands knew him only as Frank. Why pretend he was anything but Flint Mason, the notorious gunfighter? It was who he really was and obviously always would be.

When Flint appeared in his doorway, she flew at him with such wild fury that he immediately backed away from her. His face revealed his uncertainty as he watched her come at him with fists clenched and teeth bared, almost tripping on her wide skirts as she hastened up the porch steps.

"What on earth is the matter with you, Kat?" he asked once she was inside.

"You blackguard!" she screamed with a rage that was so overwhelming she no longer cared what she said or who heard her. "You lousy lying blackguard."

When Flint realized the distance her voice would carry, he hurried to close the door before any of his men could hear her. Though they were supposed to be busy in the tack room on the far side of the barn, one of them could come out at any time.

As soon as he had the door securely shut, he turned around to face her. Not realizing her intention, he didn't have time to duck before she brought her open palm down hard against his cheek. He was at first too stunned by the sharp blow to speak. All he could do was gently rub the reddened area and wonder what had come over her.

"How dare you try to make my son into your image!" Her brown eyes blazed with anger.

"What are you talking about?"

"Don't bother lying. I know exactly what you've

been up to. Jeffrey told me everything. He told me about the way you've been showing him how to use your revolver, and he also told me that you proudly showed him how fast you can draw. He said you promised to teach him to draw just as fast, if not faster. How dare you! Don't you care what becomes of your son? Is your ego so inflated that you really want him to end up being just like you—a lying murderer?"

Her words were like a knife in his heart. "It's not like that. I'm not teaching him how to shoot in order to make him into some sort of gunfighter . . ." he started to explain but she cut him short.

"The boy is only five years old! How could you stoop so low?" She was in no mood to listen to his excuses. Besides, she knew everything he said would be a lie. All he had ever done was lie to her.

"Katherine, listen to me. Let me explain," Flint pleaded with her. He reached out to take her hand, hoping to calm her down somehow, but she backed swiftly away like an injured animal. Her brown eyes narrowed with hate as, teeth bared, she continued to denounce him.

"Why should I give you the chance to tell me more of your filthy lies? You lied to me in order to get me to marry you, and you lied to me all through those years I was foolish enough to stay with you—and you continue to lie to me, even now. You've lied about everything imaginable, but the biggest lie of all was when you claimed to have changed. You haven't changed at all. Once a gunfighter, always a gunfighter! There's something inside you that needs to kill and be the best with a gun. But I'll be damned if I'll let you turn my son into a gunfighter, too."

"I'm not trying to," he again tried to explain.

"Quit lying to me," she shrieked, her hands trembling now. "Jeffrey told me all about it, and if there's one thing he did not inherit from you, it is your aptitude for lying. There's not a dishonest bone in his body."

"What he told you was the truth, but . . ."

Again she cut his words short. "At last you admit to something. You admit to trying to teach my son to be a gunfighter like you. You bastard."

"Kat, you've got it all wrong."

"No, I'm finally seeing things the way they really are. Gunfighting is in your blood. It's something you can't give up no matter how hard you claim to try. You have a strange, inexplainable lust for guns. Being the best gunfighter is all you care about, and now you're hoping to make your son into one of the best, too. You want to pass along your evil legacy to Jeffrey. You want him to carry on in your infamous tradition because you're growing older and you're starting to slow down. That's it, isn't it? That's what this is all about. You're slowing down and that's the real reason you've quit wearing your gun. You knew you'd better give it up or be killed by someone younger and faster. Now, you plan to teach your son to be just as fast as you ever were so that you can live vicariously through his bloody accomplishments."

"No. That's not true. If I thought he'd misuse what I'm teaching him about handling a side arm, I'd never have let him as much as touch my revolver."

"Please, Flint, just leave Jeffrey alone. Stay away from him. I can't bear the thought of my son living by the gun the way you have."

"He doesn't want to 'live by the gun', as you put it. The boy has no interest whatsoever in being a gunfighter. His ambitions are far more noble than that. He wants to be a Texas Ranger, and if he ever does become one, he'd damn well better know how to protect himself. That's what I want to teach him, how to protect himself."

"The boy is too young to really know what he wants. And he's far too young to be taught to use a handgun. What happens when he finds out that the real reason you're so good at it is because you're a notorious gunfighter? Don't you think that is going to influence him in any way? He admires you, and should he somehow discover who you really are, he's certain to get the wrong impression. He might not see it for the evil it really is."

"I've already told you, he's not ever going to find out about that part of my past."

"How can you say that? It's really only a matter of time before someone who knows you as Flint Mason happens to see you and tells the entire community about your past. You can't really hope to keep your true identity a secret forever."

"I can hope. Besides, even if Jeffrey was to find out, I'd explain to him right away how wrong that part of my life was and how much I suffered because of it."

"Why not just stay away from him?" Her eyes pleaded with him to agree.

"Because he's my son and I love him."

"Some love you have, teaching him to use a handgun—leading him to an early death."

"Quite the contrary. I hope to prolong his life. If he does decide to become a ranger or a lawman of any kind, he's going to need to be good with a gun. Unless he's quick and accurate and can remain calm when threatened, he won't last long. Believe me, I know."

"Is that what's kept you alive all these years—being quick and calm in the face of death? Well, now that you're slowing down, there's hope you may be killed yet, isn't there?" She smiled grimly.

It took all the restraint Flint had not to grab her and try to hurt her as much as she had just hurt him. His green eyes glinted with rage as he fought for control. "Only one thing wrong with that theory, my dear wife. I don't wear my gun anymore, remember? I've changed."

"The hell you have," she snapped back. "The only thing that's changed about you is now that you're getting older you aren't nearly as confident as you once were. You don't wear your gun anymore only because you're slowing down, not because of the undying love you claim to have for me. It's all so clear to me now."

Although Flint could agree that he had indeed started to slow down and had been aware of it for quite some time, he knew in his heart that he quit wearing his gun because of Katherine and only because of her. "I took off my gun nearly six years ago, back when I was still very quick on the draw."

"So you say," she retorted, unconvinced. "Seems to me I remember reading about a couple of gunfights you were in just a few years ago. How'd you manage to outdraw those men and shoot them dead without a gun?"

"I only put the gun back on because I was being threatened by Paul Munn who was known for drawing on unarmed men. I knew that if I didn't put my gun back on for him, he'd kill me in cold blood—before I could find you again. I had no choice. Then his brother, Michael, came after me and again, I had no choice."

"Poor Flint, always being forced to kill someone against his will. It never is your doing, is it? It's always the other man's fault. Or, as in one case we know of, the other *boy's* fault."

Flint closed his eyes to her tormenting words. Again, he could see the image of the dead boy's face, and he shrank from the pain it caused him. She was right. That boy's death could have been prevented. If he hadn't been wearing his gun that night, the boy couldn't have tricked him into a gunfight. If only he'd kept his word to her and left his gun off, the boy would still be alive. Or his death would have been at someone else's hands. Clearly, the boy was looking to get a reputation. Flint somehow doubted the kid would have given up his misguided ambition even if he had refused to draw on him. The boy would have found some other gunfighter with a big reputation to go up against. Still, it hurt to know he had been the one to kill him.

"Kat, I never willingly drew against but one man." His stony expression revealed little of his inner torment.

"Even if I wanted to believe that, it would still be one man too many. Wanting to kill even one man is just as bad as wanting to kill twenty." It angered her that he didn't show his anger. She wanted to be sure she was hurting him as much as he had hurt her.

"I haven't killed twenty. I may have wounded twenty, but I haven't killed that many."

"Excuse me if I haven't kept an accurate tally," she said bitterly.

"Kat, I don't know what I can do to convince you

that you've got me all wrong. Maybe if I explained about that first time."

"I don't want to hear it. All I want from you is for you to stay away from Jeffrey."

"I can't do that," he replied matter-of-factly. "But I will promise not to let him shoot my revolver anymore until he has your permission."

"Which will be never," she put in quickly.

"That will be up to you."

She stood staring at him a long moment, as if trying to decide if she dared believe him this time. "See that it *is* left up to me or I'll get a court order to force you to stay away from him."

"I doubt that, because then I'd be forced to tell the court how I'm the boy's real father. You wouldn't want that to happen, would you?"

"Oh, how I hate you," she said, trembling and weak with anger. She had to get away from him. She had to get far away from him as quickly as possible.

"Oh, but how I love you," he called after her as she rushed from the house, tears streaming down her face.

Not knowing what else to do, Flint followed her outside to the carriage and tried one last time to make her understand. "I'm not out to hurt the boy, Kat. I love him too much to knowingly do anything to hurt him. If I'd known you'd be this opposed to it, I'd never have let him touch my revolver. I didn't even know you disliked handguns so much until today."

"Good day, Mr. Mason," she said in a cold, level voice as she snapped the reins. Her eyes bore into him as if to issue a final warning.

"Good day, *Mrs.* Mason," he shot back as she drove

away and left him standing in a trail of red dust.

Though it was clearly against Katherine's wishes, Flint continued to see his son regularly. As February drew to an end and the temperatures became more bearable, Flint began to spend more and more time with Jeffrey. They shared afternoons fishing, crawdad hunting, picnicking, or just riding horseback through the countryside. With the coming of warmer weather, various wildflowers dotted the fields and the trees were beginning to bud. Green patches of early grass sprouted here and there on the surrounding hillsides. It was a fine setting for a father and son to get to know each other, to become the best of friends—even if the son had no idea he *was* the man's son. For the first time in Flint's life, he felt he had a true friend, someone he could completely trust.

Jeffrey had been openly disappointed to learn that he would no longer be allowed to shoot Flint's revolver, but had accepted his mother's decision and did not ask Flint to break his word to Katherine. But he did on occasion convince Flint to show him his quick draw, and listened attentively when Flint lectured about how guns should be used for protection—or for providing meat when necessary—but should never be used just for sport.

Katherine learned of these demonstrations and talks, but as long as Flint made a point of emphasizing the proper use of a gun, she said nothing to stop him. She continued to allow Flint to come by and visit with her, too—though most of his spare time was devoted to the boy now. She was relieved that he no longer seemed quite so adamant about winning her back, and had turned his energies toward winning over his son.

Jason was also glad that Flint had stopped trying to monopolize so much of Katherine's time, but wished the man would grow tired of visiting Jeffrey. He didn't care for the idea of the boy spending so much time in the company of a man like Flint, but he refrained from voicing his opinion to Katherine. After all, the boy was not really his son. He wasn't really entitled to a say in what the boy could or could not do. It was solely up to Katherine and as long as she allowed it, he had to go along with her decision. He didn't like it, but he had no choice.

Jeffrey, on the other hand, was delighted over his new friendship with Frank. He had so much fun when they were together that he had come to think of him less and less as an adult. To Jeffrey, Frank was simply his best friend. But to Edmond and Samuel, he'd become the enemy. Jeffrey no longer had time for them—in fact, Jeffrey had little time for anyone else.

Minnie also disliked the idea of Jeffrey spending so much time with Flint, but unlike Jason, she openly stated her objections. It just wasn't natural for a boy not yet six to be wanting to spend so much time with a grown man and no time at all with boys closer to his own age. She continued to do what she could to make Flint feel unwelcome whenever he came to the door, deriving great pleasure from making him as uncomfortable as possible.

"It's you again," she muttered when, once again, he appeared to take Jeffrey riding. The only days on which Flint had not shown up were two snowy days in

February when the roads were impassable.

"You are right about that, it's me," Flint agreed with a firm nod as he stepped inside. "Is Jeffrey ready to go?"

"I hope not," she told him defiantly, but no sooner had she spoken than Jeffrey came running eagerly into the room. Katherine was right behind him, her expression noncommital.

"Here I am," Jeffrey called out enthusiastically. "Where are we going today?"

"It's such a pretty day, I thought we'd ride over to your neighbor's pond and see if we can't catch us a fine mess of fish. I've got two poles and brought food for a picnic so we won't have to come back here for lunch."

"Sandwiches?" he asked eagerly, for they were a treat that he never got to eat at home.

"Three different kinds," Flint assured him and smiled at the boy's delighted squeal.

"Do you think there's enough food for three people?" Jeffrey asked quickly and glanced back at his mother.

Katherine felt suddenly uneasy.

"Sure, you know me. I always pack plenty. I've got more than enough food for three."

Jeffrey turned to face his mother, his eyes sparkling with the idea that had just occurred to him. "Why don't you go with us today, Mother? It's such a pretty day and you love picnics."

Katherine felt her heart leap in panic. The three of them going out together would be too much like a family outing, and she didn't want Flint to have even a taste of that. "No, Jeffrey. I don't want to intrude. Besides, I have too much to do today."

"Please?" he entreated.

"No, really, I have mending to do, and as soon as Silas and Mose get back from town, I'll have to put away all the things I ordered."

"I'll help you when we get back," he said, and in an effort to persuade her, he took her hand and pressed it to his cheek. "Please go with us. I want you to see what a fine fisherman I've become."

Katherine was eager to see her son's skill with a fishing pole but she thought it best to decline. She smiled down at him. "Maybe some other time. I'm not about to intrude on your friend's visit."

"He's your friend, too," Jeffrey pointed out.

"Yes, I'm your friend, too," Flint quickly interjected. "Why don't you come with us? I've already told you I have more than enough food, and if you're in a hurry to get back, we'll make it an early day. There's no hard and fast rule that says we have to stay out until three."

"Thank you, but I don't think I'd better," Katherine said, with a glance that warned him not to press the issue. But Jeffrey would not let it alone. "Please, Mother, please come with us. I'll even show you how to fish. Please come with us."

Katherine looked down into his pleading eyes and could feel herself weakening. "But I've told you, I have too much to do this afternoon."

"But I promised to help you when we get back, and Frank said we could come back early. Come on, please?"

Despite her inner misgivings, she found herself slowly giving way. "Oh, all right," she finally agreed, "but just for a little while. And remember, we have to come back early and you have to keep your promise to help me put away all the things that Silas and Mose bring back."

"Yippee," Jeffrey said, throwing his arms around her. "I'm going to catch the biggest fish ever just for you."

"You'll have to let go first, so I can change into something more appropriate," she said, prying him loose from her skirts.

Knowing she planned to put on something very drab and far less revealing for his benefit, Flint quickly asked, "Why do you have to change? What you have on is just fine."

"I can't possibly ride a horse in this," she said, gesturing to her wide skirt that flowed gracefully to the floor.

"We don't have to ride. We can walk, and what you have on is just fine for walking. Isn't it, Jeffrey?" He knew if he got Jeffrey to back him up, he'd win, and for once he'd have the pleasure of seeing her in something pretty for more than just a few minutes.

"Looks okay to me," Jeffrey agreed. "Come on, let's get going. I want to get us some fish before lunch."

Unable to find a reason for any further delay, Katherine took her shawl from the wooden peg near the door and reluctantly followed Flint and Jeffrey out the door. She could hear Minnie's low muttering as Flint closed the door behind them.

Chapter Twenty-Three

While Katherine sat watching Flint and Jeffrey fish along the rocky edge of the small lake that lay nestled in a thickly wooded area on their neighbor's property, she was busy worrying about how Jason was going to feel when he learned that she'd agreed to join Jeffrey and Flint on their outing. She was far too worried about Jason at that moment to really pay much attention to the warm and caring friendship that had developed between her legal husband and her son.

Although she knew Jason would not voice his objections openly—for he never did—she knew very well that he wasn't going to like it. Why should he? Why would any man want the woman he loved to be in another man's company, especially when that man was her legal husband who had sworn he'd win her back?

Despite the fact Flint had managed to behave himself over the past few weeks and had not tried to lay a hand on her since their argument over his teaching Jeffrey to shoot, Jason still wasn't going to like her being here—even though she was doing her best to keep her distance from Flint, which Jeffrey would be able to verify.

Hoping to hurry things along so that they might manage to get back before Jason had a chance to find out, she called out to them, "I'm getting hungry. How long until we eat?"

"What time is it?" Jeffrey wanted to know.

"Well after eleven," she answered, though she knew it was only a few minutes past the hour.

Jeffrey glanced at Flint to see what he thought about eating so early, and when Flint merely shrugged, the boy looked back at his pole, then at his mother and asked, "You want to eat now?"

"Well, as soon as you two can leave your fishing."

"We can do that whenever you want," Flint put in. "If you're hungry now, I guess we could go ahead and eat." Then to Jeffrey, he said, "What do you say, partner, you ready for a couple of those sandwiches?"

"Yeah boy!" Jeffrey responded, patting his stomach.

"We'll be right there," Flint shouted over to her.

Relieved that they were both agreeable, she immediately opened the food hamper and set out the sandwiches and orange juice that Flint had brought along. She was surprised at the number of sandwiches—a total of nine.

"I gave you both one of each kind of sandwich," she told them as they settled down beside her on Flint's patchwork quilt.

Jeffrey wasted no time in peeking inside all three of his sandwiches. "I can eat all of them," he said eagerly. "I'm hungry as a bear."

"You're only having one sandwich?" Flint asked, noticing that she had returned two of her sandwiches to the hamper. "I thought you said you were hungry. There's more than enough here for you to eat your fill."

He looked deeply into her eyes to see if she understood the reason there was so much food. Didn't she wonder why he had made three of each sandwich and why there were three cups? Didn't she realize that he always packed enough for three, hoping that one day she'd be persuaded to join them and see for herself how great he and Jeffrey got along? He wanted her to begin seeing the three of them as a family.

"One sandwich will be plenty," she assured him. "I don't want to weigh myself down with too much food. I just want to eat enough to quiet my hunger."

"She worries about getting fat," Jeffrey informed Flint between bites. "She wants to stay skinny like that forever."

"Oh, I wouldn't exactly say she's skinny," Flint said with a smile, letting his gaze travel over the curvacous figure before him. His eyes lingered on her narrow waist, then drifted upward to the creamy white skin that her modestly low neckline revealed. He wished that she was wearing one of the newer, more daring necklines, so he could see even more of the delightful view. His smile widened at the thought.

Aware of his bold stare, Katherine reached for her shawl and quickly wrapped it around herself so that she was covered from neck to waist.

"No, Jeffrey," Flint continued, "I'd say your mother looks about right. A second sandwich wouldn't hurt her at all." His eyes gleamed roguishly.

Katherine pulled her shawl tighter.

"Jeffrey, don't eat so fast," she admonished, more concerned with changing the direction of their conversation than she was with her son's eating habits.

"I'm not eating very fast," Jeffrey said, showing them his half-eaten sandwich. But when he saw that Flint had taken only one bite of his sandwich and his mother had yet to lift hers to her mouth, he frowned and began to chew more slowly.

"He's probably just in a hurry to get back to his fishing," Flint said on the boy's behalf, and reached over to pat his dark, curly head. "I remember when I was a boy, how fishing was always more important than eating or anything else."

"And I'm going to catch the biggest fish that's out there," Jeffrey said, nodding toward the sparkling lake. "You just watch." He took another large bite of his sandwich.

Within a few minutes, Jeffrey announced he was full and ready to head back to the lake. Because he had finished two of his sandwiches and eaten nearly halfway through another, Katherine felt that he had indeed eaten enough. She had no good reason to insist that he stay and finish his meal, but it annoyed her that his hurrying off to fish again left her and Flint all alone.

"This is nice, isn't it?" Flint said as he lay down on his side. Patches of sunlight filtered through the trees and danced lightly over the quilt as he sprawled out and made himself comfortable.

"What are you doing?" Katherine asked in alarm. "Aren't you going to go back fishing?" She wondered how she should handle this situation.

"Not yet. I'm not as young and energetic as Jeffrey. I think I'll rest awhile before I go back." After a quick glance in Jeffrey's direction to make sure he was having no problems getting his hook baited, Flint looked over at Katherine and noticed how uncomfortable she seemed to be, sitting with her back rigid and her shoulders and arms drawn in.

"What's the matter?" he asked with a half smile. "Are you afraid of me?"

"No, of course not," she answered a little too quickly, realizing his question had made her even more uncomfortable.

"It's not like we're completely alone. Jeffrey's right over there. He may be too far away to hear us talking, but he's close enough to hear you if you should feel the need to scream for help."

Realizing her fears were probably silly, Katherine willed herself to relax, or at least to give that appearance. Although she wouldn't think of lying down beside him on the quilt—which is what she would have done had he been Jason—she made herself more comfortable by leaning against the trunk of a nearby tree. While she tried to arrange her skirts to keep them from wrinkling, she realized he was staring boldly at her and it made her nervous.

"You are beautiful," he said finally and it was exactly what she didn't want him to say.

"Don't," she told him. "I don't want to hear it."

"Okay, then I won't tell you how beautiful you are. Can I at least tell you how much I love you?"

"No!" she shouted with sudden anger. Then, realizing she might alarm Jeffrey, she lowered her voice. "Don't tell me how beautiful I am or how much you love me. I do not want to hear anything like that from you."

"I thought you enjoyed hearing the truth," he said and quickly sat up so that his face was closer to hers. It was far too close for Katherine and she pressed backward against the tree in an effort to put more distance between them.

"I always want you to tell the truth," she responded, confused at the way he had made it sound. If she complained about hearing the truth, it would seem to condone his lies. Yet, insisting on the truth gave him an opening to speak the words of love she dreaded so much.

"Well then, if you really want the truth, it should be okay for me to tell you how much I love you." He brought his face closer.

Before she could decide on what to say to shut him up, he captured her left hand and held it lightly between his.

"Frank, don't. Jeffrey might see," she admonished and quickly withdrew her hand.

"He's too far away," Flint told her and reached for her hand again, pleased that she had called him Frank when there was no one around to cause her to be so cautious. "Besides, he can't see our hands because of that big rock. All he can see is our heads and shoulders—that is, that's all he can see as long as we sit up."

Shocked at what he seemed to be suggesting, she said in a low, angry voice, "I will not lie down with you!"

"I didn't ask you to. At least not here, when the boy can return at any moment. All I want is to hold your hand." As he spoke, he took her hand into his again and began to stroke her palm with the tip of his thumb.

A sense of ease flowed through her as he continued to tease the sensitive skin at the curve of her palm. His touch was so gentle and unthreatening that she didn't feel the need to pull away again. As long as he went no further than holding hands, she felt she was in no real danger.

"Kind of like old times, isn't it?" he mused with a nostalgic smile and tilted his head to gaze admiringly at her.

"Not that I can remember," she replied evenly. "As I recall, you weren't much for hand-holding even before we were married." She was terrified that he might kiss her and prayed that he wouldn't try.

Flint chuckled softly. "Maybe you're right about that. I was far too eager to get on to better things than to waste time holding your hand."

Katherine didn't like the way her body was starting to respond to his touch. The initially soothing effect had gradually changed to something quite different. As the feeling grew stronger, she tried to casually slip her hand out of his, but he held it fast.

"Kat, I've missed you more than you can know. Be glad that our son is as close by as he is because if he wasn't—if we were all alone—I'd waste no time in taking you into my arms and showing you just how much I still love you."

"You would find yourself with an unwilling partner," she said sternly as she stared off into the distance, refusing to meet his searching gaze any longer and wishing he'd stop teasing the sensitive skin of her palm. She was well aware of the way her body had responded to his last remark, and it was a dangerous response. She should have been angrier than she was.

"Oh, I don't know," he pressed on. "You might be surprised at how willing you'd be."

"It's time for us to leave," she said firmly and tried

again to pull her hand away. This time he let go and she thrust her hand behind her while she tried to get her racing heart under control. She didn't want him to be aware of her rising panic.

"We can't go yet," he said. "Jeffrey hasn't caught his fish yet and it's very important to him to catch that fish while you're here to see it. I'll leave you alone; just let him fish a little while longer."

She was about to protest when he did exactly as he'd promised. He rose quickly to his feet and, with only one backward glance, went to join Jeffrey at the edge of the lake. Though he continually looked back to see if she was watching them—which she was, but only for Jeffrey's sake—Flint did not approach her again. And just as he promised—as soon as Jeffrey had caught his prize fish—they headed back to Seven Oaks. He did not even linger at the house to try to draw her into further conversation. Instead, he quickly made plans to see Jeffrey during the coming weekend and then he left.

As Katherine watched him ride away, she could not identify the emotions that churned inside her. She wasn't angry, yet she wasn't happy, either. Whatever it was, she felt like crying.

Katherine realized Jason was out later than usual as she waited impatiently for him to come in from the day's work. Though she dreaded telling him how she had gone with Flint and Jeffrey on their outing, he had every right to know and she was ready to get it over with. She wanted to feel his strong arms around her, holding her protectively. She wanted to hear his reassurances that it didn't matter—how all that truly mattered was their love for each other. And she did love him so much. Oh, how she loved him. Suddenly, Katherine had a great urge to prove to him just how much she did love him.

Through the window she finally saw him heading in from the barn, covered with a thin coating of dust and sweat, his hat pushed back on his head, and she knew she couldn't wait any longer. Flinging the door open, she rushed out to meet him and was delighted when he saw her coming and opened his arms wide, scooping her up in a warm embrace that lifted her high off the ground.

"I love you," she said and rained kisses on his face and neck, knocking his hat to the ground.

"What brought this on?" he asked, laughing. Only moments ago he'd felt so tired he wondered whether he had the strength to eat. Now, he found himself full of energy and refused to set her back down.

"You. You brought this on. Your being gone all day brought this on. I missed you," she said between kisses. As she looked down into his handsome face—the face of the man she loved more than life itself—she realized she wanted more than kisses. She wanted him to make love to her, to possess her completely. She urgently needed reassurance that their love was as strong as ever. "Carry me up to our room and I'll show you just how much I've missed you."

"Are you trying to seduce me, woman?" he asked, pretending to be scandalized.

"Only if you're willing to be seduced," she replied cautiously.

"I'm certainly willing," he responded, smiling eagerly.

"Then, yes, I'm trying to seduce you," she conceded. "Think I stand any chance of success? Do you think my feminine wiles will work on a man as cagey as you?"

"They're working already, I assure you," he said with a sly glance downward at his trousers.

Her first impulse was to cuff him playfully for being so bold. Instead, she kissed him soundly on his full and sensuous lips.

At first Jason stood still, holding her tightly against him as he deepened their kiss, but then, he suddenly took off in a headlong dash, still clutching her in his arms, never breaking the kiss.

Within minutes, they were up the stairs and behind their closed bedroom door, fumbling eagerly at each other's clothing.

Katherine could not remember ever having wanted Jason so badly as she wanted him at that moment. For the first time, impatience got the best of her and she grabbed at his shirt, tearing it wide open, scattering buttons in every direction.

Jason moaned with pleasure at having his clothing literally ripped off his body. And when she had him completely naked, his pleasure mounted as he watched her tear her own clothing off in her haste to consummate her passion. As she gripped the lacy edge of her camisole with both hands and ripped the thin material down the middle, letting her swelling, eager breasts spill right out before his eyes, he thought he would burst with desire. Although she had never been shy at lovemaking, he couldn't remember ever seeing her quite this eager.

As soon as Katherine tossed the last shred of her clothing to the floor, she flung her soft, supple body against his hard, muscular frame and pressed her lips hungrily to his. She thrust her tongue deep into his mouth and pressed herself against him harder still. It was as if she could not get enough from a simple kiss, could not taste all that she hungered for. Moaning in frustration, she began to maneuver him toward the bed.

Jason was more than willing to be manipulated and when they reached the edge of the bed, he held on to her, pulling her gently down on top of him. Her position seemed to fire her passion, for suddenly, she began to push her body against his with such force it left him breathless. Frantically, her hands traveled over his familiar contours as she moved rhythmically over his body, pressing her breasts against his chest in maddeningly slow, seductive movements.

Unable to resist the temptation, he pulled her higher so that he could take her breasts into his mouth one at a time, nibbling hungrily at the hardened tips until she cried out with the almost unbearable ecstasy. She could wait no longer for fulfillment and suddenly realized she did not have to wait. She was clearly in a position to take what she needed.

Thrusting downward, she eased onto him and began the movements she knew would bring them both what they wanted. Slowly, methodically, she brought them closer and closer to the pinnacle until at last she cried out with the rapture that exploded within her. Her body shuddered with joy as she drew out the splendid moment for as long as she could. Then, almost immediately, he, too, found release and they slowly began to drift back down together. Exhausted, she lay on top of him, unmoving. Her hunger was finally sated;

her energy spent.

"I love you," she said while she continued to lie contently on top of him, her cheek pressed into his shoulder. She could hear the beating of his heart, and it made her smile.

"And I love you," he assured her as he let his hands roam familiarly over her naked back and buttocks. "And I must say, that was a fine greeting. Whatever brought that on?"

Katherine felt sudden guilt because she had intended to tell him immediately about her outing with Flint and Jeffrey, but it had just not worked out that way.

"I needed to be reassured of our love," she finally said.

"But why? What have I done to cause you any doubt?"

His brow suddenly furrowed, and she smoothed it gently with her fingertips.

"It wasn't what you did. It was what I did. Or what Jeffrey convinced me to do."

The puzzled furrow returned to his brow. "And what was that?"

"He pleaded with me to go to the lake with him and Flint, so I could see him catch a fish. I tried to get out of it, but he kept after me and, before I realized it, I had agreed."

"And you went?"

"Yes, I did. I really didn't want to, but after Jeffrey got me to say I'd go, I had no choice."

"And the fact that you had to spend a few hours in Flint's company made you react the way you did just now?"

She could see him beginning to smile.

"I guess so," she said cautiously. "Having to be with him made me realize just how much I'd rather be with you."

His smile broke full width across his face as he pulled her lips down to his for a leisurely kiss. "Well, if seeing Flint is going to make you react like that every time, maybe I should arrange for you to see him more often."

"Jason!" Though she spoke in shocked tones, her smile betrayed her, for she was very relieved to discover that he wasn't angry at what she had done. "You wouldn't dare!"

Jason was noncommital. He simply drew her down for another loving kiss while his hand played possessively with her breast. Though he knew Minnie would have dinner on the table by now, he made no move to get dressed. As far as he was concerned, the dinner could grow stone cold. And it did.

Jason was glad that Jeffrey had decided at the last minute to go into town with him. It had been awhile since the two of them had spent any time alone—really alone—and he was eager to hear what was going on in Jeffrey's life at the moment, especially the part of his life that included Flint Mason. Though he felt a twinge of jealousy at the animation in the boy's face when he talked about his friend, Frank, Jason did not try to discourage his son from seeing the man. He still felt that he had no real right to interfere and that Jeffrey might resent it if he tried.

While the two of them were in town that Saturday, Jason had several errands, the last of which was to stop off at the mercantile and pick up a few items Katherine wanted. Knowing how easily Jeffrey got bored with shopping, Jason agreed to let him purchase a penny's worth of jelly babes with the understanding that he would eat them outside the store. Jason watched through the window to be sure the boy was settled safely away from traffic before he started down the crowded aisles to find the items on Katherine's list.

After he'd completed his purchases, Jason hurried outside to find Jeffrey so they could go over to the Star Restaurant for a couple of icy root beers before heading back to Seven Oaks. He was surprised to find his son in the middle of a heated discussion with another boy. As he stepped closer, he recognized the other boy as one of Jim Haught's sons. Both boys had their hands balled into fists, ready to do battle, while they shouted loudly at each other.

"Is not!" he heard Jeffrey cry out in a high-pitched voice. Though Jeffrey stood with his back to him, Jason could tell how angry he was. He literally shook with rage.

"Is too. My pa says so," Jimmy Haught flung back at him, his dark eyes narrowed. Then suddenly, the boy caught sight of Jason headed their way and he lost no time in taking off in the opposite direction.

By the time Jason reached Jeffrey, his son was close to tears. Frowning at the other boy who could be seen still running down the street, Jason asked, "What was that all about?"

"Jimmy is spreading lies—lies about Frank," Jeffrey said quickly. His lower lip started to tremble.

Jason knelt beside his son and reached out a hand to steady the boy. "What sort of lies?"

"He says that our friend, Frank, is really Flint

Mason, a gunfighter of some kind from up Kansas way. He says Frank's killed hundreds of men because no one can outshoot him. I told him it wasn't so, that Frank's a rancher, not a gunfighter—but he says his Pa found out about it from someone who saw Frank while he was in town the other day and recognized who he really was." Tears had finally started to form in his eyes as he threw his arms around Jason's neck and pleaded, "Find Jimmy and tell him it isn't so. He'll believe you. Find him and tell him Frank just looks sorta like that Flint Mason. They may have the same last name, but they aren't the same man."

Jason held Jeffrey close. He did not know what to say to the boy. To deny the allegation would be telling him a lie, and to admit it would hurt the boy more. Suddenly, he hated Flint for having brought this moment about.

"I guess we'll just have to see what Frank has to say about it," he finally said. "And whatever he says, you will have to judge for yourself whether or not it's the truth. Would you like to ride over to his place right now?"

Jeffrey pulled away and dashed at one of the tears that had finally spilled down his cheek. "He isn't home. He had something he had to do today, but he's supposed to come by for me tomorrow after church. I'll ask him then." He sniffed his tears back. "Then, I'll get him to ride over to Jimmy Haught's house with me and tell him to his face that he isn't no gunfighter. Then, I'll make Jimmy apologize, or else."

"Don't blame Jimmy for believing what his father told him. It's natural for a boy to have faith in anything his father tells him."

"A father ought not to lie to his own son—to his very own flesh and blood," Jeffrey said emphatically with another loud sniff.

Jason fully agreed and hoped that Flint would not openly lie to Jeffrey about his past. At the same time, he hoped the man would not decide to tell the boy the whole truth—as much for the child's sake as for Katherine's.

Chapter Twenty-Four

The rumor that the new rancher, Frank Mason, was really the notorious gunfighter, Flint Mason, spread quickly. By the time services were over on Sunday, most of the congregation was aware of the latest gossip. Though none of them knew of any real connection between Mason and the Morris family—other than that they seemed to have become good friends—it was because of that obvious friendship that everyone was afraid to discuss the subject with the Morrises.

Even so, their curiosity as to whether or not Jason or Katherine knew about Frank was eating away at all of them and everyone seemed to have an opinion. But it was the children who finally brought it out into the open by quizzing Jeffrey the moment church had let out and they could get him alone.

"Do you suppose Frank Mason really is Flint Mason?" little Cody Jackson wanted to know, his eyes filled with the excitement he felt at such a prospect. "Do you really suppose he's the fastest gun in the world?"

Jeffrey had been warned not to let his anger get the best of him should other people bring up the subject. Jason had warned him that such a thing would spread quickly, and he had to grit his teeth in order to keep quiet and not tear into Cody with his fists like he truly wanted to. Instead, he pretended not to have heard the question at all.

"You know him, Jeffrey," Billy Green put in quickly, trying to edge his way through the half-dozen boys who had surrounded Jeffrey and herded him off to the side of the small country church. "Tell us about him. Have you ever seen him draw a gun?"

"Well, yes . . ." Jeffrey answered uncertainly, knowing that a churchyard was no place to tell a lie and that his friends were not going to let him keep quiet for very long.

"Is he fast? Is he really the fastest gun in the world?" Cody wanted to know and leaned forward for Jeffrey's answer, his brown eyes as wide as saucers.

Starting to realize how impressed all his friends were with the thought of Frank being a famous gunfighter, he hesitated only a moment before admitting, "He's fast, all right—real fast. Fastest I ever saw." Then he had a pang of conscience, and quickly added, "But he just learned to draw fast like that to protect himself from bad guys. I don't think he's really a big gunfighter or anything like that."

"I'll bet he is," Billy put in, thoroughly intrigued. "I'll bet Frank is really Flint Mason, the fastest gun in the whole world—and Texas, too. Boy, I'd sure like to see him draw his gun."

"Are you kidding?" Cody scoffed, shaking his head in disbelief that anyone could be so dumb. "If he's as fast as my pa says, you wouldn't be able to see him draw, not good, anyway. All you'd be able to see is when he went for his gun, right before, and then when he held it out in front of him, ready to shoot someone down." Then, realizing his last words had heightened everyone's interest, Cody turned to Jeffrey and asked, "Does he shoot from the hip or does he bring it up in front of him to shoot?"

Jeffrey wasn't sure. "Sorta in between, I think. He gets it about waist high, up close to him, and then fires."

"You sure are lucky to be friends with him," Billy said wistfully. "I wish I could be his friend. Then maybe he would show me how to shoot like that."

"He already showed me," Jeffrey put in quickly. It was unclear just when Jeffrey had started to accept the idea of Frank's being Flint Mason, but now that he had, he found he was starting to enjoy it. It was obvious a man like Flint Mason was important to Jeffrey's friends, and even to all the adults, judging by the way they seemed to huddle in close groups discussing the matter. "I've even fired his very own revolver."

"You have not," Cody challenged him, clearly doubtful. "He wouldn't let you shoot his own gun."

"He would so," Jeffrey said and doubled up his fists ready to defend his word, temporarily forgetting he was in a churchyard.

"What's it look like?" Billy wanted to know, his green eyes shining, eager to believe. "Does it have notches in the handle?"

"No, he has more respect for his gun than to mark it up like that. And it's a pretty thing. You should see it. It's shiny all over and has a pearl handle that fits a man's hand just right," Jeffrey told them, delighted with their rapt attention.

"Think he'd show us that gun?" Tommy Murray finally asked. Tommy's parents had told him not to discuss the matter until someone knew for sure if the rumor was true, but his excitement had gotten the better of him. "I'd sure like to see a gun like that up close."

Jeffrey thought about that. Even if Frank wasn't this Flint Mason his friends seemed so impressed with, he did own an impressive gun, one that would be the envy of every boy there. "Sure, he'd let you see it. He might even let you shoot it, if I asked him to."

Before further arrangements could be made, the boys' parents had started to break up their own conversations and called out for their sons to get into the waiting wagons and carriages. It was time to go home. And by the time Jeffrey had climbed into the carriage with Jason and Katherine, he had an entirely new perspective on what it would be like if his friend, Frank, did indeed turn out to be this Flint Mason everyone was talking about. He sat back in the seat, drumming his fingertips on his chin, and wondered if his friend really was the fastest gunfighter in the whole world—and Texas, too.

The trip back from Jefferson had taken a lot longer than Flint had anticipated and by the time he reached Seven Oaks, he was late picking up Jeffrey. Had he taken the time to stop at his own ranch beforehand, he'd have learned of the many rumors that were circulating about him, but because he was late, he had decided to go directly to Seven Oaks and pick up his son first.

Jeffrey was anxious to find out if Frank was indeed Flint Mason and was outside waiting for him when he rode up. He hurried to greet him.

"Hey, partner, you ready to go?" Flint asked as he swung his leg over his saddle and dropped easily to the ground.

"Yeah boy," Jeffrey said eagerly. "Let me go tell them I'm leaving now."

Jeffrey ran toward the house but when he saw Minnie come out onto the back porch, he stopped in the dooryard and called out to her that Frank had finally come and they were leaving. Minnie scowled and looked toward where Flint stood waiting beside his horse, his usual arrogant smile firmly in place. She wished she could say something to make the boy change his mind about going, but knew that nothing she could say would do any good. Instead, she turned quickly on her heel and marched back inside so she wouldn't have to watch them ride off together.

"Where we going?" Jeffrey asked as he came skipping back to Flint.

"First, I need to stop off at the ranch and unpack my saddlebags, then we can go wherever you want. What's your choice today?"

"Anywhere," Jeffrey told him. "Just as long as we're seen together."

Flint thought that was a strange answer and as soon as he was back in the saddle again with the boy sitting in front of him, he asked, "Why are you so eager to be seen with me?"

"Just am," Jeffrey responded vaguely. He had not

yet decided if he should confront Frank with the rumors he'd heard. If they turned out not to be true, his friend might get mad at him for believing such things. But then again, if they were true, he would finally know. "I like being your friend."

"And I like being your friend," Flint replied, but felt there was something the boy was holding back. He was about to probe further when Jeffrey abruptly changed the subject.

"How was your trip to Jefferson?" he asked.

"Tiring, but productive. I've got a buyer for my extra hay and alfalfa, at least for this year. All I have to do is get it over there by a certain day and I'll get top dollar for it."

It was not until they had reached Flint's ranch and he had unpacked his saddlebags that the subject of what they should do that afternoon came up again. By then, Jeffrey had decided against going over to any of his other friends' houses to let Flint show off his gun. He was afraid of what their parents might say and chose instead to have Flint show him his fast draw again. He planned to watch real close this time so that he could learn to draw just as fast.

Flint could sense Jeffrey's unusual interest, and when he moved to strap the gun on his hip, he realized that the boy's eyes were busy studying every small movement he made.

"Is there something you're not telling me?" he asked as he adjusted the weapon so that it rode his hip just right. When Jeffrey did not immediately answer, he asked again. "Jeffrey, is there something you're not telling me?"

"What do you mean?" Jeffrey asked evasively.

"I'm not sure why, but I have a feeling you're keeping something from me."

Jeffrey thought about how he should broach the subject, but finally just blurted his question out. "Are you really Flint Mason?"

Flint felt as if someone had dealt him a hard blow to the stomach. He knelt before the boy and studied his youthful face. "Where did you hear that?" he asked. His heart stopped beating as he waited for an answer.

"It's all everyone's talking about. Some man saw you last week in town and told everyone he recognized you. He told them all you were Flint Mason, the gunfighter. Are you?" Jeffrey's words tumbled out excitedly. His eyes sparkled with the prospect of what the answer might be and who he should tell first if it turned out he was really Flint Mason.

"What difference would it make if I was?"

"All the difference in the world," Jeffrey answered quickly, his excitement heightened by the fact Frank had not denied it outright. "Are you? Are you really Flint Mason? Are you really the fastest gun in the whole world? You are, aren't you? You are Flint Mason."

An ache welled up deep inside Flint as he continued to study his son's face. He did not like the deep awe he saw there. He considered his next words carefully, for he did not want to lie to the boy, but he did want to make him understand. "I used to be known as Flint Mason. But that was a long time ago."

"I knew it. I just knew it. Wait until Cody hears about this," Jeffrey said and laughed with satisfaction. "He's going to drop his drawers right where he stands."

"Who is Cody?" Flint asked.

"He's a boy from our church. He's jealous as a green-eyed toad because you and I are friends. He'd give his right arm just to see you draw your gun even once. I told him how I've not only seen it, I actually got to shoot your gun with my own hands. He wants me to talk you into letting him shoot your gun, too."

Cold apprehension clutched at Flint's heart as he realized how deeply impressed Jeffrey was with his gunfighter's reputation—impressed for all the wrong reasons. "No, I don't think it would be wise to let your friend shoot my revolver. It doesn't sound to me like he has much respect for a gun."

"You're right. Besides, why should he be allowed to have the same honor as me? He doesn't even know you."

"You see shooting my gun as an honor?" Flint asked cautiously. The muscles in his jaw tightened.

"Are you kidding? It's not everyone around these parts who can say they got to shoot Flint Mason's very own handgun!" Then, he looked down at the pearl handle that protruded from the holster at Flint's side. "Is that the same gun you used to draw against all those men? It is, isn't it? I got to shoot the very gun that you used when you outdrew all those men, didn't I?"

"How many men do you suppose I've had to outdraw?"

"Hundreds, probably. After all, you're the fastest gun in the whole world, aren't you? I'll bet if I had me a gun like that of my very own and I practiced real hard, I could become nearly as fast as you are." His eyes sparkled at the prospect. "That's what I'll do. I'll get me a gun like that and practice real hard. You can show me how you do it. I'll get so good, no one will be able to outdraw me. Everyone will try, but no one will be able to do it better. We can become a team. No one will be able to beat us."

Flint felt a sharp knife piercing his heart. Gritting his teeth against the pain that Jeffrey had unintentionally caused, his next words were ragged and hoarse, "But I don't wear my gun anymore. I've put that part of my life behind me."

"That's okay. Once I get as good as you are—maybe even better—you wouldn't have to wear your gun, anyway. I'll take care of anyone who bothers either one of us. I'll owe you that much."

Flint could not believe what he was hearing. He had to do something to change the boy's mind and in a hurry. "What about your desire to become a Texas Ranger?"

"Oh, that. Anyone can be a Texas Ranger. This would be something more special than that. Besides, I would be getting rid of all the bad guys, anyway, wouldn't I? I'd just be going about it in a different way is all. How many bad guys have you killed off?"

Bile slowly rose in Flint's throat as he realized just how serious the boy was. He tried to swallow the bitter fluid while images of a grown-up Jeffrey, face to face with another man in a deadly showdown, burned in the back of his brain. Kill or be killed. That's all Jeffrey's life would amount to once he had established himself as a gunfighter. "Jeffrey, you've got the wrong impression. There's no glory in being a gunfighter—no glory at all. There's only pain and heartache. You live your life in wariness, never knowing when or where someone is going to call you out and try to kill you just so he can steal your reputation."

"Then, why did you become a gunfighter?" Jeffrey wanted to know, unwilling to readily accept Flint's cautionary words.

"I never wanted to be one; it just happened."

"How does becoming a gunfighter just happen?" he asked, frowning suspiciously.

Flint decided to start at the beginning so Jeffrey would fully understand. "When I was a boy, my family had a small farm in Virginia. It wasn't very big compared to most, but my pa and ma worked it hard. Even so, they barely managed to clothe and feed the three of us boys. Me and my brothers helped all we could, but it never seemed to be enough to get ahead."

"What's that got to do with you becoming a gunfighter?"

"I wanted you to understand why a turkey was so important to us. One Saturday in late November we had all gone into town so Ma could sell some dolls she'd made and Pa could sell our extra vegetables in order to buy a turkey for Christmas, which was only a month away. My brother, Vance, and I helped Pa pick out a fine turkey to fatten up for Christmas and we were on our way back to the wagon with the bird when a couple of drunkards stumbled out of a nearby saloon and started to harass my pa, demanding the turkey. When Pa ignored their taunts and tried to step around them, they got rowdy and started to push and shove him around, but Pa was still determined to ignore them. He sure wasn't about to give them our Christmas turkey. That's when they started to hit him with their fists. Vance and I tried to stop them, but I was only fourteen and Vance was barely twelve, and we weren't any match for the two men. Eventually, the turkey got away and fluttered out into the street, but the men didn't care. They continued to hit our pa until he was all bloody and couldn't even stand up anymore."

"What did you do?" Jeffrey wanted to know when Flint paused to take a deep, steadying breath.

"Vance took off running for the rifle Pa kept in the wagon while I continued to try to fight as best I could, but my brother barely got his hands on the rifle when suddenly, one of the men pulled out a handgun and shot Pa in the heart—right there, while he lay on the boardwalk."

Tears burned Flint's eyes at the remembered pain but he made an effort to hide them. He continued to face Jeffrey. "Then, when I dropped to Pa's side to hold him close and beg him not to die, that same man raised his gun again and shot the turkey dead in the street, and then, he just walked back inside the saloon, laughing over what he had done. He didn't even want the bird. He left it lying in the dirt. He'd killed my father out of pure meanness."

"Didn't the sheriff arrest him for murder?"

"No," Flint said bitterly. "The sheriff was afraid of the two men, and because no one else would admit to having seen any of it happen, and the men claimed Pa threatened them by sending Vance after a rifle, they were never even taken to jail." Flint took a deep breath to steady his voice which had become shaky with telling the tragic story. "Vance was still holding on to the rifle when the sheriff first arrived, and he accepted that as evidence that the men had told him the truth. But Pa didn't even know Vance had gone for the rifle."

Flint looked deeply into Jeffrey's eyes, hoping to see a glimmer of understanding in their shining depths. "I was only fourteen when that happened, but I was the oldest son. I felt it was my duty to avenge my father's death. I saved my money and bought myself a pistol—not a revolver like this, but a side arm I could handle. I began to practice with it every day against my mother's staunchest objections. She had no idea why I was so dead set on getting good with my gun, but she sensed it meant trouble for me. She was right, because when I was sixteen and felt I was finally ready to take him on, I called that man out into the street and dared him to draw against me. When he did, I shot him."

Flint paused for only a moment before he continued. "It wasn't until after he was dead that I learned he had quite a reputation with that gun of his, and because I'd been the one to outdraw him and kill him, suddenly I had a reputation of my own and men were calling me out in hopes of taking that reputation for themselves. And because I was always able to outshoot the men who drew on me, I eventually became the man to try to beat."

"How many men did you have to kill?" Jeffrey wanted to know. Although his expression was now sullen, his eyes still reflected the awe that he felt.

"I've had to kill fourteen men since then, and each time it was kill or be killed."

"Fourteen?" Jeffrey repeated, his disappointment evident. "Is that all?"

"Is that all?" Flint asked, suddenly furious at the boy's obviously unchanged attitude. "I've been forced to kill fourteen men, usually men I didn't even know, and you ask if that's all? Would it please you to know that I've wounded at least two dozen others?"

When it did indeed seem to please the boy, Flint

realized Katherine had been right from the beginning. He could not hide his past from his son and, at the tender age of five, the boy was too easily influenced by what others thought to understand how much Flint had suffered because of the life he'd led.

He needed to do something to change the boy's misplaced esteem—if not of gunfighters in general, then at least of himself. Painfully, Flint realized the drastic steps he needed to take. He would have to break the bonds he had worked so hard to build, at least until that time when the boy was old enough to really understand what it was he was trying to tell him.

It took all the inner strength he could summon to speak his next words. "You can't really believe you would ever be able to handle a gun even half as good as me, do you? Don't make me laugh. No one will ever be as good as I am, especially not anyone like you. I don't even know why I waste my time on you. I've got so many better things I could be doing with my time."

The tears in Jeffrey's eyes were quick in coming and Flint thought he would not be able to bear the sight of them, but deep inside he knew that what he was doing was for his son's own good in the long run. Fighting back the urge to take his trembling son into his arms and comfort him, he continued. "Why don't you just get out of here and leave me alone? I've really had more than enough of you."

"You don't mean that," Jeffrey said in a small, shocked voice.

"Don't I? See that horse? Why don't you get on it so I can take you on home? I'm tired of messing with you."

Jeffrey's lower lip quivered as his eyes went to the horse, then sadly glanced back up at Flint. Slowly, he did as he'd been told and walked over to the horse and tried to climb up into the saddle without Flint's help.

Flint's heart went out to the boy but he did not go to his aid. He waited until the boy had finally managed to get into the saddle and sat wiping away his tears with the back of his hand. Then, he climbed up behind him and hurried the horse into a gallop. The trip back to Seven Oaks was made in complete silence except for Jeffrey's occasional deep sobs. When they finally reached their destination, Flint quickly lifted Jeffrey from the saddle and held him a moment longer than necessary before dropping him roughly to the ground.

"See ya around, kid," he said in a tight voice as he urged his horse into a gallop and headed back the way he had come. He had to get out of there before the boy caught sight of the tears that were streaming down his own face by the time he'd passed through the main gate and was headed back down the road. Sadly, he realized Katherine had been right all along. Because of his past reputation—a reputation he'd never wanted—he was doomed to be a bad influence on his own son and it was breaking his heart.

Flint was so overwhelmed by his misery, he could barely see the road in front of him. Holding back the pain that pierced his soul, he wondered if there was anyplace on this earth he could go where his reputation would not eventually catch up with him. Suddenly, he doubted it. There was no escaping his past. He could see that now. And now that everyone knew who he was and where he lived, he wondered how long it would take before word got around and someone would show up on his doorstep, eager to take him on.

"Well, I'll just have to show everyone how much I've

changed," he muttered aloud. "I'll just have to show them all that I'm not Flint Mason anymore. Flint Mason is dead." As he rode into his own dooryard, he was more determined than ever to work hard and show everyone that he was a rancher now, not a gunman. He'd let them know just how much he regretted that part of his life and wanted to leave it behind. And once everyone else understood that, maybe he could make Jeffrey understand it, too.

Katherine had just started down the stairs, headed for the laundry with an armload of dirty linen, when Jeffrey ran up the same staircase as fast as he could, tears streaming down his face.

"Jeffrey?" she called, after he'd passed her without so much as a word. "Jeffrey? What's the matter?"

Jeffrey flew down the hallway and into his bedroom, slamming the door behind him. Even before she reached the closed door, Katherine could hear his muffled sobs. She knocked lightly. "Jeffrey? May I come in?"

When there was no answer, she opened the door and stepped inside. She could see her son lying on his bed, his face buried deep in one of the pillows. "Jeffrey? What's wrong?"

"Everything," Jeffrey cried out, without lifting his head. Quietly, she walked over to his bed and sat down on the edge to reach out and comfort him.

"Want to tell me about it?" she asked in a soft voice as she stroked the damp curls along the back of his head. Then with a mother's touch, she gently grasped his shoulders and turned him around to face her.

"It's Frank," he said between loud, rasping sobs.

Her heart froze as she waited to hear more. Her worst fear was that he'd told Jeffrey that he was the boy's real father.

"He really . . . is Flint Mason," Jeffrey tried to explain in a voice choked with emotion. "It—it's not a bunch of lies. He . . . he really is Flint Mason."

"He told you that himself?" she asked.

"Yes, Mother, he admitted it." Then Jeffrey went on to tell her everything that had happened between the two of them that afternoon. A fresh rush of tears flooded his eyes as he concluded his story. "He doesn't want to be my friend anymore, Mother. He said so. He said he didn't have any more time to waste on me. Then, he brought me right home and didn't even wait around to see if I got safely inside. What did I do, Mother? What did I do that made him hate me so?"

"You didn't do anything," she said softly and took her son into her arms and held him close to her heart. Closing her eyes, she tried to keep her emotions under control, for she knew what it must have cost Flint to do what he had done and she realized that he had done it for the boy's sake. "It's just that you're a young boy with a young boy's dreams and he's a grown man with a grown up's responsibilities—responsibilities you can't yet understand but will someday."

"But why can't we still be friends?" Jeffrey wanted to know as he wiped away another tear with the back of his hand. His tears had slowed as he tried to listen to what his mother was saying.

"I think he was just in a bad mood and you had the misfortune of being the one he took it out on. He may have problems you know nothing about, bad problems that need his full attention right now. But give him some time, and I feel that you two will be able to be friends again." She pressed her son to her and prayed he would not yet realize the actual hopelessness of the situation.

While Katherine sat holding her son close in the small, semidark room, she went over in her mind everything Jeffrey had told her. She was overcome by a deep sense of compassion for Flint. She had never known the circumstances that had led him to become a gunfighter. She had always assumed it was what he had wanted out of life.

Sadly, she wondered if he'd walk out of their lives now, or if he would stay on at his ranch and fight to overcome his past reputation. Finally able to see his true motivations, Katherine felt a sudden pride in the man Flint had become, and for the first time, it occurred to her that he might truly have changed, just as he'd claimed to. Though she still couldn't love Flint in the way he wanted her to, she finally had a good reason to like him again, truly like him, and deep inside, she hoped he would stay and fight to gain the respectability he so deeply wanted—and deserved.

Chapter Twenty-Five

Sheriff Ragland and Zeb Fielden strode into the Redbird Saloon and settled into the two chairs directly across the table from the tall young man who had been in town barely an hour and already had caused enough commotion to set half the town on edge.

"I hear you're looking for trouble," the sheriff said without preamble.

"Only if looking to get a little personal justice is the same as looking for trouble," the young man replied in an offhand manner as he lifted his whisky glass and drained it in one smooth movement. His brown eyes never left the sheriff's face as he set the glass back down on the table and wiped his mouth with his shirt sleeve.

"Personal justice? What sort of personal justice?" the sheriff demanded. He frowned at how quickly the boy reached for the bottle, refilled his glass and tossed down another drink. That was three the sheriff had counted since he'd entered the saloon in search of the stranger. "And what's this personal justice got to do with Flint Mason?"

Leaning back in his chair, Zeb studied the stranger closely. Although the young man sat slouched in his chair and bent over to one side, Zeb could tell he was very tall and lean, with a great shock of dark, unruly hair and wary brown eyes. And, although he sported a full beard and mustache, Zeb felt he really couldn't be any older than eighteen or nineteen—still more boy than man.

Zeb frowned as he examined the boy's dark eyes more closely. It was not hard to sense the deep hatred he had for Flint Mason, and although Flint was indeed an easy man to hate, Zeb wondered what he could possibly have done to make this boy hate him quite so much. Mulling over the possibilities, Zeb leaned forward to hear the boy's answers to the sheriff's questions.

"Flint Mason killed both my brothers," the boy said as he refilled his glass a fourth time and raised it to his lips. Before he tossed the drink down, he paused and explained in an embittered voice. "The law claimed they were both killed in fair fights, but I know better. No one could take either of my brothers in a fair fight. They were too good for that. Mason killed them in cold blood." He finally downed the whisky, then added with a crooked smile, "It's taken me two long years to find that man, and now that I have, I'm here to see that justice is finally done."

"Sounds like what you really want is revenge, not justice. Look, boy, I don't want any trouble in my town," the sheriff warned. "I can't say that I'm that fond of the man myself, cause I ain't; but he's done nothing here outside the law. If he did, I'd arrest him. And until he does, I'm duty bound to protect him just like anybody else."

"You'd protect the likes of him?" the boy asked, visibly shocked. His fingers tightened around the whisky glass as he stared at the sheriff. "What sort of man are you?"

"A man who takes his job seriously," the sheriff responded in a stern voice. "And a man who is not going to let you get yourself shot up because of some foolish notion you have of getting revenge. All you're going to accomplish by going after Flint Mason is getting yourself shot."

"No, what I'm going to accomplish is putting a bullet through Flint Mason's heart and watching him die." The boy's eyelids twitched with hatred.

"If you do manage to kill him, I'll have to arrest you. What good will it do you to be in jail over something like that?"

"You won't be able to arrest me any more than Mason got arrested for killing my brothers. It'll be a fair fight. I fully intend to give him the same sort of chance he gave my brothers back in Dodge."

"Let me get this straight," Zeb interrupted in an effort to put the situation into perspective. "Your two brothers went up against Flint Mason at the same time and he managed to shoot and kill them both?"

"Not at the same time. Paul went up against him first, but Flint managed to kill him with a single bullet right through the heart. And right after that, my other brother, Michael, found out about it and he went up against Mason—for Paul's sake—only Flint managed to get him, too. He shot him through the neck, but somehow the bullet went up into his head and killed him instantly." The young man paused to reflect, then continued. "I could almost believe that Flint Mason might be able to kill Paul in a regular shootout—I hear Mason is damned good and Paul was always a hothead—but nobody ever could outshoot Michael."

"And what makes you think you won't end up getting killed just like they did?" Zeb asked.

"Because I'm faster than either of my brothers ever were. Flint Mason doesn't stand a chance in hell against me."

"What's your name, boy?" the sheriff asked as he glanced over at Zeb who was leaning back in his chair again, stroking his mustache.

"Mark Munn," he said proudly and waited for the name to sink in.

Zeb's eyebrows rose in recognition as he returned the sheriff's quick look. All three Munn brothers had reputations for being both ruthless and lightning fast. Even their mother, Vella, had been a notorious shot. Suddenly, Zeb realized that Flint Mason was in real danger this time. He wondered if the man should at least be warned.

"Well, Mark," the sheriff said as he reached for the almost empty whisky bottle and held it just out of the boy's reach. "If you continue to drink like you are, you won't be sober enough to even find the handle on your gun, much less draw it out of your holster. If I was you, I'd let up on the whisky a little."

"Well, you ain't me," Mark Munn retorted and snatched the bottle out of the sheriff's hand. "Don't worry, when the time comes to call Flint Mason out, I'll be sober enough."

The sheriff rose slowly, scraping his chair legs against the rough wood floor. "I want you to keep one thing in mind. I run a peaceful town here and I'm not about to put up with troublemakers. Maybe I ought to run you in right now and save us both a lot of trouble."

"On what charge?" the boy asked defiantly. His brown eyes glinted with rage.

"Don't rightly know," the sheriff said with a frown as he pushed his hat back and looked down into the angry young face. "But by the time I get you across the street and locked up behind bars, I'll have thought of something."

"Go ahead, but you won't be able to keep me in there forever. Eventually, I'll get out and I'll do exactly what I've set out to do."

"Shoot off a gun in this town and I'll have you arrested—whether you provoked the fight or not. We have an ordinance against shooting off a firearm of any kind inside this town without just cause."

"Oh, I'll have just cause," the boy said with a quick smile, his words beginning to slur. "And once I've killed the bastard, I don't really care what you do to me. Lock me up if you want. But no jury is going to convict me when they hear what I have to tell about how Mason killed both my brothers and caused my mother to grieve herself into an early grave."

"Don't be so sure," the sheriff warned, then sighed loudly in exasperation. "Look, why don't you just use the brains God gave you and ride on out of here now? Shooting Flint Mason isn't going to bring your brothers back, or your mother."

"An eye for an eye, Sheriff. A life for a life. And, believe me, if I could figure out some way to kill the man three times I'd sure do it." The boy turned away from them both, effectively dismissing them as he poured another drink. His youthful show of arrogance caused the sheriff even more concern as he motioned Zeb to follow him back outside.

When Zeb rode out of town barely an hour later, he and the sheriff were completely agreed that Flint Mason should at least be warned. Neither he nor the sheriff liked the man very much, but for the sake of the town, they felt Flint should be warned and asked to stay out of Daingerfield for a while. They were especially concerned that he stay away on the following day—Saturday, March 1. Half the population of Morris County would be in town that day, not only doing their regular weekly errands but also getting ready for the annual Independence Day picnic to be held on Sunday in honor of their state's separation from Mexico so many years before.

As Zeb hurried along the narrow dirt road that led to Flint's ranch, he hoped the man would prove to be as levelheaded as he wanted everyone to believe. In all fairness, Zeb had to admit that in the months he'd known Flint personally, the man had made no real trouble. Zeb only hoped he would keep it that way—at least until after the picnic. He and the sheriff would have enough on their hands with the usual Independence Day revelers.

When he arrived at the ranch, Zeb discovered, to his dismay, that Flint wasn't there and hadn't been at the ranch since before sunup. The foreman said he didn't know where his boss had gone, but claimed to have been told that Flint would be back sometime the following morning.

Fearing that Flint had gone into town for some reason—even though he usually restricted his town business to Saturdays like so many others—Zeb headed back at breakneck speed only to discover that no one in town had seen Flint, either.

Unable to warn Flint, Zeb and the sheriff decided their only recourse was not to let Mark Munn out of their sight, and they took turns watching him until he went up to his hotel room. Even then, they kept a close eye on his door, through the night and into the next morning, when it was time for Zeb to ride out to Flint's place again.

The sad expression on Jeffrey's face the last time Flint had seen his son was foremost on his mind while he drove the flatbed wagon, loaded down with his new living room suite, along the wide gravel-topped road between Jefferson and Daingerfield. After what he had suffered the past three weeks, Flint wasn't sure how much longer he could take not being able to see his son. He didn't dare to ride over to Seven Oaks even to visit with Katherine for fear of running into the boy. He knew he had hurt and confused the child by what he'd been forced to do and he didn't want to renew or prolong the boy's suffering in any way by popping in and out of his life. All he could do now was stay away and hope that someday the situation would be different—that someday he and Jeffrey could be together again.

Although he was learning to live with the loneliness, he could barely tolerate the heart wrenching pain that the memory of Jeffrey's tearstained face still brought him. He'd give anything to be able to make it up to the boy. Time was the only thing he had on his side at the moment—time for Jeffrey's heart to heal and time to prove to everyone he was no longer a gunfighter and had never wanted to be.

Rubbing his weary eyes, Flint stared ahead toward Daingerfield which lay only a few miles ahead. As soon as he had stopped in for his mail and a few supplies, he would head on out to his ranch for a much needed rest. He was having a hard enough time falling asleep these days, and trying to sleep in a strange bed in a strange room had proven impossible. He had lain awake all night in the hotel, haunted endlessly by his dashed hopes. Sufficiently tired and travel weary now, he was certain he would be able to get some sleep at last. He might not even wait for dark. He might crawl right into bed as soon as he had his wagon unloaded.

The day was a hot one for so early in the year. It was barely noon and he was certain it had to be eighty degrees—or maybe it was just the lack of a breeze that made it seem that way. He frowned as he looked up at the newly budding trees and saw that nothing moved. Wasn't March supposed to be the windy month?

Returning his gaze to the road ahead, he reached up and unfastened the top two buttons of his black linen shirt. He considered stopping to put the top up over the buckboard, but decided against it when he saw the pine-topped hills surrounding Daingerfield. He was as good as home now. He smiled to himself as he thought of his ranch, now officially named the Circle M. It had indeed come to feel like home to him and he looked forward to being there again.

When Flint finally topped the last hill and could see the town sprawled out in the valley below, he was surprised to find more people milling about than usual, even for a Saturday. He wondered what could have brought them all out, then remembered the big picnic planned for the following afternoon. Banners were already being stretched across the main street and small wooden booths, decorated with red ribbons, were being erected at the far end of town. Evidently, the picnic involved more than just eating. He would have liked to return to see the celebration but he knew it was a bad idea since Katherine was sure to bring Jeffrey to something like that.

As Flint drove through town toward Creel's Mercantile, he gradually realized that he was attracting more than usual attention from the people along the street. He had hoped the interest in him would have started to die down by now, but obviously it had not. Everyone was still curious about him.

Nodding politely to those who stared a bit too long, he tried not to let it bother him. He had to remember, that time was on his side. Eventually, they would come to accept him and understand that he never wanted the reputation he still bore. Someday, these very people might just become his friends. And once he had won the town over, he would be free to win back Katherine and Jeffrey. Such hopes kept him going.

It was while Flint was searching the crowded street for a place to park his wagon that he first noticed Jeffrey. The boy sat at the edge of the raised boardwalk just outside Creel's front entrance, happily watching the traffic that drove by in both directions. The mere sight of his son struck Flint like a thunderbolt. The pain it produced was so severe it brought tears to his eyes.

Immediately nervous lest the boy should see him,

Flint quickly turned his wagon into a dark alley across the street and then turned around in his seat so he could watch his son without Jeffrey's seeing him. He knew that if he left his wagon unattended in the shadowy alley, the furniture might be gone when he returned. He remained seated, knowing he'd have to wait until the boy was gone before he dared drive his wagon back into the street.

"Jeffrey," Flint said the boy's name softly, and with a father's deep pride, as he watched the boy lean back against a post. Flint wondered what thoughts were going through the boy's inquisitive mind. Smiling sadly, he fought an overpowering urge to run across the street and scoop the boy into his arms.

Finally, Jason came out of the store and knelt down beside the boy. When Flint noticed that Jason wasn't carrying any packages, he realized that Katherine was probably still shopping inside the mercantile. He climbed down from the wagon and waited near the alley entrance until Jason and Jeffrey had crossed the street and entered the Star Restaurant. He knew that he risked having his furniture stolen, but he was so eager to see Katherine, if only for a moment, he didn't really care what he lost. It had been so long since he'd seen her, so very long.

His heart pumped furiously as he made his way across the crowded street and stepped up onto the boardwalk. Impatiently, he waited for a group of ladies to pass in front of him before crossing to the front door that had been left open. As he paused just outside, searching the crowded aisles for a glimpse of his beloved Kat, he heard his name. He frowned with frustration, for he didn't have the time to talk to anyone just then. He had to see Katherine while he had the chance.

"Flint! Flint Mason!" the voice shouted out again, clearly impatient.

Reluctantly, Flint tore his gaze from the store and turned around just as his name was shouted out a third time. Though the young man who was calling him looked vaguely familiar, Flint was sure he'd never actually seen him before. He was instantly wary. Had the face been on a *wanted* poster?

"You want me?" he asked. He felt a cold prickle of apprehension as he noticed the holstered revolver strapped to the man's lower thigh.

"Damn right, I want you," the stranger retorted with a sneer as his eyes darted to the gathering crowd, then back to Flint.

There was a gasp from the ladies who were close enough to hear the young man's foul language. Several mothers quickly covered their children's ears and hurried away in the opposite direction. Most of the men stood where they were, or moved to a better vantage point, waiting to see what would happen.

Flint was aware of the crowd's sudden silence as he carefully stepped away from the door and asked, "Do I know you?"

If there was to be gunplay, he wanted it out in the open, not on the sidewalk where innocent bystanders might get hurt.

"Obviously, you don't know me, but I know who you are," the stranger replied.

Flint slowly worked his way out into the middle of the street which was now deserted except for the angry young man. Everyone else had either run off to hide or had formed a line on either side of the street in eager anticipation of what was about to happen. The men who remained behind were more than willing to risk a stray bullet rather than chance missing any of the action.

"You know who I *was,*" Flint corrected him. "You also should know that I'm no longer that same man."

"Yeah, I heard you were calling yourself 'Frank' now, but that doesn't change who you are. You can call yourself whatever you like, but you're still Flint Mason—the man who killed both my brothers." The boy spoke with so much hate and anger that he trembled slightly with each breath he took.

Suddenly, Flint realized who the boy was—Mark Munn. Not only did he have the same deep-set eyes as his brothers, his voice had the same husky timbre. "As you can see, I no longer wear a gun. So, if it's a gunfight you want, I'm afraid you're out of luck."

Slowly, Flint started to back away, hoping to put more distance between them. If he was to be shot down in cold blood, the farther the bullet had to go, the better his chances for survival. To his dismay, the boy started to take slow, short steps in his direction. Realizing his efforts were useless, Flint quit backing up and stood squarely before the angry young man.

"Somebody hand him a gun," the boy called out to the crowd that lined the street in either direction almost as far as the eye could see. When no one came forward, he cried out his demand again. Noticing a man off to his right with a small revolver strapped to his side, he pulled his own gun out of its holster and pointed it directly at the man's heart. "Loan Mason your gun. You'll get it back. I just want him to die with a gun in his hand like both my brothers."

The man's eyes widened with fear when he realized the boy was serious. Slowly, he moved his hands to his buckle and removed his revolver, holster and all. Taking short, tentative steps, he walked out to where Flint stood watching.

"Here, mister. I don't want no trouble," he said in a loud voice so that both Flint and the boy could hear. "Take my gun." Then, when Flint reached out and took the gun, the man leaned forward and added in a low whisper. "It's fully loaded. Use every bullet if you have to, but kill that son-of-a-bitch."

Flint waited until the man was safely back on the sidewalk before he spoke again. "Look, boy, I have no quarrel with you." He continued to hold the gun and holster out, so that everyone could see he did not intend to put it on. He wasn't going to let this boy ruin everything he had worked for. He had to think of Katherine and Jeffrey.

"Strap that gun on," the boy ordered.

Flint simply shook his head and continued to hold the gun out where everyone could see it. Suddenly a shrill voice from the crowd broke the tension.

"That's not fair. He hasn't ever used that gun. You could at least let him get his own gun."

It was Jeffrey's voice. Flint felt his heart crumble. He had hoped Jeffrey would not come out in time to see any of this. The boy already had the wrong idea about gunplay. To actually witness a gunfight and then to see everyone cheering the winner, would only reinforce his wrongheaded notions. And to watch him back away would make the boy think he was a coward.

"Jeffrey, get out of here," he said, shifting his gaze to

his son long enough to catch sight of the boy's angry expression. Was he angry at him for not fighting back, or angry at the other man for trying to start trouble? Flint wished he knew.

Just as Jeffrey was about to run out into the street, Jason broke through the crowd and grabbed the boy's shoulders. "Jeffrey, get back inside."

"I won't," Jeffrey said defiantly and tried to wrench himself free of Jason's strong grasp.

"Oh, yes you will," Jason said, his voice filled with both fear and rage.

"Oh, no he won't," Mark put in, and when Jason looked up, he found the young man's gun pointed in their direction.

"The kid stays," Mark told Jason flatly. His nostrils flared defiantly as he spoke. Then to Flint, he called out in a clear voice, "And you'd better hurry up and strap that gun on or the first bullet is going to be for the kid. One good shot and I'll have him crippled for life."

"Okay, I'll put the gun on," Flint finally conceded. "But I want you to let Jason take Jeffrey back inside. I don't think this is the sort of thing a five-year-old boy should see."

"Let the kid stay and watch if he wants," Mark said and smiled as he looked again at Jeffrey. "Let him see how a real gunfighter handles a gun. Besides, if you'd just take a quick look around, you'd discover he's not the only kid out here."

Flint did take a quick glance around at the many faces lining the street and noticed there were several young boys watching the scene with wide-eyed interest. Where were their parents? Didn't they care what their children were about to see?

"Like I said, I'll put this gun on, but Jason takes Jeffrey out of here."

"No," Jeffrey cried out stubbornly. "I want to stay and watch you shoot him down. Even with you shooting someone else's gun, he doesn't stand a chance against you." When Jason pulled him up into his arms and started to back away, Jeffrey began to wriggle as hard as he could in an attempt to get loose. Though Jason almost dropped him twice, he managed to keep his hold on the boy.

"Just put the gun on," Mark said, returning his attention to Flint. "You're just using the kid as an excuse to stall for time." A smile played about his thin lips as he watched Flint slowly buckle the holster around his lean waist. "Hurry, before someone runs and gets the sheriff."

As Flint adjusted the holster and shifted the weight of the gun, he realized that Jeffrey was right. This was not his own gun and he wasn't at all sure how it would handle. He wished he could reach down for the handle and see if it met his hand right, but he knew that doing so might incite Mark Munn to shoot early.

"Are you finally ready to die?" Mark wanted to know as he slowly returned his own revolver to its holster. His gaze flicked briefly to the many watching faces before returning to concentrate on Flint. He seemed pleased at the size of the crowd.

Suddenly realizing that Mark wanted more than revenge, Flint tried again to talk the young man out of drawing against him. "Just what's this going to prove, anyway—that you can outshoot a man who is forced to use a gun he's never shot before? That you're faster than a man who hasn't drawn against another man in over two years? Some honor that will be."

Though his attention was focused on the angry young man who stood in front of him, Flint was still able to see the way in which Jeffrey continued to struggle against Jason in a very real effort to get free. Jason had managed to pull the boy back into the crowd, but did not yet have him completely out of view. Flint knew he had to stall for more time. If this did come down to gunplay, he refused to let Jeffrey bear witness to it.

"You killed my brothers," Mark reminded him as he watched the way Flint continued to glance over at the boy. "And now I intend to kill you. It's as simple as that."

"There's no glory in killing a man out of revenge." How he wished someone had explained that to him many years ago. How different his life might be now.

"What's that kid to you, anyway?"

"He's a friend is all," Flint said and when he glanced again toward Jeffrey, he saw a wide smile spread across the boy's face as he momentarily stopped struggling. Never had a smile touched Flint's heart in quite the way that one did.

"Yeah boy! Flint's my friend and he can shoot you down easy," Jeffrey called out only seconds before Jason's hand came up to cover his mouth. Without considering the consequences, Jeffrey bit down on the fleshy palm of Jason's hand. His eyes widened in shocked surprise at what he'd done when Jason's hand was jerked away from his mouth and he was nearly dropped to the ground. Though he could have taken that moment to wriggle free, he was immobilized.

Frowning because Jeffrey still hadn't been taken

back inside, Flint tried one last time to avert a shootout. "I don't see why you're so dead set on shooting me. I never wanted to fire on either one of your brothers. They both came looking for me and they both drew first. I had to shoot in self-defense both times."

"Liar," Mark cried and went immediately for his gun.

Flint's finely tuned reflexes sent his hand quickly to the gun at his side, but as his fingers closed around the handle, he thought of Jeffrey and hesitated.

Chapter Twenty-Six

Both revolvers fired within a split second of each other just as the sheriff finally pushed his way through the crowd. Though Flint had hesitated, his keenly honed reflexes had carried him through. Even so, it was the first time in Flint's life that his opponent had got off the first shot.

The sound of the gunshots muffled most of the gasps and screams that came from the crowd during the actual shooting, but one female voice carried over the rest of the noise and caught Flint's attention at the very moment the bullet tore into the right side of his chest.

Though Flint had purposely aimed high—just inches above the young man's shoulder where the only damage his bullet would cause would be to the courthouse yard beyond—Mark Munn's aim had been true. The tiny piece of metal burned deep inside Flint as his eyes scanned the gaping crowd for Katherine.

There she was—standing motionless just outside the mercantile with her hand pressed to her mouth and her eyes wide with horror. His first thought was to go to her and try to explain that none of it had been his fault. He wanted her to understand that he had tried his level best to avoid it, but he was too stunned to move.

The crowd slowly began to press forward and as they did, they blocked out what little view he had of Katherine. He tried to ignore the pain that gripped his chest as he stared into the crowd, craning his neck, searching the many faces for her. He hoped she would come to him, but when he was unable to locate her among the many others, he realized she would not come and he understood why. Even though everyone realized they were friends, her rushing to him—even at such a moment—might raise a few eyebrows and would certainly attract unwanted attention.

Flint's vision blurred, then cleared. He felt strangely lightheaded. Afraid that he might disgrace himself by passing out in front of everyone, he turned and tried his best to walk away proudly. He would explain to Katherine later, in private. None of it had been his fault. He had tried to prevent it.

With his eyes trained on the alley where he had left his wagon, he fought the urge to bend his head and examine the wound. That, too, could wait until he was alone. Slowly, he slipped the revolver back into its holster, and, head erect, kept his hands at his sides while he continued to walk toward the alley's narrow entrance.

Though Flint had been clearly defeated, he refused to let anyone see how much pain he was in. His expression was calm and relaxed, but the pain had spread from the wound to the entire right side of his chest, and with each step that he took, the spasms were sharper and more agonizing. He could feel his right arm going numb. Yet he walked on, determined to get out of his son's sight, and out of Katherine's sight, before he became too weak to walk.

He tried to hurry his steps. But before he could make it to the far side of the street, his knees buckled and he fell face forward onto the graveled earth. Furious, he tried to push himself up, but his arms no longer had the strength to lift his own weight, and when he tried to use his right arm, the pain in his chest became too severe to bear and he collapsed again, face down in the dirt.

Frustration swept over him as he turned his head to one side and looked in the direction where he had last seen Jeffrey. He was horrified to discover the boy heading across the street with a look of deep disappointment on his young freckled face. Flint tried again to push himself up only to be met with another piercing pain through his chest.

Determined to get up, he gritted his teeth and tried once again. More than anything else at that moment, he wanted to stand on his own power and walk away with dignity. He could not bear the thought that Jeffrey's last memory of him might be that of a beaten man groveling in the dirt.

Flint's frustration grew. He could tell by Jeffrey's frowning expression that he had failed miserably in his son's eyes. He wanted to explain to the boy, but wasn't sure he had the strength to speak. Yet, he had to try.

In an attempt to call out his son's name, he opened his mouth and was appalled to taste dirt. His face and mouth were covered with gritty dirt and he didn't even have the strength to reach up and brush it away. How he wished Jeffrey would turn away and spare him this final humiliation.

Fighting the haze that began to blur his vision again, Flint watched helplessly as Jeffrey came closer. Then, he noticed Katherine hurrying to catch up with the boy. Her beautiful face had turned ghostly white and her hands trembled as she caught hold of her son's upper arms and tried to turn him away. Flint was powerless to do more than just watch as Jeffrey fought against his mother. How he prayed she would succeed.

Flint's heart struggled to keep beating as his life's blood poured out onto the street. His eyelids began to close just as he glimpsed Jason pushing his way through the crowd in pursuit of his son.

As soon as Jason caught up with Jeffrey and Katherine, he reached down, and without a word, hoisted the boy onto his shoulder. When she was sure Jason had him securely, Katherine let go, then glanced beseechingly up into Jason's solemn face. Receiving his understanding nod, she turned and rushed to Flint's side while Jason quickly escorted Jeffrey in the opposite direction.

Flint forced his eyes open again in time to see his son being led away and he felt a strong wave of gratitude. Jason's firm hand on the back of Jeffrey's neck kept the boy from turning to look back. Flint wished he could find some way to thank the man for that. Again, his vision faded, but he blinked hard to clear it. He wanted to get one last glimpse of his son before he disappeared into the crowd for good. How dearly he loved that curly headed little scamp. How deeply he would miss him.

"I shot him!" Mark Munn shouted victoriously as the crowd gathered around him, cheering him on and thumping him on the back.

Flint frowned and hoped that Jeffrey would not witness the misplaced homage the other man was receiving for having successfully shot him. He prayed that Jason would be able to hustle the boy out of sight and immediately explain to him how foolish the whole incident had been and how neither of them truly gained anything by it. Jeffrey must be made to understand. The opinions formed by his son, even at so tender an age, could be with him for the rest of his life.

"I shot Flint Mason. I've just gunned down the best Kansas has to offer!" Mark's loud bragging mixed with the crowd's cheers, and the din grew so loud it drowned out Katherine's first words as she knelt beside Flint and gingerly lifted his head. He could see her lips move, but he couldn't hear the words that she spoke.

Flint tried to smile up at her as she carefully turned him over on his left side and rested his head in her lap. It was such a tender, loving gesture—so very like Kat. He stared up at her pale beauty and wished he could reach up and touch her fair cheek one last time but his hand refused to obey.

Tears streamed unchecked down Katherine's stricken face as she ran trembling fingers through Flint's hair, pushing the thick black locks away from his face. She glanced only briefly at the ragged hole in his shirt and at how much blood had spread across his chest and pooled out onto the ground beneath him. She knew immediately he was dying and there was nothing she could do to stop it. All she could hope to accomplish now was to ease the pain of his final moments.

Most of the onlookers followed the young victor into the nearby Redbird Saloon and much of the noise disappeared with them. Flint was finally able to hear Katherine softly calling his name again and again. How sad she sounded as she tried to comfort him.

"Kitty Kat. My wild little kitten," he said, his voice weak but just loud enough for Katherine to hear. He gazed up into her sad face and tried to memorize every little detail. There was an odd comfort in knowing that her tears were for him. "Sweet, tenderhearted Katherine."

"Hush," she told him as she gently brushed the dirt from his face with tiny light strokes of her fingertips. "Someone's gone to get the doctor; just lie still until he gets here."

He glanced around to be sure no one was close enough to overhear what he had to say, and when he saw that the nearest group was huddled several feet away trying to appear as if they were not really watching, he looked back at her and spoke the words that burned in his heart. "Take good care of our son, Kat. The devil has already claimed my destiny; don't let him have my son. Bring him up right. And, please, I don't want you to ever tell him that I was really his father. Let him think Jason . . ." he paused as an extremely severe pain surged through his chest and thrust deep into his shoulder. It was several moments before the pain eased.

"Flint, don't," she pleaded with him. Tears veiled her eyes so that she could barely see him. He became a dark watery image, wavering before her. "Just be quiet and lie still."

But Flint continued, needing to talk before it was too late. "I think you were right about everything all along. It would be best if he didn't ever know about me. Let him continue to believe Jason is his father. Just promise that the two of you will make sure he doesn't grow up to be anything like I was."

His use of the past tense made Katherine bite down hard on her lower lip to contain her overwhelming grief. Flint was fully aware he was dying. Though it hurt deeply to talk at that moment, she knew she had to. There were things she must tell him—things he must know before he died.

"Flint, I was wrong about you. There *are* qualities of yours I want Jeffrey to have." She spoke in a pain-filled voice, barely above a whisper. She pressed her hand gently to his cheek and winced as she felt a tear trickle from his eye and moisten her fingertips. Softly, she brushed the tear away with her thumb, knowing it embarrassed him. "I'm not blind to what you just did. You never intended your bullet for that boy. You took your chances and missed him on purpose—for Jeffrey's sake. You didn't want him to actually watch you kill a man."

"You're a smart one, Kat," he said in a raspy tone. He tried to reach up and touch her but he was too weak.

When a tear fell from her face to his cheek, he treasured the feel of it against his hot skin and was grateful he still had the strength to talk to her. "And you're just the one to see to it that our son grows up to be a good and decent man."

Suddenly, Flint gasped for air and squeezed his eyes shut for a moment, his teeth clenched in the pain. Katherine bent closer and cried out in alarm. "Please, Flint, just lie still until the doctor gets here. Anything you have to say can wait until he's examined you."

"No, I have things I want you to know." Again, he

gasped for air. His left hand tightened but couldn't quite make a fist. "Oh, how I wish I had met you before I ever fired that first bullet. My life would have been so different. You would have seen to that." He paused again, fighting for air. "But I do want to be sure you know. I really have changed . . . I have. Just for you . . . I swear it. You can see that now, can't you?"

A few curious onlookers started to edge closer, as if they wanted to hear what the dying man had to say to Katherine, but she waved them back, her eyes filled with an angry warning to stay away. No one had offered this man a friendly hand while he lived, why should they bother with him now that he was dying? No, all they wanted was to watch a man die, hear his last words. Suddenly, she was enraged at the entire town for never having accepted him. Then, she became angry with herself, for she had behaved no better than they had.

Aching with her own shame, she finally found the strength to answer him. She smiled down at him as she spoke, "Yes, Flint, I can see how very much you have changed." Pain swelled her throat and circled downward, piercing her heart. She tried to swallow some of the ache—some of the misery that grew now to an unbearable intensity—but found she could not. "I can see that change in you so clearly now."

"Can you?" At last, he found the strength to smile fleetingly. His strength was ebbing fast.

"Yes." She sobbed aloud with the heartache that continued to build as she stroked his handsome face. Damn fate for what it had done. Flint had indeed changed, truly changed—yet it was that very change that had cost him his life.

Flint stared up at her, wondering what her thoughts were. Did she regret having refused to give him that second chance? Did she want him to live so they might yet have that chance to shape a future together? How he wished he knew what was really in her heart. Suddenly, the pain grew worse. His eyes closed tightly and he grimaced, waiting for the pain to subside. But this time it did not. It grew steadily worse with each rasping breath.

"Know this, Kat. I love you. I always . . ." Holding back the scream in his throat, Flint bit down on his lip. Every muscle in his body tensed against the agonizing pains cutting through him.

Katherine bent lower to hear his words just as he stiffened, then fell limp in her arms.

"Flint, no!"

Cradling his head to her breast, she began to rock back and forth. She was not certain if he could hear her words or not, but she had to say them. "Oh, Flint. I know you love me. And I love you, too. I want you to know that. I do love you, too."

Sadly, it was now clear to Katherine that she had never stopped loving Flint; she had only stopped trusting him. And it was the loss of that trust that had left her open to so many other conflicting emotions. To learn, only too late, that he had actually grown to deserve her trust again was almost more than she could bear. He had grown to be every bit the man she had always wanted him to be: a man of honor, a man to respect—a truly noble man. And although she knew she would not honor his dying wish not to let Jeffrey know who his real father was, she would wait until the boy was old enough to truly understand.

When the time was right, she would see to it that Jeffrey not only knew him for the father he had so wanted to be, she would make sure he understood exactly what sort of man Frank Mason had grown to be before he died—a man who would risk his own life for the love of a son he had never been allowed to claim as his own.

As she pressed his pale cheek to her breast, she looked up to see Doc Edison hurrying toward them. Moments later, Jason returned from another direction. After having left Jeffrey with Zeb Fielden, he had come back to see what he could do to help. When Katherine turned her tear streaked face up to his, he was able to see Flint Mason more clearly and knew that the man was dead. Quietly, he knelt beside her, and taking one of her hands from around Flint's shoulder, he held it gently in his.

No words were spoken as he eased Flint's head from her grasp and let the doctor take over. Slowly, Jason rose, then pulled her up and cradled her in his arms. A few onlookers who had remained behind moved forward to help the doctor move Flint's body. They did not have far to go; Flint had died only a few yards from the undertakers. Within minutes, they would have him out of everyone's sight.

As the men hoisted the body up, the late-morning sun slipped behind a stray cloud, throwing the scene into shadow. Brassy piano music trickled out into the street from the Redbird Saloon while loud, masculine cheers of victory rose and fell, accompanied by squeals of delight from the girls who worked there. The saloon was filled to capacity. Those people who had not followed Mark Munn into the Redbird, had moved down the street to the sheriff's office, waiting to see what he intended to do. The men muttered among themselves, occasionally glancing back down the street to where Flint was being carried away. The women, who had come back outside now, stood in small groups, whispering.

But all Katherine could hear at that moment, as she stood with closed eyes in the warm circle of Jason's arms, was his slow and steady heartbeat. Suddenly, she found a reason to smile, though the smile was a faint one.

The pain inside her remained severe and she realized it would be there for a long time. But she also knew now that she would have the strength to overcome the deep grief that consumed her. Slowly, she opened her eyes and looked up at Jason, knowing he was her strength. With Jason beside her, she would get through the days of torment that lay ahead and eventually sort out the turbulent emotions caused by Flint's sudden death. It would take a great deal of time, but that was to be expected.

Katherine closed her eyes as she gratefully slipped her arms around Jason's waist and held him close—for she had indeed found the high level of courage and the unwavering source of strength she would need in the coming days.

Epilogue

March 1, 1902

Jeffrey could feel the hot tears that had formed along the outer corners of his eyes as he further considered the bitter sacrifice his father had been forced to make and why. Sadly, he turned his burning face towards the brisk March wind and let it cool away some of the deep sorrow which consumed him. It was then he first noticed the dark blanket of clouds that had rolled in from the northwest and now churned angrily overhead. The wind had picked up even more and the temperature had taken a rapid drop. Jeffrey pulled his heavy overcoat tighter around him. It appeared winter was going to give them one last blast of cold air before giving way to the warmer weather of spring which was due to arrive.

Though the coat he had thought to wear was thick and made of warm wool, Jeffrey began to shiver uncontrollably and knew it was from more than just a cold lash of wind in his face or the distant rumble of thunder. It was the intensity of emotions burning inside him that caused his body to suddenly shake so violently and gooseflesh to rise along the sensitive skin of his neck and arms.

Morosely, he glanced back down at his father's grave and noticed the yellow narcissus that he'd placed there earlier. He leaned forward to touch it and frowned at the way the tiny wildflower had already begun to fade and curl along the edges, after so few hours. How very fragile life could be.

"Father!" a youthful voice from somewhere in the distance broke into Jeffrey's tumbling thoughts and momentarily drew his attention away from the grief that had overtaken him.

Slowly, he turned toward the voice and saw his own son rushing along the path that led to the cemetery. He rose to wait for him. With a deep feeling of pride, Jeffrey watched as his son burst through the rickety gate and left it standing open in his eagerness to reach his father. He was such a handsome boy. So full of energy. So full of life. Smiling, Jeffrey bent low and scooped his four-year-old son into his arms.

"What's your hurry, Frankie?" he wanted to know as he held the boy high so that he could look into the freckled young face he adored more than he'd ever thought humanly possible.

"Grandma said for me to come find you and tell you it's nearly suppertime. Grandpa's already come in and washed up. In fact, everyone is waiting for you."

"And did Minnie fix those apple pies we asked for?" he asked the child.

"Three of them," Frankie assured him with a bright smile, unperturbed by the way the cold wind tugged at his short brown curls and made his large green eyes blink. "Are you finished here yet?"

"I suppose so," Jeffrey said and turned his head so that the wind would blow his hair out of his eyes. "I certainly don't want to keep everyone waiting."

Especially not tonight. The whole family was going to be there for the first time in ages. Not only would he enjoy a leisurely evening with his parents—a treat that had come to be far too rare over the past few years—his little sister, Jessica, and her husband were bringing their three daughters from their home in neighboring Camp County just so he could meet them. Although he'd met the oldest daughter, Katy, some years back, he had not had the opportunity to see the other two since he'd returned from Washington, D.C. just a few weeks ago.

He was glad that he had decided to give up his senatorial seat and return to Texas for good. Now that Amanda was gone, he felt Frankie needed a closer link to the rest of the family. The boy needed others who loved him to help fill the void his mother's death had left.

Jeffrey had brought Frankie home to stay. He had already decided to set up a limited law practice in Daingerfield, and take over the running of the Circle M personally. He never had felt right about leaving the ranch in someone else's care, even though he knew he could trust Edmond to run it properly.

"Well, let's go," Frankie urged, linking his arms around his father's neck to let him know that he preferred being carried back to the house. When his father did not move immediately, the child seemed to sense his melancholy mood and tilted his head questioningly. "Are you all right, Father?"

Suddenly, Jeffrey wished there was some way Frank Mason could see the fine son that he and Amanda had produced. How proud his father would have been. Smiling sadly, Jeffrey glanced one last time at his father's gravestone, then hugged his son close. It was the only way he knew to pass along the powerful legacy of love that Frank Mason had so generously left behind.

"I'm just fine," he told the boy and took a playful nip at his tiny freckled nose. Laughing at the way the boy wrinkled his nose in response, he asked, "Think Grandma will let us have two slices of that apple pie if we ask her real nice?"

"Maybe if we give her a big kiss and a hug," Frankie suggested. "You know how Grandma loves a big kiss and a hug."

"You're right, but let's not take any chances. Let's each give her two big kisses and two big bear hugs just to be on the safe side," Jeffrey said with a chuckle as he shifted his son's weight to his left hip and headed for the open gate.

MORE TANTALIZING ROMANCES
From Zebra Books

SATIN SURRENDER (1861, $3.95)
by Carol Finch
Dante Fowler found innocent Erica Bennett in his bed in the most fashionable whorehouse in New Orleans. Expecting a woman of experience, Dante instead stole the innocence of the most magnificent creature he'd ever seen. He would forever make her succumb to . . . *Satin Surrender.*

CAPTIVE BRIDE (1984, $3.95)
by Carol Finch
Feisty Rozalyn DuBois had to pretend affection for roguish Dominic Baudelair; her only wish was to trick him into falling in love and then drop him cold. But Dominic had his own plans: To become the richest trapper in the territory by making Rozalyn his *Captive Bride.*

MOONLIT SPLENDOR (2008, $3.95)
by Wanda Owen
When the handsome stranger emerged from the shadows and pulled Charmaine Lamoureux into his strong embrace, she knew she should scream, but instead she sighed with pleasure at his seductive caresses. She would be wed against her will on the morrow—but tonight she would succumb to this passionate MOONLIT SPLENDOR.

UNTAMED CAPTIVE (2159, $3.95)
by Elaine Barbieri
Cheyenne warrior Black Wolf fully intended to make Faith Durham, the lily-skinned white woman he'd captured, pay for her people's crimes against the Indians. Then he looked into her sky-blue eyes and it was impossible to stem his desire . . . he was compelled to make her surrender as his UNTAMED CAPTIVE.

WILD FOR LOVE (2161, $3.95)
by Linda Benjamin
All Callandra wanted was to go to Yellowstone and hunt for buried treasure. Then her wagon broke down and she had no choice but to get mixed up with that arrogant golden-haired cowboy, Trace McCord. But before she knew it, the only treasure she wanted was to make him hers forever.

Available wherever paperbacks are sold, or order direct from the Publisher. Send cover price plus 50¢ per copy for mailing and handling to Zebra Books, Dept. 2226, 475 Park Avenue South, New York, N.Y. 10016. Residents of New York, New Jersey and Pennsylvania must include sales tax. DO NOT SEND CASH.